Taken in the Night

Taken in the Night

Janet Y. Martel

TATE PUBLISHING
AND ENTERPRISES, LLC

Published by Tate Publishing & Enterprises, LLC
127 E. Trade Center Terrace | Mustang, Oklahoma 73064 USA
1.888.361.9473 | www.tatepublishing.com

Tate Publishing is committed to excellence in the publishing industry. The company reflects the philosophy established by the founders, based on Psalm 68:11,
"The Lord gave the word and great was the company of those who published it."

Book design copyright © 2014 by Tate Publishing, LLC. All rights reserved.

Published in the United States of America

ISBN: 978-1-62746-253-2
1. Fiction / Crime
2. Fiction / Mystery & Detective / General
14.01.11

For my brother, Gerald LePage,
With love and gratitude for his encouragement and help.

And for Aunt Ella Ledoux,
Who is now in God's light with the angels.

Tuesday, December 27

6:17 A.M.

The vestiges of a dream dissolved as wakefulness took over. Antonio Ibarra shivered and blinked at the red LEDs of the radio alarm clock glowing in the darkness. What on earth woke him?

The girls? He wondered listening intently for Marissa's chatter or Liana's giggle. But the only sound was the heating system, the clicking of the base board radiators as hot water flowed through the pipes.

The children are still asleep. Good.

Determined to catch a few more Zs, he clamped his eyes shut and pulled the covers up tighter around his chin to cut off the chill of the room. But even as he snuggled deeply into his pillow he continued to feel uncomfortable; chilly.

Forget about it; you'll warm up in a minute. After all, the heat is running.

His eyes flew open again. If the heat was on, why was it so cold?

He flung back the warm covers as the reason became clear: One of the girls had opened a window, something he had warned them about once winter came and the heat was turned on. But since they lived with Carmen and her new husband, Antonio assumed *his* rules no longer mattered. They were just some inconvenience to be ignored.

Well, not if he could help it.

From the foot of the bed, he shivered and grabbed his old green velour robe. A Christmas gift from Carmen the first year of their marriage. Funny. The marriage was over, but the robe was still there.

He shrugged into the garment as he padded barefooted out of his room to face the tightly closed door across the hall. At the same time he realized the cold draft was not coming from his daughters' bedroom, but from the other end of the house.

The living room? What's going on?

Annoyed, Antonio ran to the living room to find the front door wide open, a harsh, cold wind blowing powdery snowflakes into the room. *I know I locked this door last night! What the hell!* He reached for the door and swore as a bare foot landed onto the icy wetness of the carpet. Incensed, he flung the door shut, not caring if he woke the children.

"The girls are done sleeping for today anyway," he muttered angrily to himself. "They will hear about the sinfulness of wasting hard-earned money." He stomped back to the bedroom his daughters shared and threw the door open expecting to surprise them out of their sleep.

But instead of finding the girls snuggled deep under the Barbie comforters, instead of a pair of dark curly heads rising from the pillows and tiny hands rubbing sleepy eyes awake, instead of bewildered expressions at their father's abrupt entry, Antonio found two empty twin beds.

"Marissa! Liana!" Antonio called, but no answer. Perhaps they were in the bathroom. Antonio retraced his steps down the hall to search that room, but neither child was there. Not on the commode. Not hiding in the shower or behind the door.

Where could they be?

Of course. It was a game. They were hiding somewhere.

He went back to the bedroom and he checked the closet.

Empty, except for Marissa's burgundy dress askew on its hanger, Liana's forest green one in a heap on the floor, and two pairs of black patent leather Mary Janes tossed carelessly in the bottom. Nothing else except for a bunch of empty hangers.

Next, he got down on all fours, lifted the edge of the pink dust ruffle and peered under first one bed, and then the other. But no child leapt out at him yelling, "Boo!" Only Donna, his three-year-old Lab, appeared at his elbow sniffing and whimpering.

Ignoring the dog, Antonio looked around noticing for the first time the condition of the room and his blood ran cold. Not because the open front door had turned his home into a refrigerator, but because he knew this was not how the room had been last night when he had tucked his little girls into bed. Toys and books had been knocked from their shelves and were scattered about. The Barbie lamp on the table between the two tiny beds was lying on its side. The pretty dolls Santa had brought them were cast carelessly on the floor.

Something had happened. But even as cold fingers of fear gripped his heart, he would not allow himself to speculate on what. He only knew that the girls were not in the house and he needed to find them.

"Where are they, Donna?" he asked the girls' constant companion. If anyone knew where the children were, she did.

The dog whimpered again, turned quickly and bumped into the doorjamb, stumbled but regained her balance, and then preceded him down the hallway to the front door.

"Outside?" Antonio asked in disbelief. "They went outside?"

Alarmed, he was outside calling for his children. This early, the street lights were still on, throwing round yellow pools onto the white snow at the base of the poles. The neighborhood was still asleep, but Antonio didn't care about that. With increasing panic, he yelled loudly hoping his frantic calls would reach his children's ears, but his voice seemed to fall dead in the world covered in white. All he heard were the last flakes of last night's blizzard falling gently onto the snow: *tic, tic, tic.*

They have to be somewhere!

From the center of his driveway, Antonio's dark brown eyes anxiously swept the neighboring yards for any sign the girls had gone off to visit someone. Maybe to Mary Carvalho's across the street, for some of her wonderful Christmas cookies. Or at LaRue's to play with Jenny.

A sound at the head of the driveway caught his attention.

It was Donna, snuffling excitedly in front of the vacant lot adjacent to the property. She lifted herself unsteadily on her hind legs and sniffed the air. The animal slipped and fell heavily onto her side. She lay there for a moment, then struggled back onto her feet apparently unhurt, and continued to smell the ground, her nose plowing the snow. Finally, she sat at the end of the driveway facing west. In the direction of busy Cross Street.

Please, God, don't tell me the girls went that way! was Antonio's dismayed thought. Wide-eyed, he yelled at the top of his lungs, "Marissa! Liana!"

He trudged up the driveway, his eyes intent on his dog, and became aware of someone approaching him on his left. *Some neighbor coming over to shoot the breeze.* He couldn't care less about who it might be and didn't bother to look. "No time to talk. Go away," he flung his arm out and waved them away.

The intruder, not put off that easily, grabbed him by the shoulder. Antonio roughly shrugged himself free and continued toward Donna. "Let go!" he demanded desperately. "I must find the girls."

But his assailant somehow got in front of him and blocked his way like a wall, this time gripping both his shoulders. Antonio struggled ineffectively against the hold.

"Tony!" the voice said sharply. "What's going on, man?"

"No time now," Antonio muttered. "Must find the girls."

"The girls? What about—?"

"*Si. Mi hijas,*" Antonio interrupted. "Marisa and Liana."

Antonio tried to break free but the voice insisted, "Marisa and Liana? What about them, Antonio? Where are your little girls?"

Antonio continued to struggle. "Could they have gone up to Cross Street? I must find them! I've looked everywhere and I cannot find them. They are not in the house," his voice trailed off.

"Have you called the cops?" the voice demanded. "We should call the cops."

The question struck Antonio like a thunder bolt and he finally took note of where he was. Of what he was doing. Outside. In knee-deep snow. In nothing but his green bathrobe. And that he was being held in place by the large basketball player hands of his friend and neighbor, Bob LaRue.

Antonio swallowed hard against hot, desperate tears and avoided Bob's black eyes. "No! The children have to be around here somewhere."

"And what about Carmen?" Bob persisted. "Have you called her?"

The scowl deepened further. "No! They are here somewhere. Can't call her now. I'm their father and I'll find them." Antonio gave another futile tug against Bob's hold. "Let go of me. I must keep looking," he managed between teeth chattering with cold.

"Come put some clothes on at least." Antonio felt the robe being drawn closed over his broad bare chest. "God, man! Your lips are purple, for cryin' out loud. Come on, Tony," Bob firmly turned him toward the house.

"But Donna—" Antonio insisted trying to turn back.

"Okay, Tony," Bob was saying now. "I'll get her. But first, we need to take care of you. You're frozen to the bone, man. Come in and get warmed up and I'll help you look for the girls."

"You will help me?" Antonio blinked away the snowflakes that clung to his eyelashes and finally made eye-contact with the one who was speaking to him. "Bob?" When had Bob LaRue come by? That's right, Bob was his friend. Bob promised he'd help. He could count on Bob.

"Yes, Tony. It's me."

Bob looked worried. And strange. He had not taken time to shave. And under his unzipped fleece-lined jacket, Antonio could see that Bob's shirt had been buttoned wrong; one shirt tail hung over the top of his jeans. He wore no socks and his fancy leather loafers were getting ruined in the snow.

"Your shoes, Bob," Antonio murmured and looked back up at the African-American's face. Something else was off about Bob, and Antonio squinted trying to figure it out. Suddenly he knew. "Where's your hat, Bob?" Antonio asked. It was an ongoing joke that Bob always wore some kind of a cap to cover the bald spot on the crown of his head. Yet here he was, standing before him bareheaded.

"Where's your baseball cap, Bob?" Antonio asked again.

Bob shrugged, drawing him toward the house, "I was in a hurry, man. You needed help, so I came running."

"You're a good friend," Antonio sighed. Such a good friend. Someone he could count on. Suddenly overwhelmed by his fears, Antonio collapsed into Bob's arms and melted into heart-wrenching sobs, "Marisa! Liana! Where are my little daughters?"

"It'll be okay, Tony," Bob assured him, "We'll find them. It'll be okay. I promise."

Clinging to Bob's reassurance like a life raft, Antonio allowed himself to be brought into the bathroom where Bob started a hot shower. The next thing Antonio knew, he was standing in the stall beneath a steaming stream of water. Although he could feel the hot water restoring the warmth to his frigid body, the cold sense of loss and despair still clung to his heart and soul.

6:47 A.M.

Minutes later when Antonio emerged from the bathroom fully dressed and shaved, he found Bob LaRue in the living room restraining an angry Donna who was challenging two Ridgeport police officers stepping inside the front door. Bob's assurances to the dog seemed to have no effect upon the animal and the policemen both had their hands on their pistols, ready to defend themselves.

"Cállate, Donna," Antonio ordered sharply. Immediately the dog ceased growling, whined apologetically, and when Bob let go of her collar she came to Antonio for a pat. "My apologies," Antonio offered. "She means no harm; she protects her family."

The policemen relaxed. The darker-skinned Hispanic one introduced himself as Geraldo Diaz and his blond partner as David Caron. Then as if by some secret agreement, Officer Diaz went with Antonio to the kitchen, while Officer Caron took Bob LaRue's statement in the living room.

Now, as Antonio stirred sugar into his coffee with a shaky hand, Officer Diaz sat across the kitchen table from him, a pen poised over a clean sheet of his pocket-sized notepad. Antonio gripped the mug like a lifeline, trying to get a handle on his mounting panic. He swallowed hard and regarded the cop with red-rimmed eyes.

"Where do the girls like to play besides the backyard and at the neighbor's, Mr. Ibarra?" the cop was asking.

"Sometimes we go to the river, but they're forbidden to go there alone. They must have an adult accompanying them. Especially now while the water is so high because of the rain we had on Friday." Then shocked by a sudden thought, "You don't think they went to the river!"

"I have no way of knowing that, sir," Diaz responded calmly as he jotted into his notebook, "but we'll search that area." Next question, "What did you do yesterday?"

"Yesterday, we had our Christmas." The cop seemed to be waiting for more, so Antonio explained, "I planned on having them on Sunday, Christmas Day; but of course, Carmen had them, so I was not able to take them to Mass like I wanted." He didn't try to keep the bitterness from his voice. "Instead, they got here so late Sunday night, they were too sleepy to do anything with me. They opened only one gift and then it was time for bed. We had to have our Christmas yesterday."

"So what did you do yesterday?"

"What does it matter what we did yesterday?" Antonio lashed out in frustration. All these stupid questions were getting them nowhere. "We have to look for my little girls."

"We need to draw a timeline," Diaz explained, "like a map to trace the events of the day. Who saw whom. Who did what when."

The lawman was looking at him expectantly, so Antonio finally relented, shrugged and continued his recital, quickening his pace. "The first thing they wanted to do when they woke up was open the gifts Santa had brought them." As Antonio relived the events of the previous day, the pain of today faded to the background. For the moment. "They played with their new dolls while I made pancakes for breakfast. After that, I cleaned up the dishes and started the pork roast marinating—"

"And what were your daughters doing while you did that?"

"They were in their room. They made their beds, got dressed, played with their toys, I guess," he shrugged. "When I was finished in the kitchen, we bundled up and went outside for awhile. We busted the piñata in the backyard. They love that, especially when the thing breaks wide open and everything falls out. We made sure we picked up all the prizes. By then, it had started to snow and it was too cold to stay out and play. They were disappointed to have to come inside, but I promised them that we'd make a snowman today and that we'd try out their new sleds on Collier Hill." Antonio's voice caught and he drank a bit more coffee. "So we came inside and played Candy Land and we watched that Nemo movie—"

"You mean *Twenty Thousand Leagues under the Sea*?"

Antonio shook his head and flashed the cop an impatient look. "No. The animated thing with the fish." Diaz nodded and Antonio continued, "After the movie the girls put on the new dresses I bought them for Christmas—the dresses they were supposed to wear to Mass—" The quaver in his voice made him stop abruptly and he closed his eyes, frowning. *Of course that didn't happen because Carmen had to mess up those plans.* He covered his face with his hands.

"Mr. Ibarra?"

Antonio's eyes flew open and he roughly wiped them as Diaz's voice brought him back to the present. *"Lo siento,"* Antonio said gruffly and sipped more coffee hoping his tears had gone unnoticed. "Anyway," Antonio continued when he could trust his voice, "by then it was three o'clock and time to eat our Christmas dinner. Roast pork, like *mi madre* always made when we were kids."

"And who joined you for that meal?"

"No one. Just Marisa, Liana, and me."

"And no one else lives here?" Diaz asked. "Just you and the girls?"

Antonio shook his head, "No. You misunderstood. The girls don't live with me any more. Most of the time, it's just me and Donna."

"Donna?"

"*Si. Mi perra.* My dog," Antonio said.

Diaz glanced toward the animal lying down on the floor beside the kitchen table and jotted something in his notebook.

"Loyal Donna." Antonio explained, "Since the end of August, when I lost custody of my children, I might have gone insane if it had not been for Donna's being there every day when I come home from work. That and seeing my children every other weekend are what keep me going."

"So, the children live with their mother?"

"Yes."

"And the mother had them until—"

"Around nine o'clock Sunday," Antonio said grudgingly, "Christmas *night.*"

Diaz looked at him curiously. "You seem upset with that."

"'Of course, I am!" Antonio vehemently banged his fist on the table and Diaz jumped. "I told Carmen I wanted them early enough on Sunday to make the evening Mass at six o'clock. I thought it was a reasonable request. A father should be allowed to have his children for some part of Christmas, after all. But no," Antonio sneered. "Carmen gave me a lot of attitude. She and her new husband had brought them to Midnight Mass, so bringing them to Mass again on Sunday would have been redundant, she said. So Sunday, when they should have been with me, they were over at Thibault's family. The *step*-family, if there is such a thing. The Thibaults had bought the girls gifts and Carmen wanted them to open them in front of their new relatives." Antonio's lower lip curled in a snarl, "They are *not* their relatives. Not blood." He pounded a fist on his chest, "I'm the father, you know? They belong with *me*—not with the *Thibaults*.*"

Officer Diaz made a few more notations into his pad, then steered the conversation to a more pleasant topic, "So, you spent yesterday alone, enjoying each other's company." Antonio immediately felt the rage drain away and the cop continued, "You mentioned *tu madre*. Is she living?"

"*Sí. Mama* is living. But for the past ten years or so, she spends the cold months, from November to April, in Puerto Rico. A snowbird. She lives in Troy City the rest of the time."

"I see. So what did you do after dinner?"

Antonio lashed out petulantly, unable to hide his frustration, "Are all these questions really important? Shouldn't we be out looking for my little girls? While we're in here chatting like old friends, Marisa and Liana are getting further and further away. God knows where they could be by now." He covered his face again with his hands.

Diaz sighed. "Perhaps these questions seem like a waste of time to you, Mr. Ibarra. But I assure you, they are *very* important. Something may innocently come up to enlighten us as to where they might have gone."

Antonio sighed deeply and resigned himself to Diaz's questions. The sooner they got done, the sooner they could get out there and do their job. "Okay. What more do you want to know?"

"What happened after dinner?" the cop repeated.

"We cleared off the table and they begged me to let them dry the dishes. They were so cute." Antonio's heart swelled with love as he reminisced, "Marisa kept pointing out wet spots Liana had missed. She was like a mother hen, warning her little sister not to touch the sharp knives. They left those for me—" He suddenly had to swallow a hard lump in his throat. Sensing that Diaz was preparing to ask another dumb question, Antonio hurried on, "Later, I phoned my mother in Puerto Rico so that the girls could talk to her. They don't get much of a chance to do that now that they live with their mother. My sisters, Ramona and Luisa—"

"Are they in Puerto Rico as well?"

"Yes," Antonio frowned. *Something else that Carmen screwed up!* "It's our custom to go to Puerto Rico for *la Noche Buena* to see *Mama*; a family tradition since she spends Christmas there, and we're here in the States. My sister, Luisa is a teacher in New Hampshire, so she's already off on vacation. But Ramona and I take time off from work; she's a nurse in Vermont." Then he added with annoyance, "My father is deceased; he died of a heart attack when I was fifteen years old. You have enough details now, Officer Diaz?" Antonio let the sarcasm drip, "Maybe you want my shoe size, too?"

"The more details we have, the better, Mr. Ibarra." Diaz ignored Antonio's disrespectful tone.

Antonio sighed, "I'm sorry." He rubbed his eyes hard then dropped his hands to the table once more. "Please forgive my outburst. You must understand how upset I am. This is so frustrating. I feel like we're wasting time. I want to find my little girls."

"We want to find them, too, Mr. Ibarra. And as soon as possible," Diaz assured him. "So, you spoke to your family in Puerto Rico, and—"

"*Si*," Antonio nodded grimly. "It's the best we could do this year. Carmen put an end to any hopes I had of bringing the girls to the island. This is the first year Marisa and Liana missed *la Noche Buena* with their *abuela*. So, we called them and the girls spoke with them all. Then, even though they are with her all the time, and were with her all of the Christmas weekend," Antonio heard the resentment in his voice, but didn't try to cover it, "they asked me to call their mother so that they could say hello." He shrugged, "So I let them call her." A thought struck him and Antonio moaned mournfully, "Oh, my God! How am I going to tell them about Marisa and Liana? My mother and my sisters. They will be devastated." Then shocked by the next realization, he blurted, "And Carmen! What will I say to Carmen? She will kill me for sure. I'll never see *mi hijas* again!"

Diaz left those comments unanswered and asked, "What time did you make those phone calls?"

"I don't know," Antonio answered miserably. "It was dark out by then. Maybe it was around six o'clock or so." He was so tired, as though he hadn't slept in days.

Diaz prodded again, "And then?"

"Then, it was time for their baths. I combed out the tangles in their beautiful hair and made loose braids to keep it from snarling again while they slept. Then I listened to their prayers and I read them a story," then added before Diaz could ask, "— *Winnie the Pooh*. I tucked them in with hugs and kisses. I blessed them, traced crosses on their foreheads—" His voice broke again, "And then, this morning, they were gone." Antonio squeezed his eyes shut as twin hot tears ran down both cheeks.

"Mr. Ibarra," the cop was saying as though he hadn't noticed, "we're going to be using scent dogs to help locate Marisa and Liana. I need you to find the clothes that the girls wore yesterday to give the dogs their scent. I also need a couple of good, clear photographs to copy and circulate among the searchers and to give to the media. If you could get those things for me now? I'll call this in as an urgent 'missing persons.' The FBI will be notified and I'll make sure they sound an Amber Alert. We'll call the state police and the sheriff's office to assist as well. I promise you, we will do everything in our power to find Marisa and Liana."

The strength of Officer Diaz's promise was all that sustained Antonio Ibarra as he left to do the policeman's bidding.

7:18 A.M.

Stretched luxuriantly on the satin sheets of the king-sized bed, Carmen was enjoying the extra moments of quiet. It had been a late night, after all. She and Paul had taken advantage of their alone time, and had made slow, easy love until after midnight. It was too early to get up, although she could hear Paul in the shower, getting ready for work. That was making her feel somewhat guilty; but not enough to get up just yet. Her eyes slowly closed—

Loud banging coupled with the repeated jarring sound of the doorbell startled her fully awake. The urgent, persistent pounding required immediate attention. *Someone must be in trouble,* she thought. *A neighbor has had an accident and needs help.* She sprang from the bed and flew down the stairs, barefooted and in pajamas, not taking time to grab her robe. She flung open the front door.

She was not prepared for the two Massachusetts State Troopers standing on the porch.

"Are you Carmen Thibault?" the taller one asked.

She nodded, "Yes." She clutched the neck of her pajamas more closely against the cold.

"May we come in?" the other requested.

She stepped back, still puzzled about the reason for their visit. The policemen looked serious; something had happened. *But not here,* she reasoned against a stab of fear. Paul was upstairs, safe and sound. Surely they had come here by mistake—

The taller policeman had been talking. Apparently he had introduced himself and his partner, but she had not caught their names. Now his question forced her to pay attention, "Where are your daughters, Marisa and Liana?"

"They're not here," she answered quickly. "They're with their father, visiting for the Holiday."

She saw the troopers exchange glances. The first officer was speaking again, while the other stared at her. "Perhaps you should sit down," the first policeman suggested offering his hand to help her to a chair.

This isn't a mistake! Her heart dropped to the pit of her stomach and a prickling sensation began in her head. She knocked the trooper's hand away, "No! No! I don't want to sit down! Tell me what happened!" She gasped, "You've come to tell me something awful! My God, they've been injured in an accident. They're in the hospital. Please don't say they're—"

"No, Mrs. Thibault," the other cop assured her, "At least, that's not—"

"We're here to tell you that Marisa and Liana are missing," the first one stated.

"Missing?" she repeated, trembling. "No, they're not missing. They're with Antonio—"

"—Antonio Ibarra of River Road, Ridgeport," the other cop acknowledged.

"A 9-1-1 call went into the Ridgeport Police Station around 6:30 to report that two children had disappeared. Their father had found their beds empty," the first one finished.

That was all Carmen heard above the unbearable ringing in her ears. A sickening grayness closed in from everywhere around her, and then total blackness.

*****

Paul heard the commotion as he was toweling dry. It didn't sound good; Carmen's voice sounded odd. He grabbed his pants. Suddenly, she was screaming. *She's being attacked!* He finished pulling on his jeans and came out of the bathroom shirtless just in time to see Carmen's limp form crumple into the arms of a state trooper. Paul ran down the stairs and took his wife from the cop's arms. "What happened!" Paul demanded, incensed and frightened. He carried her quickly into the living room and carefully set her down on the sofa as one of the officers filled Paul in on the disappearance of the children.

"What?" Paul shook his head, "I can't believe it!" He vigorously rubbed Carmen's hands and gently patted her pale cheeks, calling her name, "Carmen. Carmen. Wake up, darling." He took only a moment to glance up at the cops, "Those kids are her life. How did this happen?"

"The FBI has been called in," the shorter Statie said, "and an Amber Alert has been sent out. It's too early to tell, though, if the kids were kidnapped, or if they ran away."

Paul looked at them scornfully, "They didn't run away, I can assure you of that. They've been abducted. Damn Antonio!" He returned his attention to his inert wife. "God, this is going to send her off the edge."

7:19 A.M.

Strange how things happen by chance.

It was chance, for example, that fifteen-year-old Jet Tate was spending part of Christmas vacation with his cousin, Hank Robert. During the week before Christmas, his mother and Aunt Claire had made final plans for their annual trip to New York City, when they took his eighteen-year-old sister, Christine, and Hank's seventeen-year-old twin sisters, Danielle and Denise, "To see the spectacular window displays, ice skate at Rockefeller Center, and maybe catch a theater play." Since Jules, Jet's dad, had been laid off from work on the Friday before Christmas, it seemed logical to let the guys bunk at the Roberts' house, and the girls sleep at the Tates'. This would allow the women to get an early start on Monday without disturbing the men.

So since Sunday night after the womenfolk left, the men had been doing guy things. Monday morning they'd gone paintballing and had feasted on Coney Island hot dogs for lunch. They'd made it back home before the first snowflake fell and spent the rest of the afternoon playing hearts. Then over some of Uncle Phil's primo chili, they'd made plans for the next day. They decided they'd get lunch at Caroline's Corner, see a movie, then maybe go to Bigelow's and shoot some pool. The boys went up to bed excited and looking forward to spending another day together with their dads. As they had done the previous night, Jet and Hank talked, played with Hank's new video game, and watched some late-night TV. By the time they finally turned in it was well after 2:00 A.M.

Even so, Jet had trouble falling asleep. First, it was the pillow, flatter than he was used to. He folded it in half and that was a little better. Then there were sounds outside, loud enough for him to hear even through the closed windows; voices, a child complaining, car doors closing, and then a car's motor starting. A dog howled once, a long, mournful sound, and then at last—thank God—the car drove away and everything was quiet. For two minutes. Hank began snoring and Jet considered moving to the couch downstairs. But in the end, fatigue took over and Jet drifted off to sleep, only to be startled awake by a loud commotion.

Jet sat bolt upright in bed. Voices. Uncle Phil's and another male voice he couldn't identify. He checked the time on his watch.

"Geesh! Not even seven-thirty!" He yawned, plopped back down, turned over and pulled the pillow up over his ear. Yet even then he could hear them. Bleary-eyed and groggy, he dragged himself out of bed and opened the bedroom door a crack, trying to find out what the noise was all about. But from there, it was only louder, not clearer. So Jet went out and sat on the top step where he got a great vantage point.

A Ridgeport police officer was talking to Uncle Phil whose hairy legs protruded from beneath his navy blue housecoat.

"—search the area around River Road," the policeman was saying.

"Of course," Uncle Phil stated. "I'm sorry I didn't see or hear anything, Officer. I've lived in this neighborhood for about fifteen years, so I know the area well. I'd be happy to organize whatever neighbors are home today, as well."

That's how Jet got involved in the search for the little Ibarra girls.

Totally by chance.

7:53 A.M.

Word about the disappearance of the Ibarra children got out quickly, and by the time Jet and Hank came out with Uncle Phil and Dad, a good number of searchers bundled up against the cold had already assembled at River Road outside the boundaries of the yellow police tape. Some had backpacks in which they carried extra mittens and scarves, trail mix, and thermoses of hot cocoa or coffee. While they waited, they pulled woolen hats over the reddened tips of their ears, stamped their booted feet on the snowy ground, and murmured softly to each other, the foggy wisps of their breaths carried away by the chill wind. Had they been a little rowdier—or more cheerful—they might have been taken for a group of freezing fans eagerly waiting to buy tickets to a Patriots game.

The weather cooperated in one way; it stopped snowing. Yet the sun could not break through the thick battleship gray clouds that hung low in the sky. The weatherman had correctly predicted bone-chilling cold with a wind chill that would take fifteen degrees from the actual temperature. But no one was discouraged by the frigid weather.

New arrivals continued to come by car, presumably from other places too far away to walk, as more neighbors trudged through snow to join the growing assembly. These newcomers quickly found friends and acquaintances in the crowd and joined them to share news and gossip.

Just then, Jet recognized a pretty African-American girl he knew from way back in first grade at St. Augustine's, Robin LaRue. Jet knew that both of her parents were teachers; he had had Mrs. LaRue in third grade, and now Mr. LaRue was his geometry teacher. These days, Robin was in his English class at Bishop O'Donnell's, but she was not one of the kids he usually hung around with. So he was surprised when she waved and headed their way.

Jet realized that she had done something to her curly black hair. It was straighter than usual and flowed in long tresses past her shoulders and attractively followed the curve of her jaw and framed her pretty face. She was a perfect compromise between her parents; tall and slender, like her father, with her mother's delicate features. As Jet gazed at her with new appreciation, she smiled at him coyly, causing deep dimples to appear in her smooth cinnamon-colored cheeks.

Robin LaRue nodded hello as she approached him and Hank. She smiled at Jet again, and then to his disappointment, she turned her attention to Hank. The two of them took up a conversation that effectively shut Jet out. All he could do was watch and listen. He tried to convince himself that they weren't deliberately being rude and that he should not be offended. They were obviously just good friends who shared interests different than his own. And why shouldn't it be that way? They were neighbors after all, and apparently had known each other forever. Still Jet felt himself blush, embarrassed by the fact that he'd barely paid any attention to her since their days at St. Augustine's. As he stood there feeling totally flustered and foolish, he was rescued by a sound that caused all eyes to turn in that direction.

A gray-haired woman warmly bundled in a man's red plaid hunter's jacket had stepped out of the front door of the bungalow across the street and was making her way around a Mercury Sable parked in the snow beside the driveway. Leaning on her cane, she tottered out to the hastily shoveled driveway that led to a small garage set apart from the house. She pressed a button on a remote control, and the garage door slowly opened to reveal a long table on which had been set up three large urns with Styrofoam cups and all the fixings.

She waved to the crowd and called out in a gravelly voice, "Coffee, cocoa, and hot tea, everyone. Please, come get something hot to drink."

Not plagued by shyness, Hank and Jet were among the first to approach the table of hot drinks. As Jet came away with a cup of steaming creamy cocoa, the man from next door ambled over noticeably favoring his right leg. He wore a heavy old camouflage jacket, apparently Army issue, and a fur-lined leather hat with the earflaps down.

"That's Mr. Cabot," Hank whispered to Jet.

"His ankle must be bothering him," Robin observed. Then she added for Jet's benefit, "He was shot in Vietnam, you know. He usually doesn't limp that much."

"Yeah," agreed Hank. "I wonder what happened."

As though he'd heard Hank's remark, Mr. Cabot explained. "I hope you people don't mind if I sit this out," the man said solemnly. "I twisted my ankle yesterday getting down from a ladder and it's letting me know it today." It was obvious to Jet that Mr. Cabot's ankle was causing him considerable pain. It would not be wise to aggravate it by walking on irregular, slippery terrain. Apparently, others shared his assessment for many nodded wordlessly. "I thought I'd help Mary with her rest stop."

"That's a good idea, Chuck," Uncle Phil commented *sotto voce*. "Although I believe Mary could do a number on any assailant with her cane, I think it's unwise to leave her alone."

"Right," Chuck Cabot chuckled. "The whole mess could be tied up in court forever!"

"What're you two whispering about over there?" Mrs. Carvalho cackled. "I heard my name mentioned. What're you up to, Sergeant Henri Philippe Robert?" She mocked with a terrible, affected French accent meant to underline her annoyance.

Uncle Phil turned his light blue gaze upon the irritated woman. "Nothing, Mary, I promise."

"I just told him I was going to hang out with you today," Mr. Cabot came to Uncle Phil's defense. "That's if you don't mind," he added quickly as she cast angry eyes his way.

"It doesn't have anything to do with my being *old*, does it, Mr. Charles Cabot, Esquire?" she snapped. "Sixty-five ain't old, but you make it sound like I'm decrepit! I'll have you know that if it weren't for this bum hip, I'd run circles around all of you! I have more energy—"

Mr. Cabot raised both hands in mock surrender. "We know, Mary. I just figured since I can't go out there either with this accursed ankle," he winked at her, "us two cripples could keep each other company."

Mrs. Carvalho's face was transformed in a mass of smiling wrinkles. "Pshaw! Go on! A youngster like you, flirting with an old bird like me?"

"Me, a *youngster*? You an *old* bird? Did you hear yourself?" Mr. Cabot's hearty laughter made the onlookers smile; a

23

momentary lifting of everyone's heavy mood. "I'll have you know I'm not that young. I'm fifty-nine myself."

"You child," she teased back, "You're not even sixty."

Suddenly the banter ceased as everyone's attention turned to the Hispanic man emerging from the yellow house across the street. He had a black Labrador retriever on a leash and together they carefully picked their way in the tracks already in the snow.

"There's Tony Ibarra, now," Dad said. He waved and the man immediately came over, embracing Dad in a big bear hug. Under different circumstances, it might have been funny given that Dad was so much taller than Mr. Ibarra. At six-foot three-inches, Dad towered over the other man by what looked to Jet like six or seven inches. But the hug was filled with emotion and touching to watch, causing a lump to rise in Jet's throat, and he was forced to avert his self-conscious gaze.

"Thank you so much, Jules, for coming to look for my Marisa and my Liana," said the Hispanic man, his somber brown eyes filling.

Jet saw his father swallow hard against rising emotion. "It's the least I can do for one of my Union brothers, Antonio. If there's anything you need—"

"*Gracias, amigo,* I'll remember that," Mr. Ibarra said. Then the man turned to Mrs. Carvalho, embraced her and said something in her ear. She kissed him on the cheek. Mr. Ibarra took a cup of coffee and rejoined their little group while the large black dog sniffed around the garage floor with interest.

Jet hunkered down extending his hand to the retriever and she gently licked the tips of his fingers with her warm wet tongue. *How I'd love owning a dog like this.* But the thought was interrupted by some activity out at the street.

Rising, he saw that two more squad cars had arrived, followed by four K-9 units. Directly behind them trundled a white van with a satellite dish lying flat on its roof; WTCN-TV News Channel 3 was on the scene. The vehicles parked where they could along the street, the news van commandeering the area directly in front of Mrs. Carvalho's house. Dog handlers with their specially trained hounds spilled out into the road as search organizers took charge of the crowd.

For the most part, groups were made up of ten to fifteen people, families and friends being encouraged to work together. Specific assignments were laid out. A third of the people would search the area of Long River for any sign that someone had recently walked along its slick, swollen banks or gone into the water. The rest would scour the woods behind the Ibarra house. Jet's group—comprised of Uncle Phil as their leader, Dad, Hank, the LaRues, and a few more people he didn't know—was part of the latter contingent.

By eight-thirty, the teams were ready to go.

The news crew was left to film with a strict warning to stay out of the way. No one took time for an interview. Lives were at stake. There was no time to waste.

Since the Ibarra property had been cordoned off with yellow police tape, the "woods detail" proceeded through the large vacant lot adjacent to the property. Jet looked up at the tall trees on the other side of the broad, snowy meadow. These woods, a mixture of deciduous and coniferous trees, formed the northern boundary of Ibarra's, LaRue's, and all of the properties on the north side of River Road, from Cross Street all the way to Long River.

"Whew," Jet whistled. "Is this a state forest?"

"No, Jet," Uncle Phil answered. "That's Collier's Woods. They're actually part of Collier Ridge Estate and property of Jeremiah Ridge Blakely, the patriarch of our town. His mother was the great-great-great-great-granddaughter of the town's founder, Esther Collier Ridge." He added, "I might have missed a great or two."

"It's a really big deal to Ridgeport natives," Hank told him. "Every Founder's Day, Mr. Blakely is Grand Marshal of the parade. You know," Hank jogged Jet's memory, "it's when we have the fireworks at the end of August—"

"Gee," Uncle Phil teased, "and I thought it was to celebrate that all the kids were going back to school."

Hank rolled his eyes at his father.

"Yeah," Jet remembered, "and they have the blueberry pie-eating contest—"

"To commemorate that Esther Collier Ridge paid the Wampanoags for the land with a blueberry pie—" Robin explained.

"—along with a metal knife, a few strings of colored glass beads, and a peck of beans," Hank said as though he were reciting for the class.

Within a few moments, the group had arrived outside a rusty, partly collapsed wire fence. As the rest of the searchers gathered around, a stout, middle-aged woman of medium height and straight chin-length black hair made her way to the front of the assemblage. Jet could see that she was wearing a sheriff's deputy's uniform. She brought a bullhorn up to her mouth and solemnly waited until everyone had quieted before speaking. Then she gave the volunteers concise and clear instructions.

"Good morning," the sheriff's deputy said briskly, "My name is Sergeant Sheila Rothman of the Troy County Sheriff's Department and I will be coordinating the search of Collier's Woods. Mr. Blakely has graciously given us permission to search his woods, saving us the trouble of getting a warrant or court order. That's good news for us because it's saving us a lot of time. Please remember that you are on private property. Also, be aware that these woods are home to a variety of animals, not all of them harmless and gentle. Snakes are hibernating right now; however, coyotes and foxes are not. I doubt they will bother us, but as a precaution, stay within sight of other people. Do not hurry on ahead of the group or take off on your own. Does everyone understand?"

"Are there any bears in these woods?" asked a woman somewhere to Jet's right.

Sgt. Rothman inhaled thoughtfully, then shook her head slowly and raised the bullhorn up to her mouth again, "No one has reported any bear sightings in a long time. But that doesn't mean there aren't any newcomers." A murmur rumbled through the crowd but the deputy spoke above it. "Bears should also be hibernating for the winter, so they shouldn't be a problem. You just need to be careful and refrain from approaching any wild animal. That includes deer, squirrels, and other types you might think are harmless and cute. Raccoons are nocturnal and should not be out now, so their presence would be a sign of trouble. Most animals will stay clear of us, though one infected with rabies could attack."

She scanned the crowd for other questions or comments, and then continued. "In a moment we will enter Mr. Blakely's woods and search for any sign that the Ibarra children wandered here during the night. Each person will walk in as straight a line as possible, scrutinizing the area directly in front of him or her for any piece of clothing, scrap of fabric, strand of hair, broken branch, child-sized impression in the ground. Real footprints will have been covered up by last night's snowstorm. We're looking for anything that could give us a clue as to what happened to the children. Particular attention should be given to spots that might be construed as "hiding places," like low-hanging pine boughs and spaces beneath fallen timbers that might provide shelter from the elements. Be aware that some of these hiding places, the hollowed out trunks of trees, for example, could also be the den of an animal. Remember, Collier's Woods has long been used as a hunting ground, so look out also for pits or holes in the ground where a child might fall and be unable to climb out. The point is; you yourselves must be careful and vigilant. This is not a game; we don't want to have to suspend our search for the children because one of you has had an accident or an unfortunate encounter with a wild animal."

Sgt. Rothman let that sink in, then finished, "If the little girls went through here, or tried to hide anywhere in these woods, with any luck, one of you will find some indication of such. If you do, you are to call out immediately for your group leader so that your find can be carefully examined. By the same token, don't waste time by calling out needlessly." Sgt. Rothman again scanned the crowd, "Are there any questions?" When no one replied, the deputy ordered everyone over the rusted, crumbling fence. "Please face the woods and stand side by side at arm's length away from the next person."

As Jet waited for his turn to go over the fence, he noticed that Mr. Ibarra and Donna lagged behind. It didn't look as though they were coming any further.

"Wish us luck, Mr. Ibarra," Jet said.

"Not luck," Mr. Ibarra corrected him, "but the grace of God. I invoke *mi patrono*, St. Anthony of Padua, the finder of lost things, that he might help the searchers find my little girls."

Then, at Sgt. Rothman's signal, one hundred-fifty people advanced together like a long snake moving sideways among the brambles and bushes that poked up from the snow beneath the stark and leafless trees.

8:35 A.M.

With preliminary statements from both Antonio Ibarra and Bob LaRue, Officers Geraldo Diaz and David Caron had gone to work. While Caron strung yellow police tape across Ibarra's front yard to protect the scene that had already been compromised by Ibarra's and LaRue's footprints, Diaz radioed the station to request the necessary manpower to conduct a proper search and thoroughly investigate the scene. Next, they had asked the closest neighbors if they had seen or heard anything unusual in the wee hours of the morning. Everyone had been genuinely concerned and eager to help in any way they could.

The policemen returned to their cruiser as the first teams set out on their search and the crime scene investigation people were unloading their gear from the van. They spotted Antonio Ibarra coming around the west end of his house with his dog on a leash.

Officer Diaz repeated his earlier advice, "You need to stay close by in case the investigators want to ask you any questions."

"I understand. I must stay out of their way and let them do

their job," said Ibarra looking grim. As one of the crime scene investigators approached the house, Donna pulled on her leash and began to growl menacingly. As he had done earlier, Antonio Ibarra gave the dog a simple command, "Quiet, Donna," and the animal immediately obeyed.

"You'll need to keep the dog away from them as well," Diaz pointed out.

"*Si.* I will. I'll put her in the basement until they leave," Ibarra promised, but he didn't look happy about it. "Thank you, Officers."

Diaz and Caron got into their cruiser and watched the man go back into the house. "What do you think?" David Caron asked from the passenger's seat.

"Not sure," Geraldo Diaz admitted getting behind the wheel. "He seems upset—"

"Just as you'd expect a father to be when he discovers his children missing from their beds."

"And he's not happy about staying put."

"Again, understandably," Caron said. "If I were the kids' father, I would certainly feel useless sitting at home when I could be out looking for them."

"He has some mean temper, though," Diaz commented.

"Like any hot-blooded Latino," Caron teased with a sideways glance.

Geraldo smirked. Then, "I got the feeling he's not too fond of his ex."

David's eyebrows shot up, "What'd he say that makes you think that?"

"He didn't say in words exactly," Geraldo said slowly, "but when he talks about the custody arrangements, he tenses up, gets sarcastic. Almost vicious." Diaz went on to explain how Ibarra was upset over missing Christmas Mass with the children.

"And that surprises you? He's certainly not going to blame the kids, even if it was their idea to be at their new family's house." Caron shrugged, "It's easier to blame the ex-wife. Do you know any man who thinks his ex is a saint?" When Diaz didn't respond, Caron continued, "It's understandable, man. He's emotional right now; worried about his kids; maybe feeling guilty about their disappearance; maybe pissed that they went missing while *he* had them. You're married with a kid on the way. How would you feel if something happened between you and Paloma and she made it hard for you to see your kid?"

Geraldo Diaz shook his head and sighed, "I love my wife and I can't imagine anything that could change how I feel about her." At David Caron's impatient look, Geraldo finished quickly, "But if we had to share custody of a child, I guess I'd be pretty pissed if I missed out on having my kid on an important holiday like Christmas."

"Maybe this Carmen chick is flexing her muscle, pushing her ex's buttons." David Caron suggested, "Maybe she has something to prove. A score to settle."

"Or, maybe she's pushed his buttons once too often, and he's done something to ensure that the kids'll stay with him." Geraldo mused aloud. It was something he'd be sure to put in his report. "And that dog. Something about that isn't right." He drifted off in thought. *Unbelievable the way that animal can change mood just with a single word from her master.*

"What?" Caron's voice broke through his thoughts.

Diaz shook himself, "It's just that, remember how the dog acted when we first got here?"

"Yeah! I thought we were dog food!"

"Well, I don't understand how anyone could have gotten past her, let alone take those kids away. She would have torn them apart, don't you think?"

"Maybe she wasn't around when they left," Caron suggested. Then, "And remember, we haven't established that the kids were kidnapped. They could have simply walked away."

Geraldo nodded, although he couldn't shake the feeling that something didn't ring true. It was useless to speculate at this point. The crime scene people would get to the bottom of it. He shrugged it off and asked, "What'd you get from the neighbor. What's his name? LaRue?"

"Only that Ibarra was in a heightened state of anxiety,"

Caron responded. "Found him wandering outside in nothing but his bathrobe, knee-deep in snow, no shoes on, ranting about his little girls. Can you believe that? A good way to freeze your *cajones* off, if you ask me!"

Further comment was interrupted when a newsman dressed in a dark blue parka, microphone in hand, approached the police car, making a cranking motion with his free hand. He was closely followed by another with a video camera. Geraldo Diaz turned the key in the ignition and lowered the window.

"Carlos Viveiros, WTCN News," the newsman stated. "We heard about the disappearance of the children on the scanner. Did the kids wander off and get lost? Were they kidnapped? What can you give us, Officers?"

"Only what you probably already know," Geraldo answered. "An Amber Alert has been put out for two little girls, Marisa and Liana Ibarra, ages seven and five. They were here with their father yesterday, and this morning they were not in their beds."

"Any leads? Suspicions? Is it really a kidnapping? Do you suspect foul play?"

Diaz bristled at the newsman's insinuations and persistence; all they needed now was for the media to jump to premature conclusions. He started the car and answered levelly, striving to keep his ire from showing, "When we have something, we'll be sure to let you know, Mr. Viveiros. We'll need media coverage to alert the public and get people to keep an eye out for these kids and get them back, so you can be sure of a scoop." Geraldo started to raise the window, but stopped with an afterthought. "Oh, and Mr. Viveiros, I'm sure we can trust you to honor the yellow tape?"

The newsman's face dropped slightly as he took in the crime scene barrier that effectively restricted his admittance to anywhere on the Ibarra property. "We would have liked to interview the father."

"No can do," Geraldo Diaz shook his head. "The crime scene people are in there now, the man is in a terrible state, he won't be coming out, and there's no way you can cross this line."

With that, Diaz raised the window, and as he turned the car around, heard the newsman yelling, "But the people have a right to know." David Caron gave him a friendly wave as the police car passed inches from Viveiros's toes.

8:44 A.M.

In her twenty-some-odd years with the Troy County Crime Scene Investigation team, the last twelve as district head, fifty-seven-year-old Lieutenant Ruth Wilson had seen her share of disturbing crime scenes. Gore and evidence of violent death no longer shocked and horrified her as they had in the early years. A bloody weapon, blood-splattered walls, entrails and gray matter splayed over a carpet, severed body parts, a corpse sprawled in a grotesque position; none of it upset her any more. Murder was never pretty.

Her team knew better than to enter the scene before she had the chance to look it over from the doorway. She liked to envision the way the room must have been before the crime had occurred. She would imagine the movements of the perpetrator and the reactions of the victim. She could do this in a detached manner that seemed cold to her subordinates. She knew her crime-scene demeanor had earned her the unflattering nickname "Lieutenant Iceberg". No one had ever dared call her that to her face, but it didn't matter. They could say whatever they wanted. The bottom line? She knew she was good at what she did. No one could fault her on that.

Now she unzipped her jacket and got to work. As she looked at the disarray of the little girls' bedroom, her mind's eye reconstructed it as it might have looked yesterday with everything in its place. Mentally, she made up the white twin beds; fixed the rumpled pink covers and the puff quilt coverlets, set the dainty shams in place at the headboard. A few stuffed animals posed among the pillows of each bed. Between the beds, a nightstand held a Barbie lamp with a pretty pink shade. The closet door was closed, the bureau drawers were neatly shut. Dolls, toys, and books were placed carefully on the shelves and racks that lined the wall. Maybe some had sat on the chest of drawers.

It was a sweet room for two innocent little girls. One that her granddaughters—

No! Don't go there! she warned herself. *Don't let anything get in and muck up your judgment.*

She closed her eyes to banish the unwanted thought, took a deep breath and quickly expelled the air from her lungs. Once the undesirable image had left her mind, she opened her eyes again, ready to return to reality and take stock of what was actually there.

She snapped a few Polaroid pictures: The beds with their pink Barbie comforters thrown aside, the pillows askew, and the matching sheets twisted and drooping onto the rose carpet. The overturned lamp on the nightstand, its shade tipped sideways at a weird angle. The castoffs scattered about the room; toys, books, shoes, articles of clothing, and hair ribbons littered the floor. Next, she pointed the camera toward the closet; its folding mirror doors were fully opened exposing a few bare hangers on which had presumably hung the children's clothes. A pretty burgundy velvet dress hung by a shoulder on its hanger, while a smaller, dark green garment had dropped to the floor among a couple of pairs of little girls shoes. Finally, she photographed the dresser, totally devoid of anything on top, as though it had been swiped clean. Some of the bureau drawers had been left opened with sleeves and pant legs hanging out like the broken arms and legs of victims of a horrible accident.

As she shook her dyed-blond head, she sensed her second-in-command at her elbow and turned to look at him. Thirty-two-year-old Kristofer Bauer not only matched her height, but his slight frame often caused him to be mistaken for a female from behind. In addition to that, he kept his light brown curls rather long and neatly tied in a low ponytail, further contributing to the illusion. It was only when he turned around and one caught sight of his carefully groomed goatee that one realized one's error. Kris had come to her team about five years ago, and Ruth had trained and molded the eager young man into as near a replica of herself as she could get, so much so that he'd been dubbed "Ice Cube." Now he returned Ruth's grim look, his light blue eyes magnified to large orbs behind thick glasses.

"Okay, Kris. It's all yours."

The younger man nodded and muttered his thanks as he entered the bedroom and got to work. Confident that he would let her know if he found anything significant, Ruth Wilson left in search of the father of the missing children.

She found him in the living room sitting on the brown leather couch, bent forward, elbows on his knees, his head dropped into his hands. He must have sensed her presence for he looked up as she approached. She sat on the cream-colored easy chair closest to him, but used only the front edge of the seat, resisting the temptation to make herself comfortable. She leaned forward, serious and unsmiling, her chocolate brown eyes holding his, and addressed him, her cop antennae alert and searching.

"Mr. Ibarra, did you go into the children's bedroom today?"

8:52 A.M.

Antonio found himself to be in the way in his own house.

After he put Donna in the cellar, he got himself a fresh mug of coffee and brought it to the living room, convincing himself that he would simply relax and read a magazine while the crime scene investigators went about their work.

Easier said than done.

Truth be known, the crime scene investigation team had invaded his home like ants. Now that the investigators were fully entrenched, they infiltrated every room. No private place was left untouched. They swept for clues, for anything that could be used as evidence or provide them with any lead. Every scrap of paper, every article of clothing, every particle of dust was of interest to the investigators. They worked methodically, touched his most treasured possessions, intruded his most personal domain, and examined his most secret thoughts. Antonio knew they would dig relentlessly until they found what they wanted.

He tried not to think about what they were doing, but he couldn't help it.

There was nothing for him to do but sit quietly out of the way and let them do their job. He had no stomach for the coffee and it sat on the coffee table, untouched, getting cold. He dropped his head in his hands and tried to pray for the safe return of his little girls but all that did was bring on more feelings of dread, more tears of despair.

Antonio raised his head as he sensed someone approaching him. He gazed up into the dark brown eyes of a middle-aged woman with yellow hair. She looked stern—no, mean. Like she thought he did something wrong. Like she hated him.

Antonio knew the type. She was a woman who was used to having her own way, one who needed to be in charge, run the show. A woman who had to prove she was as good as any man and in the process would emasculate any man she had power over. *Humph! Even her second in command looks like a girl!* When would women realize they already had power over men? Trying to be one of the guys was just so wrong. Unnatural. And unnecessary.

A waste.

He watched her sit in the chair beside the sofa. Her eyes never left his. *She's trying to beat me down,* he thought. She introduced herself as Lieutenant Wilson and asked him a question. Accusing. He did not lower his gaze as he felt she would expect him to do but held her steady.

"Yes, Lieutenant," he shrugged, "I went in there to look for my daughters. I already explained all this to Officer Diaz—"

She nodded impatiently and interrupted, "I only want to know if you touched anything."

Bitch. "Well, of course," he shrugged again, trying to keep his cool. He wanted to say, *Of course I went in their room! I touched stuff. It's my house, after all.* Instead he explained that he had initially thought they were playing a game, hiding on him. The same as he had told Officer Diaz. "Then I went back in there to get something for the scent dogs."

"Okay, Mr. Ibarra." She seemed disappointed. "Do you remember how the room looked last night when the children went to bed?"

What the hell kind of question is that?

As though she read his mind, she reworded it, "I mean; the room has been turned upside down. I need to know if that's the way it was when the kids went to bed, or if—"

Antonio shook his head violently, "No. The room was neat when I tucked them in last night. They took baths. I brushed out their hair. They said their prayers, I blessed them, and tucked them in. Everything was in its place. Then this morning—" His voice caught, and he blinked away tears, resenting how she made him cry like a girl. *Bitch. Why is she putting me through this all over again?*

"Well, Mr. Ibarra," she ignored his pain. "Can you explain what happened to the room? If the kids didn't wreck the place, who did?"

Antonio sniffed and brought himself up proudly so that he could give this stupid woman an answer she could understand. "The kidnapper, maybe?"

She didn't flinch, but countered, "You believe they've been kidnapped?"

"Don't you?" He could feel himself losing control of his temper, but at this point, he didn't care. This woman was heartless and these questions were a waste of time. "Do you really believe my little girls wandered out of the house in the middle of the night, in the dark, during a blizzard? For what reason would they do such a dumb thing? They didn't run away or wander off. They were stolen from this house!"

She ignored his outburst and asked another stupid question. "Why would anyone want to kidnap your children, Mr. Ibarra?"

Antonio frowned. *This woman's nuts!* "Who else would

want my children other than myself and Carmen?"

"Carmen?"

"My ex-wife, the girls' mother."

"I'm asking you that exact question, Mr. Ibarra. Who else would want them besides you and their mother?" Then she suggested, "How about for ransom?"

"I certainly don't have money, if that's what they want."

"Why would the perpetrator turn the room upside down?"

Again we're back to the bedroom. Ah, Dios mío. Save me from such ignorance. "Maybe the kidnapper was looking for something in particular. Or maybe discarding what they didn't want. I don't know. Maybe the children fought back."

"But if there was a struggle, Mr. Ibarra," Lieutenant Wilson persisted, "wouldn't you have heard and come to investigate?"

For the first time since the exchange had begun, Antonio dropped his eyes. "I'm sorry, Lieutenant. I sleep heavy, like the dead. It takes a lot to wake me up. I've always been like that. Once when I was a child, I even slept through the smoke alarm; they had to come and shake me." Antonio lifted his head and met the police lieutenant's eyes. "Maybe if I had awakened, my little girls would not be missing."

"So you heard no strange sounds coming from the girls' bedroom?"

The woman was obviously hard of hearing. Hadn't he just explained this? Antonio was shaking his head before she had finished speaking, "No. Nothing at all. I only woke up this morning feeling cold." He recounted again the events of earlier that morning, just as he had related them to Officer Diaz.

Lieutenant Wilson let him speak without interruption. Then asked another useless question, "Mr. Ibarra, where are the clothes the girls wore yesterday?"

"I already told you. I gave those to the police earlier this morning for the scent dogs," he responded automatically. He didn't have the energy to be angry any more. He was too worried and frightened to care if this woman who wanted to be a man saw him cry. He simply crumpled into tears and blubbered into his hands, "Where could they be?"

9:08 A.M.

The sound of someone gently clearing his throat caused Ruth Wilson to turn. Kris Bauer stood in the doorway and motioned to her. He had found something. She wordlessly left Ibarra to his grief and followed Bauer back to the bedroom. He kept his voice low as he explained to her.

"I found blood," he pointed toward the bed to the right of the nightstand.

Ruth stepped forward and examined the round, red spot with professional interest. It spread out on the top sheet, spoiling the side of Barbie's face, and was just turning brown along the edges. Kris set down a measuring tape below the stain; four and a half inches. Ruth photographed it. Another similar spot stained the pillow. More red dots had dripped elsewhere on the bedding. Some were smeared as though someone had tried to wipe them off the sheet with a hand, or vice versa. After Ruth had snapped all the pictures she wanted, Kris removed the sheets and bundled them into a large plastic bag.

More blood was found on the rose carpet; small round spots, like drips. They made a path going out the door. Ruth and Kris followed the trail down the hallway, expecting it to take the logical path to the bathroom. Instead, the drips continued down the hall and went out to the front door. A white towel, now very wet and dirty with the passage of many feet, lay on the floor in front of the door. Ruth lifted it, looked underneath, and found yet another drop of blood. She snapped more pictures, and then stepped outside confident that Kris would get samples of all the blood and take charge of the investigation inside the house during her absence.

Outside, Ruth looked for additional drops of blood. She was able to find only two: One on the stoop, a scar on the fringe of the pristine snow along the edge of the step where no one had walked. *Snap! Snap!* Another, a two inch long drip down the yellow shingle of the house just outside the door.

Snap! Both drops had fallen where they were sheltered from last night's snow.

There had to have been more, but with Ibarra's traipsing all over the place this morning, not to mention the footprints of the helpful neighbor, the responding officers, and those of her own investigative team, those drips, if not covered with new snow, would have been trampled and obliterated. But at least these two drops of blood meant that whoever had been bleeding had gone outside.

She zipped her jacket, pulled up the collar against the cold and made her way around the west side of the house to the backyard. Although there were plenty of footprints from Ibarra's earlier search for his daughters, the yard still retained an untouched look. The swings and slide stood idle and a broken piñata in the shape of a bull hung from a branch of a bare maple tree. All seemed peaceful; snow had collected in soft mounds on the swings, the piñata, and the branches of the maple.

Ruth scrutinized the rest of the yard for any sign that the little girls might have wandered there: An above-ground swimming pool, covered for the winter; a playhouse where she imagined the sisters had enjoyed many hours having tea parties and playing mommy; another building she took for a tool shed; and farther back at the end of Ibarra's property line, Collier's Woods.

If the children had gone off on their own and entered the woods, the volunteers would find them before the end of the day. She saw no point in looking there. She walked around the swimming pool and noted that the steps that led up to the deck surrounding it were safely closed and the cover over the pool remained securely tied down with an undisturbed blanket of white spread out on top. Clearly, no one had been there recently.

Next, she headed for the playhouse. It was a twelve-by-ten structure made of wood and covered with wooden shakes, with shutters and flower boxes at the windows. She imagined Ibarra had built it himself for his little girls during a happier time and had painted it to resemble the family home.

The door showed signs of having been opened earlier that day. The snow had been scraped away when the door had swung out. Although there was only one set of footprints—large, man-sized prints—leading inside, she investigated anyway.

The doorknob turned easily in her hand and the door opened without a sound. A quiet chill had settled like a pall over the tiny house. The windows darkened by snow on the panes added to the gloom. In the dim light afforded by the open door, Ruth made out an assortment of dolls in various stages of dishabille, doll clothes, play furniture, plastic dishes. Everything remained as the children had left it. Undoubtedly, no one had been in here for some time either.

She shut the door, and made her way to the shed. That door also had been opened since the snow, and it moved now without protest. Inside was the normal assortment of gardening tools, as well as a barbeque grill, folding lawn chairs, some rags tossed into a five-gallon bucket standing in a corner. Along one wall were two bicycles just the right size for two little girls, ages five and seven. But no sign that the children themselves had been there.

She looked at her watch. Almost nine-thirty. They'd been here over an hour and had little to show for it. Maybe Kris and the team had found something inside.

Ruth followed Ibarra's footprints back around the east end of the house, up to the driveway where the neighbor had caught up with him. So many feet had passed over this area that looking for clues here would be a waste of time.

At that moment, a shout caused her to look up. Across the road, a man in a dark blue parka was gesticulating, calling out, and slipping and sliding toward her. Although she could not make out what he was saying, she scowled, recognizing exactly what this was: A news reporter trying to get a statement. She pretended she hadn't seen him and returned to the house.

Once inside, Ruth learned that Kris had finished with the girls' bedroom and was packing things up. "Isabel came up with this," he handed her a number of sheets of blue paper.

Bank statements. She examined them briefly, and then returned to the living room.

Henry Chin, the wire-tap man, was speaking with Mr. Ibarra. "It's ringer-activated," Chin was explaining, "so it will record all calls, in-coming and out-going, made on this phone."

Mr. Ibarra nodded his understanding, "So there is nothing for me to do?"

"Nope. Just talk like usual. If it's the kidnapper," the Asian cop assured him, "all you need to do is keep the person on the line for three minutes, and hopefully, the call will be traced and the perpetrator will be apprehended."

Lt. Wilson waited until Chin had packed up his stuff and left before she approached Ibarra. This time she did not sit down which forced him to look up.

"Your bank records show deductions in the amount of one thousand dollars every month beginning in September, Mr. Ibarra. Could you tell us what that is for?"

"Child support," he avoided her eyes and replied sullenly. "I pay Carmen one thousand dollars a month for the privilege of taking my children away from me. Besides that you'll notice I pay tuition to St. Augustine's Catholic School every quarter," he added with a stony look.

Ruth Wilson merely lifted her pencil-thin eyebrows, "I must ask these questions, Mr. Ibarra. Something you might tell us in passing, although seemingly quite innocent, could supply us with information that will lead to the recovery of your children."

"Yeah, yeah," he acknowledge grumpily. He'd heard that from the other cop, Diaz. Still, they were here to help find his daughters. He looked up at her, "This is most difficult. My children have disappeared. Strangers are searching for them while I sit here, useless. Then my home, my most personal possessions, all have been opened to you like a book. My privacy has been invaded and it's hard to remember that you are not the enemy."

She brushed off his comment with a wave of her hand,

Janet Y. Martel

"We're almost done in here, Mr. Ibarra. When we leave, please do not enter the children's bedroom. We may want to return to retrieve more from the scene."

"Retrieve more from the scene? What does that mean?"

"It means, sir, that we will process what we have and we may need to return if our samples are inconclusive." Then, to make certain there could be no doubt of her meaning, she added, "If you go in there, you will contaminate the scene." She wanted to add, *More than you have already.* But held her tongue. *Civilians.* Ruth scowled.

10:06 A.M.

When Lt. Wilson and her team finally left, Antonio Ibarra let Donna out of the cellar and sent her out the back door to run for a bit. An icy wind took his breath away and he quickly shut the door feeling bad for the people searching for his little girls. He needed to be out there himself.

He rubbed his arms briskly as he returned to the living room and checked the thermostat on the way by. It was set at seventy-two degrees as it should be, yet he felt chilled to the bone.

My conscience is making me feel this way, he thought.

Moments ago he had tried calling Carmen. But as luck would have it, Paul Thibault answered. It had not gone well.

"You have a lot of nerve calling Carmen," Paul remarked. He sounded angry. "I know you were a lousy husband, but damn it, Antonio, haven't you put her through enough?"

"What—?"

"I can't believe you, man," Thibault cut him off, not giving Antonio a chance to speak. "What kind of a father are you, anyway?

"But I—"

"You what? You don't think you've done enough? What'll make you happy? For Carmen to have a relapse?"

"Of course not," Antonio protested.

42

"Listen, she can't talk right now. She's been sedated and she's asleep. I won't disturb her for the likes of you."

And then Antonio was listening to dial tone.

Antonio pondered Paul's words, letting them sink in. Apparently, Carmen had been told about the children's disappearance. She must have become hysterical or something like that. Why else would she be sedated? Would calling her earlier, as soon as he'd discovered their disappearance have made any difference? It was something else to feel guilty about.

The call to Puerto Rico did not go much better. But at least, they did not hold him responsible. As least not as much as he did himself.

Stop this!

He blew into his cold hands and rubbed them together. He needed so get warm. He wanted something. Not more coffee. Maybe some hot cocoa would help. He was in the kitchen about that task when the doorbell rang.

Must be those news guys coming to harass me with their stupid questions, he thought remembering the van parked across the street. *I'll get rid of them quick!*

"Don't you have anything better to do than to bother a distraught parent? I have no comment!" he said gruffly as he yanked the front door open.

The two figures on the doorstep, however, were not news reporters, but a man and a woman dressed in black overcoats. He blinked at their identification badges.

FBI. More cops!

"Mr. Antonio Ibarra?"

Antonio nodded dumbly as he assessed his visitors. He guessed the black man to be in his mid-to-late thirties, about six-feet-two. His closely cropped black hair and sharp, dark brown eyes gave him a stern appearance. Apparently, he was the senior; he spoke for the two of them.

"FBI," the man's voice was deep and mellow, and although his tone intimated authority, it was unthreatening. "I'm Special Agent John Turner, and my partner is Special Agent Mary Ellen Kelly," he indicated the attractive blond woman who stood beside him. She was slender and almost Antonio's own height, about five-feet-seven or -eight, he thought, and she regarded him with honest, clear blue eyes the color of a spring sky. As his gaze lingered on the beautiful woman, he heard the other agent's voice. "We're here to talk to you about the disappearance of your daughters."

Collecting himself, Antonio nodded and stepped back, allowing the two agents to enter his house. "I was just going to have a cup of hot cocoa," he said. "Would you like to join me? Or maybe you'd like something else?"

Special Agent Turner shook his head, "No, thank you."

"None for me, either, Mr. Ibarra," Special Agent Kelly declined. "But don't let us stop you." She was younger than the man; late twenties, he guessed. Her voice was gentle, yet he imagined she could get mean if the need arose, just like any other cop.

"*Si. Gracias,*" Antonio nodded. "Please, sit down, make yourselves comfortable." He gestured broadly toward the living room, lit one of the lamps on the end table beside the couch, and left his guests alone.

*****

As she stepped onto the sodden towel that covered the tan carpet just inside the door, Mary Ellen Kelly took in the room before her with professional interest.

It had a lived-in feel to it: Neat, by most standards, but not so much as to make one feel reluctant to set down a glass, or sit with one's feet up on the coffee table.

A brown leather couch stood along the longer wall that faced the southern window. Two cream-colored easy chairs, also in leather, faced the couch with their backs to the picture window. Behind the two chairs, in front of the window, an evergreen tree decorated with shiny multi-colored balls and gold garland stood over a sprawling assortment of opened Christmas presents: Clothing, mostly; some children's books and puzzles; and two new sleds propped against the window sill. Dim light filtered into the room through sheer lace curtains and around the tree. In the center of the grouping was a coffee table where a Candy Land game had been abandoned in mid-play. A Junior Scrabble box and a pile of magazines, topped by *Sports Illustrated* and the *IBEW Journal,* lay in a neat stack on the floor beside the table. At either end of the couch, matching end tables held identical brass lamps with accordion pleated lampshades.

It was the east wall, however, that grabbed Mary Ellen's attention. An entertainment center surrounded by shelves lined with books took up the entire space. Placed here and there along the fronts of the shelves were the ceramic figures of a Nativity scene. But the top shelf, reserved for framed photographs, caused her to approach for a closer look. Placed prominently in the center of the shelf, a couple of eight-by-tens of two smiling little girls dressed in school uniforms stood side by side. *No doubt, Marissa and Liana Ibarra.* Around these two photographs were scattered a number of smaller pictures of various relatives. *The grandmother,* Mary Ellen guessed. *And some aunts, uncles, and cousins.*

She scanned the photos searching for those featuring the missing children. Among them was a smiling Antonio Ibarra with the two little girls on either side of him, his arms around them, gathering them in. Beside that, a five-by-seven of the older daughter dressed in a pink tutu on her toes, arms extended over her head for a pirouette. Then, the younger daughter in a ladybug costume posed for her dance number. At the other end of the shelf, the two girls stood together disguised for Halloween. The younger, a white-faced clown with a bulbous red nose and a blue smile, was dressed in a yellow jumpsuit with large red polka-dots. The elder was a purple- and black-clad witch with a sickly green complexion and an oozing, brownish pimple *(peanut butter?)* on a fake nose that would have made Cyrano de Bergerac proud. Finally, at the far end of the shelf, was an enlarged snapshot of a happy family of four; the older of the little girls, a mere toddler, stood beside a slimmer, kneeling Antonio, while an adorable infant sat happily on the lap of a stunning redhead. *The mother, Carmen.*

As the sounds from the kitchen changed, Mary Ellen took a seat on the couch noting that John Turner had already sunk himself comfortably into one of the easy chairs. At the same moment, Antonio Ibarra returned with a steaming mug of cocoa topped with a lump of marshmallow crème. Setting down his mug on a coaster, he apologized.

"Sorry about the mess," and began throwing pieces of the game into its box.

"That's quite all right, Mr. Ibarra," Mary Ellen said. "Really," she placed a gentle hand on his arm. "Please. Just sit and speak with us for a moment."

Antonio stopped and lifted his sad, dark brown eyes to hers. She nodded encouragement and finally he gave in, sighed and sat in the other easy chair, but did not speak. Instead, he wrapped his hands around the hot mug, seeming to absorb its comforting warmth. Then he slowly stirred the melting marshmallow into the hot liquid and sipped his cocoa.

Finally, he cleared his throat and said in a thick voice, "I already told the policeman this morning—"

"Yes," John Turner responded, "we understand that, Mr. Ibarra. But even though we're sure that Officers Diaz and Caron took excellent notes—and I promise you, we *will* read their filed reports—we have questions of our own."

"It happens sometimes," Mary Ellen added, "that new questions trigger a memory or a thought that was previously overlooked."

"Okay," the man shrugged. "What do you want to know?"

"To start, I'd like your permission to record our conversation on audio tape, if you don't mind, Mr. Ibarra," Turner stated. "I take written notes also, but this way, there's no question of what was actually said. If I have any doubts, I can simply review the tape." He regarded Antonio with raised eyebrows, waiting for his consent. When Antonio gave a short nod Turner pressed a switch on his pocket-sized recorder and placed it on the corner of the coffee table. In a voice that would clearly be captured by the tiny machine, he asked his first question. "Mr. Ibarra, have your little girls ever wandered off like this before?"

"No. No. Never." Antonio shook his head. "I can't imagine them leaving the house in the middle of the night. They are just little girls. Afraid of what might be hiding in the dark." He finished with teary eyes and shook his head again.

"Then, if they didn't wander off on their own, do you have any idea who might have a motive for kidnapping your daughters?" Turner barely paused before continuing, "Do you have any enemies? Is there anyone you can think of who would like to exact revenge on you for any reason?"

A worried frown furrowed the man's brow. "No," he responded after a moment's deliberation.

"Someone at work?" Mary Ellen Kelly suggested, "A rival? Someone you might have angered or slighted in some way?"

Again, Antonio seemed to consider the agent's words. Finally he shrugged, shaking his head, "If it were not that Carmen now has full custody, I might say that *she* would have the most reason to want to steal them from me. But I'm the one who gets them only part time now—"

"Is that a recent change, Mr. Ibarra?" Mary Ellen asked.

"Since the end of August. The courts gave the children back to Carmen in time for the opening of school. Apparently, they'd rather see my little girls with their drug-addicted, alcoholic mother than with their devoted father," he grumbled bitterly. Instantly, he seemed to realize he'd spoken harshly and amended, "They figured it would be less disruptive to them if the change was made before they started classes." He looked up dolefully as Turner asked another question.

"How long have you been living in this house, Mr. Ibarra?"

"Nine years. I bought it in October, right after I met Carmen," he answered. "I know because we were married on Christmas Eve of that same year. I had taken her to look at houses, and she fell in love with this one. So, I bought it. It seemed an appropriate wedding gift. We thought we'd fill the house with children..." His voice trailed off, apparently lost in thought. Then, "At least *I* did. Instead, she broke trust," he continued somberly, "I divorced her. Now she's married again, and it's just me and Donna. It makes for a lonely house." As though to punctuate his statement, there was a scratching at the back door, accompanied by a mournful whine. Antonio gave the FBI agents an apologetic glance, "That's Donna. She wants in." He made to leave, but Mary Ellen put out a staying hand.

"I'll go," she offered.

Antonio shook his head, insisting, "It's better if I go. She's not a mean dog, but she's protective. She will not like strangers in the house. I'll be right back."

He left the agents alone in the living room and was back in a moment with the dog happily trotting at his heels. However, when the animal noticed the two people seated in the living room, she stopped short and gave a number of sharp barks, followed by a low throaty growl.

"It's okay, Donna," Antonio reassured her. "These are friends."

Accepting her master's word, Donna sniffed the hem of Mary Ellen's black skirt and then the backs of her proffered fingers. The dog allowed herself to be stroked and scratched behind the ears. Satisfied that Mary Ellen posed no threat, the animal moved on to assess John Turner. Once a similar rapport was established with him, she contented herself by sitting on his feet. John made a valiant attempt at ignoring his discomfort while Mary Ellen asked the next question.

"Would you mind showing us the house? It might help if we saw where your daughters sleep, for one thing."

Antonio's eyebrows shot up, "Of course!"

As he heaved himself out of the chair, Donna got up happily from her place and came to Antonio's side. However, when the FBI agents moved, she scrutinized them seriously, barked twice loudly and emitted another menacing, deep-throated growl.

"Donna!" Antonio reprimanded, "*¡Pórtate bien!*" At that command, Donna immediately ceased her threats, although she continued to eye them suspiciously. "My apologies," Antonio offered. "As I said, she's very protective of me and my fam-

48

ily."

"Yet she didn't sound the alarm when whoever-it-was entered your house and took your children," John Turner observed. "How curious."

"Yes," Antonio frowned pensively. "That *is* most peculiar. What could it mean?"

"It could mean, Mr. Ibarra," Turner said, "that your children *did* wander out by themselves."

"Or," Mary Ellen submitted, "Donna knows whoever took them."

11:11 A.M.

Upon leaving Antonio Ibarra, Special Agents Turner and Kelly began the exhausting, tedious job of canvassing the neighborhood for any possible witnesses to the kidnapping. With most of the neighbors at work or searching for the missing children, they knew they might not find many people at home but they wanted to interview as many individuals as soon as possible before the passage of time caused memories to fade. Hopefully, those who had already spoken with Officers Diaz and Caron might have remembered something they had forgotten to mention before.

The agents found their first couple with no trouble, right across the street.

Two people sat bundled up in lawn chairs turned eastward inside the opening of the garage door, where they could be out of the cold wind. Behind them, a table had been set up with hot drinks. John Turner consulted a sheet of paper he pulled from the inside pocket of his coat.

"According to tax records, this is the residence of Mrs. Mary Carvalho, widow of Manuel Carvalho," he mumbled to Mary Ellen as the couple limped out toward them. "I believe it's safe to assume the woman is the widow Carvalho—" But the identity of the man remained a mystery. It was apparent, however, that they were close friends.

As a rule, it is normal police practice to interview people separately, since interviewees tend to feed off each other, inadvertently compare notes, and testimony can be corrupted. However, since the agents did not want to vex this older couple unnecessarily, and since neither of them was a suspect, the agents broke protocol and spoke with them together. The fact that this house was directly in front of Ibarra's was encouraging. With luck one of them might have even been an unwitting witness to what had transpired in the middle of the night.

Moments later, John Turner and Mary Ellen Kelly were ushered into the warm cozy living room of Mary Carvalho's bungalow. The furniture was old but of fine quality and in good condition. On the edge of the end table beside the couch amid Christmas elves and a jolly Santa Claus candy dish, Turner found a spot to set his little tape recorder. Mary Carvalho was not happy until she had served the FBI agents steaming Styrofoam cups of hot coffee. Once she had settled herself in a chair beside her friend and facing the FBI agents, the interview began.

"Interview with Mrs. Mary Carvalho of 1-1-3-3 River Road, and Mr. Charles Cabot of 1-1-3-1 River Road," John Turner said for the tape.

"Please. Make that Chuck," Cabot said. "I'd also like to add for the record that I am an attorney and as such, have represented Mr. Ibarra in the past, so there might be some questions I may not ethically be permitted to answer."

Turner nodded and asked, "How long have you known Antonio Ibarra?"

Mary Carvalho answered immediately in her gravelly voice, "I met him on the day he moved into the neighborhood. I couldn't tell you the exact date, but it was in autumn. I remember that because I was busy making applesauce with the apples from the trees out back. I saw the rental truck pull up, and I went over with a chocolate cake and a carafe of coffee and all the fixings. It's something I do whenever someone moves into the neighborhood. It's the best way to meet the new neighbors and it makes them feel at home."

"And it's a good way to get some gossip, too," Chuck Cabot teased. Mary Carvalho glared at him and pinched her lips together. Chuck ignored her look and continued, smiling, "I also met him on the day he moved in. Like Mary said, he came alone with a big rental truck, but I noticed he was all by himself. No helpers. Well," the lawyer amended, "he had Carmen with him. I couldn't see how he expected that little thing to help him with the bigger pieces. You know; bureaus, mattresses, a sofa, easy chairs. Bob LaRue and I went over to lend him a hand." He cast a mischievous glance at Mary, "Then we all had some of Mary's cake."

She whacked him amicably on the arm, "That was supposed to be for Antonio and his fiancée."

"I know," Cabot rubbed his arm. "Nancy said the same thing when I got home."

"Manny helped you, too, if I remember correctly," Mary frowned pensively. "And I wondered why he wasn't hungry for supper—"

"And how would you describe Mr. Ibarra?" John asked to reclaim the interview. "What is your opinion of him as a neighbor?"

"He's a good man. A hard worker. When he's not at work earning money, he's doing something around the house; mowing the lawn, painting, building something." Cabot stated, "You couldn't ask for better in a neighbor. He maintains his property, keeps the place neat. He's friendly. And he's always there to lend a helping hand. "

"But in a macho kind of way," Mary added with a sideways glance at Chuck. "Women have their place, if you know what I mean. He was the boss of the household. You always knew that. He never let Carmen forget it either. I kind of felt bad for her."

"Now, that's a pretty lady," Cabot commented ignoring Mary's remark.

Mary gave him a withering look, "Beauty is skin-deep. She was no saint, but she needed her space. That much I'll agree to. Manny used to wonder why a young thing like her married a man so much older. We weren't surprised when it ended in divorce."

"Do you think he was abusive to his wife?"

Mary contemplated that a moment before she answered, "No, he never hit her, if that's what you mean. But he did a lot of yelling, especially if something he wanted done hadn't been. Like, I remember one day not long after the second baby was born. It was summer, so the windows were open, and we got a good earful. He came home early and found the bed still not made and the breakfast dishes all in the sink. The yelling started right away. Loud enough for us to make out what he was saying."

"And what was he saying, Mrs. Carvalho?" John Turner asked.

"Well! He wanted to know what was going on. What was she doing lying around? All she had were the babies to take care of. She should be able to at least keep the house neat while he broke his back at work. That kind of thing."

The FBI agents exchanged glances. Special Agent Kelly picked up John's unspoken signal and continued the interview.

"And what did Mrs. Ibarra say in her defense?"

"We couldn't hear that part. She isn't one to raise her voice," Mary Carvalho explained.

"Mary's right. Antonio used to yell," Chuck Cabot agreed tightly. He seemed upset by something. The friendly joking was gone and the lawyer's tone was reserved and controlled. "I missed a lot of the day-to-day drama because I was at my office most of the time, but from what I could see, he was a very loving man. He worshiped the ground she walked on. He called her his goddess—"

"One that he desired to control—"

"He bought her whatever she wanted; clothes, jewelry, a car—"

"A *used* car," Mary amended. "It was a two-year-old Pontiac."

Cabot frowned at Mary's constant interruptions, "But it was a nice car just the same; a bright red Grand Prix with a T-roof." Mary shrugged off his justifications and allowed Cabot to continue the story. "The first summer they were here, he had that swimming pool put in for her—"

"It's an above-ground pool, Chuck," Mary cut him off again. "You make it sound like an Olympic in-the-ground job—"

"And no sooner did he have that done," he said over her comment, "he took her on a fancy vacation to Puerto Rico and the Bahamas."

"Then she tells him she's pregnant," Mary interrupted again. "Goodness! He was so upset—"

"Why was he upset?" Turner asked, "Didn't he want children?"

"That's exactly why he *was* upset. He so wanted kids," Cabot said with a frustrated sigh. "He never would have taken her on an airplane if he'd known she was pregnant. He figured it was too risky. I guess she suspected as much because she didn't tell him until they got back."

"And what kind of father would you say he is?" Agent Kelly asked.

"He adores those children!" Mary Carvalho exclaimed, chafing to have her turn to speak. "It's nothing but the best for them. They go to Catholic school, and they're always dressed to the nines. Designer play clothes, mind you. And fancy dresses for Mass every Sunday. They never lacked for anything. Those children are his world. They're like little princesses."

"But they're not spoiled," Cabot submitted shooting Mary an impatient look. "They are polite and well-behaved. It's always 'Please' and 'Thank you.' Very respectful. If they want something and the answer is 'No,' they accept that without making a fuss."

"And helpful, too," Mary Carvalho added. "If I'm out raking the lawn or sweeping the driveway, they offer to help. They're great kids."

"From Mr. Ibarra's statement, we've established that the children were taken out of his home sometime roughly between nine-thirty P.M. yesterday, and six this morning. I realize we're talking about the middle of the night and that you were probably asleep, but maybe one of you heard something you discarded as nothing at the time…"

Mary Carvalho shook her head, "Sorry. I spent the entire weekend with my son, Victor, and his family in Connecticut. I got there in time for supper on Christmas Eve, and I left Monday afternoon around four o'clock." Then she continued with disgust, "*That* was a mistake. Traffic was horrendous. Didn't help that I was heading *into* the storm! I should've spent one more night at Victor's. By the time I reached New London it was coming down like crazy and the highway was a like a parking lot. It usually takes me about three hours to get home; but with all the delays and a break for supper I only got back around ten that night. I called Victor to let him know I'd arrived safely and went to bed soon after. I'm a light sleeper, you know," she explained, "so I take a sleeping pill and use earplugs and a blindfold. Once I'm in bed, I don't budge. I hear nothing, see nothing, and feel nothing."

"When you came home, you saw nothing out of the ordinary?"

"No. All the usual cars around. A few extras, actually, because some of the neighbors still had visitors. But nothing was going on at Ibarra's at that time," the woman said. Then she added, "I do remember, though, that all Antonio's Christmas lights—the tree, all the lights in the windows, and those decorating the shrubs in front of his house—went out just as I was pulling into my driveway."

"What about you, Mr. Cabot? Did you hear or see anything unusual?"

Charles Cabot had been quiet, apparently in deep thought as Mary Carvalho had been talking. Now he said, "I did, but I didn't realize it could be of any importance until now. It was after midnight. I'd been in bed for a while. Even though Nancy's been gone for over a year, I still have trouble falling asleep. The bed is so empty and cold without her there."

Mary Carvalho reached over and patted his hand in sympathy, "I know how that is, Chuck. It's been almost five years since my Manny's gone, and that's why I take a sleeping pill."

Apparently over his earlier irritation with her, Chuck placed his hand warmly over Mary's and returned to his explanation. "I couldn't sleep. I had awful indigestion. So I got up to take an antacid. There was no more in the medicine chest, so I came to the kitchen where I have another bottle. That's where I was when I heard a car start up and drive away. At about the same time, a dog howled. Long and doleful. Spooky. I looked out the window but I didn't see anything out there. Everything was quiet after that and I went back to bed. I didn't think any more about it until just now."

12:06 P.M.

As they were leaving Mary Carvalho's pleasantly snug house, Special Agents Turner and Kelly were accosted by a blast of frigid wind and a curly-haired news reporter. Earlier, although they had passed the news van to get to their interview, the newsmen had been nowhere in evidence and the agents had not been hampered. Now, though, their luck seemed to have run out.

"Carlos Viveiros, WTCN Channel 3," he said by way of introduction. "What can you tell us about the search for the missing children? Any leads? Any ideas? Anything at all?" As he thrust his microphone in their faces, each agent put up a warding hand.

Mary Ellen muttered, "No comment."

John quipped, "When we have something, we'll let you know."

They turned their backs on him and returned to their black late-model, Bureau-issued Crown Victoria, the replacement for the ill-fated vehicle in another case they'd worked on in Troy City. They hoped to review the new information they had learned from Charles Cabot and Mary Carvalho without fear of being overheard or disturbed. The reporter quickly recovered from the affront and zeroed in on a group of searchers breaking for a quick bite of lunch.

"A car drives off after midnight and a dog howls," Mary Ellen Kelly commented. "What do you make of that?"

"I don't think we know enough to form any conclusions at the moment," John shrugged.

Mary Ellen nodded, opened a sheet of lined filler paper and held it in her left hand so that she could better study it. "Someone else in the neighborhood might be able to shed more light on this," she murmured thoughtfully.

"What's that?"

"A map Mary Carvalho drew for me," she explained. "Not only did she supply the names of the people who live in the houses on River Road, she was kind enough to add details about their relationship with Antonio Ibarra. You know, whether they could be considered friends? I just saw one of the neighbors go into the house next door to Ibarra. Number 1-1-3-8," she compared the map to the tax records. "According to this, the house belongs to Mr. and Mrs. Robert LaRue. Mary lists the wife as Maria LaRue, and the little girl is Jenny, Marisa and Liana's playmate."

The LaRue residence was a twin to Ibarra's except that it had been flipped end for end, placing the driveways to their respective garages practically side by side with merely a twenty-foot space separating them. LaRue's house was painted light sand with terracotta shutters and the front stoop had been lengthened to form a real porch. The blacktopped driveway and the brownish-red flagstone walkway to the front porch had been neatly shoveled, yet icy patches had formed here and there.

The FBI agents carefully proceeded to the long front stoop where a redwood bench sat catty-cornered between the house and an enormous terracotta urn. A façade of the same brownish-red flagstone covered the porch and a low wide terracotta rail that doubled as a planter ran along its front edge. Mary Ellen figured that in spring, both the urn and the planter would be filled with brightly colored annuals. Low evergreen shrubs had been planted along the contours of the house, with twin fir trees at the extreme corners to complete the effect. As they approached, strings of Christmas lights could be seen intertwined among the branches of the snow-encrusted trees and shrubs, and strung along the outline of the house. A beautiful Christmas wreath hung on the wide redwood door.

The FBI agents waited only a short moment after John had pressed the doorbell button. The elegant door was opened by an attractive woman with a clear café-au-lait complexion, sparkling smoky gray eyes below finely arched and sculpted eyebrows, and curly chin-length dark brown hair. She wore a pink turtleneck sweater, jeans, and black leather boots. She glanced quickly at their proffered FBI badges and opened the door wider allowing them entry.

"I'm sorry for the mess," she apologized as she waved them toward the living room decorated for Christmas. She shook her head, "I suppose you're here about Marisa and Liana. We hurried out of here this morning to help look for them, and we didn't have time to pick up." As she spoke, she grabbed an armful of newly-washed clothes that had been dumped on the peach-colored easy chair closest to the door and shoved it back into the laundry basket. "Jenny's just getting over a bad cold, and she and I have called it a day." She grabbed the loaded basket by its two handles. "Please, sit. Make yourselves comfortable." She disappeared down the hallway with the laundry.

Mary Ellen crossed the moss green Berber rug, heading for the couch upholstered in a rich damask of large peach blossoms and deep green foliage on a cream-colored background. She picked up a well-loved, partly bald plush Dalmatian puppy from the sofa and sat down with the toy on her lap. She noted how the spruce tree stood in a large metal drum with its rooted bottom wrapped tightly in brown burlap.

It's a live Christmas tree that they'll plant somewhere in the yard come spring.

Rather than sit on the newly liberated chair near the door, John selected its celery-colored mate across the room beside the Christmas tree. He took the liberty of moving the chair closer to the coffee table in front of the couch.

Presently, Mrs. LaRue returned from her mission closely followed by a pretty little girl with golden brown eyes and short curly pigtails tied with red bows that matched her red sweat suit. The child regarded the agents shyly as she took the middle seat on the sofa between her mother and Mary Ellen. As John Turner pulled his tape recorder out of his coat pocket and placed it on the coffee table, he explained to Mrs. LaRue the reason for their visit.

Mary Ellen took the opportunity to acquaint herself with the child.

"Hi. My name is Mary Ellen. Is this your puppy?" she asked holding out the stuffed animal. The child nodded and reached carefully for the toy. "You must be Jenny."

The little girl nodded, smiling.

"How old are you, Jenny?"

"Six-and-a-half," answered the child clutching the beloved puppy to her chest.

"Your cheeks are all rosy," Mary Ellen observed.

Jenny nodded and supplied a reason, "I went outside this morning to look for Marisa and Liana." Then she sadly cast down her golden eyes, "But we didn't find them." She added in a whisper, "Maybe we'll never find them." A tear dripped onto the stuffed dog and Jenny quickly wiped another one away before it could fall.

"I know. We didn't find them yet," Mary Ellen acknowledged sympathetically, "but we're going to keep looking for them until we do."

Jenny sniffed and looked up at Mary Ellen, hope in her eyes, her curly eyelashes still wet, "You promise?"

"I promise," Mary Ellen smiled.

By then, Maria LaRue was answering John's first question.

"It's funny you should ask that. Bob and I were just talking about that this morning," she smiled displaying deep dimples in her cheeks, giving her a young, ingénue appearance. "Nine years ago. We moved in just before Halloween, only a couple of weeks before Antonio did. You probably noticed that we both have the same house? They were built at the same time by the same contractor. When we moved in, both houses were white with black shutters. It was kind of weird until we changed the color," she chuckled. "Believe it or not, there used to be a white picket fence between the driveways; but it was a pain to mow the lawn, and no one wanted to claim ownership of it to maintain it. When the girls started playing together, we tore it down. I guess Jenny was about two at the time."

"Did you hear or see anything strange or out of place last night?" John asked getting immediately to the point.

She shook her head slowly, "Not really. I got up in the middle of the night to go to the bathroom. I'd just gotten back into bed when I heard a coyote howl. Or maybe it was a fox. You realize we have foxes and coyotes in these woods? It was only one howl, though, and I thought that was strange. Usually, it's a chorus, and it lasts for quite a few minutes." She shrugged dismissively, then added, "I remember thinking it was odd because we don't usually hear them once the cold weather comes in."

"What time was that?"

"Just before three. I noticed the time on the alarm clock when I got into bed. I remember it changed from two-fifty-four to two-fifty-five as I was pulling up the blankets."

"You say that Jenny and Marisa started playing together when they were about two years old." Mary Ellen surmised, "So you knew Carmen Thibault when she was still married to Antonio Ibarra…"

"Oh, yes. As I said before, Antonio moved into his house around the same time we did. But although Carmen spent a lot of time at Antonio's she really didn't move in until after they were married at Christmastime. Have you met her yet?" When the two agents shook their heads, Maria continued, "She's a pretty woman and Antonio was smitten by her, you could tell. On the other hand, I kind of think that Carmen saw him as a way to keep from being deported."

"Deported?" John furrowed his brow.

"Yes. Carmen was born in England. Liverpool, I think she said. Her mother is British and her father is Cuban. Left Cuba before Castro took over. So while Carmen is bilingual and her Spanish is flawless, she speaks what Bob calls 'the Queen's English,'" Maria smiled. "Carmen always felt her parents had missed the boat; that they'd never reached their full potential. She felt she had to make her break, leave that all behind. So, right after her eighteenth birthday, after she'd socked away enough money for airfare, she came to America with nothing but a suitcase and about a hundred dollars. When she met Antonio, he fell head-over-heels, and she married him two weeks after she turned nineteen."

"So the marriage was a sham," John interjected.

"Well, it sounds like that on the surface, doesn't it?" Maria agreed. "But I don't know if Antonio ever thought he was being used that way. I mean, Carmen was good for him. You realize she's fifteen years younger than Antonio?" She did not wait for the agents to acknowledge the question, but continued, "He was happy. They *both* seemed happy. And it wasn't long before she got pregnant for Marisa. So," Maria shrugged, "she may have loved him—"

"Or else the children aren't his—"

Maria seemed shocked by the suggestion, "Well, I wouldn't know about that. I never saw any evidence to indicate that Carmen was seeing somebody on the side, no strange men coming by or anything like that. Granted, I was at school all day, but during the summer when I was on vacation, Carmen was always around, either gardening or tanning by the pool. She really didn't go anywhere without Antonio. She only went out for groceries or to her job at the Shop Smart." She gave a dismissive shrug, "I really wouldn't know. I can't say I had a whole lot in common with her in the beginning. She was so young and all. But after she had Marisa and I was pregnant for Jenny, we got to know each other better." Maria explained, "Marisa was born at the end of January and Jenny's birthday is April 11th. Under doctor's orders, I had started my maternity leave in the middle of March. I needed exercise and with the arrival of spring, Carmen started taking Marisa out in the stroller. We used to take walks every day after I got Robin— that's our older daughter—on the bus. I guess you could say she and I got to be friends, even if I didn't agree with her Bohemian lifestyle."

"You just described her as a homebody. Now you say she had a 'Bohemian lifestyle.' Aren't those conflicting statements?" John Turner requested.

"Maybe that's the wrong term," Maria allowed. "What I mean is, she had a wild side, you know? She'd been a professional exotic dancer. And even before she was of legal age, she was free with the alcohol. She stopped dancing at the Lady Slipper when she married Antonio, and then gave birth to Marisa a year later. So, she stayed home a lot. Nesting. But she still had crazy ideas, always wanting to party, have a good time. Can't blame her for that, I guess. At first, Carmen and Antonio would entertain together at their house. They'd invite neighbors or people Antonio knew from work. It was fun." Maria sighed, and then added, "As long as Carmen wasn't flirting with somebody's husband." Maria met John Turner's eyes, "You really don't want to know all this, do you?"

"We need to know as much as possible about everyone in Marisa's and Liana's lives," he explained. "The more we know about the people around them, the better we can form conclusions that will lead to discovering who took them."

"Tell us everything," Mary Ellen suggested, "and let us decide what is useful and what is not."

"I just abhor gossip," Maria said looking from one agent to the other, "and this feels so much like gossip to me."

"Not if it helps us find the girls," Mary Ellen countered.

Maria LaRue shrugged again and picked up her story from where she'd left off. "Carmen used to drink too much at those parties and she'd do those dance moves; you know, bumps and grinds? It was as though she reverted to the life she had before she married Antonio. While she was still sober, although it was suggestive, it was rather compelling even for us women. But after a few drinks, even though she kept her clothes on it got somewhat obscene, embarrassing to just about everyone and infuriating to the wives. So, Antonio put a stop to the parties.

"Soon after that, she got pregnant for Liana and everything calmed down for awhile. But she started drinking again when Liana was only a couple of months old. It was summertime again and I was off from school. I could see the drinking was a problem now because she didn't need a party; she was drinking alone. For a while I tried to cover for her. This was easy enough to do because Bob was teaching summer school or taking classes for his own recertification, so he was out every day and I was up early with my own kids. I'd drop by early, within an hour of Antonio's leaving for work. She never drank in front of me so that worked for a couple of months. But one day, she wouldn't answer the door and I could hear the babies crying. The door was unlocked so I went in. I found her passed out on the couch. I took the girls home with me and left her to sleep it off. Robin was about ten at the time. She and I played house all day with the three babies as though they were dolls."

"And how old were Marisa and Liana then?" Mary Ellen wanted to know.

"Liana was practically newborn, maybe three months old. That would have made Marisa around eighteen or nineteen months." When Mary Ellen nodded, Maria continued. "Bob told me I should call Children's Services. But I didn't want to do that. Carmen and Antonio were our friends. And Antonio didn't deserve to lose his kids because Carmen was neglectful or because she had a problem. But I was going back to school in September. I wouldn't be around any more to rescue the girls. I had to do something. So, instead of calling Children's Services, I let Antonio know something was not right and he set a trap for her. The next day he left for work as usual, but he came home two hours later to find her high on crack and both babies crying in their cribs."

Overcome with emotion, Maria buried her face in her hands and took a moment to collect herself. Then she continued, "In one way, I felt so guilty; as though I'd betrayed a friend. But, then on another level—even barring the fact that as a teacher,

I'm legally bound to report suspected child abuse or neglect—I realized I had no choice. I had a responsibility to those babies. They needed to be taken care of. I'm sure Antonio would have realized the problem sooner or later. But I had to do something before someone—one of the babies—got hurt."

"You did the right thing," Mary Ellen assured her quietly.

"So, that's when Antonio forced her to move out—" John Turner prompted.

Maria nodded, "That's when it all hit the fan." She smiled wanly, "Despite Carmen's promise to give up the booze and crack, Antonio wouldn't hear it. He threw her out, got legal custody of the girls and filed for divorce. Even got an annulment from the Church. Even so, there's never been another woman for Antonio." Maria sighed, "Carmen fell into a veritable hole. She was into crack and alcohol, caught in a downward spiral until she finally hit rock bottom a couple of years later. She ended up in jail over Christmas that year, busted for possession. Luckily for her the judge was lenient. Instead of deporting her back to England, he sent her to Serenity House— detox—for six months. That was, let's see— Jenny will be seven in April..." Her sculpted eyebrows furrowed as she did the math in her head, "That means it was about three years ago. Anyway, Carmen came out of detox a changed woman. She vowed to stay clean and get her children back. But first, she had to be worthy. She applied for U.S. citizenship and took classes in accounting at Community College. She got her degree and now she's got a job with a big accounting firm. She's doing well. She continues to keep her addictions under control, she's got a new husband and full custody of her children. It wasn't easy for her and I'm so glad for her turnabout. But now, it's Antonio who's hurting."

For a moment everyone was quiet, then John gave her a questioning look, "So, when Carmen was kicked out of the house, who took care of the kids while Antonio was at work?"

"Oh! That was Adelina," Maria supplied.

"Does Adelina have a last name?" John asked, pen poised.

"Aguilar. Adelina Aguilar."

"What can you tell us about her?"

"I didn't really know her that well. But," she continued trying to answer his question, "I always thought she was a strange woman. She was only a couple of years my senior, but she seemed so much older. "

"How so?" John asked.

"In her bearing, her mannerisms, her tastes in music, in clothes. Rather old-world, if you get my meaning." Maria smiled, "A nice lady, though. Kind of pretty. Completely dedicated to the children! Nurturing. Kind. And a fantastic cook and housekeeper. She made that place shine, and I think Antonio put on a few pounds. I always wondered why Adelina had never married. She was such a great surrogate mother, and she'd have made someone a wonderful wife. When she started as the girls' nanny, she was fresh from Colombia and her English was limited. That was fine by Antonio; he wanted the girls to speak Spanish and I think her Spanish was the one asset that got Adelina the job. Although Carmen used to abide by Antonio's wishes when he was home, I know she used to cheat and speak English to the babies when he was out. 'They're American, after all,' Carmen would say. I guess Antonio must've suspected she was speaking to them in English because as a young toddler, the few words Marisa was trying to say sounded like a mixture of both languages. Anyway, Antonio hired the Spanish-speaking nanny, figuring it was one way of insuring the girls would continue to speak Spanish in the house." Maria rolled her large smoky eyes, "Ironically, Adelina wanted to learn English, so she signed up for night classes at Community College. Goodness, how she struggled!" Maria glanced self-consciously at the FBI agents. "I mean, I'm a teacher, and I helped her as much as I could. I took Spanish in high school and I'm far from fluid but my Portuguese helped a lot. I tried to help her with her homework a couple of times but because I was at school all day, she naturally made friends with Mary Carvalho across the street who's always home. Their personalities were better suited to one another anyway. Since she hit it off with Mary it was only natural that she'd turn to her for help.

I was glad to see Adelina do well. She's a lovely person."

"How did she get around?" Mary Ellen asked abruptly. "Did she use the Grand Prix Antonio had bought for Carmen?"

"Oh, no," Maria frowned shaking her head at the absurd notion. "Carmen took that car with her when she left. It was hers, after all, registered in her name. Although she doesn't have it anymore," a pensive note entering her voice. "I think I saw her recently driving a white late-model Dodge minivan." She chuckled, "Can you *imagine*? How children do change us! Carmen's become totally domesticated," she laughed. "Anyway, it doesn't matter," she blinked, and returned to the topic. "Antonio helped Adelina buy a car of her own to use for errands. It was a Plymouth, I think. Bob used to remark about it all the time because Plymouths make a distinctive sound when they start. He'd always say, 'There goes Adelina.' Or something like that."

1:09 P.M.

Carmen woke up in bed.

Her eyes felt grainy, as though filled with sand. So heavy. *So sleepy,* she thought. She let them close again, but her parched throat demanded immediate attention. *A glass of water.*

She tried to sit up, but fell back heavily onto the bed.

What the heck is wrong with me? she wondered.

The house was quiet. *Paul must be at work,* she thought.

Now she forced her gritty eyes open and stared at the ceiling. Something about the light was wrong. Something about the direction of the light and the shadows. It didn't feel early—

It felt *late.*

Had she slept away the entire morning? How could that be? Her groggy mind would not cooperate.

She recalled having had a very bad dream. Two state troopers had come to the door asking about Marisa and Liana. Something awful had happened to them. But of course, they were just down the hall.

"Marisa!" she called sleepily, "Liana! Come see Mummy." But there was no response. No child came running to her bedside. "No, that's right," she murmured, "They're with Antonio. To celebrate Christmas."

But no, there was something else that she wasn't remembering. She rubbed her forehead with her fingertips and forced herself to concentrate. As her brain shook off the remnants of sleep it all came crashing back to her.

Marisa and Liana are missing!

Panic stabbed her heart and she bolted upright on the bed and tried to free herself from the tangle of sheets. "Marisa!" she screamed at the top of her lungs, "Liana!" The force of screaming hurt her throat, but she continued to cry out for her children as hot tears burned her eyes and slipped down her face. Then suddenly, Paul burst into the room and gathered her in his arms.

"I'm so sorry, darling," he murmured in her hair, holding her close so that her tears were absorbed into his sweater. "I only stepped out for a moment to answer the telephone."

"My babies," she cried against his strong chest, "What has become of my babies?"

2:26 P.M.

When Charles Cabot saw the blue Troy County Crime Scene Investigator's van pull into Antonio Ibarra's driveway shortly before two-thirty, he knew it was a bad sign. He knew they'd spent a good hour and a half at the house earlier and a return visit could only mean that the police were beginning to think the children had not simply wandered off, but that they had been kidnapped, or something worse. In either case, it did not bode well for Antonio who seemed to be the prime focus of their investigation. Their return could only mean trouble.

Cabot immediately recognized the boss; the slender, fifty-something-year-old dyed blond was Lieutenant Ruth Wilson.

More trouble. Her reputation as a ball-busting detective meant that if there was anything to find that could implicate Antonio in the disappearance of his children, she would sniff it out and ruin him.

As expected, she had in her possession a warrant that included examining any and all vehicles registered to Antonio Ibarra, which she readily showed Cabot upon his request. She seemed to gloat as she watched him examine the paper for any irregularity.

"Hmm," Cabot stated, "Everything seems to be in order." One point for their side; but he wasn't going to let her claim a total victory, "As Ibarra's attorney, I wish to observe the proceedings of your investigation."

She nodded curtly, but any reply was interrupted by the WTCN-TV 3 News team who had also noticed the return of the crime scene investigators. They ran over to Ruth to try to get some information from her. In spite of his ire, Cabot had to cover a smile as he watched her neatly and politely thwart their efforts.

"Sorry, guys," she said with a crooked smile and a flash of her chocolate brown eyes. Cabot knew she wasn't sorry at all. "This is a police investigation. No one crosses the police tape except for authorized personnel."

"Can you tell us—?" The reporter's question was left hanging as Ruth Wilson turned her back on the news team.

"No comment," she called back as she walked away.

Special Agents Turner and Kelly appeared and joined Cabot in front of the garage at the east end of the house. At Ruth's nod, one of her technicians raised the door. Inside they found Ibarra's two-year-old dark blue Dodge Ram 2500 Diesel pickup. The bed of the truck was empty except for a large shiny metal tool box fastened along the cab wall.

Each member of the five-man team ignored their observers as they pulled on latex gloves and set to work. One of the team climbed into the bed of the truck while Ruth and another investigator opened the doors on either side. The two remaining began a thorough search of the garage, workshop, and laundry room. The FBI agents and Cabot watched from the sidelines, staying well out of the way of the investigators.

Under Lt. Wilson's expert leadership, the team worked slowly and methodically, sweeping and combing, tweezing and swabbing, dusting and scraping, gathering and labeling all types of clues; dirt, fiber, and stain samples. Apart from what they had found earlier in the house, among the findings from this new search which they considered most significant were three separate instances of blood evidence.

A child's bloodstained jersey was found wrapped in a plastic shopping bag and tossed in the garbage can in the garage. A man's navy blue sweatshirt in the laundry hamper, still damp from being rinsed out, bore traces of blood. And more blood was found in the truck; on the floor, on a child's car seat, and on the cushion of the back seat. These and other evidence were carefully sealed in plastic and placed in the blue Troy County Crime Scene Investigator's van. Everything would be taken to the lab for further tests and analysis.

Cabot turned troubled eyes toward the agents, "As Antonio's attorney, I hope you will avail me of your findings, although I truly believe you are wasting your time while the real perpetrator gets farther away and the trail gets cold."

"Your concerns are duly noted," John Turner replied. "A copy of the report will be forwarded to you if we find anything that incriminates your client or puts him under closer scrutiny."

"You understand that we must go with what we find," Mary Ellen Kelly said.

"Hmm," Cabot grunted as he moved away from them, "as long as the evidence isn't twisted to fit the mold of your choice."

3:05 P.M.

Paul had forced her to eat a light lunch and after that Carmen felt better. At least as well as one could be when one's children had been abducted—or murdered.

68

"Are you sure you're going to be okay?" He looked back at her worriedly from the doorway, holding the tray of lunch dishes.

"Yes, Paul," she assured him. "Go on. Take the dirty dishes to the kitchen. I promise I won't jump out of the window or slit my wrists in the loo."

"Not funny," he regarded her gravely.

"Sorry," she apologized, "That was in poor taste." She tried a smile, "I'll be fine, really."

He reluctantly left her alone, then. Alone with her thoughts.

Much of what had transpired earlier was still a blur; dream-like, as though it had happened to someone else. Or as though it were not real. Details were sketchy and difficult to recall.

She was vaguely aware that she had been picked up and carried, put down on the sofa. Then, for whatever reason, Dr. Solomon had appeared. Very unusual, that. She must have scared the bloody hell out of Paul to have him call her therapist to the house. She remembered hearing someone screaming hysterically.

Oh, yes. That was me screaming.

Lucky thing she hadn't wound up in the psych ward at the state hospital; straight-jacketed in a padded-room, catching flies. She was suddenly overcome by a case of the giggles; another side-effect of Dr. Solomon's drug.

She looked at the needle mark in her arm, sighed deeply, and then started to cry.

God, she hated this medication! It made her daft as a brush, really. And thirsty!

She dragged herself out of bed and made it to the adjoining bathroom, feeling much steadier on her legs than she had before she ate. Earlier, she had managed to take a shower without falling in the tub; but she had not dressed, instead wrapping herself in her pink silk dressing gown. Now, she brushed her teeth and when she was done, ran the cold water in the sink until the faucet was wet with condensation. She pulled a small Dixie cup from the wall dispenser, filled it with water and drank deeply, refilling the paper cup again, again, and still again.

Now, a very pale woman with a mane of wild red hair stared back at her.

"God, you look like bloody hell," she said to her reflection

She splashed some of that icy water on her face, grabbed a fluffy white towel from the bar, and patted her face dry. As she brushed out her long coppery tresses, she realized there was something she needed to do.

By the time Paul returned from the kitchen, she was already dressed.

"You're up! Feeling better?"

I won't feel better until I have my children back, she would have liked to say. Instead, Carmen said, "I want to go to River Road."

"That's not a good idea," Paul said, "Dr. Solomon—"

"Screw Dr. Solomon!" Carmen surprised both of them with the vehemence of her response. "I need to go to River Road to see about Marisa and Liana. Will you drive me there?" When Paul hesitated, she added, "Or shall I drive myself?"

3:56 P.M.

Doug Ferris held his camera steady on his shoulder as he filmed Carlos Viveiros's interview with yet another volunteer. They'd been at it since this morning and he was beat.

After wasting a lot of time, trying to get the story from cops and neighbors—and honoring that blasted yellow police tape—the news team had hoofed it over to Long River to see what they could get. At least, they weren't restricted too much there and it turned out to be better than they had expected. They had lucked out.

They'd been on the scene when, around noon, a scent dog had uncovered a child's pink sweatshirt not far from the river bank. Doug had gotten great footage of that. The garment was dirty, frozen-stiff, encrusted with crumbling leaves. But to him, it had the look of something that had been discarded for a long time; not a shirt that a child might have lost only last night.

Nonetheless, a special team was called in to drag the river. Doug filmed the divers in wetsuits, who were securely tethered to the shore by means of long safety lines. They braved the icy waters only to return a short time later shivering and with discouraging news. The current, they reported, was too swift. They concluded that if the girls had indeed entered the swollen river, death would have occurred within minutes and they would have been quickly swept away. By now their tiny, lifeless bodies could be as far as the Troy River or even carried out to the bay.

Another stroke of luck occurred after lunch when they were allowed to follow one of the groups with the stipulation that the news team stay out of the way and refrain from trampling areas that had not yet been searched. Doug got to film the progress and dogged determination of the police and volunteers who covered every inch of the area looking for the little girls. The searchers tirelessly examined the insides of hollowed tree trunks, explored any irregularity in the snow-covered ground, poked under heaps of fallen branches and piles of sticks. Nothing had been overlooked as a possible hiding place where two young children might be huddled against the cold.

Doug filmed everything while Carlos interviewed anyone who would talk to him. It wasn't really hard to find a willing talker; many were hoping to see themselves on the six o'clock news. Doug marveled at the perseverance of the searchers. As minutes became hours and the girls were not found, the volunteers refused to give up hope. Many promised to return the next day, even though the general consensus was that the area had been completely scoured. If the girls had wandered off on their own, everyone believed they would have been found if they were anywhere near River Road. No one wanted to state the obvious: If they were indeed out there somewhere and had been missed by today's search, there was little hope of finding them alive tomorrow.

Now as the searchers were beginning to leave for the day, the news team had positioned itself back in front of Ibarra's house, and Doug hoped Carlos was almost done. He'd had enough and as far as he was concerned, it was time to call it a day.

Doug hoped it wouldn't be too hard to convince their field director, Peter Flaherty, of that. He could just picture the large black man, a former defensive lineman for Notre Dame, making fun of them both, "Aw, whatssamatta wit de babies?" Then he'd turn serious and add, "Come on. This is a big story. We stop when the story's finished." Sure. What did Flaherty care? He'd been inside the nice warm van all day, watching the monitor and giving orders, while Doug and Carlos froze their butts off!

Doug noted that the light was changing. Heavy clouds had blocked out the sun all day long and dusk was rolling in earlier than usual. If they didn't finish soon, he knew it would be necessary to set up the high-powered lights to film the final footage. To make matters worse, an arctic, breath-robbing wind now screamed mercilessly down River Road, whipping Doug's brown hair into his eyes and making tears stream down his face. He was surprised they weren't turning to ice on his cheeks.

And his ears! He could barely stand the pain. His ears felt like they were going to fall off. He tried to hold the camera with one hand as he struggled to pull his stocking cap over them with the other. The task proved impossible to accomplish and he was forced to give up. No doubt about it, this was torture. He didn't get paid enough for this crap.

He needed a distraction from his discomfort and he found it across the street. Every so often, he glanced over at Ibarra's property, looking for his chance to get something out of the crime scene people. It looked like they were wrapping things up. Earlier that blond boss lady had cut them off quickly enough, but maybe one of her underlings would slip up and inadvertently give something to the press. That's if Carlos finished up before they left! He envisioned the angry look that would cross the witch's face. She'd rail and object, but there'd be nothing she could do about it; freedom of the press and all.

Although he was cold and tired and couldn't feel his toes anymore, he'd tough it out for that one last interview. It would certainly be a feather in their cap.

And then he noticed movement out of the corner of his eye. Movement going in the wrong direction.

Not waiting to make sure Carlos had wound up the interview, he swung the camera to catch the scene unfolding before him. He only vaguely noted Carlos' irritated expression and motioned across the street with his free hand. At the same time, Peter Flaherty commanded from the plug in his right ear, "Get that across the street."

But Doug already had the whole thing framed and in perfect focus.

He'd noticed the woman dressed completely in black leaning against a bright red Mustang GT parked along the front of the Ibarra property. Now, she headed toward a large group of exhausted searchers. It was unclear whom she was seeking, but something in her high-booted stride—besides for the flash of shapely leg that appeared occasionally between the flaps of her long leather coat—attracted his attention.

Could be a story.

The object of her concern became clear in a moment as one of the searchers stopped short, frozen in his tracks upon seeing her. The heavy-set dark-haired man of average height looked stunned. His hands opened at his sides in supplication. The woman, a tiny thing just over five feet, advanced on him, her long coppery tresses bouncing against her shoulders, hands deep in the pockets of her coat. As she approached, the man seemed about to speak when suddenly, without warning, her right fist came out of the coat, connected with his chin with surprising force and sent him sprawling into a snow bank. Then, just as quickly, another taller man came up beside her, slipped an arm protectively around her shoulders and led her away as she leaned into him.

Without a word, Doug kept the camera running as the WTCN-TV News team sprinted toward the man who was rubbing his jaw, trying to sit up in the snow. But when the man saw them coming, he rolled away from them with unexpected agility, slipped once but managed to come up on his feet, ducked under the police tape, and hurried into the house.

Undeterred, the news team went after the red-haired woman. They found her sitting sideways in the passenger seat of the Mustang with her legs outside the car. The bottom half of her leather coat was unbuttoned so that it fell away on either side revealing her pretty legs all the way up to the hem of her black miniskirt. She dabbed at tears with a tissue.

"That was quite a punch," commented Carlos Viveiros as an opener. He smiled displaying his perfect white teeth and trademark dimples.

She looked at him with large gray-green eyes, red-rimmed from crying, but turned away quickly when she saw the camera. The man who had led her away intruded from the side.

"My wife is upset right now," the man said.

Through the camera lens Doug appraised the man quickly; neatly cut black hair, stern blue eyes, over six feet tall, protective stance. Carlos had better tread easy on this one. No use getting a punch in the nose. As though reading Doug's thoughts, Carlos smoothly stated, "We realize that, Mister ah—" He fished for a name to tie to the story.

"Thibault," the husband stated. "My wife is the mother of Marisa and Liana Ibarra. So you can understand that she is not in any condition to grant you an interview."

"We understand, Mr. Thibault," Carlos gave the man his most sympathetic look. "But can you tell me who the man was that she clobbered?"

"Yeah," Thibault shrugged as he waited for the woman to swing her shapely legs into the Mustang, and then closed the door. He straightened up and looked Carlos in the eye. "That was Antonio Ibarra, her ex, the little girls' father." He went around the other side of the car, "You must excuse us. It's been a long day."

He got in and started the car with a roar. At the same moment, the passenger window came down. The red-haired woman's nostrils flared and her angry eyes flashed at Carlos and the camera. Her cultured British accent lent a note of credibility to the harsh accusation she spat out with venom.

"He swore that he would never allow my daughters to live with me; that he'd rather see them dead. So tell me why he has not been arrested! He's murdered them! I know he's murdered them!"

Her further comments were cut off as the window slid up. Thibault hit the gas and the tires spun briefly in the snow. When they finally caught, they threw up a spray of ice and pebbles.

"Did you get all that?" Carlos asked.

"Sure did."

4:22 P.M.

Jet's team had reached a five-foot high red-brick wall topped with an additional three feet of heavy black wrought-iron fence shortly after three-thirty. Even in the poor light among shadows made deeper by dense pine trees laden with heavy snow, it was evident to everyone that the children had not gone onto the estate. Regardless of the fact that none of the snow on the wall itself had been disturbed, there was clearly no way the children could have scaled the wall and climbed over the fence that edged the protected grounds of Collier Ridge. They'd reached a dead end, and with the quickly gathering gloom the searchers had no choice but to abandon their task and turn around.

Whereas it had taken most of the day to reach Collier Ridge as they searched the woods, their return to River Road was much quicker since it did not involve the painstaking scrutiny of every little branch and twig, every depression in the boggy semi-frozen snowy ground that might be a child's footprint. They arrived less than three-quarters of an hour later, exhausted and dejected, knowing that not a trace, not a scrap of a clue had been uncovered. The little girls had not been found. It seemed the children had literally vanished into thin air.

As they emerged from the woods, Donna came out from Mr. Ibarra's back door and immediately made a beeline for the front of the house. Jet saw her run past someone collecting yellow plastic police tape from where it had been strung across the yard. The dog sniffed the air and actually lifted herself on her hind legs. Then she dropped down on all fours and snuffled along the street. Nose to the ground, she zigzagged among the many vehicles that had parked there while the search was going on. With the return of the searchers, many of these vehicles were now leaving for home, yet Donna threaded her way around them, miraculously avoiding getting run over. She ignored the cars and plowed deep in the soft snow with her muzzle and then stopped short in front of the vacant lot west of Ibarra's property. Something seemed to draw her attention to that spot, Jet noted. After a while, she abandoned that activity and returned to the end of the driveway where she sat at attention and faced west toward Cross Street.

"What is she doing?" Jet asked his friends as they approached the front yard.

"I don't know," Robin LaRue said. "My dad said she did the same thing earlier this morning, too. She was like that when he came out to get Mr. Ibarra. Daddy says Mr. Ibarra thinks that Donna believes the girls went up toward Cross Street."

"Cross Street!" Hank exclaimed. "I don't think so. Or, at least, I hope not!"

"You'd think somebody would've noticed two little girls walking around alone up there and done something about it," Robin reasoned.

"Or else they'd've gotten hit by a car!" Hank blurted.

"Really!" Robin agreed. "They *wouldn't* have gone up there alone."

"They weren't alone," Jet muttered pensively.

If anyone responded to his observation, Jet didn't hear it. His attention was focused on Mr. Cabot up on Mr. Ibarra's doorstep, telling him something in a low tone. Jet watched Mr. Ibarra's expression change from one of surprise, to disbelief, to displeasure.

"I did not hurt my own daughters!" Jet heard the man say with an angry scowl.

Mr. Cabot quickly glanced toward the many people who still lingered around the property and gave his neighbor a warning look. "Not so loud," Jet heard Mr. Cabot caution Mr. Ibarra. Mr. Cabot motioned with his head toward the WTCN-TV 3 News team busily getting statements from a number of individuals. Despite his painful ankle, Mr. Cabot pushed his way into Mr. Ibarra's house and closed the door. Presumably, the men had something urgent to discuss in private.

At that juncture, a sound in the garage caught Jet's attention. A man with a ponytail and a neatly trimmed beard emerged from the garage, carrying a type of case. As he approached the police van, the news crew fell upon him like vultures. Until that moment Jet had not noticed the activity going on inside the garage.

"Looks like the cops have been searching Mr. Ibarra's truck," Robin commented voicing Jet's thoughts.

"Yeah. I wonder what they're looking for," Jet mused.

"They probably won't know themselves until they find it," Hank said becoming absorbed by what was going on in the garage.

Jet made no response but turned his attention to Donna once again. On the pretense of going to pat the dog, he squatted beside the animal and observed the investigators placing their evidence cases back into the blue van emblazoned in gold lettering: Troy County Crime Investigator. He wondered what they had retrieved from Mr. Ibarra's truck. What kind of evidence could they find that would link Mr. Ibarra to the disappearance of his daughters? Jet couldn't imagine.

He had never met Mr. Ibarra before this morning when everyone had assembled for the search. Yet even in that short time, Jet felt that Mr. Ibarra could not have done anything to his little girls. He'd seen the pained expression in the man's eyes, the deep emotion when he greeted the volunteers, the way he'd embraced Dad. Jet had heard the distress and heartache, as well as the love, in the man's voice when he spoke of Marisa and

Liana. The man had been truly hopeful this morning as they departed into the woods, and now Jet witnessed the man's distress as the day's search ended and it became evident that the children had not been found.

Yet the CSI was here again. Did that mean they had reason to believe there was something to find that would incriminate Mr. Ibarra of some crime? Why else would they return to look at his truck?

Jet was startled out of his thoughts when he felt something warm and wet gently touch his cheek. He smiled as he realized that Donna was licking him in gratitude for the attention he'd been unconsciously bestowing upon her. He ruffled the thick fur around her neck, jangling the tags on her collar.

"You're such a good dog," he said. Her tail began to thump enthusiastically on the driveway, sending snow and loose gravel skittering. "You're a smart dog, too, aren't you, Donna?" She stood up and gave a single bark.

"There you are!" Hank said coming up on the pair.

"We wondered where you'd gone off to," Robin said reproachfully.

"Yeah," Hank added. "I turned around for just a minute, and the next thing I knew, you were gone."

"I was just talking to Donna, here," Jet said. "You know, she's the only one who knows what happened to those kids?"

Donna barked again and wagged her tail.

"Too bad she can't talk," Robin commented.

4:49 P.M.

"You should put ice on that," Chuck Cabot advised his friend.

Antonio examined the damage with a hand-held mirror. A deep red mark traced the left side of his jaw line, visible even through his black whisker shadow. He gingerly touched his stubble-rough jaw. "For sure, man," he answered angrily. "All my teeth ache from banging together. I can't believe Carmen hit me!"

"And with such force!" Cabot couldn't hide his amusement. He followed Antonio to the kitchen where the latter put a handful of ice cubes into a Ziploc bag and placed it carefully where it hurt the most.

"It's not funny, man," Antonio scowled. "I feel so stupid, letting such a little woman knock me down like that—"

"With one punch."

Antonio shot Chuck Cabot an annoyed look cutting off any more unwanted comments. With his free hand, Antonio took two mugs out of the cabinet and a couple of teabags out of the tin on the counter. He dropped a bag into each mug and looked at Cabot.

"She came at me like *una mula loca*. I swear I saw fire in her eyes. Then out of nowhere, her fist comes out like a hammer, and I find myself on my ass in the snow. I feel like I've been kicked by a mule. I even bit my tongue, man."

"She's upset," Cabot said. When Antonio gave him another irritated look, Chuck let the matter drop. The kettle started to whistle on the stove and Chuck, taking over the role of host, poured hot water over the tea bags. He brought the mugs to the kitchen table, sat down, and changed the subject. "Listen, getting back to what I was saying before," Cabot stirred a spoonful of sugar into his tea and looked up at Antonio. The man met Cabot's eyes with grave concern. The lawyer knew his client was paying attention, "Those CSI people are like rat terriers when they get onto something they think is important."

"What do they think they have? I didn't do anything," Antonio retorted.

"I didn't say you did, Tony," Chuck frowned at Antonio's defensive tone. Someone who didn't know him like Cabot did might think Tony was feeling guilty. When Tony had calmed down, Chuck continued, "They found blood in the truck—"

"I can explain that—"

Cabot held up a hand, silencing his client, "—and something else in the trash can. I haven't seen the report. But if they come back—" Then he amended, "If *anyone* comes here—and

Janet Y. Martel

by that I mean the cops, the FBI, the media, *anyone*—don't talk to them unless I'm present."

5:32 P.M.

Maybe Paul was right. Perhaps going to River Road had been a mistake.

Instead of talking to Antonio and finding out what she could about what had really happened to Marisa and Liana—or at least, Antonio's side of the story—all she'd done was hit him.

Carmen repositioned the icepack on her hand, winced, and smiled wryly. She had hurt herself; the knuckles of her right hand were swollen and bruised. But it had been worth it to see him sprawled out on the snow. Although the shocked surprise on his face had been a beautiful thing to behold, it had not given her the satisfaction she had expected.

When she first decided to go to see Antonio, she had not intended to hit him. Becoming physical with her ex-husband was the furthest thing from her mind. She had wanted to share with Antonio the grief over the loss of their children that had been with her all day. She knew that Antonio had to have been feeling the same worry, the same fear, the same dread, as she. Perhaps they could share those feelings, support each other, commiserate. She and Antonio would include Paul in this because he loved the girls, too. It was a time for the people who loved Marisa and Liana to be together.

When she and Paul arrived in front of her former home, Carmen was overwhelmed by the number of volunteers who had come out to help find Marisa and Liana. She was filled with a deep sense of gratitude for all these strangers who had given up their time when they could have been at home with their own families. In a way, she also felt cheated that she had not been among the searchers; although she knew that if she had come upon the children's lifeless bodies huddled in the woods, it would have been her undoing.

And then, moments later, she saw him, swaggering back from Long River, she supposed. All full of himself, flaunting his macho "I'm the man" attitude. The father, the provider. The responsible and perfect parent.

Ha!

And all of the old resentment and animosity flooded through her, drowning all of her earlier indulgence toward her former husband. She was reminded of how Antonio had treated her when she was in trouble with the alcohol and the crack. There had been no mercy, then; only recriminations and accusations. He had feared, Antonio said to the judge, that something would happen to the children when they were in her care. That's how he had taken them away from her in the first place. But now, ironically, it was he who had lost the children, he who turned out to be the defective parent. They had gone missing while *he* had them, taken away in the night while he *slept*. And that, in Carmen's book, made him culpable!

Suddenly, she was angry.

No; that was too small a word to describe how she felt. Suddenly she *hated* him beyond words, and she wanted to let him know what she thought of him.

She couldn't remember walking over to him, but the next thing she knew, her fist had connected with his jaw, and he was on his arse in the snow. Neither of them had said a word, but in that moment, she felt that Antonio suddenly knew how it felt to be the loser, the pathetic weakling, the incompetent parent, the failure.

And then Paul was taking her away, and putting her into the Mustang. Unfortunately, her ire had not been entirely spent with the blow to Antonio's jaw—and ego—and she had further lashed out at her ex-husband via the media.

Good enough! she shrugged.

Let him see it on the telly and think about what he'd done to her. To her children. His remorse was not enough. She wanted him to pay, and he deserved a lot more than a simple punch in the mouth.

Her behavior, she knew, had truly upset Paul. On the way

home, she could see him from the tail of her eye, continually looking her way so that she wondered how he was able to keep the Mustang on the road. It seemed she couldn't stop the tears, unsure at times for which reason she shed them; whether out of anger with Antonio, or worry over the children. All she knew was that despite sleeping half the day, by the time they got home, she was completely exhausted and a major pounding had begun behind her eyes.

Paul had gotten her some aspirin for the headache, along with one of Dr. Solomon's little white pills, and had insisted that she go up to their room to lie down again. Perhaps she would sleep.

Actually, there was nothing else she could do, under the circumstances. Since she couldn't do anything to help find her own children, she might as well sleep the time away until they were returned, one way or another. As long as the nightmares stayed away...

She needn't have worried about bad dreams.

Sleep did not come. Over an hour passed as she lay on her back, staring at the darkening ceiling, replaying the awful events of the day, beginning with this morning and the ringing doorbell and the pounding on the door.

And for every scene she replayed in her mind, her anger and hatred of Antonio mounted.

6:44 P.M.

By the time Special Agents Turner and Kelly arrived at 72 Hollywood Drive, all light had been squeezed from the sky. But with the aid of the street light on the telephone pole across the street, coupled with the soft glow from the front porch lantern, the two FBI agents were able to make out the details of the property.

Nestled behind a white, snowcapped picket fence was Thibault's cranberry and white Cape Cod. Upstairs, a soft light shone from the eastern dormer, while a Christmas tree glittered in the bay window downstairs. An American flag flapped lazily from a staff that had been mounted on one of the vertical supports for the porch roof. A large, leafless, snow-encrusted tree complete with a tire swing took up much of the front yard. A roughly-shoveled, gravel driveway went up the west side, leading up to a two-stall garage painted to match the house.

"As wholesome and patriotic as a Norman Rockwell print," commented Agent Kelly.

John Turner shot her a wry look as the FBI agents exited their car. Agent Turner opened and held the gate for his partner and the two carefully proceeded along the icy brick walk. They pulled out their ID badges as they climbed the steps of the neatly swept front porch. The doorbell was immediately answered by a handsome dark-haired man wearing blue jeans and a black turtleneck sweater, a striped dishtowel slung over his left shoulder.

"Mr. Paul Thibault?" Agent Turner asked.

"Yes." The man's blue eyes quickly took in both of the agents and their IDs.

As he did with Antonio Ibarra, Turner introduced himself and his partner, and then stated, "We would like to ask you some questions about Marisa and Liana Ibarra."

"Of course." Thibault opened the door wider and let the agents pass by the foot of the stairs that presumably led to upstairs bedrooms. He gestured toward the living room.

The spacious room was carpeted in navy blue and decorated in a patriotic motif. Two brick-red wingback chairs were evenly placed at either side of a Christmas tree that twinkled with red, white and blue decorations. The tree was centered to the south wall's bay window hung with elegant white draperies. Instead of presents on the floor beneath the tree, a large number of tiny Nativity figures had been arranged on a blanket of white cotton.

A fireplace of red brick took up most of the east wall and an inviting fire crackled and spit in the hearth. Centered on the white cotton-covered mantelpiece among the pieces of a Christmas village, an antique clock finished chiming the quarter hour.

A white sofa shared the blue north wall with a good copy of that well-known painting of Washington crossing the Delaware hung above it. Attractive needlepoint pillows with patriotic motifs were nestled into both corners of the couch. Conveniently positioned at either side of the sofa, two cherry wood end tables held white ginger jar lamps, both turned on. At the west end of the north wall was an archway that led into the deeper recesses of the house.

Potted red poinsettias and Christmas cacti in full bloom sat on both ends of the wide window ledge, on the end tables, and on the floor beside the fireplace. The room was immaculate and had the unlived-in, untouched feeling of one kept for company only. To further support that conclusion was the room's lack of a television set, stereo system, or opened presents under the patriotic Christmas tree.

"Please. Come in," Thibault indicated the sofa, smiling, "Sit." The agents crossed the deep blue plush carpeting and sat at either end of the sofa. "Can I get you something to drink? Coffee, tea, cocoa? Or would you prefer soda?" The perfect host.

As at Ibarra's, they refused any kind of beverage and directed their attention to the business at hand. Paul Thibault sat in the wingchair closest to the fireplace.

"Some of your people were here earlier to install taps and recording devices on our phone."

"Good," Agent Turner acknowledged, then asked, "Is Mrs. Thibault at home?"

"She is," Thibault's expression turned serious, "but as I explained to you earlier on the phone, she's in bed. Has been pretty much all day. Doctor's orders. This has really been awful for her, you understand."

Special Agent Turner nodded, "We do need to speak with her eventually, but we can put that off for now. In the meantime, we'd like to ask you a few questions." Then he asked for permission to tape the interview.

"Fine by me," said Thibault, and the questions began.

"How long have you known your wife, Mr. Thibault?" asked Agent Turner.

The man thought for a moment, then, "Just short of a year. We met in January and were married in July, just over five months ago."

"Newlyweds," Agent Turner smiled.

Thibault nodded and blushed, "Yeah, I guess so."

"I'll bet having two little girls around all the time must get in the way of the honeymoon," Turner said coolly.

Thibault's eyebrows came together in a frown, "I wouldn't say that, Agent Turner. Carmen and I have plenty of opportunities for honeymooning, as you put it. The children certainly are not in the way. When I married Carmen I considered the girls a part of the package. There's never been a moment when I suggested we leave them behind. In fact, we took them with us on our actual Honeymoon; we went to Disney World." Thibault seemed to be getting more upset by the minute, "I couldn't love those kids more if they were my own, and I resent your insinuation that I find them a nuisance or a hindrance."

"I'm sorry," Turner looked embarrassed, "I didn't mean to say—I just meant—" Turner shrugged, "Forget it." He sent Special Agent Kelly a quick glance.

"How did you meet your wife, Mr. Thibault?" she asked taking John's cue. This last bit of his was a favorite ploy, used to goad an unsuspecting person into making a rash but truthful statement. Often, it was the person's initial reaction that gave a hint to the underlying truth, leading to quick results. But sometimes, when an inappropriate suggestion or outrageous question failed to yield the desired results, John would feign embarrassment, pretend he'd misspoken, and Mary Ellen would take over, giving the person a chance to relax again.

Thibault gave her a charming, crooked smile, "It was fate. I'm a locksmith. She locked herself out of her car and I got her in."

"Her knight in shining armor," Agent Kelly's blue eyes sparkled, smiling. "I think that's rather romantic."

"I guess she thought so too."

"And Marisa and Liana. Are they happy with having a new stepfather?" she asked lightly. Thibault, it seemed, was a talker with a healthy ego; he liked sharing his accomplishments. Agent Kelly played on this trait, getting him to relax, and perhaps reveal some information of consequence.

Paul Thibault smiled, displaying deep dimples, "If they like me as much as I like them, then I'd say yeah. As I said before, I love those kids. We hit it off right away. They call me Paul-Daddy," he chuckled. "We bonded like a family even before Carmen and I got married," he reflected. "Of course, we all didn't move into this house until after Carmen and I were properly married. She didn't want *anything* to get in the way of her custody hearing. We got busy fixing up two of the bedrooms for them, though, so that when it happened, they'd have their own space. They were thrilled! Carmen's place was so small; just a one-bedroom apartment. On the weekends she had them, she used to give up her room and she'd sleep on the couch. So you can imagine what having each their own room means to them. I mean, even at Ibarra's they share a bedroom. This house was meant to have a family in it. Before we fixed them up, those rooms were just collecting junk."

"How long have you lived here, Mr. Thibault?" Agent Kelly asked.

"In April it'll be," he paused, thinking, "three years. It was my Aunt Aurelie's house until she passed away that February. It went to her only child, my cousin Elise, who is married and living in Michigan. It needed a lot of work; a new roof, repairs to the porch, paint, not to mention yard work. It was too much for Elise to deal with from way out in Michigan, and she wasn't about to move here—uproot her family, make her husband give up his job, and take the kids out of school and all— for the sake of a house. After the title cleared, she decided to put it on the market, and I made her an offer." He chuckled, "I'm afraid if she saw what I did to the place, she'd feel I gypped her."

"You made improvements, then?" Agent Kelly smiled.

Thibault nodded, "First thing I did was raise the roof in the back. I had to put on a new roof anyway. It wasn't much more work to raise the trusses. It makes those back bedrooms—the ones we made up for Marisa and Liana—so much more spacious. At the time I did the work, though, I thought I'd fix the place up and resell at a profit," he said. "Little did I know I'd have a wife and family to put in it only a couple of years later."

"Those repairs must've been expensive," Agent Kelly observed.

Thibault shrugged, "I took out a loan and did most of the work myself."

"You're pretty handy, then," she commented.

"Yeah, I guess. I enjoy a challenge. I like to tackle problems and make them right. Turn a messed up thing into a good one."

Agent Turner shifted in his seat on the sofa. Agent Kelly understood the signal and allowed her partner to take over. It was time to get to the more serious questions.

"So, you feel the space you've afforded the girls is better than what they have at their father's?" Turner surmised.

Paul Thibault flashed him perturbed look. "I don't get what you mean. All I said was that here they have their own room. They love it."

Turner nodded and took a different tack, "Do you go to Ibarra's often?"

"Well, other than to go with Carmen to pick up or drop off the girls, no, of course not. What would be the point?" He shrugged, "I've never even really gone inside except to stay around the front door while the girls got their things. I might've sat down in the chair closest to the door while I waited. I couldn't tell you what the girls' bedroom looks like, even, or where it is in the house, for that matter. I mean, I know it's somewhere down the hall, but I couldn't tell you which room it is. I haven't seen any part of the house other than what you can see from the front door."

"What about Donna?"

"Donna?" Thibault looked puzzled, as though he didn't understand the purpose for the question, but offered information anyway, "The dog? Yeah, she's a beauty. Really loves those kids. I had a yellow Lab when I was a kid. Every kid should have one."

"She lets you in the house?"

"She was a bit skittish the first time," he conceded, "Possessive and guarding. But after a while, she accepted me and never made another peep." He chuckled, "She wags her tail and greets me like an old friend, now. I don't think Antonio knows what to make of it. I think he sort of resents that Donna likes me."

Turner nodded again, "So, you don't like Antonio Ibarra?"

Thibault's smile vanished, "I didn't say that. Don't put words in my mouth, Agent Turner. I don't *like* him, and I don't *dislike* him. I'm not in competition with him. For the sake of the girls, I try to keep things…" he searched for the word, "calm. Polite."

"I see," said Turner. "What can you tell us about him?"

"I only deal with him when he comes here or we go there to transport the girls. We're not part of his social circle, you know? I mean, Carmen introduced us and all, and he acts civil to me. Doesn't talk much, but he minds his manners, even though he doesn't like *me*. After all, I took his woman; doesn't matter that *he's* the one who threw *her* out. I don't really know him, except from what I know from Carmen." Thibault explained, "According to her, he's a strong-minded individual. A real martinet, the way she describes him. He never cut her any slack. She was young, immature. Irresponsible, even. But he treated her like a man would a child, not a wife. He dictated what her behavior should be, what she should wear, how she should talk, who she could talk to, where she could and could not go. He never let her do what she wanted to do. You can't squash a spirit like Carmen's, not for long anyway, before she'll bolt. It makes me wonder what kind of a father he's going to be to his daughters when they start asserting themselves and they aren't so pliable to his will," Paul Thibault stopped abruptly, glanced up at the FBI agents as though suddenly remembering they were there.

"I truly believe that you should be asking *me* the questions about my ex-husband," said a female voice with a significant British accent.

All eyes turned toward that voice and fell on the woman emerging from the shadows of the archway. Although small in stature, Carmen Thibault was a powerful figure even in her nightclothes. Despite all evidence that she'd been crying, she stood erect with her chin up, her long coppery red tresses flowing over her shoulders like a shawl. Below the hem of her long pink silk dressing gown modestly cinched over her shapely figure, could be seen the bottom few inches of matching pajamas and her tiny feet with perfectly polished toes poking out of pink marabou slippers. Paul Thibault was up and at her side the moment he heard her, and with a protective arm around her shoulders, led her to the chair in which he had been seated.

"You shouldn't be up, Carmen. Dr. Solomon assured me that pill would put you to sleep," her husband gently admonished.

She gave a mirthless laugh, "Sleep! I should be able to sleep, you think, when my babies are dead. Murdered by that man who thought *I* was such an unfit parent!" The statement was made with much ire and the emphatic manner in which she poked her breastbone with the tips of her manicured fingers should have been painful.

"Who do you think murdered your babies, Mrs. Thibault?" Agent Kelly asked softly.

"Antonio!" she answered sharply, her gray-green eyes flashing with malice.

"And what makes you think that?"

"When the judge granted me custody," she snarled, "he yelled out in court that he'd rather see them dead than let them live with me." She lowered her head into her hands and ended with tearful conviction, "They are dead. He's murdered them. I pray to God that I am wrong, but I already know it is so in my heart."

10:51 P.M.

Freshly showered, wavy black hair slicked back, a pajama-clad Jet stretched out full-length on the frilly violet coverlet of the twin bed, hugging a cuddly pink plush bunny to his chest. Since Danielle and Denise were not using their beds, it seemed only right that the boys should, otherwise one of *them* would have been sleeping on the floor in Hank's room. Besides, by using the girls' room, it left Hank's empty bed for Jet's dad who otherwise would have been relegated to the sofa in the living room. It all just made good sense. Practical.

And the boys didn't mind using the girls' room. So *what* if the room was papered in lavender and light blue nosegays! And ruffled curtains with satin ribbons hung at the windows! "When you're asleep, your eyes are closed," Hank pointed out, "and you can't see them."

Or the buff, bare-chested pinup taped to the back of the bedroom door, Jet thought.

Besides, Jet and Hank were well-aware that it drove the twins nuts to know that the boys were using their room. All the more reason to settle in as comfortably as they could. It was all part of the age-old battle between younger brothers and older sisters that has gone on since time immemorial. And despite all the fussing, the boys were heeding Aunt Claire's warning and were being careful not to mess up the room—too much.

Jet was exhausted. Considering the restless night he'd had yesterday, the early morning rise, the day-long search, not to mention fighting the bitter cold, it was no wonder his energy was totally sapped. Yet his brain wouldn't quit. It kept reviewing the events of the day, trying to work out the mystery of the Ibarra girls' disappearance.

Earlier, after supper, Jet had sat on the floor in the twins' bedroom, with his back leaning against the foot of Danielle's bed to watch the Channel 3 News. Hank propped himself against Denise's bed, while Robin was sprawled on her stomach on top.

Sylvia Chan, the evening anchor, was on. The pretty Asian

woman's almond-shaped black eyes sparkled with enthusiasm as she gave her report. The lead story concerned an overnight fire that had turned a number of families out of their apartments; five people had died, including two children. This kind of tragedy was always terrible, but seemed worse at Holiday time. The Red Cross was there to help the survivors who had pretty much lost everything. People who wanted to make donations of money, food, or clothing were told to call the telephone number at the bottom of the screen.

Then Chan was introducing Carlos Viveiros with a story he had concerning an Amber Alert that had been issued for all of New England.

The handsome young news reporter appeared bundled in a dark blue parka with a fur-lined hood, worn up so that only a hint of his curly black hair could be seen. Around his neck was tied a red and blue muffler. As he spoke, his breath turned to fog and was carried away by the chill wind. "Thank you, Sylvia," he said with an uncharacteristically serious expression in his dark brown eyes. "The little sisters, Marisa, seven, and Liana, five, either wandered away in the middle of the night, or were stolen from their beds while their father slept in his room across the hall." As he spoke, the picture changed to show Ibarra's yellow and brown ranch house, apparently filmed from Mrs. Carvalho's across the street earlier that day. The bright yellow police tape across the front yard vibrated in the brisk wind.

"While police are trying to determine which of the two scenarios is true, fear that the girls are out somewhere in this cold has prompted a desperate search. Despite the below-freezing weather, close to two hundred volunteers combed the woods of Collier Ridge Estate today, yet no clue was found to suggest what might have happened to the girls." The scene changed each time Viveiros brought up a different phase of the search. Now a long line of searchers moved side by side, scouring Collier's Woods. Jet recognized some of them even if he didn't know their names. He, however, had not been captured on film. It was just as well; Jet hated that kind of notoriety, especially when school chums might see him and make a big deal out of it.

"A pink sweatshirt was uncovered along the banks of the swollen Long River, prompting a dive search. However, with this awful cold, you can imagine how difficult that was. The icy water, coupled with the swift current of the river, made even more treacherous after last week's heavy rains, forced the divers to give up. They've concluded that if the girls fell into that river, they would have been quickly overcome by the severe cold of the water. Authorities further believe that their bodies would have been swept away by those swift currents and they may not be found until late spring after the waters recede, or maybe not at all. Although with each passing hour it becomes less likely the girls will be found alive if they *are* in these woods, the volunteers are coming back to help."

Then Jet recognized the raspy voice of Mary Carvalho even before he saw her round face. "These wonderful people have taken time from their jobs and their own families to help Tony Ibarra find his little girls. Food and monetary donations have been pouring in." The camera scanned two long food-laden tables that stood end to end in Mrs. Carvalho's garage. Some of the volunteers were helping themselves to a snack before they set out again to resume the search. "Everyone's generosity and caring is too much for words, although I can't say it's unbelievable. I always knew they had it in them. It's too bad that tragedy had to befall one of us to bring out the good in people. Of course at this time of year, people tend to be more caring, more generous. But the outpouring of love from total strangers is truly remarkable and wonderful."

Mary Carvalho's further comments were cut and Carlos Viveiros continued, "Even as searchers had hoped to find the girls huddled somewhere in the woods, authorities must consider the possibility that the children were kidnapped. For that reason, an area-wide Amber Alert has been issued for the two sisters in the hope that someone out there has seen them. Although the police have not officially charged anyone with the disappearance of the two Ibarra children, clearly there are some who have their own suspicions."

The camera zoomed in on a pretty red-haired lady wearing a long black leather coat. She walked quickly up to a man, seemingly picking him out of a crowd of returning volunteers. As the crowd dispersed, Jet could see that the man was Mr. Ibarra. Who the woman was, Jet had no clue. It seemed to him that Mr. Ibarra was about to say something when without warning, she swung out and punched him in the face. Though much larger than the lady, Mr. Ibarra landed heavily on his butt in the snow.

"Whoa!" Hank lurched forward. "Did you see that?"

But Jet did not answer because abruptly the picture had shifted to show the same copper-haired woman inside a red car. The window slid down so that one could plainly see her eyes flashing angrily through her tears, and hear her harsh words flavored with a British accent.

"He swore that he would never allow my daughters to live with me; that he'd rather see them dead. So tell me why he has not been arrested! He's murdered them. I know he's murdered them!"

"Geesh!" Jet exclaimed using his favorite expression. "Who was that?"

Robin looked at Jet with her head supported on her crossed arms, "That was Mrs. Ibarra—"

"You mean Mrs. Thibault," Hank corrected her.

"Whatever," she sighed. "She was pretty ticked off! To say those awful things about Mr. Ibarra. I mean, I guess it's understandable. People get all bent out of shape with the stress. They start attacking and blaming each other. I feel so bad for both of them. If Jenny went missing..." she cut herself off. "I don't even want to think about it. It's just too awful."

The boys nodded. There were no words they could add to Robin's. For a moment, the three teenagers were silent as Carlos Viveiros finished his report.

"Thank you, Carlos," Sylvia's golden face came back on the screen, and she directed her words to her viewers. "As Carlos reported, it is unclear whether the children simply wandered off or if they were kidnapped. Because either possibility exists, an Amber Alert has been issued for all of New England." Her face was replaced with pictures of two dark-haired girls, one apparently older than the other, but not by much. Chan's voice continued, "These are photographs of Marisa and Liana Ibarra. Police ask that you study these pictures carefully. Marisa will be seven years old in January. She has curly dark brown hair, dark brown eyes, is about four feet tall, and weighs around fifty pounds. Liana, age five-and-a-half, has curly brown hair with red highlights, tawny brown eyes, is approximately three-and-a-half feet tall, and weighs about forty pound. When last seen, the girls were wearing light blue pajamas. It is possible that they were also wearing pink and purple double goose-down hooded jackets. Any information concerning these girls should be reported to the Ridgeport Police Hot Line. That number appears at the bottom of your screen."

The pictures of the two Ibarra girls remained on the screen with the RPD Hot Line number as they went to commercial.

"Geesh!" Jet said again.

"Yeah, creepy," Robin agreed. "Do you think they just wandered off?"

"I don't know," Jet answered deep in thought.

"If those kids *did* wander off, then I don't think the chances are good that they'll be found alive," Hank observed. "It's way too cold outside for them to survive. I mean, they're just little kids. What would they know about how to keep warm?"

"In nothing but pajamas and goose-down jackets," Jet mused.

"My dad said the door was not forced," Robin said. "Mr. Ibarra found it unlocked and left wide open."

The threesome fell silent while a silly commercial flashed before their unseeing eyes.

"I don't get it," Hank finally broke the silence. His voice was filled with frustration, "We've looked *everywhere*! Why haven't we found them? Or *something*, at least!"

"I know what you mean," Robin frowned sitting up cross-legged on Denise's bed. "You'd think by now *something* would have been uncovered. Some clue for the police to form some kind of theory, a hunch they could go on."

Jet's companions had voiced his thoughts exactly. "I agree," Jet stated. "If Marisa and Liana wandered off on their own, some sign of them should have come to light by now. Some clue should have been found to suggest where they went. A scrap of cloth caught on a branch. A footprint. Something to give authorities a hint as to what happened." Jet abruptly fell silent. It made no sense at all. It was as though they'd simply vanished.

But of course, people don't simply vanish.

"To think that those kids just took off in the middle of the night…" Robin said. "It's crazy!" She swung her legs over to the side and set her stocking feet on the floor between the two beds. "I know Jenny never would do anything like that, and she's no 'fraidy-cat. I can't imagine them going out in the dark. In the snow."

"I'd've been scared to death!" Hank avowed. "I mean, I know my backyard like the back of my hand, but I wouldn't *think* of going out there at night without turning on the flood lights, or at least using a flashlight. Like behind Ibarra's house, it's all woods back there. There's no telling what might be lurking in the dark!"

"Are we sure it was nighttime when they went out?" Robin asked.

"Had to have been," Hank reasoned, "or else, they'd have left footprints in the snow."

"Right," Jet agreed. "Mr. Ibarra saw no trace of where they had gone when he went looking for them. Their tracks must've been covered with fresh snow after they left. So it couldn't have been much after midnight."

Jet stopped talking as his mind worked on the puzzle. It was highly unlikely that the children would have ventured out alone in the middle of the night. Not only would it have been frightening, it would also have been horribly cold. Jet shook his head, "They didn't go out alone. Someone led them away. Someone woke them from their sleep and convinced them to go with them. Someone they knew and trusted." *Maybe even someone they loved,* Jet thought.

Jet launched himself from the floor and dug into his duffle bag. He knew he had a spiral notebook and a pen in one of the side pockets. A moment later he found the objects of his search and sat at the twins' desk, carefully moving items aside until he had a flat surface on which to write.

"What're you doing?" Robin asked.

"Don't ask." Hank laughed, "He's got that look in his eye."

"What look?" Robin's brown eyes darted quickly from one cousin to the other.

Jet ignored her question. He was busy heading up pages in his notebook. In a moment, he swung away from his work and regarded his companions seriously. "First, let's list everything we know about Marisa and Liana's disappearance," he suggested. "When was the last time anybody saw them?"

"I saw them breaking a piñata in their backyard yesterday," Robin volunteered getting into a more comfortable position on Denise's bed. "Jenny wanted to go out too, but she's getting over a cold and my mother wouldn't let her. They didn't stay out very long, anyway."

"And that night," Hank added incredulously, "they leave without taking any of their new Christmas presents!"

Jet's eyes met Hank's, "How do you know that?"

"I heard the skinny CSI guy telling the mean-looking blond lady that Mr. Ibarra said nothing was missing from under the tree, except for the dolls they'd taken to bed with them. But the CSI guy said those dolls were in the bedroom," Hank explained. "What kid in his or her right mind does that?" Hank watched in satisfaction as Jet wrote it all down.

"They were wearing light blue pajamas?" Robin offered, "And purple and pink parkas?"

Jet's eyebrows shot up. He nodded and wrote that information down.

"They did *not* go in the woods. I don't know why we even looked there. There were no footprints leading there in the snow," Hank reasoned.

"But like Jet said before, they might have been covered with new snow, Hank," Robin argued gently.

"Well, just the same, if they *had*, we'd've found them," Hank insisted forcefully.

"Not the river, either!" Robin exclaimed with round brown eyes. "Tell me I'm in denial, but I won't believe they went there."

"So, where did they go?" Jet asked with his pen poised above the paper, "In their pajamas and jackets?" Then, "Nobody said anything about shoes, but I can't believe they went out barefooted."

"Maybe somebody carried them," Robin suggested.

"Hmm!" Jet nodded, jotted into his pad, then looked at his friends, "We keep saying where they *didn't* go. So, where *did* they?"

"In a car?" Hank shrugged. "That would be the easiest way to get a couple of kids out of sight quickly. I doubt the kidnapper could have carried two kids very far."

"Especially if they didn't want to go along," Robin added. "Kids are kind of slippery. I know I can't hold onto Jenny when she wants me to leave her alone. I'm thinking those kids had to know the person they were with, and they had to be okay with going with them, or they'd have called out for their dad."

"Maybe there were two people; one carrying each kid," Hank suggested.

Jet said nothing, noting that his companions had quickly abandoned the theory that the children had wandered off and were ready to believe they had been kidnapped. He busily jotted down all of these observations.

"Donna keeps sniffing around the street in front of the vacant lot," Jet mused. "She did it this afternoon, and according to Mr. Ibarra and your dad, Robin, she did it this morning, too. I wonder what she's smelling for. . ?" That was something he needed to find out in the daylight. He continued, "Then she sits at the end of the driveway and looks up toward Cross Street."

"As though the car they were in drove up that way?" Robin

suggested slowly.

"And she's waiting for them to come back?" Hank finished.

"Because..." Jet encouraged.

"She expects them to?" Hank shrugged.

"Because whoever they went with usually brings them back?" Robin ventured.

Excitement lit Jet's light blue eyes, "Okay. If Donna thinks whoever has them is going to bring them back, I think it's safe to assume whoever took them is close to them."

"Right," Hank nodded. "Remember, Donna didn't bark when whoever-it-was went into the house. That would mean that she knew them."

"Wait a minute," Robin warned. "She doesn't simply *know* whoever took the girls." The boys regarded her waiting for her to continue. "Look, even though she knows *me*, whenever I go there to get Jenny, she still barks once or twice when I enter the house. Then Mr. Ibarra tells her to be quiet, and she doesn't make another sound. It's not an angry, threatening bark, the way a watchdog would bark at a stranger. It's more like a friendly hello, but with a 'heads up', like she's making sure I know she's in charge." She shrugged dismissively, "It's understandable. I don't live there and I'm not part of the family." She finished thoughtfully, "No. For family, she scrunches down playfully with her tail wagging like crazy, and she makes these whimpering sounds. She lets them know she's happy to see them."

"That means whoever took the girls is *family*?" Hank said incredulously.

"Geesh!" Jet's eyes went wide with shock. "You've just implicated Antonio Ibarra as the kidnapper of his own daughters."

"It's a good thing Mr. Cabot is a good lawyer," Robin said quietly. "I think Mr. Ibarra's going to need him."

That was hours ago and Robin had gone home. Now, Jet and Hank were getting ready for bed and unwinding in the twins' bedroom.

"How about some TV?" sandy-haired Hank asked with the

remote poised in his right hand.

"Sure," yawned Jet as the screen came to life. Hank aimlessly flipped channels. If he was looking for something, Jet had no idea what. But Jet knew what *he* wanted to see, and when he recognized the image he was looking for, he bolted upright on the bed and threw the pink bunny at Hank's hand. "Stop!" he commanded the bewildered Hank. "Go back."

"Whaa-a-a?" Hank cast him a startled blue-eyed glare but complied, not really knowing how far back Jet meant. Although Hank was three months Jet's senior, the younger cousin had the more forceful personality. Bound by blood, the cousins had always been close, but the bond of friendship had truly tightened when the two boys entered Bishop O'Donnell High School as freshmen last year. They considered each other best friends; but sometimes, like at that moment, Jet made demands and Hank automatically bristled.

Jet noticed his cousin's irritation, and apologized, "Sorry, Hank." He chuckled at his cousin's bewildered expression. "But hurry up and go back to the news. They might have something more about the Ibarra kids," Jet explained.

Hank pressed the channel button until the golden face of Sylvia Chan appeared. He caught her as she segued to Jet's favorite meteorologist, redhead Tim Riley. As usual, Riley flashed his green eyes, and gesticulated and pointed in front of a map of Southern New England.

"Cold, cold, and more cold, at least until Thursday for us in Southern New England. Although yesterday's snowstorm was a good one, it was nothing like what they got in the snow-belt. That's the region north of the Mass Pike, and up into Maine, New Hampshire, and Vermont. The storm that started yesterday afternoon—the second in three days for them—continued through the morning hours, dumping nearly three feet of the white stuff in some places. The heavy snow took out electrical service in some areas and made driving hazardous, if not impossible. Crews worked quickly to restore power and plow roads and by supper time, most places were almost back to normal. Kudos to them. And while we were lucky here in Troy

County and only got eight to ten inches, it still gets us skiers thinking it's time to head for the hills! North of us, Mother Nature has been busy since Thanksgiving, and here in Massachusetts and neighboring Connecticut and Rhode Island, ski resorts have been making the man-made stuff. So, all you skiers and snowboarders, wax the equipment, find your goggles and mittens! The slopes are open and waiting!"

"That sounds like fun," Hank interjected.

Jet merely nodded and listened attentively to the rest of Tim Riley's forecast.

"Good news for tomorrow! *The sun'll come out—tomorrow.*" Riley sang the first line of the song from *Annie*, then said, "But although the sun will make an appearance both tomorrow and Thursday, don't expect temperatures to reach much above twenty degrees until Friday. Then, we *might* hit thirty-two, and that at least, is freezing."

It wasn't good news for the searchers; definitely not good news for the little Ibarra girls if they were out there. Hank seemed to be thinking along the same lines.

"I'm wearing my long johns tomorrow."

"At least it won't snow again," Jet sighed. More snow would complicate the search and make it that much harder to find clues or traces of where they went.

Hank tossed the remote to Jet who caught it smartly. "I'm beat," Hank yawned and got under the covers. "You can watch TV if you want." He reached over from his bed and switched off the bedside lamp.

"Naw. I'm turning in, too."

Jet was about to press the off button when the Amber Alert was repeated. The pictures of the missing Ibarra girls came back on the screen. He stared mutely at the two sweet faces. Liana's tawny eyes glowed as she smiled unabashedly, showing small pearl-like teeth and two perfect dimples in her round cheeks. Marisa, her head slightly tilted, gazed impishly at the camera, displaying a space where her front teeth used to be. Both of them were so full of life.

After today's exhausting search, Jet knew they weren't in

the Collier's Woods. But had the mischievous Marisa led her little sister to Long River to play? Had they accidentally fallen into the water and drowned? It was so hard to think that way.

Jet knew he'd been a cut-up as a child. Yet would he have ventured out in the middle of the night in the freezing cold with a wind-chill below zero to go play near water? No. He didn't think so. His instincts for self-preservation were way too strong. He'd never done anything like that even in his wildest days. When he was ten or so, he'd snuck out of the house to look at the stars; but that was in the middle of summer when it was too hot to sleep and crickets' chirps were so loud they kept him awake. The cool grass had felt so good to lie on.

A flash on the TV screen brought him back to the present. The *Eleven O'clock News* was over, and some obnoxious commercial was playing. Jet turned off the set and pushed the frilly bedspread down to the foot of the bed in the dark. He crawled under the blankets, lay on his back, and closed his eyes.

The unbidden image of the lost girls came to mind almost immediately.

So alive. How could they be dead?

How could they have left their warm beds in the middle of the night to venture out in such awful cold? What could have possessed them to do that? The snow? No. He couldn't believe they'd gone out alone. They'd been taken in the night by someone else. Someone older. Someone they trusted. They were out there somewhere. He could feel it.

"Where are you guys?" he whispered in the darkness.

Wednesday, December 28

Streetlamps were still glowing when Special Agents Turner and Kelly rolled into the Ridgeport Government Complex. They parked their Crown Victoria in the guest lot in front of the police station and went in through the glass doors with large covered cups of hot coffee in their hands. To their left, the Chief's glass-enclosed office still lay dark behind the open slats of the mini-blinds; to the right, the War Room would be empty for another few minutes before the change of shifts.

The desk sergeant's desk and switchboard stood directly in front of them. A slightly overweight, red-faced, balding man in his late fifties, looked up questioningly as they approached. The name plate on his desk identified him as Sgt. Max Machbitz.

The agents showed Sgt. Machbitz their IDs and he nodded at them jovially, his gray walrus mustache twitching, "You've been assigned a couple of cubicles I think you'll find comfortable; A-3 and B-3 at the end of the first aisle."

He jerked his thumb indicating a large room that had been

102

divided into sixteen six-by-eight workspaces set in rows of four with a common aisle in between. A few fluorescent lights recessed into the ceiling illuminated cubicles where detectives and officers were finishing up paperwork at the end of their shifts. All of the work areas were similarly equipped with a counter on the long wall serving as a desk for a computer, a printer, and a telephone. Short stacks of filing cabinets supported the countertop, with a three foot wide space in the center for a knee hole. In addition to an office chair on rollers, there were also two visitor's chairs.

Machbitz was right. The five foot high walls surrounding the cubicles would afford the agents enough privacy to do their work unhampered by the routine hubbub of the busy police station, yet without the claustrophobic feeling of a tiny office space.

Mary Ellen Kelly removed her black wool coat and hung it on the metal hook near the doorway of cubicle A-3. She set down her briefcase on the countertop, popped the clasps, and took out what had occupied her mind for the last twenty hours: The Ibarra case. With colored pushpins, she started fastening the various items from the case to the inside walls of her cubicle. This would serve as their evidence board.

At the top of the center wall, directly over the computer station she pinned the school photos of the missing girls. Beneath them were their vital statistics.

Marisa Anita Ibarra; age seven; Height, 4'1"; Weight, 49 lbs.; Eyes, Dark brown; Hair, Dark brown. Distinguishing characteristic: Missing two front teeth.

Liana Maria Ibarra; age five; Height, 3'7"; Weight, 37 lbs.; Eyes, Light brown; Hair, Brown w/red highlights.

Off to the right of the girls' pictures she pinned the floor plan of the house at 1136 River Road: The Ibarra residence. On it, she had carefully labeled the rooms. Antonio's room was the only bedroom on the south side of the house, facing the street. Marisa and Liana's room was directly across the hall from Antonio's. The room adjacent to the girls' room had been the nanny's, Adelina Aguilar. The nanny had been dismissed after

Antonio lost custody of the girls. It seems that Donna slept in the girls' room when they were home. When they were not, she slept either in the kitchen or in Antonio's room.

Next, Mary Ellen Kelly unrolled a long strip of banner paper on which she had started a timeline. John helped her pin the clumsy length of paper to the wall and she left him to read it while she continued with her work.

On the opposite wall she posted three glossy, unflattering eight-by-ten Registry of Motor Vehicle pictures of those who had seen the girls most recently: Antonio Ibarra, Carmen Thibault, and Paul Thibault. At the right edge of the wall near the corner, she pinned the photos of Carmen and Paul side by side. To the left of them, she put up Antonio's picture and that of a black Labrador retriever.

"It's not really Donna," she explained to John, "I got this photo from the Internet; but it will do for our purposes."

"You've been busy," Turner commented with approval. "Did you sleep at all last night?"

She gave him a dour look. "You know me," she sighed. "When there's a hot case, I work in my sleep. I got up at three. Aunt Tillie wasn't happy about it. She grumbled a lot and wanted me to turn off the computer. You know how she is. But I won out, made notes about all of our friends here. You want to hear them?"

"By all means." He sat down in Mary Ellen's office chair with his coffee cup, "Please proceed."

She smiled wryly back at her partner of three years and began her presentation. Mary Ellen pointed at the first picture with the back end of her pen. She spoke mostly from memory, only occasionally referring to some written notes which she held in her other hand.

"Antonio Ibarra, age forty-two, five-foot nine-inches tall, one hundred and ninety-five pounds, electrician, I.B.E.W. Local Union five-thirty-one. Was last to see the girls at nine-thirty P.M., December 26. The children are with him for a scheduled visit: They arrive at his home at nine P.M. on Sunday, and they are supposed to go home Wednesday night. Ibarra notices they're missing around six A.M. on Tuesday morning. Front door is open. No sign of forced entry."

"That in itself is suspect, don't you think?" John commented. "If he locked the door before he went to bed, how'd it get unlocked? Could the children do that for themselves?"

"Possibly. All they would have had to do was turn the bolt. I measured the height of that bolt. Maybe not Liana, but Marissa could have reached it on her tiptoes. She takes ballet lessons; she could have stretched. Anyway, CSI dusted for prints. I'm waiting on their findings." She continued with her narrative, "Realizing the children are not in the house, Ibarra goes off looking for them. Bob LaRue says the man was only in his robe, walking in deep snow in his bare feet. In LaRue's words, the man was totally out of it. LaRue reports the girls missing around six-thirty—"

"Why him?" John asked. "Why did the neighbor make the call and not Ibarra?"

Mary Ellen shrugged her slender shoulders, "Apparently, Ibarra thought the kids were playing a game, hiding on him. LaRue had to convince him that the police would help him find the children."

John frowned, "I don't buy it."

Mary Ellen's eyebrows shot up, "I get it. After speaking with Mary Carvalho and Charles Cabot, I can see how Ibarra thinks. He's the macho type; losing the children is a black mark against his parenting skills. Calling for help is a sign of weakness and in his opinion, diminishes his masculinity. Think how stupid he'd have felt if the girls had shown up all smiles. He'd have looked like a fool. He can't allow his ex-wife to see him in that light." She shook her head, "I don't agree with him, but I can understand where he's coming from." She shrugged, "When we spoke to Ibarra, he seemed genuinely upset. The two uniforms they sent out," she checked her notes, "Diaz and Caron say the same; reactions were reasonable and as expected."

"Unless he's a good actor."

Mary Ellen had nothing to say to that remark. The pen went

to the next picture. "Donna, three-year-old black Labrador retriever. Said to be the children's faithful companion. Does not bark when the perp enters the house. That's assuming the children were kidnapped, and did not just wander off."

"Do you think that's possible?" Turner interrupted, "They just left the house of their own accord?"

"Ibarra feels that it isn't, and I agree. I think going out alone in the dark might be a scary thing to do at seven and five years old. Besides, I would think if they *had* ventured out by themselves, they would have come back in once they saw how cold it was." She shrugged her shoulders, "But you never know with kids. They do silly, stupid things sometimes. I also feel that if indeed they *were* out there, they would've been found by now. This gives me mixed feelings. At this point, with the cold we've had the last two nights, the chances of finding them alive are slim."

"Mmm," John nodded, "I agree: If they've been exposed to the elements this long, they're probably already dead."

Mary Ellen sucked in a breath and turned away to hide the dread she knew showed on her face. "No," she said with conviction, when she knew her voice would not betray her, "they're *not* out there. I believe they were taken away."

"But depending on who has them, they might be better off if they *were* dead. Lots of crazies out there. Do you think maybe a pedophile—?"

She frowned, "For their sakes, I hope not!"

"But it's always a possibility."

"We need to find them fast." Mary Ellen cleared her head of the horrible thoughts. "Anyway," she continued with her dissertation, "the dog is their constant companion, and she's at the house when Antonio discovers they're missing. I can't put my mind around the fact that they left voluntarily and she didn't follow. I can't imagine why she didn't put up a fuss. Donna would not have allowed the children to leave with anyone—"

"—unless she knew the person who took them."

"Or she was sleeping and she wasn't aware of them leaving."

John gave her a dubious look, "I don't know. It's possible, but I think Donna is more vigilant than that."

Mary Ellen nodded once, accepting his point. She tapped the next photo with the pen. "Carmen Thibault, age twenty-eight, five-foot two-inches, one hundred and ten pounds, former exotic dancer, according to Maria LaRue she has a wild side—"

"Had," John corrected, "Maria also said she's become 'domesticated.'"

"True," Mary Ellen conceded, "but does a leopard change its spots? She's a recovering alcoholic and crack-addict. How long will she stay on the wagon? Crack addictions are almost impossible to overcome or control. I think we need to keep a watchful eye on her." John nodded encouragement and she continued, "She's a new U.S. citizen, and holds a position as an accountant with Brent Accounting Services."

"According to Maria LaRue, she married Antonio to avoid deportation," John pointed out. "Is Marisa's paternity questionable? We haven't established that, but a simple DNA test would answer the question, should the need arise."

"I agree. It needs to be addressed; might have bearing on the case." Mary Ellen shrugged, "Carmen has issues with Antonio Ibarra stemming from her resentment over his unmerciful treatment of her; the divorce, the custody of her children, *et cetera*."

"Question," John broke in. "Would she have kidnapped her own children?"

"Motive?"

"Because Ibarra really *isn't* the father and she can't bring herself to tell him, so she makes the kids disappear, and—"

"Stop right there," Mary Ellen put up her hand. "You could write fiction."

"Okay. Maybe she wants to hurt Antonio."

Mary Ellen winced and shook her head, "I thought of that. She has full custody of the girls. Even if we don't believe her every word, it's obvious she's worked hard to get where she is now. How would kidnapping them give her more than what she has?"

"Revenge?" John supplied.

"No, I don't think she'd risk doing something that would cause her to not only lose her kids for life, but land her in jail as a consequence. Not after she's won." She shook her head again. "There are other ways to get revenge without making the girls disappear. Besides, she wouldn't want to harm them or endanger them in any way. They've bonded. They're mother and child again. Last year at this time, maybe I'd agree with you, but not now. She's got nothing to gain and everything to lose." Mary Ellen turned to face her partner, "I see her as a suspect because at this early stage of the investigation, we can't rule anybody out. Maybe she *did* steal them to punish Antonio, although I have trouble making that work. My instincts tell me that what's happened to the girls has something to do with Carmen, but I haven't figured that part out yet."

"Interesting," John commented. "And then there's Paul Thibault."

"Yes, charming and handsome Paul Thibault." She moved the pen to his picture. "Age thirty-four, six-foot three-inches tall, one hundred ninety-eight pounds, works in the family locksmith business. A handyman. Likes to fix problems. Seems to really love Carmen, would do anything to make her happy. Possibly in competition with Antonio. Does not like or *dis*like Antonio Ibarra, he says. I wonder about that. It seems to me Paul's been influenced by his pretty wife into believing that Ibarra is a nasty man. He definitely has a negative opinion of Ibarra, but for the sake of the girls, tries to keep things civil."

"It's interesting that he's a locksmith, too," John mused, "How convenient that the door should be opened, not forced."

"Paul certainly would have the know-how and the tools to open Ibarra's front door without damaging it. And since Donna likes him—"

"It looks to me that you have a nice list of viable suspects," John said approvingly. "All we need to do is narrow it down to one."

"But we're lacking motive in every case," Mary Ellen

pointed out.

"How about custody?" John suggested again, "I keep coming back to that because to me, it works for either parent. Antonio would like to see things back the way they were before. He resents Thibault, which came out nicely in his interview with Officer Diaz. He said something about Thibault not being related to the children; that he, Antonio, was their father, not Paul. He's also angry that Carmen has taken the kids away from him. He's invested a lot of time and made a lot of sacrifices. He's not only supplied those children with the necessities, he's gone the extra mile, putting them in private school, giving them dance lessons… And did you get a load of that play house in the backyard? Now, after all that, Carmen waltzes in and takes the kids away from him."

John shifted in his seat, "Then, there's the other possibility; Carmen and Paul abduct the children. They're in it together. Carmen resents the ill-treatment she's received at Antonio's hands. She blames him for losing the kids in the first place. You know how alcoholics and drug-addicts are; nothing is ever their fault. They are always the victim of some misfortune caused by someone other than themselves. So she doesn't see that her alcoholism and drug-addiction played any part in her losing them. It's just Antonio being mean. Now she's back, married to a man who'll do anything for her. She plans her move wisely. Waits until Antonio has them. Then she kidnaps them herself—with Paul's help—in a way that will cast suspicion on Antonio. It's perfect revenge. She'll never again have to share the girls with Antonio."

"So she'll make Paul give up the house, his business, his family, and move away?" Mary Ellen shook her head. "Because to stay here would mean the girls can never be out in public. They'll change their identities so that Antonio will never find them." She gave him a haughty look, "I can write fiction too, John.

"You're right," John conceded. "We need to find out more. I don't see how anybody wins by stealing those kids."

"That's if they've been stolen by one of these people,"

Mary Ellen pointed out. She pulled a white sheet of paper from the tray of the printer and mounted it to the evidence board. With a wide tip black marker, she drew a large question mark on it. "The question is: Who *would* benefit by kidnapping the children?"

"Right," John nodded. "There's always the possibility they were kidnapped by someone else. Someone we haven't thought about."

"I guess we'll have to wait to see if there's a demand for ransom. Seems odd that no one called yesterday."

"Mmm," John agreed, "our guys monitoring the phone taps listed a number of calls on both Ibarra's and Thibaults' phones, all from concerned friends and relatives, the girls' teachers, Sister Angela, the principal at St. Augustine's. Antonio got a call from his priest, Father Gomez. And then the business agent from the Union called him, too. But that was it. The longer we go without a ransom demand, the more it looks like the kids were stolen by one of our three suspects."

Mary Ellen fell silent and turned her attention to the evidence board looking for something she'd missed before. Yesterday, they'd gotten some bits and pieces that needed to be checked out today. For one thing, they would have to speak to Mary Carvalho and Charles Cabot again, this time separately. And Paul Thibault, too.

"How about a doughnut?" John's voice startled her out of deep thought. "Sorry. Didn't mean to make you jump." He offered up a paper plate holding about a half-dozen assorted doughnuts. There was everything from sugared to frosted to filled to glazed. Apparently he'd skipped off and gotten these from the break room while she'd been engrossed in thought. "Mm-m-m-m," he mumbled as he bit into a gooey jelly-filled concoction, "these are great. Have one."

Succumbing to temptation, Mary Ellen selected a honey glazed doughnut, silently vowing to herself that she'd only have this one. Munching delicately, she used her black marker to add something she'd just remembered to the timeline: Monday, 12/26, 10 P.M., Lights go out at Ibarra's (M. Carvalho) and Tuesday, 12/27, 2:55 A.M., Fox or coyote (M. LaRue) howls.

"Chuck Cabot said it was a dog," John reminded her as set the doughnut-laden plate on her desk and picked up his coffee cup.

"We're assuming they heard the same thing but identified them differently?"

"Sure!" he shrugged, noisily slurping his coffee. "Maria LaRue lives closer to the woods; it's natural for her to think it was a fox or a coyote. But remember she said it was different? They usually howl in choruses, but this one was alone? I think that's because Cabot was right; it was a dog, not a fox or coyote."

On the timeline, Mary Ellen obligingly entered a carrack before the word 'howls' and printed 'or dog (C. Cabot)' above it.

Evidently satisfied, John continued, "Cabot also said he heard a car start up and drive away just before the dog howled." He removed the straight-backed visitor's chair from Mary Ellen's cubicle to make room for his own more comfortable office chair. "So I think we could say that happened around two-fifty-four."

Mary Ellen added that new bit of information to the timeline, "Thanks."

"You're welcome!" He popped the last of his jelly doughnut into his mouth, licked his fingers, rolled his chair into Mary Ellen's cubicle, and turned his attention again to the plate of doughnuts. "What'll I have next?" he deliberated. He chose a chocolate frosted and sat down.

She sat in her office chair and turned it to face John so they could speak while they ate. "If we can establish that the kids were in the car that started at two-fifty-four A.M., then we've pinpointed the time of the abduction."

"All we need now is a 'who'," John said before he took another bite. "You should add to Ibarra's character profile, that besides being macho, he's domineering, possibly violent. At least, according to Mary Carvalho and Carmen, verbally so."

"And into Carmen Thibault's that she's self-centered and manipulative. Maybe even deceptive," Mary Ellen said, "or at least she was before the divorce." As she made the notations into the respective files, she muttered, "How much can a person change?"

"While we're at it, how much do we know about Paul Thibault?" John said after he swallowed.

"You mean besides that he's charming and debonair? Likes to 'fix' things?" Mary Ellen smirked, "Not much. I did background checks on all of them, and came up with zip."

They sat in silence for a while, eating their doughnuts, each lost in their own thoughts, mulling over the few facts they had. Instead of getting up, John rolled to the counter to get one more doughnut from the plate. "Ready for another?" he asked.

"I really shouldn't."

"Aw, come on! The job'll burn off these calories before lunch."

Mary Ellen rolled her eyes and took a cinnamon-covered doughnut. "This is *it!*" She said forcefully, "Now get those things away from me."

John snickered and instead of getting up, rode his chair back into his cubicle to put the plate on his counter far out of Mary Ellen's view. "I have a question," he rolled back beside his partner with a crème-filled. "Why did the dog howl? According to Chuck Cabot, it was a long, doleful sound. 'Spooky', he said."

Mary Ellen shuddered involuntarily, "I got shivers when he said that. In my mind I heard the Hound of the Baskervilles."

"Sounds different than a coyote or a fox, doesn't it?" John smiled crookedly. "And I guess we both thought of Donna when Cabot said that. But really, Mary Ellen," he persisted, "Why does a dog howl? Why did *Donna* howl?"

She regarded him quizzically, "You're serious. You realize you're asking me to profile a dog."

Since his mouth was full, John merely nodded.

To humor him, she answered, "Well, I've heard of a dog howling at the death of his master. Or at his master's grave."

She chuckled, "Even at music."

"Everyone's a critic," John shrugged and chased the doughnut down with a gulp of coffee, "So what was Donna feeling when she howled?"

Mary Ellen studied her partner's face for a moment. The look in his eyes was serious. This wasn't a joke; apparently he was going somewhere with these questions. Most likely he'd already formed a conclusion, and was pushing her to get there herself for corroboration. "I don't know. I don't know much about dog psychology," she said. Noting a trace of impatience knitting his forehead, she quickly added, "But if a dog were capable of the same feelings as a human being, I'd say it was an expression of deep emotion."

"Like…" He urged.

"Well, in the case of a deceased master, the dog would feel deep sadness. A sense of loss and overwhelming grief," she shrugged. "What are you getting at?"

"Yesterday at Ibarra's. When I said it was strange that Donna didn't bark, you said it was because…"

"She knew who entered the house," she finished. "So? I still think if the girls didn't just wander off but were stolen, it was by someone they—and she—knew."

"So why did Donna howl?"

"Because the children were going away?" she fumbled about searching her thoughts. "Someone was taking the children away."

"And. . ?"

"She was upset because she couldn't go with them."

"You're missing the obvious, Mary Ellen, and being quite obtuse."

Obtuse! Mary Ellen scowled.

John tried to smooth over his last comment. "Look, Donna has had to watch those kids leave since August when Carmen got full custody of them. So, shouldn't she be used to the idea of the girls going away without her? Marisa has been going to school for two years now. And certainly, there are many times when she can't go with the family on outings; when they go to

Mass, for instance." John shook his head. "It's been that way since she was a puppy. There are times when a dog has to stay home. Does she howl then, too?"

"I'd say no, since no one made that point," Mary Ellen responded thoughtfully, "I mean, if she were in the habit of howling when the family left her behind, I'd think the neighbors would've complained about it long ago. And Mr. Cabot would've said 'Donna howled,' not 'a dog howled.' So I'd say her howling is unusual."

"Exactly. And if Cabot had known it was Donna he heard, he might have also realized something was the matter and would have investigated, or notified the cops, or at least called Antonio. We could be looking at an entirely different case." John said, "Anyway, the fact of the matter is, a dog who never howls, did just that. And do you know why?"

When John did not explain, Mary Ellen was forced to ask, "Well, are you going to enlighten me?"

Before answering, John rolled back to get another doughnut, but finding the plate empty, had to content himself with a sip of his coffee. Then he answered with obvious satisfaction, "Donna howled out of sheer frustration. Something about *how* the kids left, or *who* they left *with*, was *unusual*. Something about it was not right, and the dog knew it, but was powerless to do anything about it. They say dogs have ESP, and although I don't think they can foretell the future, I believe they can sense when things aren't kosher. This feeling distressed Donna so much, that she howled."

Mary Ellen thought about John's theory as she finished the last of her doughnut and wiped her fingers delicately on a paper napkin. Finally, she asked, "So what was so unusual? If something was off, why didn't she defend the children? I mean, Diaz and Caron both said in their reports that the dog would have torn them apart if Ibarra had not intervened. And while we're at it, why didn't she wake Antonio?"

"Well, Mary Ellen," John said, "when we know all that, we'll be well on the way to solving the case."

6:24 A.M.

A white and blue telephone maintenance truck crept down the street, apparently looking for a particular utility pole. It stopped beside the one across from 72 Hollywood Drive. A man wearing a white hardhat got into the bucket and the long telescoping arm gently raised him up to the crossbar at the top of the pole.

That a telephone company truck should appear anywhere in Troy City was not an unusual occurrence, even this early in the morning. It was merely the reassuring sign that crews were repairing communication lines downed by the recent snowstorm, replacing cable corroded by weather and time, or merely troubleshooting. Therefore no one wondered why the truck was there. Apparently, someone's phone was out somewhere and that was all there was to it.

If anyone *had* looked a little more closely, one might have noticed a small device no larger than a tube of toothpaste being mounted on the pole under the crossbar. From the ground it was all but invisible. Yet from its position beneath the crossbar of the utility pole, the gadget would have an unobstructed view of whatever fell within the scope of its lens once the tiny camera was hardwired onto an extra pair of wires.

In another place miles away, a blurred image appeared on a monitor in a small, dimly-lit room filled with electronic apparatus. A technician spoke to the man performing the installation over a headset and typed information into a computer. Seemingly of its own accord, the camera moved slightly to the right, placing a red house in the center of the screen. The camera focused and the picture sharpened. The technician keyed in a command and the picture zoomed in, placing the front door in center screen.

"That's a go," the technician told his man.

"Roger that," the man answered. Before lowering the bucket, he mounted a cover that would not only weatherproof the camera, but protect it from squirrels noted for chewing through electrical wiring and from birds who liked to build nests in odd places.

At the same time, another telephone truck was working on the pole in front of 1136 River Road, unhampered by the volunteers who were assembling close by. Presently, the image of a yellow house with brown shutters appeared on a different monitor. The technician tapped in instructions until the picture was crystal clear.

Presently, the crowd parted to allow a black Dodge Caravan to enter the driveway and five people, two males and three females, got out. As the five proceeded to the front door, it opened and the actual subject of the surveillance came out to welcome and embrace his visitors. Within moments, everyone was inside the house and the door closed behind them.

*****

John Turner answered his desk phone on the second ring, "Turner, here."

"Cameras are both working perfectly, Special Agent Turner," the technician said. "We can provide twenty-four hour surveillance from here, and alert mobile units whenever someone leaves the premises."

"Good work, Marty," John replied. "Let me know immediately of any developments."

"We've already had one at Site A." The tech informed him of the arrival of the five people in the Caravan.

"Any idea who they are?"

"Mmmm. They looked pretty friendly, hugs and kisses all around. Emotional. My guess is family."

"Can you zoom in on the license plate?"

"Let me see if I can read the tag." John heard keys being tapped on a keyboard. "Focusing in on the back end of the Caravan. People keep getting in the way... Okay, it's a Rhode Island registration."

"Can you make out the characters?" John grabbed a pen from his desk.

"I'll try. As I said, volunteers keep getting between the

camera and the back of the car."

As Marty haltingly read off the figures, John wrote them down. "Thanks, Marty. Keep me informed." Turner immediately dialed another number. Within moments, he was speaking to Support. "Carl! John Turner, here."

"Yes, John," came the friendly response, "What can I do ya for?"

John smirked. Carl; always ready with a catchy retort. "Run a check on this plate number, will you?" Turner read off the information. "Let me know as soon as you find anything." John turned toward Mary Ellen who had her back to him, studying the evidence board, "Ibarra has company."

"Probably family," Mary Ellen answered in a distracted, unconcerned tone, seemingly unable to break her focus on the evidence board. "Hispanics are very family-oriented. Anyone has a problem, they all converge."

That gave John an idea; but his hunch needed facts to back him up. He swung around to his desk and punched a few keys on his computer.

6:51 A.M.

By the time the telephone truck left River Road, a good number of volunteers had already assembled. They stamped their feet, pushed up the collars of their heavy winter jackets, and pulled knitted caps down over their ears, trying to keep warm.

At least today will be a sunny day, thought Jet surveying the orange-pink glow brightening the eastern horizon.

As he joined the others, it was immediately obvious to Jet that something had happened to bring down the optimistic mood of the previous day. Where yesterday there had been hope, today there was a sense of loss and despair. The early morning sunshine did little to lift the spirits of the searchers. Already before the grim-faced group leaders had emerged from their vehicles, a general sense of foreboding had fallen over everyone.

The scuttlebutt was that Long River would be dragged again today; only further downstream. If the girls' bodies had been dumped in the swollen tributary, its swift current might have dropped them at the bend where the flow was slowest as it turned to join the Troy River. They might have gotten hung up on one of the pylons that supported the bridge there. However, if the bodies had passed both the pylons and the bend in the river and made it to the rough, tumbling waters of the Troy, they would have been swept out to the bay with nothing to stop them. There was no telling where they might surface then. With luck a fishing trawler might snag one of the sisters in its net; otherwise, there was little hope of finding them at all.

As she had done yesterday, with a bullhorn up before her mouth, Sgt. Rothman stood before the volunteers to give them today's instructions. The WTCN-TV News team was there to record her announcement.

"Okay people, listen up." Sgt. Rothman waited a moment as the pockets of chatter ceased. When she was satisfied that she had their full attention she began, "Sadly, we believe that if the children were exposed to the severe cold of the past two nights, there is very little chance that they have survived."

Many people gasped or moaned in disappointment as their worst fears were confirmed. For Jet, hearing her put into words what he and his friends had concluded last night struck a somber and depressing chord in his heart. Hank stared at him in shock and Robin's eyes filled with tears. The deputy was suddenly interested in something at her feet, shuffled and kicked it away, cleared her throat and continued in a businesslike manner, although the tremor in her voice gave away her true feelings.

"If they had come into these woods voluntarily, we would have found them yesterday. Now we believe there is a good possibility that the children were murdered and their bodies disposed of in these woods." More gasps and groans. Sgt. Rothman took a deep breath and continued in a steadier voice, "So our mission is no longer a rescue operation, but rather a recovery effort. Cadaver dogs will be working today instead of the scent dogs we used yesterday. These dogs are specially trained to find corpses. We'll be looking for signs of recent digging. We expect the graves to be shallow, due to the frost in the ground. The earth will be fresh, most likely covered with leaves to hide the newly turned soil. The snow is going to make your job harder and since we trampled it all yesterday, you're not going to be able to tell right off if it looks suspicious. You're going to have to look *under* the snow to find any clues; but as you were cautioned yesterday, please refrain from touching anything suspect. You don't want to disturb or corrupt the scene. I know this sounds gruesome but we must recover these little girls as soon as possible so that their family can plan a funeral and find closure to this awful time." She ended abruptly and coughed. She turned her back on the searchers, but not before Jet saw her quickly wipe her eyes.

As they had done before, the searchers lined up and advanced into the woods. But today, completely subdued by the new aspects of the case, the camaraderie and banter that had punctuated yesterday's hope-filled search was totally gone. No one spoke. No one laughed. Everyone went through the motions solemnly and in low spirits.

Jet pushed aside a pile of dead branches with a long stick and used this quiet time to reflect on the new developments of the case without interruption. In his heart he felt the girls were still alive somewhere. The problem was they were looking in the wrong place.

7:58 A.M.

Charles Cabot came to the door with a mug of coffee in his hand and invited them into his spacious kitchen. It smelled deliciously of toast and coffee. Clearly he had been having his breakfast; a half-eaten poached egg and toast remained in his plate. He courteously offered them a seat and a cup of coffee. The FBI agents declined the coffee but accepted the seats around the table. After he had quietly closed the kitchen door, he sat back down to his meal.

"You don't mind if I finish my breakfast, do you?" Charles Cabot smiled, "Cold eggs are pretty awful."

"Of course not, Mr. Cabot," Mary Ellen said.

"Do you mind answering a few questions for me as you eat?" John Turner asked as he set his little tape recorder on the table. "It's about something that happened at the custody hearing last August. The one where Carmen was granted custody of Marisa and Liana."

The forkful of egg stopped halfway to Cabot's mouth. "Well, as I told you yesterday, Agent Turner. As Antonio's attorney, there are certain things I can't divulge. They are held in confidence; attorney-client privilege."

"I'm sure that's true much of the time," John allowed. "However, what I'm asking you I believe is public record."

"Really?" The lawyer looked doubtful. The egg finally made it into his mouth.

"Certainly," John assured him. "You represented him at that hearing, correct?"

"Yes, I did," the lawyer acknowledged.

"And whatever was said in court is public record, is it not?"

"Yes," Cabot narrowed his dark brown eyes suspiciously.

"Can you tell me exactly what Antonio Ibarra yelled out in court when the judge ruled in Carmen's favor?"

Cabot visibly blanched and stopped chewing. His manner became guarded. "It was in Spanish. I doubt his exact words were noted for the record."

"But *you* know," Agent Turner insisted meeting the lawyer's dark brown eyes. "*You* understood what he said. And there are others who understood as well. If you can't tell me, I'll find someone else who can. Perhaps if I hear it from you, though, it won't sound so..." he seemed to search for the appropriate word, "nasty." Cabot remained silent and seemed to debate whether or not to tell Turner what he knew. Turner raised his eyebrows and pressed on. "Carmen Thibault told us he threatened to kill the girls."

Now, Cabot's eyes blazed and he reddened. He wiped his mouth with a paper napkin, "No. That's not what he said. Exactly."

"Maybe you could clarify by telling us his exact words, then," Turner persisted.

Cabot sipped some of his coffee. His brown eyes met Turner's squarely and he sighed heavily, "The judge had just awarded Carmen full custody of the girls. I had tried to prepare Antonio for that possible outcome, but he had convinced himself that it wouldn't happen. Understandably, Antonio was not only shocked but devastated. He was very upset." Cabot searched the agents' faces for some hint of compassion or understanding. He sighed again and finished, "A rough translation of his actual words were: 'Not if I can help it. I'd rather see them dead than be with their whore of a mother.' I managed to shut him up and Bob LaRue grabbed him and hustled him out before the judge could find him in contempt."

"Do you think Antonio could have murdered his daughters?"

Cabot's chocolate brown eyes glinted angrily, "I know Antonio as well as I know my own brother, so I can tell you truly that murder is not in his nature."

"In your opinion," John Turner added.

8:28 A.M.

When asked the same question Mary Carvalho responded with an equal amount of indignation.

"Antonio Ibarra is many things. He's domineering, possessive, quick-tempered, and emotional. And although those traits sound rough and maybe even threatening, his outbursts are fast and loud and out there for all to hear. Then just as quickly, it's done. It's over. He doesn't hold grudges. He's not spiteful." She finished through clenched teeth, her brown eyes flashing, "He did not kill his little girls to punish his ex-wife—or for any other reason! I'll never believe otherwise."

"Thank you, Mrs. Carvalho," Turner said leaning back in

Mary's comfortable living room couch. "We're sorry to have upset you." He glanced Mary Ellen's way and she changed the subject.

"What do you know of Adelina Aguilar?" she asked softly.

"Adelina. Oh, how I miss her," Mary Carvalho said wistfully. "She was the live-in nanny," Mary explained. "Besides minding the girls when Antonio was at work, she also took care of the household; did the cleaning, the laundry, the cooking, the grocery shopping. That type of thing. I know for a fact that Antonio hired her specifically because she spoke Spanish. He wants the girls to be bilingual, and for that to happen, you've got to start young, before they even go to school. Kids pick up English so quickly." She realized her digression and came back to the subject, "Anyway, Adelina knew only a little English, and she wanted to learn so badly. We were able to communicate with each other pretty well; my Portuguese helped. You know that Spanish and Portuguese are similar; many words are alike. If she spoke slowly I could understand most of what she said. When I didn't get it, she'd write it down and I'd get the gist. She took English classes and I helped her with her homework if she got stuck. By the time Antonio let her go she could carry on a simple English conversation, though heavily accented."

"What was her relationship with Mr. Ibarra?" Agent Kelly asked.

"Relationship!" Mary Carvalho exclaimed. Her initial shock gave way to amusement and she almost laughed as she explained, "There was nothing sexual going on there, if that's what you mean. Their 'relationship' was purely business."

"How do you know that for certain?" Agent Turner wanted to know. "You seem so positive. How could you know what went on behind closed doors?"

"Well. How can I say this?" She sighed, "Have you met Carmen, his ex?"

"Yes, we have," Turner admitted.

Mary Carvalho nodded, "Well, then, let me help you understand. Adelina Aguilar and Carmen Ibarra—I mean, Thibault—

are complete opposites. While Adelina is more Antonio's age—She's forty-five, and Antonio is forty-two—Carmen is fifteen years younger than Antonio. What attracted him to Carmen was her petite size. I think she wears a size five shoe! She's sexy, feminine, and has curves to kill. Maybe it was her small stature that made him feel manly and protective. On the other hand, although she is an attractive woman in her own right, Adelina is tall and big-boned, about six foot tall and weighs at least a hundred and ninety pounds. She's *taller* than Antonio. And although I know there are some successful marriages where the woman is larger than her husband, that's just not Antonio's turn-on. He was not attracted to her, and vise versa. Besides, Adelina had a boyfriend," then she frowned, "although I can't remember his name."

"And she was let go when Antonio lost custody of the girls?" Mary Ellen asked.

Mary Carvalho nodded sadly, "Adelina had weekends off, except if Antonio was to work overtime, which was very rare. Since the children were no longer here during the week and Antonio is capable of doing his own house cleaning and cooking, there was no need to keep her on. When he came home that day and told her, it was the saddest thing." Her eyes moistened as she recalled the event, "She was so upset. She ran over here and poured her heart out to me. It was so pitiful. That poor woman loved those little girls like her own. When Carmen got custody, it was as though Adelina had lost her own children. She grieved as though they'd died. That night, even though Antonio told her she could get herself established somewhere else before she moved out, she packed up her things and left. No one has seen her since."

"Where did she go? Do you know?" was Agent Kelly's next question.

"She told me she was going home; back to Colombia."

9:05 A.M.

Special Agent Turner pushed open the door to 1508 Pleasant Street, Troy City, amid a jangle of raucous jingle bells. Turner held the door for Special Agent Kelly, noting a white-haired man in a heavy overcoat standing in front of the service counter perusing a brochure for home security systems. The place was pleasantly warm and smelled of filed metal and penetrating oil. As the door to Thibault & Son Locksmith closed with another barrage of bells, the old man looked their way curiously, then apparently finding the newly-arrived couple of little interest, returned his attention to his reading material.

The agents made themselves inconspicuous by examining the merchandise. Wall safes of varying sizes, doorknobs with special keys, heavy-duty dead bolts, anti-theft devises for motor vehicles, and various types of alarms were only some of the items for sale. Over the displays, signs promised money-back guarantees or offered reasonable installation fees.

Presently, Paul Thibault came out of the back room. The elderly man replaced the brochure into the stand on the counter as Paul handed him a number of keys.

"Here you go, Mr. Ouellette. I made an extra full set for you just in case Mrs. Ouellette misplaces hers again. Keep this other set in a safe place."

"Oh. Thank you. That's an excellent idea. How much do I owe you for this, Pierre?" Mr. Ouellette asked.

"It's Paul, sir." Thibault corrected him, "Pierre is my father."

"Oh, yes. Paul," Mr. Ouellette murmured.

"That'll be ten seventy-five for the five keys you asked me to make for you. The extra set is on the house."

"Oh, thank you," Mr. Ouellette unfolded a number of bills from his pocket and dropped some change on the counter. He counted out the exact amount and slid the money over to Paul. "Say hello to your father for me."

"Sure thing, Mr. Ouellette."

The old man left in a carillon of bells as the door slammed behind him. It was only then that Paul Thibault noticed the FBI agents. The smile immediately faded from his handsome face, replaced with a look of consternation.

"What's happened?" He asked urgently, "Have you found the girls?"

"Unfortunately not," Turner said.

"We're here to ask you a couple of questions," Agent Kelly supplied.

"I don't have a lot of time," Paul began.

Agent Turner looked around the store, his eyebrows lifted interrogatively, "I don't see any customers—"

Paul shrugged, "You may not see them, but I have orders to fill for clients. Being a locksmith isn't just making keys, you know. If it were, I'd never be able to make a living."

"Especially if you give them away."

Paul shrugged dismissively, "Mr. Ouellette has been a customer longer than I can remember. He used to own a number of tenements and was one of my father's most faithful clients. His wife is in the beginning stages of Alzheimer's. It's sad. She keeps losing her keys—or rather putting them in crazy places—and it's driving him nuts. Last time, he found them in the freezer under a carton of ice cream. God knows where he'll find them this time. If it'll help out the old guy—" Thibault shrugged again. "But I do have contracts. I'm currently designing a security system—"

"We understand that you're a busy man and that we're interrupting you in your place of business," Mary Ellen Kelly soothed. "We won't take up much of your time."

"You must have heard that Ibarra says he found his door wide open on Tuesday morning," John Turner began. "We were wondering what it would take for a person like you to break in without damaging the door, or the lock, for that matter."

Paul blinked his blue eyes at them, yet he answered after only a moment's hesitation, "I don't know why you ask that. I've never considered trying to get into Antonio's house. Just as I never would try to enter any of my neighbors' houses, their cars, or any other place that's locked. Not without their permission," he stated, an indignant frown creasing his handsome face. "I'm insulted by your implications. We locksmiths have standards, you know; a code of honor."

"Okay," John nodded, "I get what you're saying, and I apologize for offending you. But suppose—"

"But hypothetically, yes, I could get into Antonio's house if I wanted to," Paul shrugged and shook his head, "but I wouldn't need to break in or use any of my tools to get inside. Carmen still has a key."

9:29 A.M.

One of the first things Mary Ellen learned from John Turner was that ringing cell phones can really mess up interviews. Not only were unexpected calls annoying to the agents, they flustered the interviewee and interrupted the flow. It was practically impossible to regain momentum after the break and the interview quickly disintegrated. So before beginning an interview both agents routinely turned off their ringers allowing all calls to go to voice mail. Upon leaving Thibault's store the agents checked their phones. There was nothing for Mary Ellen, but John found he'd missed one call.

The caller had left a message. It was Glenda Baldwin, Chief of Forensics for Troy County. The FBI agents got into their Crown Victoria where John returned her call and turned on the speaker so that both of them could hear what the she had to say.

"You wanted to know when I found something." They had met Dr. Baldwin yesterday, and as the woman spoke, Mary Ellen could envision the sophisticated five-foot-nine scientist with the burgundy hair worn in a neat and professional twist. She could also see from the expression on John's face that the violet-eyed beauty had had a particular affect on him. The fact that Dr. Baldwin was a good ten years older than John's thirty-six years made no difference; the man was apparently smitten.

"Yes, Doctor. Go on," Turner said.

The forensic scientist's husky feminine voice came over the line, "I've got the results from the blood samples Ruth Wilson's people took yesterday. I had people working on it all night long. Thanks to Mr. Blakely's donation—you know, the patriarch of the Collier Ridge family?—the overtime was a non-issue, since the money is earmarked specifically for any extra expenses incurred for the Ibarra case. Anyway, the bloodstains on the sheets and pillow case, the damp sweatshirt, the child's jersey they found in the trash, as well as what they got in the back seat of Antonio Ibarra's truck; it's all Liana's."

"So Liana was murdered?" John couldn't hide his excitement.

"Maybe, but not necessarily," Glenda Baldwin cautioned. "There were good-sized bloodstains on one set of linens; bottom and top sheets as well as the pillow case. And the sweatshirt still had a lot of blood that hadn't washed out. But even though it all seems like a lot of blood, it's not really. Certainly not enough to prove a murder was committed. Not a life-threatening amount even for a child." The scientist sighed and continued, "Photographs by CSI show a trail of blood that goes down the hall and leads out to the front stoop. Presumably, it led down to the driveway, but of course, the snow covered the trail. I don't know what you want to make of this other than the fact that she was bleeding when she left the house."

"It's a good guess those kids didn't leave the house alone if one of them was bleeding," Mary Ellen mused aloud. "Why didn't they wake up their father? Why didn't they call out?"

"Maybe they didn't call out because there was no need," Turner said. "Maybe their father took them out."

Mary Ellen's gasp of objection went without comment because Glenda was speaking again.

"Besides Liana's blood, the sweatshirt also had a few hairs and sweat that I was able to match to Antonio Ibarra's DNA. So he can't deny ownership. You have that much, at least."

"With the blood on the sweatshirt, he can't deny touching

her when she was bleeding, either. He knows more than he's letting on," John said triumphantly as they ended their conversation. He turned his attention to his partner. "It looks like our search is narrowing down," he smiled.

Mary Ellen couldn't help being shocked, "How does this narrow down the search? Please explain this to me. I don't see how you can arrive at any conclusion so quickly."

"We've got our man!" Turner answered. "The evidence is piling up on him."

"There wasn't that much blood," Mary Ellen reasoned, "And Glenda didn't mention anything about Marisa's blood being found anywhere at all."

"That only means both girls weren't murdered at the house. Ibarra maybe did Liana at home, and Marisa somewhere else," John reasoned. "Or maybe he strangled Marisa; no blood."

The thought sickened Mary Ellen, "I think you're moving too fast—"

"What?" He seemed perfectly satisfied with his conclusion. "You said yourself that you didn't believe the kids wandered off by themselves. And they didn't because they were murdered. Ibarra had opportunity: They were in his house with him alone."

"And motive?"

"Revenge."

"I don't see how that fits," Mary Ellen argued.

"It fits fine," John insisted. "Antonio was angry that Carmen got full custody, and killed them out of revenge: If he couldn't have them, then neither could she. He said he'd rather see them dead than be with her. It fits fine," he repeated. "What more do you want?"

"Something more definite," she countered still not convinced. "If he killed them, I'd like to find their bodies." She let her frustration show, "I'd like proof."

"All in good time, Mary Ellen," John Turner said. "Without the bodies to determine time of death, I'd guess he killed them sometime on Monday night, maybe after he'd put them to bed. He kills them in their sleep and then disposes of them quickly.

He either digs shallow graves in the woods behind his house figuring the snow will cover the evidence and hide the graves. Or maybe he dumps them in the river. That gives him about eight or nine hours to tidy up—"

"So why did he leave so much evidence behind?" Mary Ellen interrupted. "Why were the dirty sheets still on Liana's bed? Why leave blood-soaked clothes where they could be found, and stains in his truck? Why the charade of running around barefooted in the snow? Why report them missing so soon? Why not give himself more time to at least to throw suspicion in a different direction?" Mary Ellen frowned. "Why leave evidence that points directly at him?"

"You ask a lot of questions," John chided. Mary Ellen could tell he was trying to control his temper. "Look. He had to make it look good. Bob LaRue's the one who called the cops, not Antonio; which, in my opinion, indicates that Ibarra was stalling." Mary Ellen's lack of conviction must have shown because John continued, "It works, Mary Ellen. Ibarra made a lot of mistakes because he's an amateur and instead of thinking things through, he rushed. He murdered the girls out of revenge and envy. He was getting back at his ex, teaching her a lesson. But he botched it because he was in a hurry. Hey, look! Maybe he was drunk when he did it and he didn't do a better job of cleaning up because he couldn't think straight or he passed out. It doesn't matter. He did it and it had to look like a kidnapping, hence the open door; which, by the way, has not been corroborated by anyone else and could have been staged. The kids are abducted in the middle of the night, the dog doesn't bark. A clear indication that she didn't think anything was wrong—"

"Until she howls. 'A long and doleful sound,'" she interjected.

"Right."

They were interrupted by the melodic chimes of John's cell phone. This time John didn't put the speaker on, so all Mary Ellen got was a one-sided conversation. There wasn't much she could make of what John was learning. His eyebrows knit together in a scowl, then they rose in surprise while he gave

whoever it was on the other end a number of "ohs" and "ahs".
"Thanks!" he said at last when whoever it was finished talking. He shoved the cell phone into his pocket and the Crown
Victoria started with a roar. With the flashing blue light on the
top of the car and the siren going, the tires squealed as he leapt
out onto Pleasant Street. Cutting off a number of cars, he quickly
negotiated a neat U-turn and headed back the way they had
come.

10:03 A.M.

The low spirits of the searchers seemed to be contagious;
Jet was depressed. As he poked and prodded piles of leaves
with the end of a stick, his thoughts returned to last night's dis-
cussion with Hank and Robin. The conclusion it had drawn
was most disheartening for the evidence seemed to point to Mr.
Ibarra as the culprit.

But Mr. Ibarra was innocent. Of that much Jet was certain.
He could feel it in his gut.

For one thing he couldn't establish motive. Even if the man
hated his ex-wife with the most extreme passion Jet couldn't
believe Mr. Ibarra could have murdered his daughters. For
what reason? Getting even? It didn't make sense. How did killing your own flesh and blood get revenge on another person? It
seemed a really dumb thing to do in Jet's estimation. By de-
priving the wife of the joy of having her children, so did Mr.
Ibarra punish himself. Unless the guy was totally loony; then
maybe there was a chance of that. Even after only one day's
acquaintance Jet could see that Mr. Ibarra loved his children
too much to have murdered them out of revenge on his wife.
Wouldn't it have been more feasible, more logical, more *grati-
fying*, to kill the ex-wife and keep the kids?

A large pile of snow about twenty yards behind the Ibarra
property caught Jet's attention. Yesterday, when they were
looking for two little girls huddled in the woods, he'd seen that
mound but like everyone else, had dismissed it as an unlikely if

not impossible hidey-hole. Now with the new directive, it took on an unnatural and sinister aspect. It could very well be concealing the signs of digging and covering up a shallow grave. Jet knelt down beside the mound and brushed away the icy chunks of snow. His efforts revealed a pile of leaves someone had apparently raked up from their lawn last fall and dumped here. Yet, maybe there was something underneath. He was in the process of pushing the leaves aside when a commotion out front distracted him.

From where he was, he could plainly see along the east end of the house, as well as a narrow piece of the front yard, but only as far as the edge of the driveway. A blue and white Ridgeport police car blocked his view of the street itself. Yet the disruption continued; shouting, barking, screaming, wailing. In a flash Jet left his task, hurdled over the broken-down fence, and darted to the front yard, partly out of curiosity but mostly from a desire to lend a helping hand in whatever drama was unfolding there.

When he reached the corner of the house, he saw the WTCN-TV News team already taping the event. It took Jet only a moment to come to a regrettable conclusion: The cops were here for Antonio Ibarra. Jet advanced no farther, realizing that from this vantage point he could see everything that was happening and still stay out of the way.

Four people were arranged in a rough semi-circle in front of the porch steps forming an effective barrier to any attempt at escape. Jet recognized the Hispanic policeman as the one who had come to the door yesterday morning, and the blond CSI lady who had headed the investigation in the garage. The man and woman in black overcoats had their backs to him, so he couldn't see their faces and didn't know who they were. Although he had not seen any officers as he ran along the side of the garage, Jet assumed that some were placing themselves around the house to prevent Ibarra from leaving by any other exit. But the precaution proved unnecessary.

Mr. Ibarra was standing on the porch wearing no coat; just his beat up Nikes, a pair of jeans, and a blue flannel shirt. The wind blew his hair around but he paid no attention to it. He faced the people who had come to arrest him.

The CSI lady was reading Mr. Ibarra his rights with unfeeling routine as the uniformed policeman patted Mr. Ibarra down for weapons, then took his prisoner's right arm to cuff his wrist. All the while people's voices wailed and shouted in protest from inside the house. The cop had only gotten the handcuffed Mr. Ibarra down the two steps to the snowy lawn when a woman came out waving a winter jacket.

"You must let him have his coat!" the dark-haired woman insisted. "He will catch his death of cold."

A second, older woman emerged, hugging a sweater around her shoulders, "And we will sue the town if he does!"

The policeman rolled his eyes to heaven and dutifully stopped, but the woman was not allowed to approach the prisoner. Instead, the CSI lady grabbed the garment and squeezed it from top to bottom, presumably feeling for weapons. Satisfied that the pockets were empty, she draped it around Mr. Ibarra's shoulders while the other woman brought her hands up to her tearful face.

"We know you're innocent, Antonio," said the woman through her tears. She backed off, and the policeman pressed Mr. Ibarra toward the waiting police cruiser.

He didn't get far for just then Donna charged out of the house barking wildly. She circled Mr. Ibarra and the officer, preventing them from going any further. The dog braced herself in front of them, snarling viciously, jaws quivering, ready to attack. When the officer attempted to move Mr. Ibarra toward the car, the angry animal lunged forward snarling and growling menacingly only inches from the cop's hand. It was a guttural, frightening sound that caused the policeman to pay attention. He froze.

"You'd better call off your dog, Mr. Ibarra," he warned, "or I'll be forced to shoot her."

Mortified by the policeman's threat, Jet forgot about staying out of the way. "You can't do that!" he exclaimed as he ran to the front of the house.

But Mr. Ibarra already had the situation under control. "*¡Cállate, perra!*" he said, "*¡Pórtate bien, Donna!* Lie down!"

Donna lifted doleful, pleading eyes toward her master. Clearly she thought he was wrong to let himself be taken away by these people, but she instantly obeyed. She immediately stopped her ferocious display, bowed her head, and whimpered as she brought herself low to the ground. Yet she continued to regard the officer disdainfully. The younger of the two women took hold of Donna's collar and murmured gently to her, but the dog continued to growl and mutter softly, her body tense with restrained emotion.

"What's going on here?"

Jet jumped as Mr. Cabot rushed past him to run to his client's assistance. The lawyer was moving a lot better than he had yesterday; apparently his ankle was feeling better.

The CSI lady handed him a sheet of white paper, "We have a warrant for the arrest of Antonio Ibarra for the abduction and possible murder of his daughters, Marisa and Liana Ibarra."

"Please, Chuck. Help me. I didn't do anything to my little girls," Mr. Ibarra pleaded.

"It's okay, Tony," Mr. Cabot reassured him, "Go along quietly with them. Remember what I said yesterday. I'll be at the station in a little while."

Satisfied that the dog was not about to attack, the policeman nudged Mr. Ibarra toward his squad car, but his prisoner resisted. He looked Jet's way and said, "Please, Julian, could you take care of Donna for me while I'm away? My family is here only for a few days and I'm afraid if I leave her with a neighbor, she'll spend her time on my front steps, worrying. If she has a change of scenery, she won't suffer so much."

Jet opened his mouth to answer, but heard Dad's voice reply from behind him. "Of course, Tony. Though I doubt we'll have her long. You'll be out of there in no time. They'll figure out they've made a mistake and let you go."

"You're a real friend, Jules," Mr. Ibarra said.

The cop tugged on him a bit roughly but it was not necessary since Mr. Ibarra now allowed himself to be directed toward the police car. As he passed the newsmen, Mr. Ibarra noticed the camera and quickly averted his face. The CSI lady opened the back door of the cruiser and the uniformed officer guided Mr. Ibarra into the back seat, placing one hand on his head so that he wouldn't bump it on the frame of the car. But before the cop could close the door the news reporter boldly stuck his microphone in Mr. Ibarra's face.

"Is there anything you'd like to say, Mr. Ibarra?"

Mr. Ibarra seemed resentful of the intrusion and at first Jet didn't think he was going to say anything. But that initial reaction quickly passed and the man lifted sullen brown eyes to the reporter and the camera. His statement was short and full of ire.

"The police are making a mistake."

Any other comment he might have made was cut off when the policeman decisively shut the door.

At the same time, a loud, high-pitched, heart-stopping yowl sent chills up Jet's spine. It seemed that everyone halted what they were doing as all eyes instinctively turned toward the sound that blocked out all others.

All chatter ceased.

All engines died.

All birds quieted.

Jet located the source of the noise immediately.

Donna sat beside the woman who held her by the collar. The black dog's head was tilted back, her slightly open muzzle pointed up toward the sky, and her mournful howl seemed to drag on forever. Finally, when the dog had finished her doleful cry, time seemed to resume from where it had stopped. The policeman got into the squad car and slowly backed out of the driveway.

Jet turned worried eyes toward his father and was surprised by how many people had assembled behind them. He'd been so engrossed in what was happening, he had not realized that a number of searchers had also been distracted by the commotion brought on by Mr. Ibarra's arrest and had followed Jet out to the corner of the house. Even as he noticed them, now that the excitement was over, their numbers began to recede as they returned to the search.

Dad placed a comforting hand on his shoulder and Jet met his deep blue gaze. His usually smiling eyes were serious, the laugh lines surrounding them flat. "It'll be okay, Jet," Dad said softly. "There's no way Tony killed his kids. He's a good man. And Chuck Cabot is an excellent and astute lawyer. I wasn't just trying to boost his morale when I said he'd be out soon. I meant it. We just have to keep faith."

"Thanks, Dad," was all that Jet trusted himself to say without breaking down.

The crowd had completely dispersed by the time the blue and white police car quietly started up River Road. As Dad followed the rest of the searchers, Jet turned for one more look at the squad car and noticed the black Crown Victoria right behind it.

It reminded him of another Crown Vic and the agents he'd met the last time the FBI was in the Troy City area on a different abduction case. Of course this wasn't the same car. This was a newer model. Besides, if he remembered correctly, the other one had met with an unfortunate end. But he wondered if these agents might be the same ones who worked that other case. Jet had been so completely focused on Mr. Ibarra's arrest that he had neglected to pay them any notice. Now he kicked himself. Wouldn't it be something if these agents were the same ones he'd met a year and a half ago!

What were their names? He couldn't seem to remember, no matter how much he tried. Yet, in his mind, he could see their faces.

The man was a tall African-American; serious, stern, and business-like. At the time, Jet had found him rather scary. Now that he was older, though, perhaps Jet would not be as intimidated by the man. The agent had given him a call card. It might be in his desk at home.

The lady, he remembered better. She was beautiful, blond and blue-eyed. A nice smile. Soft-spoken. Jet had been in love. She'd been slightly taller than Jet, but he'd grown since then, and that might no longer be the case. He could practically taste her name on his tongue. Something with a K, but the answer flitted away like a nervous butterfly.

Why couldn't he call those names to mind? *Geesh,* he wondered, *am I going senile at fifteen?*

"Where are you going?" Dad's voice cut into his ruminations.

Without realizing it, Jet had followed Donna to the area in front of the vacant lot. Now Dad was looking at him strangely; as though the man thought that Jet had lost his mind. "Nowhere, Dad," he said. "I was just thinking and walking, following Donna. You go on and continue the search. I'll be there in a minute."

10:53 A.M.

Why in heaven's name did I agree to this? Carmen thought as yet another sound man attached one more microphone to the podium. When they had first proposed the idea, it seemed like a good one. After all, if it would help get Marisa and Liana back, it certainly was worth a shot.

"One more minute, Mrs. Thibault, and we'll be ready," she was told.

One more minute, my sweet arse, she thought dismally. That's all she'd heard for the past half hour as she stood here on the porch of her house, freezing to death despite her leather coat and purple muffler. And they had not yet begun. Paul, the dear, sweet man, seemed to read her mind and placed a comforting hand on her shoulder. She patted it and smiled at him wanly.

Just as she was about to call the whole thing off someone gave her the okay. Paul dropped his hand and Carmen began her half-rehearsed lines.

"First of all, I want to thank everyone who's had a part in the search for my little girls, Marisa and Liana. The state police, the county sheriff's office, the Ridgeport and Troy City police, not to mention the FBI, have all put forth a stupendous effort; but they could not have done any of it without the help of the volunteers, people I—we—don't even know," she paused for a deep breath, dabbed her swollen, teary eyes with a tissue, then continued. "My husband, Paul, and their father, Antonio Ibarra, and I thank you all. You can't begin to know what it has meant to us and to see so many people giving up their time to volunteer.

"Next, I am here to make my plea to anyone who thinks they might have seen my little girls. Anyone who knows—or thinks they know—where Marisa and Liana are, please come forward. Call your local police, even with the smallest of tips. Your information could result in Marisa and Liana coming home to us," she stifled a sob. Paul placed his hand on her shoulder again, and she clutched it like a lifeline. She gave up trying to dry her tears as she finished. "And whoever took them, please, if you're watching this, if you can hear my voice, please, return them to us. Please, whoever you are. I beg you. Please return my babies safely."

As her voice caught, the reporters took this to be the end of her statement, and someone from the crowd at the foot of the porch steps called out a question.

"Do you hold you ex-husband responsible for the disappearance of your children?"

"Well," she frowned, not knowing exactly how to respond, "They were at his home for a visit, you know—"

"Do you think he had anything to do with their disappearance, then?" someone else asked.

"Really, I couldn't say—" What the hell was this all about?

"How do you feel about the arrest of Antonio Ibarra?"

"Excuse me? Arrest?" she was totally confused. Someone was trying to move her away from the microphones, trying to get her into the house, but she shook off his hands. "I'm sorry. I'm sure I have no idea what you're talking about."

"Mrs. Thibault, didn't you know? The Ridgeport police and the FBI arrested Antonio Ibarra about an hour ago, for the abduction, disappearance, and possible murder of your daughters."

The words burned into her brain like a hot branding iron. *My God,* she thought. *How could they have arrested Antonio?*

Too stunned to speak, too shocked to resist, she allowed the gentle guiding hands to bring her into the safety of the house.

11:38 A.M.

Antonio Ibarra was booked and processed at the Ridgeport Police Department. He silently endured the procedure in a detached manner as though it were all happening to someone else. He was searched again and relieved of his watch, the belt on his jeans, and the shoelaces on his old Nikes; whatever might be creatively fashioned into some kind of weapon, removing from him any way to do harm to anyone including himself. The meager contents of his pockets—a ring of keys, a pocket comb, a fingernail clipper, a couple of wire nuts, a pocket knife, a set of black Rosary beads, loose change amounting to seventy-three cents, his wallet containing his driver's license, a VISA card, the debit card for his checking account, his Union health insurance card, his social security card, a paid dues receipt, a couple of pictures of Marisa and Liana, and forty-seven dollars in cash—were placed into a large brown envelope as each item was documented on a long sheet of paper. He signed the inventory sheet and it was inserted into the envelope which was labeled with his name and case number. He watched the stony-faced officer slip the envelope into a large cardboard box, along with his winter jacket. Finally, the lid was placed on the box and carried away to another room.

Next he was photographed and fingerprinted, and then taken in handcuffs to a room where the two FBI agents he had met yesterday were waiting for him.

It was a small room measuring only about eight by ten. The walls and the door were painted battleship gray so that the recessed fluorescent light seemed to brighten only the center of the room, leaving the rest of the place somber and dull. A large mirror took up almost the entire back wall of the room. A pitted and scarred four-foot-square wooden table and two chairs stood directly beneath the light in the center of the room. The furniture was bolted down to the floor. The pretty FBI agent sat in one of the chairs; the other was vacant.

"The handcuffs will not be necessary," the tall African-American agent said to the policeman who'd led him there.

The cop gave the agent who casually leaned against the wall a dubious glance, but unlocked the handcuffs as he'd been ordered. Antonio's wrists immediately felt better once the cuffs were off, and circulation quickly returned to his cold, numb hands. The officer stepped out of the room and closed the metal door behind him. The lock engaged with a resounding clang.

Antonio was left alone to face the two agents, trying to remember their names.

*****

"Come in, Mr. Ibarra," Mary Ellen Kelly invited from her chair facing the door. Her hand held a pen delicately poised over the blank sheet of a spiral notebook. Beside her notebook, John Turner's little tape recorder whirred.

Turner pointed to the vacant chair that faced the mirror, and watched as his prisoner obediently sat. Both of the FBI agents assumed their interrogation faces now; serious and unreadable. They studied their suspect who seemed to be measuring each of them in turn. To Turner, Ibarra seemed neither angry nor frightened, just insufferably aloof and blasé with the proceedings.

Turner purposefully remained leaning against the wall to the left of where Mary Ellen sat, and began to speak with the tone of one carrying on a civil conversation; no threat, no anger, no intimidation.

"You know why you are here, Antonio." It was not a question, but a statement. When Ibarra did not reply, Turner continued in the same tone of voice. "Blood was found in the girls' bedroom; more precisely, on Liana's bed linens and on the carpet. Can you explain that for me?"

No answer. Antonio Ibarra, his hands folded in front of him as though he were in prayer, had his eyes riveted to a spot on the table.

Turner's eyebrows came together in a frown and he strolled to the other side of the room taking the path behind Ibarra's chair. This maneuver served two purposes; it made it impossible for the suspect to see him unless he looked up into the mirror where the culprit's expression would be caught on film, and it gave Turner time to compose himself and get a hold of his quickly mounting irritation. He was not entirely successful on the latter effort; his voice came out a fraction louder than before and carried a slight edge. "A bloody shirt—a *child's* bloody shirt—was found in the garbage wrapped in a plastic bag. Can you explain *that*?"

Again no answer. Ibarra did not move.

Turner took a deep breath to calm himself. He wanted to hit the guy, but he couldn't allow himself that pleasure. He pushed his clenched fists deep into his pants pockets, and then pressed his back firmly against the wall; the coolness of the smooth surface through his shirt helped calm him down. He tried once more when his anger was carefully under control. "And a sweatshirt with your DNA on it had traces of the same blood type. Evidently you tried to wash it out without much success."

Antonio Ibarra still made no response. It was as though he hadn't heard him.

Like hell! He hears me fine, Turner thought angrily. *This is all an act.* How could the man be so cool? How could he do what he had done and not show some emotion? What the hell kind of a father could kill his children and be so—

Suddenly, John Turner found himself across the room, his face inches from Ibarra's downcast head. His fist came down heavily on the table top. The tiny tape recorder clattered to the floor.

Ibarra flinched and blinked up at him in surprise, as though he'd forgotten where he was and what he was there for. "*¡Lo siento!*"

"Answer the question, Ibarra!" Turner demanded, yelling now. His black eyes glinted as he leaned over the table, his fist still on the pock-marked surface where it had landed. *He's lucky it's just the table I hit!*

"What question?" Incredibly, Ibarra cast his rat-like eyes from one agent to the other, "I'm sorry. I did not hear what you asked me. Please repeat."

Like hell! Turner thought again, *This creep is something else!* John squeezed his eyes shut and took a deep breath. He willfully pushed himself away from the table and gave Mary Ellen the unspoken signal. Then hands back in his pockets, he purposefully distanced himself from the prisoner, a safety measure to insure that he wouldn't hit the scum. God knew once he got started, there'd be no stopping.

He closed his eyes and listened as Mary Ellen took up the questioning, her voice almost friendly and conversational, "Where are your daughters, Mr. Ibarra?"

Ibarra regarded her in confusion, "I don't know."

What an actor! John thought in disbelief. But he managed to restrain himself and allow Mary Ellen to ask her questions.

"Mr. Ibarra," Mary Ellen was saying in a soft voice, as though she were coaxing a frightened kitten from a tree. *Molly-coddling,* John thought. Mary Ellen continued, "Why don't you tell us what happened? We know you want what's best for Marisa and Liana. They might be cold or hungry, don't you think? If you told us where they are, we could get them and feed them. Wouldn't that be best?"

"*Si.* That would be wonderful," Ibarra nodded without looking up. But then, he shook his head, "But I can't tell you where they are."

Mary Ellen shifted in her chair, a small frown creasing her forehead, "Mr. Ibarra, you said the last time you saw them was Monday night."

"Yes, I listened to their prayers, blessed them, and tucked them into bed," the man smiled and Turner was sickened by his gall. "They were so happy to be spending part of their Christmas vacation with me."

"And then what happened?" she asked gently.

Ibarra finally moved. He looked at Mary Ellen with what Turner perceived as anger and disrespect, "We've been through all this before. Why are you asking me the same questions over again? I told you. I took a shower and went to bed myself. But I woke up yesterday morning to find their beds empty. They had been taken in the night."

That's it! It was all Turner could take. This scum had the audacity to sit there and act like the victim while his little girls— God only knew what he'd done to them!

"Look, Ibarra," Turner's voice boomed from the other side of the room and it gave him smidgen of pleasure to see the man jump. *Idiot forgot I was here!* "Why don't you come clean?"

"Clean? What are you talking about?"

"We found blood," Turner stated, "on a sweatshirt that belonged to *you*."

Ibarra frowned in puzzlement, but this time, he had an answer. He nodded, "Yes. Liana's blood."

"How did Liana's blood get on your sweatshirt, Antonio?" Turner demanded no longer trying to hold back his anger.

Ibarra shook his head, his hands turned palm up on the table in a manner that said that the reason for the blood should be plain to the FBI agents. "She had a nosebleed—"

"All that blood was from a nosebleed?" Incredulous and frustrated, John pushed himself away from the wall and Ibarra regarded him with what the agent took for defiance. This guy was going to be tougher than he'd thought. *He knows I can't hit him.* The realization was fuel for John's rancor. "You've jerked us around long enough, Ibarra. I want a clean answer from you. We know you killed them," Turner insisted bending close to him, placing his dark face mere inches from the suspect's. Turner watched the man's pupils dilate in their dark brown irises as he enumerated Ibarra's probable motives one by one. "You were angry with your ex-wife. You were frustrated with the court for giving the girls to her. You figured that if you couldn't have them, then neither could she. You said so in court, didn't you? Didn't you say you'd rather see them *dead* than be with their mother? So at your first opportunity, you killed them. What'd you do with the bodies?"

That's when Turner saw something change in Ibarra's eyes. Something he'd said had broken through the barrier of the man's defenses and now Ibarra was shaking his head and covering his ears with his hands. Tears flowed copiously down the man's cheeks and he started to bang his head against the tabletop, mumbling.

"*Si. Si.* They are gone. I was responsible for them and they are gone."

Suddenly, an indignant new voice cut across the room startling both agents. "That's quite enough, Special Agent Turner. My client has already been advised against talking to you without counsel, so anything you got from him will not be admissible in a court of law. I'm asking you to leave us alone now, so that I may confer with him in private." And then Charles Cabot inclined his head toward the mirrored wall, "I trust you'll make certain that both the camera and microphone will be turned off."

12:29 P.M.

Mary Ellen Kelly preceded John Turner out of the Interrogation Room fuming. With her shoulders tense and her back rigid she reached the stairs in only a few long-legged strides.

"Mary Ellen," John called after her, keeping his voice down so as not to attract the attention of the officer standing guard. "Special Agent Kelly. Would you wait up a second?"

She halted with one foot on the first step, left hand clutching her notepad to her chest, right hand on the rail. She turned only her head. "What?" she demanded a graceful eyebrow arched high in irritation.

John Turner stopped short, "What's the matter?"

"You're asking *me* what the matter is?" she asked incredulously. "I'm not the one who lost it in there. What the heck was that all about?"

"What?"

Apparently, she had put him on the defensive, but she was too angry for that to give her any satisfaction. "You were totally out of line," she said shaking her head.

"You think I was a little rough?"

"A little rough, you say?" The sarcasm in her voice took on a sharp edge. "I thought I was at the Spanish Inquisition! Tell me something, Special Agent Turner. If Charles Cabot hadn't shown up, what were you planning next, thumb screws?" She started up the stairs dismissing him. His footstep sounded on the stairs behind her.

"I was using conventional interrogation techniques," John answered.

"As per Hitler's Gestapo, maybe?" she replied wryly without stopping or turning around.

"Come on, Mary Ellen," John frowned jogging behind her, "I've been rougher. What's this all about?"

Any answer she would have given him was interrupted by the appearance of a young rookie cop at the top of the stairs. He was tall and good-looking with golden blond hair and bright blue eyes. He couldn't have been much more than twenty-one. He smiled at them displaying two even rows of perfect white teeth. "Special Agents Kelly and Turner! You're just the people I was looking for."

Mary Ellen quickly climbed the rest of the stairs, momentarily putting aside her irritation with John. "What is it?" she read the officer's brass name plate, "Officer Olsen?"

"You have a visitor." At Mary Ellen's questioning look, Olsen elaborated, "Wouldn't tell me anything. Said he needed to speak with you guys in person. Said it had to do with the Ibarra case."

12:31 P.M.

As Officer Olsen indicated, they found the youth sitting in cubicle A-3, waiting. Something about the curly dark-haired boy seemed familiar to Mary Ellen, and when he turned around and regarded her with his light blue eyes with their startling black rings, she instantly remembered. Jet was his name, an acronym for Julian Edmund Tate, Jr.

She smiled and extended her hand in greeting, "Jet! What a surprise to see you!"

The boy had manners. He rose and shook both agents' hands, then waited until they had taken seats before sitting back down in the same chair as before. Mary Ellen thought he looked nervous.

No. That wasn't the word for it. He looked upset.

"How long has it been?" she smiled trying to help him relax.

"It'll be three years in May, ma'am," he answered quickly. Apparently he'd figured it out earlier.

"The Knight case," John supplied.

"You've gotten taller," Mary Ellen remarked, ignoring her partner, "About six inches, I think."

Jet smiled and nodded.

"How's the leg?" John asked.

Jet glanced at his left leg self-consciously, "Thanks for asking, sir. It's all better. Good as new," he said. "I played baseball the past two seasons with no trouble."

"Babe Ruth League?" John asked.

"Yeah, during the summer. But I play for Bishop O'Donnell during school time," Jet said. "Shortstop, mostly." He seemed to have anticipated John's next question, glanced down at his hands, then looked directly at the FBI agents with serious—accusing?—eyes and said, "I saw you earlier, arresting Mr. Ibarra." He shrugged, "I was out with the volunteers, but afterwards I couldn't get Mr. Ibarra out of my mind. I needed to speak with you so I rode my cousin's bike here. I hope you don't mind."

"Of course not, Jet," Mary Ellen assured him taking control of the interview again. She realized they were getting to the reason for his visit so she ventured gently, "Officer Olsen said you had something to tell us about the case?"

"Yes, I do," he answered. "I think you already know part of it, but there's something else."

"What part do we know already?" she asked wondering how accurate his information could be. As she remembered, the kid had great insight and a knack for getting down to the truth.

"That Donna howled around three o'clock in the morning on Tuesday. You also know that Marisa and Liana Ibarra went missing at that time. You realize that Donna howled because she was upset about the girls leaving and couldn't prevent it. Yet, apparently, she knew the kidnappers well enough to allow them—"

"Them?" John interrupted.

Jet's blue eyes met Turner's dark ones. He shrugged, "Yeah. I figured the kids were carried out by whoever kidnapped them. There had to be two people involved."

"Continue, Jet," Mary Ellen shot John a warning look. "You were saying something about Donna?"

"Yeah," Jet's eyes went back to Mary Ellen, "She let them into the house without barking, without alerting Mr. Ibarra." His expression became even more intense. "I came here to tell you that I heard Donna howl, too."

John put up his hands, "If I remember correctly, you live in Troy City. How could you have heard—?"

"I've been at my cousin's since Christmas," Jet broke in looking somewhat perturbed by John's second interruption. "My Uncle Phil owns the house on the other side of the vacant lot from Ibarra's. It was when she howled today as you arrested Mr. Ibarra that I made the connection with what I'd heard."

"Well, as you've already pointed out, we knew all this before," Mary Ellen stated. "You've corroborated information we already had—which is good. But what is it that you felt we needed to know?"

"That we've been wasting our time looking for the girls in Collier's Woods," Jet said with conviction.

Mary Ellen's eyebrows knitted in a frown. "Why do you say that?"

"Let me put this another way," Jet sighed. "The girls are not in the woods because the kidnappers didn't bring them there. Donna would have known it if they were there, if they'd ever gone there. But she's not telling us to look there. She keeps sniffing around the street in front of the vacant lot. Something happened *there*. That's where we need to look."

"With Antonio Ibarra in custody, we should know a lot more soon enough," John said.

But Jet was shaking his head, "No, you won't. You won't get anything out of Mr. Ibarra," he avowed. "He's not the kidnapper. You've arrested the wrong man."

Now John scowled, "And how do you know that?"

Mary Ellen could tell her partner was not happy. She sat back and watched, wondering how this would all play out but ready to jump in if John lost his temper. She found herself looking from one to the other like a spectator at a tennis match.

"Because I heard something else the night the girls disappeared," Jet squarely met John's angry eyes. "I heard a car start up and drive away."

"So did Charles Cabot," John countered, nodding.

"Mr. Ibarra doesn't own a car," Jet pointed out. "He owns a pickup truck, a Dodge Ram with a Cummins engine. It's a diesel with a very distinct sound."

John's eyebrows made a steeple in the middle of his forehead. "Yes," he said slowly, "and the significance of that is?"

"The vehicle that drove away in the middle of the night," Jet began calmly, holding the FBI agent's eyes with his own, "with the Ibarra girls inside—"

"You *presume* the girls were in the car—" John interrupted.

"Yes, *presumably* with Marisa and Liana inside," Jet nodded patiently, "was not a diesel truck, but an automobile—"

"Okay," John cut in again impatiently, "We checked but there are no other vehicles registered to Antonio Ibarra."

Mary Ellen remembered something else she'd learned about Jet last time they'd met: The boy knew cars. She took John's interruption as a chance to speak herself, "And there's something particular about this car?"

Jet turned his troubled blue eyes on her, "Yes, Agent Kelly. I know there was something special about the car I heard, but I can't put my finger on it. Maybe it's because I was on the verge of sleep and not awake enough to realize what it was. But I know I'll eventually think of it. And when I do, I'll let you know."

1:28 P.M.

It was after lunch by the time Jet returned to River Road and rejoined the searchers in the woods behind the Ibarra house. Jet flipped over a thin snow-covered half-sheet of plywood. Once satisfied that it wasn't concealing anything sinister, he continued pondering the case.

He'd told the FBI agents everything he knew, and he hoped he'd contributed something to the case. Agent Kelly appeared to be open to Jet's observations, so not *everything* he'd said had fallen on deaf ears. Agent Turner seemed to be of the opinion that Jet didn't know what he was talking about and refused to value anything he had to say. To Agent Turner, Jet's input was of no more importance than the unfounded rants of a child.

Apparently, Agent Turner believed he had his man. Worse, the Ridgeport Police shared Agent Turner's conviction that Mr. Ibarra had done something to his own daughters. What did they think he'd done? Murdered them? What did they have to support their case besides circumstantial evidence? What had the investigators uncovered that could be so damning? He'd heard someone say that blood had been found in the house and on some clothing.

Okay, so blood was blood. It happens. A kid skins a knee, cuts a finger, there's blood. It drips on the floor, gets on clothes. How much blood were they talking about?

He remembered when he was seven he'd fallen out of the apple tree in the backyard and had received a gash over his right eye that had required eleven stitches. Not a big deal. But the bleeding had been alarming. Blood had run down his face in a steady stream, entering his eye and completely soaking the front of his T-shirt in the short time it had taken him to run into the house to get the first adult he could find; his grandmother. Mom had driven him to the hospital emergency room while Grams had held his head tightly against her bosom with a kitchen towel pressed firmly on the wound. Yet that also had been drenched with blood by the time they'd reached their destination only fifteen minutes away.

Despite what had seemed like a frightening amount of blood to him and to Mom and Grams, none of the medical personnel who treated him seemed overly concerned. No one suggested that he needed a blood transfusion or an IV to replace fluids. They hadn't even kept him in the hospital under observation. He'd been sent home with no other directive than to keep the stitches dry. There was never any question that Jet would survive his injury without any further treatment. So much for that.

Jet also remembered that Dad regularly donated blood for the Union blood drive. Jet had asked him once and Dad had said that a healthy adult could donate a pint of blood with no adverse effects every eight weeks.

The question was, was it the same for a child? When did blood-loss get to be a life-threatening amount for a child?

How much blood had the investigators found? Enough to prove murder had occurred? Or were they looking at stains and spots, enough to arouse interest and suspicion; enough to convince them that *something* had happened but that the actual murder would have happened elsewhere? That is, if a killing had been committed at all.

If Mr. Ibarra hurt them, say, stabbed them to death, then where was the weapon? And if, as Sgt. Rothman said, they were looking for a grave, where was the dirt-encrusted shovel? Would the killer have even been able to break the dirt now hard with frost? Had they found soiled clothes consistent with digging in dirt?

Or maybe he had tossed them into the river. Yesterday's news had reported that a child's shirt had been found near the banks of Long River. Could Mr. Ibarra have stabbed the children and dispensed of the bodies by throwing them into Long River? Jet tried to imagine what that might be like; killing someone you love, then watching the river take them away. It seemed like a cold and heartless thing to do. But of course, a killer would be desperate to get away with the crime and might do anything to get rid of incriminating evidence. Is that what the police were thinking?

The more Jet thought about it, the more he felt the children had not been murdered and that they were being held somewhere against their will. Jet feared that in an effort to incriminate Mr. Ibarra, the authorities were abandoning that line of thought. In so doing, they were putting themselves on the wrong track. By accepting that the children were dead, everyone was wasting precious time looking for the girls in these woods—

"—while the kidnapper gets farther away and the trail gets cold."

3:51 P.M.

John answered his phone on the first ring. "Turner here."

It was Carl from Support. "That Rhode Island registration belongs to a rental car agency at T.F. Green Airport," the tech stated, "rented to a Dr. Wyatt Tibbs of Springfield, Vermont."

"Thanks, Carl."

Chalk up another disappointment. Tibbs was family, John knew. Mary Ellen had been right. Again. Usually he loved that she had quick instincts and near-perfect intuition. So why did it bother him that she was right this time?

He glanced over her way.

She still hadn't spoken to him since the Tate kid left. John had been surreptitiously watching her from his cubicle while he went through the motions of doing paperwork and eating his lunch, a foot-long Italian sub and an extra large Coke.

He knew he'd upset her but he didn't know what to do

about it. Actually, he didn't really know what sin he'd committed to distress her in the first place. Evidently, she objected to something he'd done or said during his interrogation of Antonio Ibarra.

She knew the score. She was well-aware that the interrogation of a suspect was not meant to be a stroll in the park. There was a certain brutality to the technique, calculated to achieve the ultimate result of obtaining information, and if lucky, maybe even a confession. There was nothing polite or gentle about questioning a suspect. And he had not strayed from FBI-sanctioned protocols. He'd gone right by the book.

But somehow, she disapproved of something.

His submarine sandwich was long gone and she still had her blond head bent over the lists of questions and observations the boy and his friends had compiled. He had a copy of the same lists, and he didn't see anything there that struck a chord in him. For whatever reason, though, Mary Ellen seemed to feel that what these kids had to offer was important, or maybe whatever *he* had to say was not.

This is stupid! We're partners, he thought irritably. *How can she stay mad at me?* He found her behavior quite unprofessional. While it was true that they treated each other as equals, the fact of the matter was that he was her senior, her superior. He didn't want to have to pull rank on her, but he would if she continued to be illogical.

For the time being, John put off voicing his unhappy observations. He had something else to be concerned about. He was busy trying to find something that would support a theory he had forming in his mind.

He read the information that appeared on his computer screen. Ibarra, Antonio Miguel, born in Troy City, would turn forty-three on January 17th.

"Ibarra has two sisters," John called over to her, more to break the silence than to share information. "His father is deceased, but his mother, a retired teacher, lives at the South End of Troy City, on Park Street."

"Didn't he mention all that to Officer Diaz?" Mary Ellen

answered in a weary tone without looking at him, "His mother goes to Puerto Rico for the winter and his sisters were visiting her on the island for Christmas? If you bother to check, they probably went for *la Noche Buena*. A very important celebration among Hispanics."

"If it's such a big deal, then why didn't Antonio go too?"

"Probably because of the girls. He didn't want to miss his time with them," her explanation was thought-out and logical. "He would have had to get there before Christmas, and I doubt Carmen would have permitted the girls to go with him and miss the holiday with her and Paul. He certainly couldn't legally take them to Puerto Rico without her consent."

Delighted and encouraged by the volume of words in Mary Ellen's response, John tapped a few keys and read the information aloud from his computer screen, "Ramona Estrella Maria Ibarra Tibbs. Married to Dr. Wyatt James Tibbs for twenty-four years. They have two children: A daughter, Samantha Luisa, age twenty-three and a son, Matthew Wyatt, age twenty-one. The daughter is a 2008 graduate of Vermont University. She's pursuing her studies of medicine in Montpelier. The son postponed college to join the Marines; he's currently in Iraq. Mrs. Tibbs is a pediatric nurse, and works in her husband's private practice. They reside at 265 Meadow Lane, Springfield, Vermont."

With a click of the mouse, he shifted screen, "And Luisa Maria Isabella Ibarra Bernard. She's been married to Marcel Louis Bernard, a civil engineer, for eighteen years. They have one child, a son, Marcel, Jr., age seventeen. He's an honor student at Franklin Delano Roosevelt High in Suncook, New Hampshire. Residence is listed as 43 Larkspur Road, Suncook." He looked over at Mary Ellen, "That's all there is."

"Hmm," she sighed. "No sinister characters there, huh?"

Her sarcastic tone caused John to look up, "What's your problem?"

"We've been through it before," she barely glanced his way. "I can't see the point of rehashing it all again."

John smirked, "You still think I was too rough on Ibarra?"

"Not only that, but I think the culprit could be someone other than your main suspect," she informed him. "I think you've narrowed your search too early in the case. We still have a lot to investigate. I fear we might have arrested the wrong man."

"So who's made *your* list?" John was curious to know.

She turned to face him, fixing him with serious blue eyes. "Don't know yet," she admitted. "But I'm not so sure it's Antonio Ibarra. I mean, think about it. Could Antonio ever get away with stealing his daughters or killing them? Either way, he loses. By kidnapping them, he can't live openly with them. By killing them, he loses them permanently."

John nodded, "Yeah, that's if he hasn't gone off the edge."

She rose from her chair and came to stand in the doorway of his cubicle, "What about Paul Thibault?"

John shook his head, "I don't think so. If Paul did anything like that, even to punish his wife's ex, he'd lose Carmen. He wouldn't want to jeopardize his relationship with her in any way."

"Unless Carmen's the brains behind it and he's in it with her."

John's raised eyebrows told her he found that notion preposterous, "I can't see either of them as the perpetrator of this crime."

"Well, why not? You're willing to believe Antonio Ibarra is the perpetrator," she argued. "Carmen and Paul Thibault are a more logical choice than is Antonio Ibarra. They'd have had the perfect set up. They could've unlocked the door with Carmen's key. The dog doesn't bark because she accepts them in the house. They steal the kids while Antonio has them, and he bears the suspicion and guilt because he had them last."

"But Mary Ellen, you said yourself that it doesn't work," John reasoned. "They'd never be able to enjoy the children publicly, unless they left Troy City and went far away. And that's highly unlikely given the work Paul has done to his house, not to mention his business."

"They could live well on the profits from the sales of both

the house and the business," Mary Ellen argued. "Even with the loan Paul took out to renovate the house, I'm sure his improvements increased its value. And certainly, the business must be worth quite a bundle. They could buy another house somewhere and set up a new business."

"But what about all the evidence we have against Ibarra?"

"You mean the blood in his truck and on his sweatshirt?"

"Yeah. How do you explain that?"

"Antonio mentioned a nosebleed," she shrugged off John's dubious look. "I don't know what it means for sure, and neither do you. Glenda Baldwin said it wasn't enough blood to be concerned about. We listened to Ruth Wilson and jumped the gun. We arrested Ibarra on flimsy circumstantial evidence."

"Ruth's record is impeccable."

"Maybe. But I think there's more to this case we haven't found yet. I think there's something about the preliminary findings of this case that struck a chord in Ruth Wilson, maybe because it involves young children. I don't know, but whatever it is, it caused her to strike quickly and arrest Antonio Ibarra prematurely. I think she has lost her objectivity on this one."

"Speak for yourself, Mary Ellen."

"What's that supposed to mean?"

"Simply that you yourself seem to have a lot of personal feelings getting in the way of sound judgment," he told her exactly what was on his mind, "I think you've lost *your* objectivity."

She stared daggers at him then and he saw her jaw clench before she said tightly, "You're out of line, Special Agent Turner."

"Am I?"

"Yes, you are," she retorted vehemently. "Just because I feel that we acted too soon doesn't mean that I am personally involved. I just think that we have not looked at all the evidence." Then to John's relief, she admitted, "I do have trouble seeing Antonio Ibarra as the murderer of his own children—"

"He wouldn't be the first—"

"—at this time," she turned her back on him and shook her

head again, this time pensively. "There's just one thing that bothers me," she murmured softly as she returned to her own cubicle. "There's been no demand for ransom. That in itself could be an indication that the children were taken by a family member."

"So I'm checking out Ibarra's sisters—" John nodded. Couldn't she see the logical, orderly progression of his investigation?

"Who I'm sure have solid alibis," she rolled her eyes.

"That brings us back to square one," he said.

"We *have* to get off square one, John!" Mary Ellen's heated retort caught him by complete surprise. "I know until I find some solid evidence to point us in the right direction, we have to keep both Ibarra and the Thibaults on our list of suspects. But unless we stop wasting our time and start chasing the *right* suspect, unless we stop arguing with each other, jumping to erroneous conclusions and following bum leads, we'll never find the actual perpetrator." She abruptly cut short her tirade and turned her back on him.

John wondered if she was crying. If so, he could understand her own embarrassment with her lack of professionalism, so he didn't try to get a closer look and he let her continue her pretended study of the evidence board.

Could Antonio Ibarra be innocent? he wondered.

Normally, he liked that Mary Ellen saw the good in people; that she dissected every bit of evidence making certain they were on the right track; that she was reluctant to make accusations until completely, totally, irrefutably convinced of the suspect's guilt. He had nothing to complain about. In the short time they'd been partners, all of the cases she'd helped crack had been upheld in court. None of them had failed.

But this case involved children. He suspected that by accusing Ruth Wilson of that very problem, she was actually revealing her own true feelings. It was getting to her that two beautiful, innocent, little girls had been murdered by their own father. He wondered how that would further affect her judgment and how it would impact the outcome of this case.

He didn't have long to ponder this for presently Mary Ellen grabbed her coat off the hook. "Come on," was all she said.

Apparently she was onto something. He had no idea what, but if he wanted to find out, superior rank or not, he had no choice but to follow.

As they left the police station, John was surprised to see that dusk was already settling over the town. Mary Ellen uncharacteristically got behind the wheel of the Crown Vic and took off before John had even shut his door.

She headed down Cross Street and he remained silent for the entire trip, not daring to ask her where they were going. Instead, he watched familiar landmarks go by and tried to guess their destination. At first, he thought they were going to River Road, but they passed that street and crossed the bridge into Troy City. Next they headed north on Eastern Avenue; but it was only when she made the turn onto Hollywood Drive that he realized they were going to see the Thibaults.

Mary Ellen slid the shift lever into Park and when she pulled the key out of the ignition, the courtesy light automatically came on, throwing its soft glow across their faces. John reached over and grabbed her wrist and his brown eyes locked with her blue ones.

"Listen, Mary Ellen," he said quietly, "we need to talk."

She wrenched her wrist out of his grip, turned away, and grabbed the door handle. For a moment he thought she was going to ignore his request, but at the instant when she would have pushed the door open, she looked back at him. "We'll talk after we speak with Paul and Carmen Thibault. I need to clear up a few questions first, if you don't mind."

"We're partners, you know," John reminded her, biting back the urge to add, *and I'm your boss.*

"I know we're partners," she pushed the door open and got out of the car. "It's nice when I'm not the only one who remembers that."

4:25 P.M.

She felt the tension immediately when Thibault opened the door. Although Paul politely ushered them into the patriotic living room, tonight he seemed more reserved; not yesterday's genial, smiling host. Apparently he was still bristling over their earlier meeting at the store.

On her part, Carmen had left the room and had avoided speaking with them at all, practically snubbing them. This behavior spoke about much more than simply the reactions of a worried, heartsick mother. Perhaps Paul had shared his view of their encounter at the store, and Carmen resented them for implicating her husband. Whatever her problem, she didn't make it known, and although they had declined the offer, she presently returned with a tray laden with a teapot, dainty cups and saucers, cream, sugar, lemon, and a plate of English cookies.

"Paul and I were about to have tea and biscuits," she said coolly. Although she wasn't crying at the moment, her eyes were puffy and her voice was thick. "You're welcome to join us, or not. Suit yourselves." She took a seat beside her husband on the sofa and began pouring tea into the cups. In the end, the FBI agents accepted Carmen's offer. It seemed easier to humor her than to argue.

While John sat back in one of the red wingchairs, enjoying his tea with plenty of sugar, Mary Ellen began her interview. She was relieved that he seemed content to play the role of spectator, the casual onlooker. He had to be curious about what they would learn; he was a good detective, after all. In the past, he'd never been too arrogant to admit he'd made a mistake, or that a case should have been handled from a different angle. He'd often said that an opposing point of view sometimes shed new light on things. He had to be as intrigued as she was by the Thibaults' cool treatment of them just now.

Mary Ellen watched John casually reach for a cookie as she asked her first question; "How is it that you still have a key to your ex-husband's house?"

Carmen's perfectly shaped eyebrows rose and she quickly

swallowed her sip of tea. "I never returned it when I moved out." She hastily explained, "It was on the key ring, along with my car keys. So when I left, the key came with me. By the time it occurred to either of us, I was already out of rehab and having weekend visits with the girls. Antonio told me to just keep it, that it might be better if I had my own key in case the girls needed something at home and he wasn't there."

"How many other people have a key to Antonio's house that you know of?" Mary Ellen demanded.

"Well," Carmen said, thinking. "When I lived there, Charles Cabot had one. And of course, Bob LaRue." Apparently her earlier frigid demeanor was thawing. Although nothing of a smile had as yet touched her pretty face, she was becoming more talkative, more cooperative. Whatever had prompted the chilly reception of the FBI agents had evidently receded into the back of her mind.

The British and their tea. Mary Ellen thought. *The cure-all for any ailment.*

"Doesn't Mary Carvalho have one too?" Paul questioned interrupting Mary Ellen's thoughts.

"Yes, indeed she does!" Carmen nodded. "So, I guess *three* more people have keys to the house besides me." She regarded the FBI agents triumphantly.

John reached for another cookie as Mary Ellen asked, "How do you explain that Donna, who is so protective, treats you like family, Paul?

Paul laughed briefly. "I told you before; it drives Antonio a little crazy that Donna loves me. I assume it's because I make a point of playing with her whenever I see her. She used to bark up a storm when Carmen and I first started going there, but she and I quickly became friends. She hasn't barked at either of us since—" Paul looked at his wife for corroboration. "When would you say, darling? Since May?"

"Oh, yeah," Carmen agreed. "It's been a long time. Since before we were married."

"As I said," Paul smiled. "It drives Antonio nuts because she still barks at the neighbors, whom she's known all her life, yet she doesn't bother either of us. As you say, she accepts us as family, I guess."

Mary Ellen gave John a pointed look, but he seemed not to notice. She continued with her next question, "Do you know of anyone else she considers family?"

Paul shook his head, and Carmen simply shrugged, saying, "As far as I know, we're the only people who don't live in the house that she doesn't bark at."

John sipped the last of his tea as Mary Ellen undauntedly asked, "I understand that Liana is prone to nosebleeds. What can you tell me about that?"

Carmen had started nodding before Mary Ellen had finished speaking, "Oh, yes! Dreadful episodes, they are, too. That was the first thing I learned about when we started visitations: How to stop them. But, sometimes, they're scary. I know I jumped the gun a couple of times and brought her to the accident department—um, what do you call it?"

"She's still learning American terminology," Paul said casting an affectionate look her way, "It's the emergency room, darling."

"Yes, thank you, dear. I've brought her to the emergency room for nothing. But you know, it just looks like so much blood—" Her voice caught, and as she dabbed at her eyes with a tissue, Paul reached over and slipped a comforting arm around her shoulders. In a voice shaking with emotion, she added, "You'd think she was bleeding to death!"

"Do you know what causes them?" Mary Ellen inquired.

Carmen sniffed and collected herself, "Dr. Winter, the girls' pediatrician, says it has to do with low humidity and the dry air from the heating system. If we use a humidifier in her bedroom, it helps."

"Does Antonio have a humidifier?"

"Of course!" Carmen flashed a disdainful look that said Mary Ellen should know better than to ask. "He's the one who insisted I buy one of my own. Once we turn on the heating system, Liana needs the humidifier. Otherwise, she gets the nosebleeds. It's that simple."

"Liana's blood was found on Antonio's sweatshirt," Mary Ellen stated. "What do you make of that?" The question caused John to lurch forward in surprise. Luckily, she silently observed, his teacup was empty, or she feared he might have splashed hot tea over the brim. He gently placed the teacup and saucer on the end of the coffee table and listened to Carmen's answer.

Carmen shrugged her slender shoulders, "How do I know? Most likely, she had one of her nosebleeds and he carried her to a place where she could sit down and hold her nose for awhile. Or that's all he had to catch the blood. I wouldn't make a big deal out of that." She looked at them with sudden awareness, and as she spoke, Mary Ellen felt she understood Carmen's earlier chilly reception of them. "This is what you have on him! Here I was blaming myself for his arrest, thinking you'd gone after him based on my hateful words. But no. You're basing the arrest on the blood from one of Liana's nosebleeds!" She shook her head and said with conviction, "As much as I despise him for everything he's done to me, Antonio would never hurt the girls. Strangle *me*, perhaps, but not the girls. So," Carmen finished icily, "if that's all you've got, you're wasting your time. You've got the wrong fellow."

5:38 P.M.

Back in the car, Mary Ellen took the wheel again. There was something else she wanted to check out.

"I need to make sure my assumptions are sound," she told John. Then, unable to resist, added sarcastically, "I wouldn't want my lack of professional objectivity to cause me to jump to unsubstantiated conclusions."

Although John said nothing, she could see him watching her from the corner of her eye and she knew he was burning to question her. *Good! Burn!* she thought.

When they turned onto the bridge over the Interstate and into Ridgeport, he couldn't stay quiet any longer. "Well? Aren't you going to say something?"

Mary Ellen intentionally avoided looking at him and kept her eyes on the road. "I don't think there's anything to say." She glanced his way briefly, then shrugged and stated matter-of-factly, "Unless you want to hear 'I told you so.' We've arrested the wrong man."

John instantly rose to the bait and asked, "You're basing that on—?"

"On what we just learned from the Thibaults," she heard the exasperation in her voice. Couldn't he see it as plainly as she? When he didn't respond quickly enough, she enumerated.

"Fact One: Antonio gave the key to *at least* three other people besides Carmen. Almost *anybody* could have gotten into that house without breaking in. How many more people are there with a key to Ibarra's house?

"Fact Two: Donna doesn't bark at family, yet she barks at neighbors. She considers the Thibaults family, and they don't even live in the house! Is there anyone *else* she trusts enough not to bark? Anyone, I mean, who doesn't live *in* the house?

"Fact Three: Not only was there not enough blood at the scene to support a murder-theory, but it could easily have come from a nosebleed, as Antonio Ibarra claims it did. This is a fact that can be confirmed by forensics. If there's any mucus in that blood, it would support the nosebleed-theory."

She finally took her eyes away from the road to give him a stony look, "Face it, John. You've arrested the man on very flimsy evidence. We don't have enough to hold him."

"Maybe not for murder," he conceded, "but for kidnapping."

"How do you figure that? It seems to me everything we had has just been shot down!"

"Here's the scenario." Evidently John was still trying to convince her. "Ibarra takes Marisa and Liana away in the middle of the night and puts them someplace he considers safe. Then he comes back to pretend they've been kidnapped, plays the over-wrought and worried father. He even leaves the front door open, wets the living room carpet with snow, and tosses the girls' room just to lend credibility to his story."

She shot him a contemptuous glance, "You expect a jury to believe that preposterous story? A good defense attorney—and I'm sure Charles Cabot will be up to the challenge—would shoot holes in all of our so-called evidence. Please!" she argued. "If Antonio has kidnapped his children, please explain to me how he plans to take care of them while he's in jail?"

"He didn't think he'd be arrested," John reasoned, "and now it's a complication he hadn't planned on. It's all because he's an amateur and didn't think it through. I would have found everything out if Cabot hadn't shown up!"

"Don't even go there," she shook her head vehemently, angry again. "You lost control of that interview! I don't know what you were doing, but it had nothing to do with finding out what he'd done with the girls. It was angry and vindictive and cruel, not to mention totally insulting to *me*."

"You?" He looked as though he really had no idea what she was talking about.

She went on before he could say anything else. "I had just painted the picture of them cold and hungry someplace—in a place where he might have hidden them if he *were* guilty, mind you—and he reacted like a truly heartbroken parent. If he had them somewhere and knew they were going to suffer now that he couldn't go to them, he would have spilled it right then and there. That was *his* chance to tell us where they were. But you ruined everything by butting in like a madman—"

"—unless he has an accomplice who'll care for them until he gets out," John pointed out, interrupting her.

"So you think he had help?" Her words were barely audible.

"Your pal, Jet seems to think there were two kidnappers. Why couldn't they be Ibarra and a helper?"

Could John be right? She needed time to ponder that possibility and she said nothing as she turned into a now quiet and empty River Road.

As though in complete defiance of the crime that had been committed on this street, Christmas lights cheerily glowed in the evergreen trees and shrubs around the houses, and Christmas trees illuminated many front windows. As Mary Ellen pulled into the driveway of number eleven-thirty-six, she saw that Ibarra's house, too, joined in with the celebration, as though that family refused to be brought down by the awful events of the past few days.

She parked behind the Caravan the technician had reported earlier. Apparently it had not moved all day; it was parked in the same place as before when Antonio was arrested. When she turned off the ignition, she shifted in her seat to face John squarely. "Okay. Who?"

"Who?" He looked surprised by her question. John adjusted his overcoat while she waited for an answer. Mary Ellen recognized this tactic; he was trying to get his thoughts together. "That's what we need to find out," he finally answered. "I want to dig further into Antonio Ibarra's lifestyle, find out if he has a new girlfriend, or if anybody has been spending a lot of time at the house lately. Find out if he made travel plans recently—"

Mary Ellen shook her head. "Okay," she cut him off. "I can see where you're going with this, and your idea has merit and deserves to be investigated."

"Thank you," he said sarcastically.

She ignored his tone and spoke over him, "But I have misgivings and ideas of my own that I think are equally valid. Are you going to allow me to proceed and work on my instincts?"

"We're a team," he drawled.

"Right now we're not acting like one." She got out of the car and slammed the door. As though on cue, the front porch light went on, and someone peeked in the space between the sheer curtains and the Christmas tree to see who was calling.

"Are you going to tell me what we're here for?" he asked as he got out and looked at her over the top of the car.

Realizing their voices would carry on the cold air, Mary Ellen tried to keep her voice down as she replied in an angry whisper, the car acting as a buffer for their conflict. "The same way you told me why Antonio Ibarra suddenly became the prime suspect in this case?" Sarcasm coated her words. "It seemed to me that you let Ruth Wilson call the shots there."

John was instantly on the defensive, "She felt we had enough to charge him."

"Since when do you let anyone decide how much evidence is enough?" she countered. "I thought that as *partners*," she sneered, "*we* were supposed to discuss *all* evidence and its viability, not rely on the opinions of the local constabulary."

"The Ridgeport PD would have made the collar alone," John answered. Mary Ellen thought he sounded weak and uncertain and it fired her up.

"Oh, I see," Mary Ellen fought to control the quaver in her voice. She wouldn't shed her angry tears here in front of him. "You wanted us to be in on the collar, no matter if it was a bad one. Well," she turned her back on him and advanced to the front steps. Motion renewed her resolve, restored her composure. "No thank you, Special Agent Turner," she said without a trace of tears in her voice now. "This time I think you let yourself be carried away by a well-meaning, over-zealous crime scene detective who made a mountain out of a mole-hill. For whatever reason—maybe she's bucking for a promotion—Ruth Wilson needed to nail somebody fast, and her enthusiasm carried you along with her."

"As I said before, she has an impeccable record," John said quietly, "noted for accuracy."

"Not this time." Mary Ellen pressed the doorbell. "This time she made a mistake. And I hope by listening to her we haven't wasted valuable time, further endangering those children's lives."

Whatever John might have said to that was interrupted when the door opened just enough to reveal a pretty, fifty-ish, salt-and-pepper-haired woman of medium height and build. Mary Ellen imagined that a smile on that face would render it lovely. The attractive woman silently regarded them with solemn, questioning chocolate brown eyes.

"FBI, ma'am," Mary Ellen produced her ID badge. This was still her show, and she was making the introductions, "I'm Special Agent Mary Ellen Kelly, and my partner is Special

Agent John Turner."

"Yes," the woman recognized them and answered reproachfully, "you were here earlier when Antonio was arrested."

"That's correct, ma'am. May we come in?"

The woman hesitated and looked back over her shoulder as a handsome, blue-eyed man with snow white hair and beard came to stand beside her.

"What do you want?" His soothingly mellow voice held an authoritative, yet unthreatening quality. He was not a tall man, only an inch taller than the woman, and looked healthy and fit. Despite his athletic build, Mary Ellen could picture this man in a Santa Claus suit, delighting children with his kind and gentle manner.

"I'm trying to find evidence that will clear Antonio of the crime for which he was arrested."

"Why would you do that?" the man persisted.

"Because I believe he's innocent."

At those words, the door opened wider to admit the two agents. They carefully stepped around luggage piled near the door and followed their hosts into the living room where they joined three other people seated on the couch. At one end was a brunette a few years younger than the woman who had answered the door; at the other, an older woman with steel-gray hair and dark eyes who bore a remarkable resemblance to Antonio Ibarra. It was apparent that both women had been crying. Between the two women was a young, dark-haired man in his late teens. Even seated, it was obvious that he was taller than the rest of his family.

The FBI agents were invited to sit, and as the white-haired man got more chairs from the kitchen, the woman who had answered the door made introductions, "This is my sister, Luisa Bernard and her son, Marcel, Jr."

The youth half-rose from his seat and extended his hand to both agents, "Everyone calls me Butch."

"And at the far end of the sofa is our mother, Estrella Ibarra," Butch's aunt finished.

"We are Ramona and Wyatt Tibbs," the white-haired man said. "I was just about to bring *mi suegra* Estrella to her apartment in Troy City, and then drive Luisa and Butch to the airport." Dr. Tibbs explained that upon receiving word of Marisa's and Liana's kidnapping, they had cut short their visit in Puerto Rico and had changed their return flights to land at T.F. Green so that they could lend moral support to their younger brother, even if it was only for a couple of days. Mrs. Ibarra had been lucky enough to get a ticket on board the same flight and would be staying as long as need be to offer whatever help she could to her son.

"You understand that it has been a long and stressful day. Especially for *Mama*," Luisa Bernard said. "She just turned eighty in October. The stress of seeing Antonio arrested—"

"I'm right here, Luisa!" objected the elderly woman who did not look her age. Her English was perfect and accent-free. "I'm not deaf, nor am I senile. How dare you talk in front of me as though I were not here! I can speak for myself." Chastised, Luisa fell silent, and Mrs. Ibarra locked her dark eyes on the two FBI agents, "You have the wrong man. My Antonio did not hurt his little girls. By accusing him you are wasting valuable time."

"We are still investigating, Mrs. Ibarra," Mary Ellen assured the woman. "We're here to learn more about Antonio and the children. And about you, his family, as well." Somewhat mollified, Mrs. Ibarra nodded and dabbed fresh tears from her eyes.

And then Dr. Tibbs confirmed everything the FBI agents had learned from John's online search. He had a practice in pediatric medicine which he ran with his wife, Ramona, who was a nurse. He had already called his office to reschedule his routine appointments, and to have any emergencies referred to a colleague until next Monday when they planned to be back in Vermont.

Mrs. Bernard and her son were both expected back in school on the Monday after New Year's as well. "If it weren't that my husband, Marcel, is going off on business to Iraq next

Tuesday," the stunning brunette explained dabbing her red-rimmed hazel eyes, "I would stay on as well since we're on vacation this week. But we were apart for Christmas because he couldn't get away at the last minute, and now he's leaving. I don't know when he'll return. I'm so torn. I want to support Antonio, but I also need to spend time with Marcel before he leaves—"

"That's okay, Luisa. You go on home with Butch tonight as planned," Ramona assured her younger sister as tears threatened again. "There's nothing any of us can really do for Antonio right now, other than offer up our prayers. Your place is with Marcel. Didn't Antonio say the same thing this morning? She turned to the FBI agents, "You must forgive us for being so suspicious of you." Ramona Tibbs wrung a tissue in her hands. "With everything that has happened; first the girls' disappearance, and now, Antonio—"she stopped abruptly, unable to continue.

"We are all truly distraught over everything that has happened," Dr. Tibbs said. "And if cooperating with you can help clear Antonio, then we're at your service."

"Thank you," Mary Ellen said, "And with that in mind, I would like to look at the girls' bedroom again, if you don't mind."

"Of course," said Wyatt Tibbs.

"What are we looking for?" John asked as he stood behind her in doorway of the pink bedroom.

Mary Ellen knew he was waiting for an answer as she cast her eyes slowly over the room. It was as she remembered it the last time she'd seen it; the semi-opened closet with the empty hangers, the bureau with its partly opened drawers, the many articles strewn across the floor. She took in the beds that had been stripped of their covers. Now they were nothing more than floral mattresses with blue-striped pillows tossed upon them. CSI had left little plastic numbered markers indicating where evidence had been found. They had treated it as a murder scene in spite of the lack of a body.

Where could it be?

John repeated his question, "What—"

"It's not here," she cut him off with her reply.

"What?"

"The humidifier."

She carefully stepped between the plastic yellow tape that cordoned off the doorway and crossed the room, cautiously picking her way among the plastic markers. She was heading for the place where it would make the most sense to put a humidifier: Well out of a young child's reach, yet close enough to the bed for the moist air to provide the best results.

The chest of drawers. She found a likely place on top of the bureau. The painted surface was scarred with a circular ring; a watermark.

"It *used* to be here," she observed without touching it. "Did the crime scene people have the humidifier on their list of confiscated items?"

"I don't remember seeing it," John said, "but I have the list on my desk back at the station."

"I didn't see it listed on there either, so I don't believe they took it." Mary Ellen mused, "I wonder who did?"

"Ibarra's accomplice?"

Although she was not happy with John's suggestion, she had to admit he might be on the right track after all.

11:06 P.M.

Jet stretched out on top of his bed, fully dressed except for his sneakers, while Donna lay contentedly curled like a doughnut on Grams' old rag rug on the floor. He had the *Eleven O'clock News* on TV, but his attention was elsewhere. Something was bothering him.

When they got back to Hank's house shortly after four o'clock that afternoon, he was pleased to see that Mom, Aunt Claire and the girls had returned to Ridgeport from their New York trip. Uncle Phil called out for pizza and the Tates and Roberts caught up on each others' news around the dining room table. That's when Dad surprised everyone with the suggestion that they to go to Tate Lodge for some cross-country skiing.

"Work is slow right now, and I'm on a temporary lay-off. I've already checked with my sister, Rachel, and there's going to be plenty of room," Dad explained to Uncle Phil. "Sue and I can take the kids up tomorrow in the Voyager for an early start on the weekend. You and Claire could meet us there—"

"Sounds great to me. Seniority has its privileges," Uncle Phil commented. "I get off at noon on Friday and I don't have to be back 'til Tuesday." He turned to Aunt Claire, "How about you, honey?"

"Well, I've got a full day on Friday, but nothing planned for the weekend," Aunt Claire answered brightly. "I thought we'd have a little party, but we can welcome in the New Year just as well in New Hampshire as we can here. We can leave here first thing Saturday morning."

Uncle Phil frowned thoughtfully, "You got room for five rowdy teenagers, all their stuff, plus ski equipment?"

"Hey!" Denise and Danielle objected.

"Who are you calling rowdy?" Christine wanted to know.

"Certainly not you quiet and demure young ladies," Uncle Phil teased, "Indeed! I was referring to the boys."

Jet's and Hank's replies were interrupted when Dad answered Uncle Phil's question. "As long as everyone remembers he or she is packing for only four nights, and not four weeks," he laughed.

The rest of the evening was spent making plans for the weekend. Then Jet and Hank took Donna for one last walk in her neighborhood before the Tates brought her to Troy City.

As Jet had seen her do before, Donna sniffed with great interest at a particular spot in front of the vacant lot that separated Robert's from Ibarra's property. Earlier, Jet had searched there for the cause of her unusual preoccupation, but could find nothing except for tire tracks in the dirty crusty snow along the street and in the brown meadow grass flattened by the passage of many feet. If anything had been there, it had most likely been carried away by the wind, or ground into the earth.

But then, of course, the first time he'd examined the area he'd had things on his mind and hadn't really looked very hard. He'd mentioned it to the FBI agents but since they already thought they had their man, he doubted they'd act on it. If only he could convince them to get the forensics team to check it out. Perhaps if they gathered up the stuff along the road or if they raked through the dead grass poking up through the snow, maybe there was a trace of something still there that would give them a clue.

That evening, Donna had again dug at the snow-covered grass, whined a little as she sniffed the air, gave a few low-toned barks and then made to return to Ibarra's yard. Jet had all he could do to hold her back.

"No, girl. I'm sorry," he said gently, "We're not going there. We're going to my house." He stooped to ruffle the thick fur around her neck. "But you'll be back here in no time. I promise."

"That's if they find something that'll clear Mr. Ibarra," Hank added.

"Yeah, but that's doubtful," Jet said scornfully. "Usually, once they have their mind set on something, they do their best to build a case to support that idea no matter what."

"Yeah," Hank agreed, "The State Police are like that too."

"I guess it's a cop thing," Jet commented, "They need to make their case otherwise a guilty person could go free to commit whatever crime all over again."

"It goes with the job."

"I just hate when they've got it all wrong and they stubbornly won't look in a different direction. It's as though they're wearing blinders sometimes." Jet led a resistant Donna back toward Hank's house.

"Well," Hank walked beside him, "we're just kids. What do we know?"

They left the Roberts around eight o'clock. Christine went with Dad in his old Chevy work truck, while Jet rode home with Mom to get some time with the parent each child hadn't seen since Christmas.

That proved to be a good idea. Jet hadn't realized how much he'd missed his mother. It took a little getting used to having Donna's stout head jutting through the space between their seats, her long tongue dripping on his shoulder, or licking his face when he turned to speak to his mother. When they got to their County Street home, everyone stopped downstairs to see Grams and Gramps Robert, bring them up to date on the Ibarra case, and introduce them to Donna before going on up to their own apartment.

Gramps loved Donna instantly.

"Oh, my goodness!" he knelt on the floor to bring himself to her level. Gramps' watery light blue eyes, the exact shade as Jet's and Mom's, twinkled and he laughed as Donna licked his face and knocked off his wire-rimmed spectacles. He picked up his glasses and wiped them with his handkerchief. "She's just like Ebony, the black Lab I had as a boy."

But Grams seemed a little bewildered by the large black dog that was going to be a temporary guest upstairs. "Be careful, Henri," she warned.

"She's just a big baby, Liz," Gramps said rising from the floor.

It was Donna's personality that took care of Grams' misgivings when she genially smiled with her ears back, wagged her tail, and licked each of his grandparents' hands in turns. Finally, she plopped herself heavily on the rag rug in front of the door. Donna yawned and stretched out luxuriously on the carpet, refusing to move. In the end, Grams insisted they take the rag rug with them.

"It's just an old thing I made years ago," Grams said, her topaz eyes glinting happily from behind her rimless eyeglasses. "It shakes out and washes so well in the washing machine. I have another one I can put in front of the door. Since Donna seems to like this one, it'll be her rug while she's here."

Up in his room, Jet unpacked his duffel bag of dirty clothes, and repacked it with everything he needed for the weekend trip to the mountains. He tossed his laundry into the hamper in the bathroom. Finally, he checked his alarm clock to make certain it was correctly set to wake him at six. Yet, even with those things taken care of, there was still something on his mind, bugging him. But he couldn't seem to put his finger on it.

Does it have anything to do with leaving tomorrow? he wondered. He and Dad had already brought up the ski boots, poles and skis from the basement. Everything was polished and neatly laid out on the front porch to be tied onto the Voyager's roof racks in the morning. Was he fretting over tomorrow's trip?

No, he decided, *that's not it.*

He figured it must have something to do with the Ibarra case.

He'd promised Donna she'd go back home soon, but how could that happen if Mr. Ibarra was in jail on kidnapping charges and the FBI was doing all they could to prove his guilt? He was presumed innocent until proven guilty, wasn't he? But if the evidence they gathered was misinterpreted or arranged in a way that pointed to his guilt, might a jury convict an innocent man? Might he be sent to a federal prison to spend years for a crime he did not commit?

Jet knew they often offered "deals" to suspects who professed their innocence while a mountain of circumstantial evidence made the person appear to be the culprit. The accused was urged to plead guilty in exchange for fewer years in prison. Jet imagined innocent people pled out just to avoid the maximum jail time they might get if a jury believed the incriminating evidence and found them guilty. It seemed like a lousy system to him, but maybe Hank had said it best, "We're just kids. What do *we* know?" Jet wondered how many persons were serving time for crimes they had not committed while the real perpetrators enjoyed freedom at their expense. It was indeed an imperfect system.

He sat up abruptly, startling Donna who woofed and half-rose from her place on the rag rug. "It's okay, girl," Jet patted her head as he got up. She immediately collapsed back on the rug and watched him go to his desk. He booted up his computer.

Earlier, at the police station while he waited for Agents Turner and Kelly to return to their cubicles, out of curiosity and for lack of anything better to do, he'd read their evidence board. It seemed they didn't have much more than what he had himself. Granted, he didn't have a forensics lab to back up his assumptions, but he couldn't help notice that the evidence they had could go either way. In his opinion, the most damning piece of evidence on Mr. Ibarra was that he had the children last. He was the last person to see them, speak to them, touch them.

The evidence board indicated that the FBI knew Donna had howled close to three in the morning; that pinpointed the time of the kidnapping. By that time the perpetrator had already entered the house, presumably with a key, since there was no sign of force. Or maybe one of the children, probably Marissa since she was taller, had unlocked the door herself and allowed the kidnapper in. In that case, it opened a whole other realm of possibilities.

But whichever way it had happened, the children had been hustled into a waiting car outside. Then Mr. Cabot had heard a car start up just before Donna howled, just like she had today when Mr. Ibarra was taken into custody. Was it safe to assume that both times she howled because she was upset by something happening? Something she had no control over? This time, she didn't want the cops to take Mr. Ibarra away. The other night, could she have howled because she didn't want whoever-it-was to take the *children* away? Because she didn't want them to go? If she didn't want them to leave, then why didn't she "tell" Mr. Ibarra?

What was there to make of this?

Jet opened a document file and started typing his thoughts:

```
    Question #1: Why didn't Donna "tell" Mr.
Ibarra that something was wrong?
    Possible Answer #1: She didn't think any-
thing was wrong. This is what the FBI is
```

thinking. But what if she started out by thinking everything was okay, then changed her mind later? -> She howled.

Possible Answer #2: She couldn't tell Mr. Ibarra because-- She was muzzled? Could she howl if she were muzzled? Was she muzzled when Mr. Ibarra found her? The kidnapper would have had to remove it—a very risky thing to do if the dog felt her family was being threatened.

Possible Answer #3: She was ordered to be quiet. Mr. Ibarra ordered her to be quiet when she threatened the policeman who arrested him. It was hard for her to restrain herself, but she did it. Would she obey someone else as well—even if she thought the person was doing something wrong?

Possible Answer #4: She was drugged? How?

Chloroform? Too fast. Would prevent her from howling at all, even the first time. She'd be unconscious.

Sleeping powder or a knock out potion, as seen in movies, hidden in the villain's fancy ring. He mixes it in the victim's drink, then whamo! Guy's out for the count. Does it really work like that? If it's too fast, Donna wouldn't have been able to howl then, either.

Or what about some kind of tranquilizer?

Question #2: Did Mr. Ibarra notice anything odd or peculiar about Donna's behavior on Tuesday morning that would support the tranquilizer theory? Was she sluggish? Sleepy? Unsteady?

Jet felt he had to be onto something. Someone had found a way to make Donna be quiet. Otherwise, judging by the way she behaved when they took Mr. Ibarra away, Donna would have protected the children. She'd have made a lot of noise. She definitely would have hurt the kidnapper.

He typed a conclusion.

```
    Conclusion #1: Mr. Ibarra is telling the
truth; his children were kidnapped by some-
one—but not just any someone. It has to be
a person well-known to Donna; someone she
loves and trusts as much as Mr. Ibarra him-
self. Someone who could get close enough to
her to subdue her. Someone the children
trust, too. The kidnapper could not be a
stranger.
```

The only other alternative was:

```
    Conclusion #2: It was an "inside job";
Mr. Ibarra orchestrated the whole thing him-
self, and then reported the girls' disap-
pearance.
```

This second scenario seemed to be the way the FBI was leaning.

Yet motive was the pivotal point to all this. If he could figure out the reason the kidnapper took the kids in the first place, he was sure that would lead to the actual person who committed the crime.

Jet headed up a new page:

```
        Possible Motives for Kidnapping
                M. & L. Ibarra
    Motive #1: Ibarra was upset with new
custody arrangements: Wanted full custody
himself.
    Question #1: Why didn't he just run away
with them?
    Possible Answer: To throw suspicion
elsewhere.
    Besides, how would he ever be able to
enjoy having them if he couldn't be out in
the open with them? That wouldn't have been
a very good life for the girls—although
people have done it before.
    Question #2: Where would he hide them
```

```
until the heat dies down?
    Possible Answer: Not anywhere near River
Road. Somewhere isolated. Somewhere away
from Ridgeport. Maybe even out of state.
Out of the country?
    Question #3: Who would take care of them
while he was in jail?
    Answer: A friend? A relative?
```

Jet didn't like the way this was turning out. He could see how the FBI was thinking. Despite what he'd told them earlier, they still seemed bent on proving Mr. Ibarra's guilt.

Jet had to think of more wrenches to throw into the works. If he could come up with enough arguments, conflicting circumstances, other possible scenarios, they'd have to pay attention to him and find the real perpetrator.

Somebody has to prove Antonio Ibarra's innocence, Jet figured, *and it's all up to me.*

```
    Motive #2: Ransom.
    Question #1: Has there been a demand for
ransom?
    Answer: Unknown. Probably a police tactic
to keep some information away from media.
Although if someone has asked for money, why
would the police arrest Mr. Ibarra?
    Question #2: If no demand has been made,
why not?
    Answer: Kidnapper wants everyone to
sweat.
    He wants Mr. Ibarra to get the blame.
    He's waiting for something to happen.
    He's a pedophile and there won't be a
ransom demand.
```

Geesh! This was starting to weird him out. He hated to think those two little girls were with some pervert. Didn't pedophiles usually grab only one kid at a time? Didn't they work alone; if two people took the kids like he thought, then it couldn't be a pedophile, right? He hoped. He wondered if Agents Kelly and Turner had considered and ruled out this possibility.

He continued typing as another motive came to mind.

```
Motive #3: Someone else close to Donna—
not Ibarra— wants them.
Question #1: Why?
Answer: Loves them?
Question #2: Who would that be?
Answer:
```

Jet watched the cursor flashing, waiting to continue, but he couldn't come up with anything to type.

11:20 P.M.

It was late when Mary Ellen finally slid the key into the lock of the tiny Riverton apartment she shared with Aunt Tillie. As usual, the gray one-year-old tabby greeted her at the door with a low, reproachful meow, rubbed herself along Mary Ellen's legs, and led the way to the kitchen, her tail held in a high question mark.

Aunt Tillie was a godsend who had appeared on the third floor balcony one morning last December, a shivering, hungry ball of gray fluff. How she got there, Mary Ellen never did find out despite all her efforts to locate the kitten's proper owner. Like her namesake, Mary Ellen's childhood babysitter, the cat kept the FBI agent grounded to reality, giving her a reason to come home at night, and a companion to whom she could tell her troubles. Aunt Tillie was the perfect confidant. She listened attentively, narrowed her golden eyes in a wise and pensive manner, and rarely spoke.

Although, occasionally, like now, she scolded when Mary Ellen neglected her.

"Sorry it's so late, Aunt Tillie," Mary Ellen said as she put down her briefcase and picked up a plastic Christmas tree ornament from the middle of the kitchen floor. "Had yourself a little party, I see."

The cat meowed loudly in response and watched with grave interest as her human hooked the gold ball on the two-foot plastic Christmas tree on the table in front of the living room window. Tillie brushed insistently against her owner's legs as Mary Ellen went to the cupboard to get a can of cat food. Mary Ellen opened the can, scooped its contents into Tillie's bowl, and set the dish back down on the floor. Immediately, the cat hunched before her bowl and started in on her meal without ceremony, purring as Mary Ellen lightly stroked her. She often wondered how a cat could do that; purr and eat at the same time. Mary Ellen stood up, stretched and yawned, and left the cat to her supper while she got ready for bed.

It had been a long day and she was beat.

When they were done on River Road, she and John had returned to the station where the two of them had tried to make sense of the strange pieces of information they'd collected thus far. She hated having to admit that John had the only plausible explanation to the children's disappearance: Antonio Ibarra did it with an accomplice.

To his credit, John had tried to help her form a variety of scenarios, but his original theory was the only way the pieces fit; Donna not barking, the unforced door, the missing backpacks and clothes. The stolen humidifier. It was not mentioned on any of the investigators' lists, so they could only conclude that it had been taken by the perpetrator. It all left her with a disquieting thought: The kidnapper apparently knew about the children's individual needs and cared enough about them to make sure they had what they needed. As a parent would.

It made so much sense to think as John did. Maybe he was right after all.

Yet, her gut instinct told her that Ibarra was innocent. He seemed sincerely and appropriately distressed over his daughters' disappearance. Bob LaRue had told Officer Caron how he'd found Antonio "out of it," he'd said, searching for the girls on Tuesday morning. *Was that only yesterday?* And in the Interrogation Room, to Mary Ellen's trained eye at least, Ibarra had been in complete shock, seriously distraught, understandably preoccupied, and definitely worried. If he wasn't true blue, then he deserved an Oscar for Best Performance by Scum.

So why couldn't she prove he had nothing to do with his daughters' abduction?

It all hinged on that persistent impression that whoever had taken them, really cared for them. Loved them. And if the kidnapper was neither Antonio nor Carmen, then who loved them as much as they? Relatives? Like grandparents, aunts, uncles? What would prompt a relative to steal a child from kin? The valiant rescue of an abused or neglected grandchild or niece? That might have been true *before* Carmen went into detox; but certainly those fears were allayed now that she was drug free, had a good job, and seemed to be on the right track. Her new husband was completely devoted to and supportive of her.

In her flannel pajamas, Mary Ellen booted up her computer and sat down at her desk. Aunt Tillie leapt up onto the desk and nudged her human's hand with her nose.

"Only for a couple of minutes," Mary Ellen assured her. "I have to look up something before I go to bed."

She had looked at Antonio's file on her computer at the station. She knew he had no other siblings than Ramona and Luisa. She'd just met those two sisters, one of his brothers-in-law, a nephew, and his mother, all of whom had alibis. John had already called Support to have those alibis checked out as soon as possible. That left the Marine in Iraq—with a solid alibi—the brother-in-law leaving for Iraq on Tuesday, and a niece in med school.

As a New Hampshire native herself, Mary Ellen knew how long it took to make the drive to her parents' home in Sugar Hill. Now, she consulted her road atlas and calculated the distance for each trip. From Springfield, Vermont, a trip of roughly two hundred miles to Ridgeport could be reasonably made in just over three hours by car. From Suncook, New Hampshire, about one hundred twenty miles away, it would take only about two. Anyone could have made the roundtrip journey in the middle of the night without being missed the following day. She really believed the family was telling the truth and that they had actually been in Puerto Rico as they claimed. Could the same be said for the senior Marcel Bernard and Samantha Tibbs?

The question did nothing to soothe Mary Ellen's mind. It only helped bolster John's theory that Antonio Ibarra had an accomplice.

Out of earshot of his wife and sister-in-law, Dr. Tibbs had voiced his own concerns over Liana's frequent nosebleeds. If the kidnapper didn't know how to handle them, the continuous loss of blood could become a significant problem. Everyone seemed reasonably and genuinely stressed over the children's abduction, but that could mean they were simply good actors. Somehow, though, Mary Ellen felt they were all, like Antonio, sincere.

It was only a matter of planting an element of doubt in John's accomplice theory.

A click of the mouse, a few words keyed in, click again, and the first file opened before her.

> Thibault, Carmen Rosa Maria García. Born, Liverpool, U.K.
> Mother: Beverly Iris Fletcher—lingerie model/stage actress, U.K.
> Father: Alberto Manuel García—longshoreman, Cuba (emigrated 1955)
> Siblings: Conrad Alberto García, automobile salesman, Troy City, MA

A brother! Right in Troy City! Mary Ellen wondered how John could have missed this. *Humph,* she shrugged. *John has tunnel vision; his sights are so narrowly focused on proving that Antonio did it, that he has missed what was right in front of him.*

A click of the mouse brought up the brother's file and Mary Ellen quickly perused the information.

"Ha!" Mary Ellen's sudden outburst startled Aunt Tillie. The cat hissed and scooted under the bed. "Same birth date as Carmen. Funny. Maria LaRue didn't mention a twin brother."

Mary Ellen jotted down the address, then read the rest of

the file on Carmen's twin. Conrad had a wife, Cynthia Ann Webster. Apparently he'd also married an American, probably for the same reason as Carmen married Antonio; although his marriage was still intact, according to the file. Maybe they *had* married for love after all. The couple had no children, as yet.

That sent up a flag in Mary Ellen's mind: Could Conrad have kidnapped his sister's children?

She could paint a scenario as well as John could:

After a number of years married, Conrad and Cynthia find themselves childless. They see that Conrad's sister has already lost custody of her daughters once due to her questionable life-style. Now Carmen has a new husband and the court has granted her custody once more. But in their eyes, she is not worthy. She could mess up again. Who knows what might happen to the children the next time she falls off the wagon? Those little girls would be better off with them.

She would have Support check out Conrad and Cynthia García tomorrow. She knew she was grasping at straws, but if John was intent on finding a connection to Antonio, all she had to do was throw up a few "alternatives" of her own.

Recovered from her fright, Aunt Tillie walked across the keyboard, brushing Mary Ellen's chin with her fluffy tail.

"I know," Mary Ellen stroked the cat as she turned around to touch noses with her mistress. "It's time for bed."

She shut down the computer and got into her queen-sized brass bed. As she pulled up the thick quilt, Aunt Tillie sprang up and found her spot between the pillow and the headboard where she slept every night. Mary Ellen turned off the bedside lamp and lay on her back in the darkness. She let her tired body relax and as she drifted off to exhausted sleep, Mary Ellen had one last thought.

"I wonder who else out there loves those little girls like a parent does."

11:49 P.M.

Despite Dr. Solomon's little white pill, Carmen's mind would not shut down, but continued to torture her with images of Marisa and Liana in countless scenarios, each one more horrifying than the last. She tried to shut her burning eyes, but the next moment, they'd be open again, staring at the long weird shadows cast upon the ceiling by the streetlamp outside the window.

And the endless video replayed in her head. The children were hurt, bleeding, or being molested by the monster who'd taken them. They were cold, hungry, frightened, being kept in the dark.

Or maybe they were dead and their suffering was over.

Neither thought was acceptable. She had to stifle a sob.

Momentarily disturbed, Paul's gentle snoring ceased as he rolled over in his sleep. She slipped out of bed and pulled on her silk robe over her nightgown. She quietly dragged the old, threadbare Queen Anne chair over to the window, and wrapped herself in the woolen throw she kept folded over its back. Then she curled up in the chair and stared out the window at the street below.

At least now she wouldn't disrupt Paul's sleep. No need for both of them to look like wrecks tomorrow.

In court. For Antonio's arraignment and bail hearing.

They had arrested Antonio!

She couldn't believe they actually thought he had something to do with their daughters' disappearance. But she'd made a quite a scene, though, at the house, in front of the TV camera. She had seen herself on the telly, hauling off and landing him a good one. Then her horrible words so filled with animosity. It was no wonder the authorities had come to the conclusion that Antonio had done something to his own children.

Yet, it made no sense if you knew the man. He may have been a lousy husband; bossy, overbearing, a real chauvinist in the true sense of the word. But he was a good father; loving, caring, nurturing. He was a fair and just disciplinarian too, judiciously giving out punishment, always making certain the child knew what she had done to deserve it, but most importantly, always forgiving.

Of course, with *her*, Antonio had been quite the opposite. He had struck out with a vengeance when he'd found her strung out on crack that day. Funny, but all Carmen could remember was that Antonio had come home unexpectedly. She couldn't remember where the babies were, although she imagined she must have had them in a safe place, like in their cribs.

And at that moment, it suddenly dawned on her why Antonio had been so ruthless. Why he had cut her out of all their lives.

He was trying to protect the children.

Why else? Up until then, he had been such a loving husband, so devoted to her, so protective. She had been young, and he was trying to make a lady out of her. Looking back, she understood why he had demanded that she quit dancing at the Lady Slipper. He considered it demeaning work, if not dangerous. The same went for the alcohol and the drugs. It wasn't an atmosphere he wanted his children exposed to or raised in. Carmen realized he had wanted something better for *her*.

Why couldn't she see that before? Why did she have to lose everything she had before she could see what Antonio was trying to do for her? He was offering her the very life she had been looking for when she left Liverpool.

She had been so stupid.

She glanced at Paul's sleeping form. She had grown up. She had been lucky to find another man who could love her, and whom she could love in return. She wouldn't make the same mistake she had made with Antonio.

Antonio had been right to be angry. She had betrayed him, in a way. Not by cheating with another man, but by breaking trust, lying to him, going behind his back, and endangering their children. All he had asked of her was to be respectable, and she had not even been able to do that for him.

God forgive me, she prayed, *if my spiteful, angry words had anything to do with Antonio's trouble now.*

The tears she shed now were not for her children, but for Antonio.

Thursday, December 29

Antonio Ibarra woke; or rather, since he didn't think he'd actually ever fallen asleep, opened his bleary eyes to the reckless banter, the loud raucous laughter, and the banging of metal doors common to locker rooms.

Must be the change of shift, he thought closing his eyes again. *Not much to see but the cement wall.* Maybe they'd get their stuff and go away and he could finally get some sleep. He had spent better nights.

Yesterday, when he had seen the holding cell where he was to spend the next twenty hours or so, he'd become completely disheartened; yet Chuck Cabot had assured him that this was better than most. The cell was nothing more than a large, windowless cement-block enclosure with a cage door, meant to hold up to ten men or women until they could be arraigned or released, usually not longer than overnight. Metal benches anchored to the bare concrete floor lined two walls of the cell. In one of the back corners was a small open space with a metal toilet, seat and bowl molded together as one. No walls or door

185

Janet Y. Martel

for privacy. Beside it was a small metal sink. No towel; presumably, one dried one's hands on one's pants.

"Welcome to the Palace," the stout, middle-aged policeman escorting him said. "You've got the place all to yourself."

"You're lucky you got busted on a weekday. Not too much going on, now. But on weekends, now that's a different story," the tall, younger cop stated with a chuckle. "I've seen this cell packed on Saturday with everyone waiting until court convenes on Monday morning. Nothing like spending the weekend at the Palace." This one swung the door open while the other removed Antonio's handcuffs.

Antonio stepped inside the holding cell with trepidation, and gripped the chain link with both hands as the cage door was locked behind him.

"You'll be okay. It's only for one night," Chuck Cabot tried to reassure him. "I'll be back in the morning to get you ready for court. I don't see any reason why we can't get you out on bail."

Antonio didn't trust himself to speak. He merely met his attorney's serious dark brown eyes, and clamped his lips tightly together trying to control the quivering of his chin. Chuck touched the fingers of Antonio's right hand where they wrapped around the chain link; all he could manage for a handshake.

"Get some sleep," Chuck advised him.

And then Cabot turned and walked away. Antonio swallowed hard as he took in the fact that he was alone in this awful place. How had this happened? How could they think he had anything to do with his little girls' disappearance?

Antonio impatiently brushed away hot, angry tears and pushed away from the cage door. He squashed his feelings of self-pity, determined not to let the police break his spirits. He distracted himself by taking in the amenities—or lack thereof—of his bare cell.

Get some sleep? Not likely.

Antonio tested one of the benches. It felt hard and cold, even through his clothes. There was no pillow, no blanket.

How could he sleep? Nonetheless, he stretched out on his side, folded his arm beneath his head, and closed his eyes. Although there was no light in the cell itself, a harsh spotlight burned in the hallway right outside. It glared obnoxiously in his eyes. He repositioned himself so that he faced the cinderblock wall. Hopefully, once his body warmed the metal bench, it might not be too bad.

He must have dozed off, because sometime later—he had no way of knowing what time it was since they'd taken his watch—he started and sat up quickly. The older policeman was opening the cell to admit a limp form being half-dragged half-supported by the younger cop. The semi-conscious man was gently placed on the bench closest to the door.

"There you go, Harvey," the older cop said genially, "You sleep it off. We'll let you out in the morning."

Harvey mumbled drunken gibberish, belched loudly and passed out. The cops chuckled and the cell door jangled shut again.

Antonio settled himself on the bench, trying to find the position he'd had before but couldn't seem to get comfortable. For one thing, during the short time he'd sat up the metal bench had cooled off and now his body had to warm it again. He managed to put his discomfort out of his mind, but by then Harvey had started snoring loudly, a deep-throated sonorous rattle punctuated by high-pitched squeaks and whistles. Antonio folded his free arm over his ear to block out the noise. He had started to drift off when he was shocked to full-consciousness again, this time by a horrible retching and the sound of gallons of liquid splashing on the floor. Antonio recognized what it was even before the sickeningly sweet smell of booze-puke reached his nostrils.

To hell with them all! he thought, refusing to call for help. The way things were going, he wouldn't have been surprised if they had made *him* clean up Harvey's mess. He hunkered himself down and covered his nose with his free hand.

That was the last he remembered until the day shift started to arrive. Maybe he had slept after all, out of sheer exhaustion.

Realizing he wasn't going to sleep anymore, Antonio gingerly sat up on the bench and stretched his cramped, aching muscles.

"Humph," he muttered, noting the drunk still sleeping it off on the other bench. He'd finally stopped snoring. *Figures, now that it's time to get up.*

He rose slowly to his feet and mindful of Harvey's mess on the floor, carefully skirted the half-dried vomit, surprised that it had sounded worse than it actually was. Nonetheless, he was in enough trouble now without adding stepping in semi-dried puke and carrying that stench into the courtroom.

He made his way to the toilet area where he took care of business. Next, he splashed cold water onto his face and flinched as he rubbed the bruise Carmen had given him. The water felt good on his tired, burning eyes, though. He figured they must be bloodshot from the bad night he'd had. He didn't need a mirror to know that his five o'clock shadow had to be looking like ten after eleven. He rubbed the side of his index finger against his front teeth, slurped water from the faucet, swished it around his mouth, and spit it out. For lack of a comb, he ran his wet fingers through his disheveled hair. If he could at least get the hair to look better, maybe he'd appear less grubby, less unsavory, less mean.

Less guilty.

He sat back down on the edge of his bench, and with his elbows resting on his knees, dropped his face into his hands.

7:26 A.M.

Jules Tate, the master packer and stacker, looked at the array of ski equipment and suitcases strewn around the Voyager and wondered how he had thought he could get everything in there, and still have room for seven people and a large dog. But since he had boasted to Phil that he could, do it he would or die trying. Failure was no option; Phil would never let him live it down.

Just then, Phil's Explorer pulled up to the curb, and his

three teenagers tumbled out of the vehicle with *their* gear and even more bags. Jules waved and smiled, hoping he didn't look as flustered as he felt.

"Gee, this looks like an awful lot of stuff," Phil commented. "Are you sure you don't want me to take some of this up on Saturday?"

"No, I think I can get it all in," Jules tried not to bristle. "It's all a matter of finding the right shaped package for the right shaped hole."

"Well," Phil said, misgiving sounding in his voice, "just remember that if you can't, the offer holds." Then his brother-in-law sauntered toward the house, leaving Jules alone with his problem. "Let me know if you need any help," Phil called from the porch.

"Sure thing!" Jules waved back gritting his teeth.

A half hour later, with Jet's and Hank's help, Jules set the last bag in place, closed the Voyager's hatch, and stepped back to admire his accomplishment. He'd done it! Granted, lots of stuff was tied down to the roof racks, making the minivan a bit top heavy, but if he took it easy on the highway there shouldn't be a problem.

When Phil came out, he whistled, "Great job, Jules. I never thought you'd get it all in." Jules happily accepted his congratulatory slap on the back. Then Phil, pretending to look under the vehicle, teased, "You didn't kick some stuff under there, did you?"

By now, everyone was outside and ready to go. His in-laws came out to the driveway to see them off with last minute hugs and kisses, and Elizabeth Robert shoved little plastic bags of her chocolate chip cookies into everyone's pockets.

"To snack on," she said. "Eating helps relieve the boredom."

"So where's the milk to go with them?" Jules teased. He laughed out loud at his mother-in-law's perplexed expression, "Just kidding, Ma."

"We'll call you at Midnight on New Year's Eve," Susan Tate promised as she kissed her father goodbye.

Moments later, everyone was belted in, and the loaded minivan trundled off to begin the two-hundred-twenty-mile trip.

9:38 A.M.

Mary Ellen Kelly's day was not going well. It had started out badly and no matter how well she'd planned for all contingencies, everything seemed to be going downhill.

Although she'd slept well enough and had enjoyed the extra time in bed this morning, she felt groggy when she jolted awake to the strident shrieking of the alarm clock. She staggered to the shower, got the coffee going, and fed Aunt Tillie all on automatic pilot, her sleepy mind consumed by the puzzling pieces of the Ibarra case.

She only really woke up when the blow dryer started to act up. First, there was the sickening smell of burning hair immediately followed by blue and yellow sparks. She yanked the plug from the wall as her thumb turned off the bewitched appliance. *Why today of all days?* She tried combing her still-damp hair in her usual style; what her mother liked to call a pageboy. But although it curled under nicely, it refused to fluff, and looked rather flat. She wasted a few more minutes before she finally brushed it all back and made a French twist.

Her luck continued its downward slide as she dressed, beginning with the run she put into her hose before she even had them on. She tore them off and managed to get on the second pair without mishap. Last night, she had selected her navy blue suit to wear, coupled with a neat white blouse and pearl studs and matching solitary pearl pendant. This morning, after she had made her bed, she had carefully laid out the suit. However, when she picked up the skirt from the bed, she was annoyed to see that Aunt Tillie had apparently made herself comfortable on it while Mary Ellen had been in the shower, leaving behind a generous amount of fur. She was able to remove the bulk of the cat hair with a lint brush, and hoped she wouldn't look like a frump.

She headed out to the small kitchen for breakfast. Determined that today she'd get a grip on the facts and make them mean something that would help rather than hurt Antonio Ibarra, she decided she had to have more than a cholesterol-filled doughnut on the way to his arraignment. She prepared a bowl of Cheerios and milk, then added some sliced banana. Next she poured herself a glass of orange juice and a mug of coffee and placed everything on a tray which she brought to the coffee table in the living room. She clicked on the TV set and sat on the sofa to watch the last bit of morning news while she ate her breakfast.

Nothing new, it seemed.

The weather would not be as cold as yesterday. Although there had been snow overnight in the mountains, the sun was expected to shine and temperatures today would reach thirty-two degrees, maybe even forty along the coast.

The weather was followed by a short piece about the missing Ibarra girls. Their pictures were shown on the screen as the anchor segued to the next item: The Ibarra arrest. The footage showing Antonio Ibarra being led away in handcuffs was immediately followed with the tape of Carmen's outrageous accusation of Tuesday afternoon.

Mary Ellen couldn't bear to watch it or listen to anymore of the reporter's insinuations. She pushed the off button on the remote with a little too much enthusiasm and somehow managed to knock the breakfast tray off the coffee table. The contents crashed onto the hardwood floor. The coffee mug and cereal bowl sloshed the remains of their contents across the room and the empty juice glass shattered into a thousand pieces.

Shoot!

Aunt Tillie immediately began lapping up the spilled milk with happy alacrity. Mary Ellen matched her speed and scooped up the animal to shut her in the bathroom where she would stay out of harm's way while her mistress cleaned up the mess with many paper towels and a dust pan and broom.

Just then, a car horn sounded in the street below: John.

The quick clean up had to be good enough for the time being. The floor would have to be washed later. Hopefully, the numerous, tiny shards of glass had all been picked up so that Aunt Tillie would not cut herself.

Aunt Tillie flew out of the bathroom in a flurry of fur as her human opened the door to that room. Mary Ellen quickly brushed her teeth and applied a touch of lipstick. Then, grabbing her coat and briefcase, she hurried down the stairs to her waiting ride.

John seemed to be in a good mood. He'd been busy. As he drove to the courthouse for the ten o'clock arraignment, he filled her in on everything he'd already accomplished.

He'd called Support and was only mildly disappointed to find out that the sisters' story checked out. They'd arrived in Ponce, Puerto Rico, on Friday night and had left on the last flight out on Tuesday, arriving in Providence early Wednesday morning. That meant there was no way either of them could have been Antonio's accomplice.

"But, that's okay. They're checking out Marcel Bernard, Sr., and Samantha Tibbs as we speak. We're narrowing down the field," he said with confidence. "Sooner or later, we'll find Ibarra's partner in crime." He glanced toward Mary Ellen and happily continued as he parked the car in the lot behind the courthouse. "I even spoke with Anita Pimental. She assured me that the Commonwealth would prosecute Antonio Ibarra to the full extent of the law."

Mary Ellen was not happy to hear this. Although Anita Pimental was the newest addition to the D.A.'s office, she had already proven herself a vigorous prosecutor with the tenacity of a pit bull. If she had her mind set on bringing down Antonio Ibarra, then he was all but buried.

John finished after they'd gone through the security gate in the lobby of the courthouse, "The longer Ibarra resists telling us what he's done with the children, the worse it'll be for him. Eventually, he'll cave and tell who's helping him."

Although Antonio's case was first on the docket, he would not be the only person arraigned this morning. Spectators, attorneys, plaintiffs, and witnesses in other cases were scattered throughout the courtroom. John took the lead down the center aisle.

On the way to their places, Mary Ellen saw Carmen and Paul Thibault seated together halfway up on the left behind the defense. Both were subdued and clutched each others' hands in mutual support. That Carmen had been crying was evident by her puffy, bloodshot gray-green eyes. The couple acknowledged Mary Ellen's whispered greeting with grim, silent nods.

She followed John into the row of seats directly behind the prosecutor's table. Ruth Wilson slid over to allow them room. John preceded her into the row to sit beside Ruth, and Mary Ellen sat on the end.

Mary Ellen glanced across the aisle and noticed that Dr. and Mrs. Tibbs and Antonio's mother occupied the seats directly behind the defense. There was no one else in the row. Apparently, Luisa and Butch Bernard had flown back to New Hampshire last night as they'd intended.

Mary Ellen nodded their way as a kind of greeting. But Mrs. Ibarra had her eyes closed, her hands in her lap fingering her prayer beads. Although Dr. Tibbs smiled wanly back at her, Mrs. Tibbs shot her a murderous look. There was no use trying to explain that these proceedings were compulsory and had nothing to do with her personal viewpoint on the case. Yet she was certain that to Antonio's loved ones, Mary Ellen's presence on this side of the courtroom screamed out that everything she'd told these people last night was a lie. Mary Ellen was distressed by the woman's justifiable anger, and sadly directed her attention elsewhere.

Anita Pimental had her back to them. She was a pretty woman whose short amber curls, green-eyed smile, and small build belied not only her age, but her resourcefulness and ability as a prosecutor as well. One who didn't know her might perceive her diminutive stature and perky personality as signs of youthful naiveté, unassuming softness, or even childlike weakness; all to their unfortunate chagrin. At a half-inch over five feet tall, the thirty-nine-year-old attorney was the complete opposite of the image she portrayed. Anita Pimental had an impressive twelve-year reputation as a successful criminal defense attorney. Three years ago, sick of defending and exonerating the guilty and saving them from well-deserved punishment, she'd switched sides of the courtroom. She was tough and ambitious. Some would even call her ruthless. Troy County had done well to acquire her as its newest assistant district attorney.

Mary Ellen watched the A.D.A. professionally attired in a white wool skirted suit and light brown silk blouse. Gold stud earrings gleamed beneath her soft amber curls, and a wide gold chain peeked behind the V-neck of her blouse. As she shuffled documents in her opened briefcase, the woman sensed their arrival and turned to greet them with a friendly smile. John placed a hand over hers on the rail between them.

"Good luck," he said.

"Thanks, but I don't need luck, Special Agent Turner," she smiled broadly. "We have the facts on our side." The A.D.A. graced Mary Ellen with a quick smile and a nod and turned her attention to the front of the courtroom as the bailiff called the room to order.

All rose as the Honorable Judge Javier Rivera quickly entered the courtroom, his black robes billowing out around him like the wings of a great bird of prey. Mary Ellen recognized the name from the arrest warrant but had never met the man personally. Now she looked him over with acute interest.

Judge Rivera was tall enough, perhaps six-one or -two, and of slender build with a mass of dark brown hair interspersed with silver. As he approached the bench, he alertly surveyed his court with sharp dark brown eyes, spaced a little too close to his aquiline nose. His lips were set in a tight, grim line, partly hidden by a salt and pepper Van Dyke. The beard was painstakingly trimmed to a point, giving one the impression that he possessed an angular chin. He had a reputation for swift, sound judgment and strict but fair sentences.

Mary Ellen next turned her attention to the pitiful form of Antonio Ibarra standing beside his counsel, Charles Cabot, Esq. While Cabot looked dapper in his three-piece charcoal gray suit, crisp white shirt and blue silk tie, Antonio looked like he'd slept in his clothes; which she supposed he probably had. He wore the same blue flannel shirt they'd arrested him in yesterday. Today it was rumpled, but neatly tucked into his beltless jeans. His hair had been plastered down with lots of water and severely slicked back. He'd apparently shaved and groomed his pencil-thin mustache, but whatever razor had been afforded him did not measure up to his usual clean shave. Instead, the shadow of his beard still darkened his face. Coupled with the bright purple-red bruise that outlined his left jaw, he looked surly and disreputable. He regarded the judge with somber, bloodshot eyes.

Once the judge was seated, the rest of the assembly also sat. Antonio's name was called and he and Cabot stood as the charge was read aloud: two counts of kidnapping.

"How do you plead?" asked Judge Rivera.

Antonio and his counsel rose. "Not guilty, Your Honor," Antonio answered for himself. His voice was steady and confident, yet humble and without arrogance. Cabot had schooled him well. After he'd entered his plea, both men sat down again.

Anita Pimental immediately stood up and asked that bail be denied. Her argument was concise and to the point. As she'd said earlier, she had the facts. Mary Ellen was not surprised that the A.D.A. was ready to use everything they'd found so far in a way that would incriminate Antonio Ibarra of kidnapping his little girls. Besides the evidence found in his home and vehicle, his lack of cooperation with police and the FBI was being viewed as belligerence, further compounding the case against him.

Charles Cabot had his hands full.

When it was his turn to speak, Cabot stood and gave a number of reasons why Antonio Ibarra should be allowed to post bond, emphasizing the fact the he had no previous record, and with his job with the electricians Union, flight was unlikely.

Yet the judge had the final say, "The court understands that up until now, Mr. Ibarra has been an upright citizen, a hard-working individual, and an honest person. However, the court must also take into account the fact that Mr. Ibarra has not been forthcoming with the police in their investigation into the disappearance of Marisa and Liana Ibarra—"

Mary Ellen could see where this was going. Apparently, so did Charles Cabot. He did a very risky thing. He interrupted the judge, "If I may, Your Honor, Antonio Ibarra is a rule-follower, and certainly will not break the law. It's a cultural thing. For Mr. Ibarra, breaking this trust, breaking the law, would bring dishonor to his mother—"

"Mr. Cabot, that's a very beautiful sentiment," Judge Rivera's smile did little to hide his ire, "although, I imagine there are many Hispanics in prison who thought little of cultural ethics when they broke the law that landed them behind bars. Save it for your closing argument." Cabot clamped his mouth shut and Mary Ellen saw a smug smile curl up the corner of Anita Pimental's lips. "Assistant District Attorney Pimental has a point," the judge continued. "Mr. Ibarra's lack of cooperation is a tangible sign that he has something to hide, an indication that he knows more than he is saying. And that only increases the possibility that he would indeed flee, despite his high regard for the Fourth Commandment." Cabot flushed. "Besides that, the court must take into account the evidence that has been presented," Judge Rivera glanced toward the A.D.A. who now was making no effort to hide her joy. "Due to the severity of the charges against the defendant, the court must find in favor of the prosecution. Bail is denied. Perhaps some time in a jail cell will encourage Mr. Ibarra to be more helpful." With a slam of the gavel, Antonio was immediately remanded into custody. He would spend the time from then until his trial in the county jail.

Triumphant, Anita turned to face John and Ruth. They were so occupied chatting like old friends that neither of them noticed that Mary Ellen was not taking part in their little celebration. It was just as well. Mary Ellen felt sick and really had nothing to say.

She watched Antonio being led away in handcuffs. He

looked to be in shock and merely shook his head. If he said anything, it was not within her range of hearing. She did hear Charles Cabot try to reassure him.

"It'll be okay, Tony," Cabot promised.

As the judgment was given, there had been audible gasps and moans from the other side of the courtroom. Now, Mary Ellen could see Dr. and Mrs. Tibbs physically supporting Mrs. Ibarra, moving her toward the doors as she sobbed into a crumpled tissue. The Thibaults, Paul's arm protectively around his wife's shoulders, followed the family. As they exited the courtroom, Carmen turned and shot Mary Ellen a final tearful glance. To Mary Ellen, they all looked pitiful and helpless and she felt like a cad to have been a part of this sham.

This wasn't justice. She knew in her heart that Antonio had not kidnapped his children. There had to be a way to prove that. She had the same facts John did. It's just that they were looking at them in different ways. If John was going to do all that he could to help the prosecution, there had to be something she could do to aid the defense. What she needed to do was focus on what she knew—on what they all knew—about the case, without embellishment or twisting of the facts.

Before she knew it, she was dodging patches of ice, puddles, and Bedford Street traffic, trying to keep up with the other three. At Anita Pimental's insistence, Ruth Wilson and the FBI agents were joining the A.D.A. for lunch at The Court Café which occupied the ground floor of the Adams Building where Pimental had her office.

In warmer weather, the popular restaurant on the corner of Bedford and Main offered lunch on wrought iron chairs and tables with parasols that dotted the cobblestone walkway, reminiscent of a Parisian sidewalk café. But winter was no time for eating outdoors and the group hurried into the warmth of the foyer. A smiling hostess met the foursome at the door and despite the lunch crowd that already packed the place, they were immediately seated at a table reserved for members of the D.A.'s staff.

Mary Ellen absent-mindedly scanned her menu while Ruth,

John, and Anita happily chatted like school chums. It seemed to have become a celebratory lunch, although Mary Ellen believed they were jumping the gun. They hadn't proved Antonio's guilt, nor had they found the Ibarra children; facts that seemed to have gone unnoticed or ignored by the three of them.

When the waitress approached to take their orders, Mary Ellen's three companions quickly requested full course meals that included soup or salad, yet she found herself still undecided. The problem was she just wasn't hungry. She settled for a chef's salad and a Diet Coke.

"Watching your figure?" Anita Pimental's green eyes glinted as she picked a cat hair off the shoulder of Mary Ellen's suit jacket.

Mary Ellen smiled, hoping it appeared genuine, and did not betray her true feelings.

11:52 A.M.

Elizabeth Robert needn't have worried about the boredom of the long trip to Tate Lodge. Jules regaled everyone with his preposterous stories and silly jokes, and the miles sped by. They stopped only once north of Concord for gas and a nature-call for everyone, including Donna. The teenagers got involved in their own conversations after that, leaving Jules free to concentrate on driving.

So involved were they in their chatter that no one realized it when Jules left the Interstate and turned south on Route 302. Now he took a left turn and drove the Voyager under a canopy of pine branches and onto a wide paved driveway between high mounds of plowed snow.

Soon, Jules caught sight of Tate Lodge. His own great grandfather, Cornelius Tate, had built the original Swiss chalet for his beautiful bride almost a hundred years ago. The chalet had been home to other Tates and over time two large wings were added on converting the over-sized log cabin into an inn: Tate Lodge. It always gave Jules a surge of emotion when he saw what he thought of as the "Old Homestead." For Jules, it wasn't an inn; it was home.

Now he could see the place had been decorated for Christmas. All of the low shrubs and evergreens close to the building had been strung with tiny white lights, each window glowed with a white candle, and twin wreaths with big red bows hung on the double front doors. From the number of vehicles parked in the lot, it looked like the Lodge had plenty of Holiday vacationers.

He parked the Voyager close to the paved walkway that led to the large oak doors, and everyone helped unload the car. After the comfortable, heated interior of the Voyager, the cold New Hampshire wind was like a sharp slap in the face, and the group hurried up the sidewalk, eager to enter the Lodge.

Sick of her long confinement in the minivan, Donna was happy to be out and frisked off across the snow-covered yard where she picked up the scent of a rabbit. Her paws left large traces and her snout plowed a trough in the previously untouched snow. Excited with her find, she chased her quarry into the woods, her nose to the ground.

"You'd better go after her, son," Jules advised Jet. "We can manage this stuff without you."

Jules watched the boy run after the dog with a leash as the rest of the group went inside. He was certain he was doing the right thing by taking his loved ones away from the heartrending and hopeless drama unfolding in Ridgeport. Everyone had been so deeply affected by the disappearance of the little Ibarra girls; but it had been hardest on Jet who seemed to be hell-bent on solving the problems of the world. Jules didn't know which would impact his son more; finding the children's dead bodies, or not finding them at all. He hoped this trip would get Jet's mind off the case, even if only for a little while.

Jules sighed and followed the others inside to be enveloped with the comforting warmth of the place, and the enticing smell of homemade chicken soup. He closed his eyes and inhaled deeply as he set down his bags, taking in the surroundings of his childhood.

Janet Y. Martel

The sitting room had not changed, although it had been decorated for the Holidays. Two monstrous poinsettias stood sentry on either side of a cheery, snapping fire blazing in the hearth of the enormous fieldstone fireplace. Above the hearth, the heavy dark walnut mantel still held the softly ticking antique anniversary clock; but around the clock, placed on white cotton snow, were the dainty figures of a Christmas village complete with a miniature Nativity scene. Mounted on the massive stone chimney was the head of an elk, presumably shot by Cornelius Tate himself. Someone—probably Rachel—had exercised a bit of Holiday levity by hanging six shiny red Christmas balls on each point of the elk's antlers.

The orange glow of the fire reflected off the polished hardwood floor between two brown leather couches. Red poinsettias were scattered about the room and graced various flat surfaces, including the coffee table in between the couches that faced each other; a comfortable place for conversation.

Curving upward to left and right were twin staircases that led to the guest rooms. Their long banisters had been wrapped with garlands of holly interspersed with tiny white lights. Standing on the living room floor inside the bend of each stairway were two huge Christmas trees, at least fourteen feet tall, trimmed with white lights, gold metallic streamers, and red velvet bows.

Between the edge of the stairs and the front windows of the Lodge were identical short passageways. They led to matching archways decorated with mistletoe. Beyond the archways could be seen dining tables covered in green and red linen tablecloths and napkins with more poinsettias as centerpieces. Soft music and the voices of diners spilled from one of the dining rooms, apparently the source of the wonderful aroma of chicken soup.

As the clock chimed noon, Rachel and Greg Barlow rushed out to greet their family and guests with introductions, and hugs and kisses all around.

Greg Barlow was a jovial, burly, barrel-chested man, slightly shorter than Jules, with the round, freckled face often attributed to redheads. For as long as Jules had known him,

Greg kept his fiery red hair in a brush cut. As he clasped hands with his brother-in-law and hugged him ferociously, Greg's flushed face seemed to make the ends of his bristly hair glow orange and sheer pleasure shone in his dark brown eyes.

"Welcome home! Welcome home!" he chortled.

Then it was Rachel's turn; Jules's little sister. At five-foot seven-inches, Rachel was taller than the Tate women who had come before her; but she, like them, was slender and small-boned, giving her a delicate, feminine appearance. Her fair complexion, black hair and deep blue eyes were true Tate features. She turned smiling eyes up to her brother and squeezed him tightly.

"You guys just don't come up often enough!" she gently reproached him.

Rather than give her a lame excuse—work, responsibilities, the kids, no time, blah-blah-blah—Jules simply agreed with her, "I know, Rachel."

Further comment was interrupted by the sound of running feet on the wide wooden stair treads. Jules's attention was drawn to the tall, gangly youth, barreling down the stairs as though someone had yelled "Fire!" The boy's feet thumped solidly on the landing.

"Patrick!" Rachel gave him an admonishing look, "Remember we have other guests."

At fourteen, true to his Tate heritage, the youth had the trademark thick black hair and blue eyes. He looked at his mother apologetically and advanced on the company with a bit more reserve. As he made the rounds with kisses and hugs, his older sister made her entrance.

Although she descended in a hurry, she managed to step lightly on the bare treads, making hardly a sound. Eighteen-year-old, red-haired, tawny-eyed Rebecca was indeed her father's daughter, but nature had graciously given her Rachel's build and grace. She also was spared her father's freckles; none were visible on her pretty face.

"But where's Jet?" Rebecca inquired.

"I'm afraid we have another guest with us; a black Labrador retriever." Jules explained, "She went after a rabbit and he's out there chasing her."

The adult Tates and the three girls were shown to adjacent rooms on the second floor of the original homestead, while Jet and Hank, in consideration of Donna, were assigned the closest available cabin to the Lodge. There was little opportunity for mischief this far away from civilization, so putting them out there without adult supervision seemed a safe thing to do.

"Once you're settled in, round up the kids and come back downstairs," Rachel told Jules and Susan. "You're just in time for lunch."

2:37 P.M.

Jet smiled as he watched Donna happily romping ahead. She frisked across the snow-covered trails, rolled in the new powder that had fallen last night, snuffled under the low boughs of evergreen trees, and enthusiastically tracked the scent of an unseen rabbit.

Jet wished he had her energy. Cross-country skiing was hard work, especially when one had to go uphill. Thankfully, a rewarding gentle downward slope followed the effort. Of course the chance to rest and coast was short-lived; there was always the next grade to ascend.

Jet was a bit out of shape, as he always got between the end of baseball season and the beginning of ski season. This year, he'd gone out for track, believing it would help. He supposed it did somewhat; he was keeping up with Becky and Pat who were much more accustomed to this activity than any of the others in the group. Yet Jet's breathing was labored, his lungs and muscles were burning, and he could feel a trail of sweat trickling down his back inside his ski suit. He and his Barlow cousins had outstripped the other teenagers and the adults. The others lagged a good hundred yards behind.

"Hey, you guys," he called out to Pat and Becky, trying not to pant, "What d'ya say we wait up for the others?"

"Whassamatta?" demanded Patrick beaming, "Tired?"

"Naw, not really," Jet lied, letting himself fall on his behind in a pile of snow, "Just bein' polite."

"Yeah, sure."

"Jet's right, Pat," agreed Becky brushing off a rock to sit on, "We ought to wait for the girls and Uncle Jules and Aunt Sue. I don't want to look like a snob, and besides," she added, "we wouldn't want them to get lost."

"You wuss," Patrick chided. "They can't get lost if they keep to the trail." But he gave in and the threesome sat together catching their breath.

Donna, however, continued on her happy romp, heedless that her people had stopped. When Jet called to her, she immediately halted to look back at him but did not return to where he sat. Instead, she turned her attention to something going on ahead. She stood like a statue; her nose pointing forward, smelling the air; her tail out, curled gently upward, not wagging; the right front paw raised from the ground.

"She's pointing," Patrick said knowledgeably.

"I've never seen her do that before," said Jet.

"Must smell a deer or an elk."

"I'd better go get her," Jet struggled to his feet and skied toward the dog. But as he got within reach, Donna bounded forward. "Come on back, you stupid dog, or else next time I'll put you on your leash!"

Donna ignored him. She ran ahead and disappeared over a hill. There was nothing for Jet to do but follow her; it wouldn't do to let her get lost in the woods. What would he tell Mr. Ibarra?

Jet pumped up the knoll and as he reached the top, he saw the black dog, leaping over mounds of snow, kicking up clouds of white powder. Jet pushed off after her. He heard her yelp excitedly as she ran toward one of the log cabins.

There was some kind of activity going on down there involving a group of three people; a man and two kids. One of the children was yelling something. Then the adult was scooping up the smaller one and grabbing the other by the hand. In the commotion, the latter one fell and the man literally dragged the child into the cabin. As the dog scrambled toward the door, it quickly closed, shutting her out.

She sat outside and howled.

By the time Jet glided down to her, Donna was sniffing the ground outside the cabin, concentrating intently on the flattened snow around an unfinished snowman. She picked up a scent and followed it to the cabin door where she whined loudly and began to dig.

Movement at one of the windows caused Jet to look there. He was met with two large brown eyes filled with emotion. But it was only a quick glimpse, for a hand gripped the child's shoulder and pulled him away, and as the red chintz curtains were tightly pulled together, Jet heard a man's voice order the boy to stay away from the window. Other than a thin plume of smoke rising from the chimney, there was no sign of life, no further sound coming from within. Whoever the people were, they had been frightened by the dog. Jet could picture the two children huddled in the arms of their parent, trembling in fear.

Mortified, Jet grabbed Donna by her collar. "Sorry!" he yelled to the people inside the cabin, "It won't happen again." Then he scolded the dog as he led her away, "Come on, you bad dog. This isn't where we live." Donna was reluctant to come with him and kept trying to return to the cabin so that he had to get firm with her. "Come on, I said. If you can't behave, we'll have to leave you tied outside the cabin when we go skiing."

Finally, the dog gave in and allowed Jet to guide her away. At the same moment, the rest of the group caught up with him and after he'd explained what had happened, Dad said, "I think you're right, Jet. If she can't be trusted not to bother the other guests, we'll have to keep her inside the cabin, or on a leash."

3:13 P.M.

When they returned to the Lodge, the Barlow kids had to get to their daily chores, so were not part of the group enjoying the warmth of the fire. Jet and Hank sat cross-legged on the floor in front of the fireplace, allowing Jet's parents, Christine, and the twins to sit on the two sofas. With cups of hot cocoa all around, the family laughed and talked enthusiastically about their outing.

But Jet did not take part in the lively conversation. Instead, his mind wandered off to thoughts of Donna. In consideration of guests who had allergies to animal hair, the dog was not brought into the main house, but was safely locked inside the boys' cabin.

What had gotten into her? Why had she charged those children? She'd interrupted the little boys making a snowman. Apparently, she'd heard their voices before she'd actually seen them since when she'd "pointed" the kids had still been out of sight. Then, when they came into view, she'd shot down that hill as though possessed, yelping as she ran. Funny, it hadn't sounded threatening in any way. At least, not to Jet it didn't. But *something* had scared those kids; or rather their father. He'd grabbed the smaller one and tucked him under his arm, then dragged the other boy by the hand. He'd hurried them all into the cabin and slammed the door.

Then Donna howled. *Again.* Crazy. A dog who'd never howled before in her life had done so three times in as many days.

"Earth to Jet," Hank stood over him and nudged him with the side of his foot.

Jet shook himself. Everyone had left. Only he and Hank remained in the living room. Even his sticky mug had disappeared. Someone must have relieved him of it while he was daydreaming.

"Sorry," he muttered as he took Hank's extended hand and got up from the floor, the top of his ski suit hanging at his waist. "I phased out."

"Big time," Hank agreed.

Jet pulled on his ski suit and went out the front door with Hank close on his heels.

"What's up, man?" Hank asked. "You're really spaced

out."

"Thinking," Jet aimed his steps toward their cabin.

"About what?"

"Donna." Jet frowned at his cousin, "Does she seem threatening to you? I mean, besides when Mr. Ibarra was arrested, have you ever heard her growl at anyone?"

"Yeah," Hank said emphatically. "She used to growl at me when I delivered the newspaper." Then his tone softened, "But she hasn't done that for a long time; though she still barks at me."

"And does that sound menacing?"

"No." Hank smirked at that preposterous notion, "She's accepted us as friends. And now since we've been around her so much, we're practically family."

They'd arrived at their cabin and Jet said nothing more as he slid the key into the lock. At the sound of their footsteps, Donna had started barking loudly; a clear challenge to any stranger entering the place. Jet turned the key in the lock and opened the door. Immediately, Donna's bark changed from one of alarm and warning to whimpers of happiness. She hopped about like a puppy, her tail wagging fiercely. Her yelps were full of delight and welcome. They sounded a lot like those she'd made as she scrambled toward the cabin earlier. Jet couldn't believe the man had thought the dog meant to attack his sons. But for some reason, he'd acted as though he needed to get the children away from the dog at all cost. As though their lives depended on it.

Jet wondered why.

3:19 P.M.

Ever since Judge Rivera's decision to deny bail for Antonio Ibarra and the ensuing victory lunch with Ruth Wilson and Anita Pimental, John had been insufferable. Upon returning to the Ridgeport PD, he'd gone about giving orders to everybody, throwing his weight around, trying to dig up as much dirt as possible on Ibarra, under the guise of getting a lead on the whereabouts of his missing daughters. He mercilessly and tirelessly delved into the man's private life. Who were his friends? Did he have a girlfriend? Did he own other property or rent storage space? Had he recently made any travel plans?

Although Mary Ellen knew it was all part of chasing down evidence against the suspect, she was sickened by John's determination in nailing, in her opinion, an innocent man. She'd been in on the collar, and now to alleviate her feelings of guilt for letting Ibarra down, she buried herself in her work, frantic to find something that would point the finger at someone else, something she'd overlooked before. She was determined to prove Antonio's innocence.

Around three o'clock, she got on the computer in her cubicle, hoping she'd find what she needed online. She needed to do some sleuthing on her own, without John looking over her shoulder.

She really liked having him as a partner, but at the moment, she couldn't help but feel angry and frustrated by John's smug attitude. Even though she realized it wasn't serving anyone to let the wound fester, she couldn't talk to him about it because she feared it would start another argument; or, more disturbingly, that she'd cry. She therefore internalized and hid her true feelings from him and spoke to him with nothing more than abrupt questions and short retorts. The result had been that they'd stopped talking to each other. She was surprised by how painful that was; they were acting like a married couple on the brink of divorce. It wasn't good for the partnership, and it certainly didn't help the case.

As the online connection was made, a chime alerted her to new email. She automatically typed in her password and opened her mailbox. She scanned the list of new mail, discarding or scrolling past most items as unimportant and to be read later.

Suddenly, her eyes spotted a new sender which caused her to gasp. It was simply called JET, and the opening message said he was forwarding her "something that could mean something."

She looked about her surreptitiously, making sure that John was busily occupied before opening Jet's email. With one ear listening for someone coming up behind her, she scanned the message, regretting that she felt insecure and nervous reading it at the office, and wishing she could do this at home instead. The experience of working with Jet in the past had taught her that the kid had amazing insight coupled with a purity of thought; a certain innocence that lent a whole different perspective to the meager facts they had with which to work. She felt she couldn't put off reading the email until later.

Mary Ellen was surprised by how close he was to what the FBI had actually come up with. He'd said in a short note that he was only sounding off and that if he happened to suggest something the agents hadn't previously thought about, he trusted her to follow up on it.

She was amused by his diplomacy. He knew how to say things in a way that would not bruise sensitive egos; an uncommon trait in one so young. She quickly scanned all of the attachments he'd sent her.

Jet still insisted there was something to be found in front of the vacant lot on River Road. Why else would Donna continue to examine the area days after the kidnapping? If the dog were the last one to see the children—and if she could speak—certainly the FBI would have questioned her at length as an important witness. But Donna couldn't speak, so her testimony was being overlooked, disregarded. Maybe in her way, she was trying to tell them something. Suppose her testimony would lead them more quickly to the kidnapper? Wasn't it worth looking into?

Mary Ellen decided it was worth the taxpayers' money to check it out. But she had to find a way to get Ruth Wilson in on it without seeming to undermine John's authority. First, though, she emailed Jet's message back to herself at home, then deleted the copy from her office mailbox just in case someone should use her password and get into her inbox.

The action made her feel guilty, as though she were hiding

something from her partner. Yet she felt justified since John had shown such dogged determination in arresting Ibarra so quickly, haughtily ignoring her warnings against it. Now that they'd gone ahead and done it, everyone would have to live with the outcome; and she knew there was going to be a good deal of humble pie to eat if it turned out they'd made a mistake.

Moments later, she was standing in the doorway of Ruth Wilson's temporary digs at the RPD. The older woman lifted her head from her paperwork and seemed not to mind Mary Ellen's intrusion.

"I have a question," Mary Ellen said in answer to Ruth's questioning look.

"Shoot!" the older woman said.

"When you swept Ibarra's place for clues, you had people working outside, too, right?" Mary Ellen also understood the importance of diplomacy.

"Of course. I did the initial investigation myself. We found a trail of blood."

"Hmm. I remember that," Mary Ellen acknowledged, "Did the trail continue? I mean, where did it end? I remember the report said there were of drops of blood leading down the hallway carpet and out the front door. Did the trail continue down the porch and out to the street?"

"Well, now that was difficult to determine because snow covered everything, but it would be a logical assumption since the trail went out the door and onto the stoop. It's possible it continued to the driveway. There was no way of telling if a car had been waiting there for them to get into, or if they went out to the street. Whatever evidence there was had been covered by snow," said Ruth, remembering. Her penciled eyebrows puckered her forehead. "Then when Antonio Ibarra walked through the snow in the driveway, he trampled any evidence there might have been. Of course, we took pictures of everything we found. You're welcome to look at those. Since then, lots of people, including my crew, have trampled that area; I doubt we'd find anything new."

"Hmm," Mary Ellen pretended to contemplate Ruth's information, then, "Did anyone check the area in front of the vacant lot that borders the west side of Ibarra's property?"

"I don't think so," Ruth replied slowly, thoughtfully. "There didn't seem to be a need."

"Would you mind checking there for me and let me know what you find? Please concentrate on the area along the road in front of the vacant lot and, say, the first three feet or so into the meadow. It'll probably mean you'll be picking up the snow piled up by the plow. That sounds like a lot of trouble..." Mary Ellen affected an apologetic tone.

Ruth Wilson was quick to take the bait, "Not a problem. You have any idea what we're looking for?"

"Not really. But I'm sure you'll know it when you find it. It might be something the kidnapper dropped as he left the scene."

Those final words had the desired affect on Lt. Wilson. "We'll get right out there while we still have light. We'll pick up all the snow in buckets if we have to. Once it melts, we can sift through whatever's left." She capped her pen and poked it into a ceramic cup on her desk. "Paperwork is an important part of my job, and I really don't mind it; but I'd much rather be in the field." She smiled, relishing the work she was about to undertake. "I hope whatever we can dig up is another nail in that bastard's coffin."

Mary Ellen was surprisingly lighthearted as she went back to her cubicle. She felt something good would come out of the search, namely a break that would prove Ibarra's innocence.

Now she burned to read more thoroughly what Jet had sent. Under the pretense of a killer headache, Mary Ellen asked John to take her home. When he dropped her off in front of her apartment fifteen minutes later, he looked at her with concern. She suffered a pang of guilt when she saw his worried expression.

"See you tomorrow," he said apparently unaware of her distrust of him. "Get to bed early and feel better."

She nodded as she got out of the car and waited for him to drive off; but he seemed to be waiting for her to go inside. She turned on her heel and used her key to get into the security door. Halfway up the stairs to her apartment, her cell phone rang.

3:46 P.M.

As they walked along a paved path in North Park, Carmen Thibault regarded her with a mixture of wide-eyed excitement and worried misgiving. Moments earlier, when Mary Ellen arrived at the park in her white Chevy Impala, the front door of Carmen's Dodge Caravan had immediately flung open. Carmen had quickly gotten out of the car and walked briskly over as Mary Ellen parked behind her.

Since the morning wind had subsided considerably and the afternoon sun had brought a comfortable feeling to the winter day, the two women took a walk. It was still too chilly for outdoor activities, though, and the park was practically empty. They paid no attention to the navy blue sedan with dark tinted windows pulling up along the curb and followed the path deeper into the park, away from the street. The only sounds to be heard amid the distant rumble of traffic were the cries of blue jays and the crunching of the women's boots on the sanded sidewalk.

Mary Ellen sensed the woman's reluctance to speak frankly where they might be overheard, so she engaged in small-talk, "How are you holding up, Carmen?"

She took a deep, ragged breath, "Not well, actually. I can't sleep. All I can think of is the children. And now Antonio." She met Mary Ellen's eyes as tears filled her own. "You know, it was a lot easier hating him when I felt like I was the victim. Now that he's been arrested and charged, I can't help but feel somehow responsible. That if I hadn't said those hateful things, perhaps the police would not have gone after him so diligently. Perhaps the blood they found would not have seemed so incriminating."

Carmen glanced about furtively and dug into the pocket of

her black leather coat with her gloved hand. She pulled out a long white envelope that had been folded in half. "I feel so stupid!" she said as unchecked tears fell from her gray-green eyes. Her voice trembled as she explained. "If I'd found this before court this morning, things might have gone differently for Antonio. It undoubtedly came in yesterday's mail, but I was so upset when I heard about his arrest, I didn't look through the pile until today. Just before I called you, actually. This was buried under a lot of other things, and I didn't notice it right away. It frightened me so much when I saw it that I knew despite the warning against involving the police, I needed to tell someone right away. But the police have been such bloody—" She stopped abruptly and pressed her lips together. "But you're different, kinder. I wanted you to be the first to see it. Paul went to work after lunch; he hasn't seen it and I haven't told him yet."

She handed the envelope to Mary Ellen. It was a white, postage-paid envelope with an adhesive strip. There was no return address. But that was not what caused the FBI agent to frown.

Mary Ellen was looking at an envelope that had been addressed using pasted cutout letters from various newspapers: A childhood stunt she'd used with her friends years ago. As she removed the folded sheet from the envelope, she belatedly realized it was lucky she had on gloves of her own.

The message was short and to the point:

$250,000 in unmarked, used billS, fifties & Twenties. LeaVe in Dumpster near Ball field, South Park 12:00 noon Friday NO CoPS!!!

Under different circumstances, she might have laughed it off as a kid's prank. It was the worn out cliché of cunning characters in cheap dime-store mysteries. Yet, as with all the "hot tips" they'd received through the Amber Alert and since Carmen's plea over the media—all of which had turned out to be nothing but dead ends—this message could not be ignored.

The childish mode of communication had been employed now with sinister intent and must be deemed genuine. That meant the terms had to be met and the delivery of ransom made on time.

"Who could have sent this?" Carmen demanded, interrupting Mary Ellen's thoughts. "It's the kidnapper, asking for ransom, right? It means if we pay this money, the children will come back unharmed, right?"

Mary Ellen met the woman's searching, imploring gray-green eyes. Not wanting to mislead her with false hope, yet equally unwilling to shatter her spirits, the FBI agent carefully chose her words, "It looks like a ransom demand." She gently replaced the letter inside the envelope, then encased the entire thing in a plastic zipper bag she had in her shoulder pouch. "You realize I'm going to have to let John know this came in, and the Ridgeport Police as well, so that we can plan a strategy?" She let her voice trail off, leaving her sentence unfinished. "With luck, they might find fingerprints, DNA, or whatever trace evidence might link the letter to its author." But Mary Ellen had a sneaking suspicion that whoever it was, had taken care to cover his or her tracks. "In the meantime, is there any way you can get this kind of money together before tomorrow's deadline?"

Carmen looked troubled and thoughtful, "I don't know." She checked her watch, "There's still time to get to the bank before it closes, but *I* certainly don't have that kind of money. I don't imagine there's enough equity in the house to get another loan. But maybe Paul's business..." Her eyes came up to Mary Ellen's, searching for an answer. "Maybe Antonio— But he's in jail..."

Mary Ellen saw her opportunity to find out something she'd been wondering about, "Can your brother, Conrad, help you?"

Carmen frowned and gave Mary Ellen a sideways glance, "Who told you I had a brother?"

"It's a matter of public record," Mary Ellen said simply.

Carmen turned her eyes away, "I haven't spoken to him

since—" She shrugged, shook her head, and stated sarcastically, "No use trying to keep secrets. You probably can find this out too, since it's a matter of public record." She pronounced the word 'REH-chord'. "I haven't spoken to Conney since Antonio threw me out of the house." She regarded Mary Ellen sadly, "He's my twin brother, you know? We used to be close. It hurts so much that he'll have nothing to do with me now. There's absolutely no forgiveness in his heart. Not that I've asked for it," she made a final shrug, "or deserve it."

"Are you sure you haven't spoken to him more recently than that?" Mary Ellen prodded. At Carmen's puzzled look, the agent continued, "Didn't you purchase your brand new Dodge Caravan from his dealership?"

Carmen smiled crookedly, "Not I." She corrected, "My husband." She went on to explain, "Conney did an advert on the telly for his business, and I off-handedly mentioned to Paul that he's my twin, but that we'd been estranged since the end of my marriage to Antonio. The silly man decided it was time that Conrad and I patch things up. So last summer, right after we were married, Paul went to the dealership and asked for him by name. That didn't go over well, mind you. The salesman didn't like being stiffed out of his commission, but he went along with it in the end: Not a good thing to get in bad with the boss. Paul then picked out the Caravan for me, bought it under the name of Carmen Thibault, and the first time Conney saw who *that* was, was when we picked up the machine. The expression on his face was indescribable. I would have spoken with him then—you know, using my commitment to A.A. to break the ice—but he walked away from me like I was the Tenth Plague of Egypt." She looked up at Mary Ellen with raised eyebrows and a trace of tears in her eyes, "So, Miss Smarty-Pants FBI agent, would you call that being on speaking terms?"

"I'm sorry, Carmen," Mary Ellen placed a comforting hand on the smaller woman's shoulder, "It's this job. You get so that everything you see or hear has a double meaning, an ulterior motive, a sinister design. Every omission, no matter how innocent, becomes suspect." She regarded the woman intently, "Under the circumstances, though, perhaps he would help you. How does he feel about the girls?"

"Oh, well, now. There's the thing. He and Cynthia used to be over often before the divorce. He absolutely adored Marisa, and Cynthia thought Liana was a living doll. They don't have any children of their own, you see, and they couldn't forgive me for losing my daughters in the first place. Conney'd warned me about the alcohol and the crack; he was always the more sensible of the two of us. I resented him poking his nose in my business, and I'm afraid perhaps he hasn't dared to call because I told him I never wanted to speak to him again." Carmen's expression became pensive, "But, maybe under the circumstances. To help the girls. Perhaps it's time to take that first step and give him a call."

4:31 P.M.

When Mary Ellen got back to the police station the sun was just lowering behind the leafless trees. As she drove her Impala into the lot, she noticed the Crown Victoria was still there.

"Good," she muttered, "He hasn't left yet."

She went straight to John's cubicle, but he didn't give her a chance to speak.

"Headache gone?" Something in his tone caused the warning bells to go off in her head.

"John, I—"

"What'd Carmen have to say?" He punched a button on his keyboard and on the monitor Mary Ellen saw Carmen hurrying out her front door, getting into her Caravan, and backing out of her driveway. At the same time, she heard the recorded voice of Carmen's earlier phone call telling her she had an urgent need to see her, followed by Mary Ellen's suggestion that they meet at North Park. "You should remind her that her phone is tapped—" His bitterly whispered words did not mask his barely-controlled temper, "And *you* should remember that these people are under surveillance. Didn't you notice the car that showed up at the park as you and Carmen went off on your little walk? Do you know how this makes us look?"

His brusque manner and the glint in his brown eyes told her that he was furious; and perhaps he had reason to be. But he had no right treating her like a naughty school child being sent to the principal's office. His attack caused her own ire to rise, yet she beat it down as well as she could to avoid a scene that would attract the attention of the officers and detectives working in other cubicles. Instead, she pulled the envelope enclosed in the plastic bag out of her purse, and tossed it in front of him on the desk.

"She gave me this," she said in as soft a voice as she could manage. "After I left Carmen, I swung by Ibarra's and I caught the Tibbses just as they were leaving for the airport. Didn't you get that on tape, too?" She continued before he could respond, "They hadn't thought to check Antonio's mail for the past two days." From her coat pocket she pulled out an identical envelope to the first, also in a plastic bag, and set it on the countertop beside its twin. "We found this in the bottom of the mailbox, under yesterday's newspaper."

He gave her an incredulous look, "Ransom notes?"

"Looks like."

He slipped on fresh latex gloves he got out of a side drawer and carefully examined the letter Carmen had given her. Mary Ellen watched him read the demand. "Why didn't you call me?" he asked.

She wanted to say, *Because you've been such an ass!* Instead she sighed and said, "You heard the tape. Carmen called *me* and asked for *me* to see her *alone*. She obviously didn't want to talk to you." She rushed on before John could interrupt her, "I was already on my way back here when it occurred to me that maybe Antonio had received a similar letter himself. It was all on the spur of the moment. I came here right away afterwards." This was making her tired. "I really don't want to fight with you, John. When I saw what Carmen had, I immediately knew you had to see it. Don't make me out to be some kind of a turncoat."

John regarded her intently for a moment. As he put Carmen's letter back into the plastic bag, he said, "The camera caught your little visit to Ibarra's. But surveillance spotted something else of interest going on there. Apparently, Ruth Wilson is back over there looking for something in front of the vacant lot beside Ibarra's property. I saw you go over to her cubicle earlier. Then I saw you walk over to her at the scene. You care to enlighten me on that?"

"Ruth Wilson is checking out that area at my request." Mary Ellen said with a sigh, "It was something Jet said about Donna—"

"Jet!" John let his anger show, "Jet is a *kid*! What does he know about police investigation?"

"Well, apparently, his idea had merit." She pulled a plastic zipper bag from the other pocket of her coat. "Ruth found this."

John examined the item without taking it out of the bag: A dark green velvet hair bow.

"It was snagged on the branch of a holly bush, above eye-level. I guess with the snow, and being green, the bow blended in with the leaves of the tree. The dog might have been able to pick up its scent above her head, but she wouldn't have been able to reach it to pull it down." Mary Ellen answered John's unasked question. "Even if she'd gotten up on her hind legs, which she might have done, she couldn't have reached that bow."

"How do you think it got up there?" John asked.

Mary Ellen shrugged, "A kid might've thrown it there. A person might have brushed by and the bow got caught on the tree without their realizing." Then she got another idea, "Or maybe, someone was carrying a child who had the bow in her hair."

4:48 P.M.

Ruth Wilson's team had just returned to the police station

when the FBI agents got to Dr. Glenda Baldwin's office.

"Ah!" Wilson smiled, "I was just going to call you." She held out another plastic baggie, "We found this half buried in the mud under melting snow along the road in front of that vacant lot. Looks like it's been stepped on a few times, what with all the searchers. Does this mean anything to you?"

Mary Ellen examined the item without taking it out of the bag. It looked to be a piece of jewelry; a delicate, narrow gold chain upon which dangled a crucifix and two charms, also made of gold. The chain had broken about two inches from the clasp, and mud had dried in its links and on the cross and charms. It was a wonder that the mud-encrusted charms had not been lost when the necklace dropped to the ground.

Mary Ellen gently jiggled the bag so that the items spread out, giving her a better look at them. If she could only make out what they were.

"Let's get a closer look," Glenda Baldwin took the baggie from Mary Ellen's hand and retrieving both charms with tweezers, placed then side by side on a glass plate for magnification. "Dim the lights, please," she requested as she turned up the light on the projector. Soon, the scientist had the items in focus and projected onto a screen wall in front of them. The oval objects were embossed with some kind of figure.

"There's something written on the charms," John observed.

Glenda selected the cleaner of the two charms. Caked-on mud covered some of the letters, and the group tried to make out the fragments of the words they could see. They could read "San" and "ertran" along the top edge. Along the bottom was "Or", then a speck of dirt covered a group of letters. However, the ending "obis" was clean.

Mary Ellen suddenly knew what she was looking at. "These are religious medals!" she said excitedly, "I can't tell for which saints, but the writing along the bottom curve definitely says *'Ora pro nobis.'* It's Latin for 'Pray for us.'"

5:18 P.M.

By the time they came out of the police station, the sun had already dipped below the trees and the sky above had turned a soft purple. Mary Ellen got into her car and watched her partner drive off in the Crown Victoria. The new evidence did nothing to change his mind. Both he and Ruth still stubbornly clung to the accomplice theory and refused to consider that Antonio Ibarra was not involved in the kidnapping.

She gave a derisive shrug. Actually, those items really didn't point to an individual acting alone and separate from Antonio; they merely brought up the possibility that something of interest had occurred in front of the vacant lot. The bow might have gotten in the tree at some other time and might not be related to the kidnapping. The jewelry could belong to anyone; perhaps even to one of the volunteers. Mary Ellen could understand how John and Ruth needed more proof to accept that these items had anything to do with the case. She had to admit to herself that the only reason *she* viewed them as evidence was because she was willing to believe that Donna was trying to point out a clue to the children's disappearance.

As she put the key into the ignition, Mary Ellen realized she had never turned on her phone today. What with court and all, she'd completely forgotten. Now she took the instrument out of her purse and as the phone came up to power, she was immediately alerted to new voicemail. Instead of starting the engine, she dialed up her messages.

Predictably, the first one was from her mother: "Your father and I just wanted to tell you again what a lovely Christmas we had at your little apartment," she said in the polite and formal—condescending?—tone she used on the phone. "You've turned into quite a cook! Now we're hoping to return the favor and that you'll join us on New Year's Eve. We're having a few friends over so bring something nice to wear for dinner. Call me either way. Love you!"

Very subtle, Mom. Evidently, her mother was trying to set her up with a blind date. *Again.* Try as she might, Mary Ellen

couldn't seem to make her mother understand that she could—
and would—find a suitable mate without her help. She wryly
shook her head. It was no secret that her mother thought being
an FBI agent was not only dangerous, but a career completely
unbecoming any daughter of hers. Her mother also deemed
anyone in law enforcement a poor prospect for marriage. Mary
Ellen knew that her mother hoped she'd marry a doctor or lawyer, maybe even a congressman or senator, that she would
"quit that awful job" and settle down to make some grand-
babies for her and Mary Ellen's father; a much more suitable
undertaking than making the country a safer place to live.

Now, Mary Ellen felt like she was stuck between opposing
loyalties: If she refused the invitation, her parents would be
hurt thinking she was avoiding them; probably with just cause.
Yet if the case were not solved by then, she had the responsibility of her job and the very lives of those two little girls on
her shoulders. How could she, in good conscience, take time
off to go to New Hampshire just for fun? Even for New Year's
Eve.

She didn't have time to deliberate; the next message was
playing. She immediately recognized the young male voice.

It was Jet. He was talking fast. To make matters worse, the
reception was sporadic and there were many blank spots. Mary
Ellen played the voicemail over a number of times and finally
was able to make out what the boy was saying.

"Agent... ly. It's... on ten o'clock... heading to New
Hamp... for the weekend... First time... signal. Hope you...
this. I know what it was that I couldn't... member the other day
when I saw you. Remember... something peculiar about the car
that drove off in the... dle of the night? Well, when my dad
started up the Voyager... all came back to me. The car I
heard... the same sound when *it* started. That... the... napper
used was an old... Chrysler... before... with Daimler... a
ninety-something or older Plymouth or Dodge."

6:25 P.M.

The third floor of the Troy County Jail was reserved for those awaiting trial and unfortunate enough to have been denied bail or unable to make it. Even though none of them had been tried and convicted of any offense, everyone was treated as though he were guilty, since there was no way of knowing what was actually true about any of the detainees. The first thing Antonio Ibarra learned when he got here was that he was just a number; another lawbreaker, guilty until proven innocent.

The place was strictly regimented. There was a set routine for everything; a time set aside for meals, bed, recreation, personal grooming, and visitors. Everything was uniformly regulated, timed, portioned, or allotted with no exceptions. The only ones who might see Antonio off-hours were cops and his lawyer.

Chuck Cabot did not let him down. Soon after Antonio arrived at the jail, the lawyer came by to offer him some encouragement and hope, "We'll appeal this, Tony." Cabot said, "The Commonwealth doesn't have anything but circumstantial evidence. I don't know what the judge was thinking when he denied you bail. The only thing I can think of is that he owed Anita Pimental a favor."

Antonio only half-listened and made no response. What could he say? Antonio thanked him, and after Chuck left, for lack of anything better to do, Antonio had taken a nap in his bunk. And the day had dragged slowly by. To Antonio, the biggest crime committed here was the waste of time; and maybe the slop they claimed was food.

The next thing Antonio learned was that he would not make friends here.

For the most part, the inmates were angry: Angry because they were guilty and had been caught, or angry that they had been accused of something they hadn't done. It didn't matter. Angry was angry. Some of them acted badly, picked fights, taunted others weaker than they. These were punished, relegated to their eight-by-eight-foot cell and locked in. Those who behaved themselves got recreation room privileges where they could read, watch TV, or play cards or checkers.

After supper, the guys who deserved a little time out of their cells went to the rec room. Antonio figured he'd watch some news on TV; maybe he'd hear something about his little girls.

But no. A group of punks with holes in their ears, noses, lips, now devoid of the jewelry they wore on the "outside", had gotten there ahead of him and for all intents and purposes, had commandeered the television set. The CO had set the TV to the channel of their choice and now what was playing was some horrible noise that passed for music.

A group of tough guys with disturbing tattoos was playing spades. The game had just begun and already it was getting loud. Nothing good could come of that.

Antonio passed them by and he sat down on a bench in the corner, off by himself.

He wasn't in the mood for socializing anyway. He was depressed. His babies were still out there somewhere, probably being abused or hurt and *he'd* been arrested on suspicion of their disappearance. Nobody cared. What was there to be happy about?

He dropped his head into his hands. That was the third thing he'd learned in the short time he'd been here; don't make eye-contact with anyone. Having his head in his hands was the safest position in which to think or pray. God forbid that his eyes should rest on another inmate and his meditative expression be mistaken for a challenge, interest, or loathing.

He groaned deep in his throat. He was miserable. He didn't even have a picture of his babies to look at because yesterday, when he'd been processed by the Ridgeport Police, all of Antonio's personal possessions had been taken away from him. He had to content himself with closing his eyes and picturing their beautiful little faces in his mind.

As he'd predicted, the game of spades erupted and suddenly the deck of cards was everywhere. Two guards in khaki uniforms Antonio knew only as Murdock and Hayes approached the group with murder in their eyes. These guys were taller and bigger than Antonio, built like the bouncers from the Lady Slipper. The card players immediately dispersed, leaving only one poor slob to pick up the mess. Antonio held his breath, wondering if privileges would be revoked. But the moment passed, the guards relaxed, and the inmates settled back into some quiet activity.

Antonio could see that guarding these men was a stressful job. The unarmed guards themselves were edgy and easily annoyed. If even one incidence occurred, it could mean lockdown for everyone. Anything, no matter how small, could set them off, making them surly and disrespectful for the most part; as though every inmate deserved to be ill-treated.

They're like schoolyard bullies.

The thought of Carmen leapt up in Antonio's mind. Is that what Carmen thought of him? That he was a bully? All he had ever wanted was to have a happy family with good, obedient children, and a loving wife. But maybe that was an old-fashioned idea and June Cleaver was gone forever. Women today had careers and didn't greet their husbands at the door with a roast in the oven and chocolate cake for dessert. But had he been wrong in wanting at least a sober wife who didn't take her clothes off for a living?

He dropped his head into his hands again. Maybe if he had used more diplomacy, more kindness, more love…

"Hey, Ibarra!" growled a voice.

Antonio looked up in bewilderment. Murdock and Hayes scowled at him with dark eyes beneath heavy eyebrows and caps with visors. He wondered what he had done to merit their attention.

"Come on! Move yer ass," Murdock, the taller one said, "We don't got all day."

"What's going on?" Antonio asked as he warily approached them.

"You got company," Hayes said as he put shackles on his wrists and ankles.

"Who?"

"Cinderella," Hayes said. Some of the inmates chuckled. Murdock laughed, "Yer fairy godmother." More laughter all around.

They all stopped laughing when Antonio didn't ask again.

Murdock firmly gripped Antonio's upper arm and led him out of the rec hall, down a brightly-lit passage, and through an electronically controlled security gate, where he handed him off to another guard Antonio had never seen before. This one brought him down a hall lined with many metal doors. What lay behind the doors, Antonio could only guess. Each was painted the same somber gray as the walls with only a small square hatch of a window in the upper third. The guard finally stopped in front of one of these doors, reached in front of him to turn the knob, and pushed it inward.

Antonio was wary about entering a room that so closely resembled the Interrogation Room at the Ridgeport Police Department. He tentatively stretched his neck to get a better view.

"Come in, Mr. Ibarra," said a gentle, female voice he recognized. "Come sit down."

The guard urged him forward and Antonio stepped into the room to face the lady FBI agent. He couldn't help but feel suspicious and wondered why she had come.

"Please remove the shackles," the FBI agent requested.

Antonio kept his eyes on the woman as the guard unlocked both sets of restraints and left the room closing the door behind him.

"I'm sorry you were denied bail," she began.

Antonio continued to regard her sullenly. He didn't believe her. He had thought she was different, but no. She was one of *them*. He had nothing to say to this person. Or to any other cop, for that matter. They were all pigs, and he would spit on them if he thought they wouldn't beat him.

His little girls were still missing, but that didn't matter to them. They had stopped looking for them. They didn't care. His Marisa and Liana could freeze or starve to death, or maybe they were already dead; but all these people cared about was making trouble for him.

Why? He asked himself. What made him less than human to these people?

And now this Agent—What was her name? Kelly. Yes, now they send Agent Kelly to him for some reason. Well, he didn't care what they wanted. They could all go—

He frowned, reeling as something she said penetrated his brain. "What did you say?" His angry thoughts had so occupied his mind that he'd only half-heard her. He certainly hadn't heard right.

"I said, Mr. Ibarra, that Carmen received a letter demanding ransom of two hundred-fifty thousand dollars. It apparently came in yesterday's mail," she said, "and there was also a similar letter in *your* mailbox."

"Ransom?" Antonio looked at her in disbelief. His mind raced. If there was a demand for ransom, wouldn't that prove he had nothing to do with his daughters' disappearance? He wanted to ask her about that, but she was still talking.

"Do you think you can help Carmen amass that amount of money before then?"

"When?"

"Noon tomorrow," she repeated patiently.

"I have some money put away, but not *that* much. A quarter of a million! Maybe the bank will give me something against the house; but from jail, what can I do? And it's such short notice." Antonio met her blue eyes, allowing himself to trust her one more time, "Maybe I can give Chuck Cabot power of attorney and he can get the money first thing in the morning."

"Good. I'll call him as soon as I leave here," she promised.

"Maybe the ransom letter will help in our appeal to get me bail?"

"Maybe," Agent Kelly said, "But you're going to have to be patient about that. The lab has both letters now, examining them for whatever clues they can find. Even if they find nothing, the D.A.'s office could argue that you mailed the letters yourself to throw off the cops."

Antonio gritted his teeth. It made him so angry to think of how much energy they were putting into proving something that wasn't true. He shook his head and covered his face with his hands, trying to compose himself.

Agent Kelly was not done, "I want to ask you something about Tuesday morning, specifically about Donna."

"I don't understand," Antonio confessed.

"How was Donna that morning?" Agent Kelly asked, "What I mean is, was she her usual self? Or did you notice anything off, not right?"

Antonio frowned, thinking. "I woke feeling cold because the front door had been left open by whoever took the children. Or maybe, Donna had nudged it open with her nose, and had let herself out?" He tried to remember. "I noticed her at the end of the driveway, pointing up toward Cross Road. She kept slipping in the snow, having trouble standing up."

"Are you sure it was because of the snow?" Agent Kelly asked, "Was she really slipping? Or was she stumbling, having trouble holding herself up?"

"She was… tripping." Antonio looked at the FBI agent with sudden recall, "She was clumsy, bumped into the wall. She led me down the hall to go outside, and once or twice, I remember she sort of tripped over something. But there was nothing I could see to trip on." Antonio shook his head, "I don't understand. What does that mean?"

Agent Kelly sighed, "Mr. Ibarra, I don't know for certain, but I think maybe Donna was drugged."

"Drugged?" What was she talking about? Who would drug his dog? Then the dawn: "The kidnapper drugged Donna so she wouldn't—"

"—so she wouldn't make any noise—"

"—so she wouldn't wake me—"

"But she *did* make a noise, Mr. Ibarra," Agent Kelly contradicted him, "and she tried to alert you—or anyone paying attention. She howled. She stayed awake long enough to howl, just as she did when you were arrested."

7:13 P.M.

Instead of going home from Troy County Jail, Mary Ellen took the opportunity to do a little more detective work without the fear of interruption or discovery. She returned to the Ridgeport Police Department to avail herself of their computers and their link with the Commonwealth's Registry of Motor Vehicle's data base. Following Jet's tip about the perpetrator's car being a Plymouth or a Dodge, Mary Ellen needed to know how many of Ibarra's acquaintances owned either make. She already knew that Carmen had a Dodge Caravan, purchased by Paul from her brother, Conrad's dealership last summer. But it was too new; Jet had said it was an older model, from before the merger with Daimler. Mary Ellen figured that meant 1999 or earlier.

What about Conrad and Cynthia García? It so happened they owned an antique 1965 Plymouth Fury III and a brand new Dodge Journey. The information came as no surprise, since García owned a Dodge dealership; why shouldn't they own the newest crossover Dodge had to offer as well as a showy classic model? But still she wondered. Could they have stolen Carmen's children? She recalled the scenario she had considered when she'd discovered Carmen had a brother in the first place. Here was another connection that could help throw suspicion in another direction.

John was having Support check them out, he'd said, but she felt she should have paid the couple a visit herself. Maybe if she got done here at a reasonable hour…

Mary Ellen typed in the names of Antonio Ibarra's neighbors.

Chuck Cabot owned a new Lincoln Towncar. Mary Carvalho had a two-year-old Mercury Sable. The LaRues had two cars; an aging Cadillac Seville and a newer Buick LeSabre. Antonio had the Dodge Ram pickup, with a Cummins diesel, Jet had said. The Roberts also owned two cars; a Ford Explorer and a Ford Taurus.

This was going nowhere.

This was giving her a headache.

The Tibbses had rented a Dodge Caravan from a rental agency at the airport: They also had solid alibis for Sunday and Monday, and had stuck around until late this afternoon. They were not acting like people who had to hurry off to take care of children they might be hiding from the authorities. But what about the two members of the family who had not gone to Puerto Rico?

Mary Ellen checked the New Hampshire and Vermont DMVs and found that the Tibbses had four cars; a Chevy Lumina, a Jeep Cherokee, a Monte Carlo, and a Dodge Neon.

Yes! The Neon was registered to Samantha Tibbs. With dismay, Mary Ellen realized this did nothing to disprove John's accomplice theory. She wondered if he had come across this information, although he wouldn't have any way of knowing about the connection since she hadn't told him about Jet's latest tip. By rights, she should let him in on what she knew, but not yet. She had to look further.

The Bernards had three cars; a Chevy Blazer, a Chevy Malibu, and a Dodge Shadow. The Dodge was registered to Marcel, Jr., who had been in Puerto Rico with his mother. Could Marcel, *Senior*, have used his son's car to kidnap the Ibarra children?

Mary Ellen shook her head in frustration. This was serving to do nothing more than raise more questions. She needed to check on the whereabouts of the senior Bernard and Samantha Tibbs on Monday night and Tuesday morning. Remembering that John had been following that particular lead, she called Support.

"We sent that report back to John earlier." The sexy male voice identified himself as Frank Snell. He sounded peeved by her question and explained to her in a demeaning tone, "You're lucky to catch me in; I was just leaving for the day." She heard paper rustling over the line. "Samantha Tibbs worked the graveyard shift at Memorial Hospital from eleven Monday night to seven Tuesday morning. And Marcel Bernard, Sr. was at Fort Dix in New Jersey over Christmas, involved in meetings and briefings until the wee hours, and only flew back home on Wednesday night. I don't know how you FBI people get anything done when you don't talk to each other."

Stung by his rudeness, Mary Ellen didn't dare ask him if he had anything on the Garcías. She meekly thanked him and hung up. Her next call was to Glenda Baldwin.

"Have you found anything on any of the new evidence we gave you today?" she asked the Chief of Forensics.

"I've had all my staff working overtime. We're not done, but I'm just sitting down to write a preliminary report. It'll be on your desk in the morning." Glenda Baldwin said, "But here's what we've got so far. With regard to the bow found in the holly tree, there were a few hairs on it; a couple of them had the root. They're new, and they're Liana's. There were also a few fine hairs caught in the links of the gold chain; but no roots came with those specimens. So the best we can do is say who they *don't* belong to, but not decisively to whom they *do*. All we know for sure is that they do *not* match Liana's DNA. I've got one of my best people running tests against samples Ruth picked up at Ibarra's. But like I said, we can narrow down the field, but not really finger the perp."

"And let me guess," Mary Ellen remarked, "All of the hair found at Ibarra's is either Antonio's or the girls'."

"Well, now, it's interesting that you should say that," the scientist said slowly. "We do have a couple that we can't account for, but we're still working on it. We'll get you those results ASAP." Then Dr. Baldwin went on to something else. "With regard to the ransom notes, there were a number of prints on the envelope, and as far as we can tell, they were all from Post Office personnel. They all have their fingerprints on file, so that part was easy. From those fingerprints, we found out the letters were picked up and sorted at the South End Post Office in Troy City on Tuesday—"

"Wait a minute," Mary Ellen interrupted, "On Tuesday? You're sure?"

"Yep."

"That means they must have been mailed at the time of the

kidnapping?"

"Seems so. Local deliveries should have been made on the same day, but perhaps due to difficulty getting to mailboxes because of the snow, or whatever, they didn't get delivered until Wednesday. So much for 'through rain or sleet' or whatever..." Then she proceeded to tell Mary Ellen exactly what the FBI agent had feared. "All fingerprints we were able to lift have been accounted for; the perp must've used gloves. And because the perp used postage-paid, self-sealing envelopes, neither the stamp nor the flap of the envelope was licked by the perpetrator, and therefore, did not carry his or her DNA." Glenda Baldwin sighed and continued. "The eight-and-a-half by eleven paper used for the message bore no watermark. It's common bond, the run-of-the-mill stuff used in copy machines. Unless we can find the actual ream it came from, it's going to remain untraceable." Mary Ellen heard the rustle of paper in the background. "With regard to the news type, the various letters came from the *Troy City Herald* and the *Riverton Journal*."

Those were two local papers with circulations in the thousands among the neighboring cities and towns, Mary Ellen knew. In short, the papers could have come from anywhere within a twenty-five-mile radius.

Aren't we going to ever get a break in this case?

Mary Ellen realized that Glenda Baldwin was still talking and forced herself to listen. "There was trace of coffee and grease on a couple of the letters used in one of the notes. The grease turned out to be mayonnaise. My guess is the newspapers were fished out of a trash bin."

That, or the perp is a messy eater. Mary Ellen kept the thought to herself.

"The glue was regular rubber cement. But we *did* find something inconsistent with the glue." Up until then, Dr. Baldwin had seemed rather subdued, but now, Mary Ellen detected a note of excitement in her tone. "I don't know if it's going to amount to anything, but we found traces of sodium hypochlorite and alkyl dimethyl benzyl ammonium chloride—"

"I'm sorry, Dr. Baldwin," Mary Ellen interrupted, "I don't

know—"

"They're ingredients found in bathroom cleaners. For bleaching and disinfecting."

"I still don't get it," she rubbed her forehead between her eyes. She was so tired. "What's bathroom cleaner got to do with—"

"Apparently, the gloves the perp used had been previously worn to clean bathrooms."

Mary Ellen shook her head and sighed, "Thanks, Dr. Baldwin. I use gloves to clean my bathroom, too. I can't see how this is going to help us."

She heard the scientist draw breath at her end of the line. "Well, *you* most likely wouldn't use these particular products to do *your* cleaning, since they're not readily available for use by the general public. Not in this concentration. What we're talking about here are industrial strength products, made with higher concentrations of powerful cleaning agents and disinfectants, specifically for professional cleaning companies. I'd venture to guess the letters were sent by someone who works for one of the cleaning companies based in the Greater Troy City area."

9:31 P.M.

Mary Ellen parked her white Impala across the street from the raised ranch at 469 Forget-Me-Not Lane, part of a new development at Troy City's South End. In comparison to its neighbors, it was a modest endeavor, but the house was by no means small.

Situated on a hill and set back from the street, all details of the pale gray and burgundy house could be plainly discerned, even this late at night, thanks to a bright spotlight that shone on it from the front yard. Two large laurel wreaths trimmed with bright red and gold ribbon hung on the double doors, partially obstructing the oval etched-glass windows. The twin railings curving up either side of the neatly-shoveled red brick porch had been wrapped in laurel as well. Lit candles stood in each window, and in the enormous bow-window to the right of the doors a Christmas tree sparkled. Pristine white snow covered the lawn.

A brass lamppost also festooned with green laurel stood at the end of the long plowed out driveway that meandered up to the two-stall garage in the house's lower level. On an extended brass arm, a sign swung gently in the frigid December breeze: GARCIA.

Mary Ellen checked her watch: nine-thirty-four. She'd called John and filled him in on everything she'd learned, finishing by telling him where she was going.

"It's late," he pointed out, "Tomorrow's soon enough."

Mary Ellen bit back an angry retort, instead opting for sarcasm, "Need I remind you that time is not a luxury the Ibarra children can afford?"

He begrudgingly acquiesced; he was on his way. She wondered if she'd have to wait long.

As though the thought spawned reality, the black Crown Victoria made the turn onto Forget-Me-Not Lane. She waited until it slowly pulled around her Impala and stopped at the curb before she got out of her car. John said nothing as he joined her on the graded walk to the front door. She could tell he was not happy.

She'd called ahead; they were expected. The FBI agents did not need to ring the doorbell; the door swung open as they gained the top step on the front porch.

"Come right in." Carmen's twin brother was a sandy-haired man, about five-ten, and of medium build. He spoke with the same clipped British accent as his sister, and had identical gray-green eyes. "Please, forgive the appearance of the house. My wife and I just got in the door, as you probably can tell." He wore the pants of a navy blue suit, but the jacket was nowhere in evidence. His powder blue shirt was creased and wrinkled from the day's use, and his blue and silver striped necktie hung loosely around his neck. As the FBI agents stepped over the threshold into the warmly lit foyer, his right hand jutted out in greeting. He wore a heavy gold college ring centered with a bright red stone. "Conrad García," he said by way of introduction, "And this is my wife, Cynthia."

He indicated the woman who gracefully floated up the stairs from the darkness of the lower level and joined the group in the foyer. Cynthia García was an attractive woman with long, silky blue-black hair that reached the middle of her back. She wore it parted in the middle and simply brushed away from her china doll complexion. She had a slim, straight nose and fine, heart-shaped, raspberry-colored lips. Her most striking feature were her large, exotic eyes; honey-colored irises encircled by rings as dark as kohl. Cynthia's fine wool dress clung to her slender figure and her black stiletto pumps made her legs look long and shapely. She was a stylish lady; unlike Conrad, she looked crisp and fresh.

Now, she approached her husband where he stood welcoming the FBI agents like invited guests. A few inches shorter than her husband, the exotic beauty took her place inside his extended arm, and he drew her close to him. A show of affection? Protection? Possession? Mary Ellen could not determine which.

"It was good of you to let us come speak with you, Mr. García, Mrs. García," Mary Ellen said after the FBI agents had shown their badges. "We realize it's late."

"No bother at all." Conrad García released his wife and she led the way up the few steps to the living room. "As I said, we just now got home. Thursdays and Fridays are the usual late nights at the showroom. To compound that, it is not only the end of the month, but year's end as well. So we're having a sale and have extended our hours all this week, you see. Tonight was a veritable zoo. People trying to cash in on the end-of-year clearance, you understand." He straightened up some magazines on the coffee table as he spoke and grabbed his suit jacket from the arm of a leather fauteuil. "Please, sit. Make yourselves comfortable," he indicated the burgundy leather sofa in front of the fireplace. "We were just about to have some dessert and coffee. Can I get you anything?"

When both agents declined his offer, Cynthia sat primly on

the edge of the chair from which Conrad had retrieved his jacket. Conrad took its matching mate beside his wife, and Mary Ellen began the interview.

"Tell us about your relationship with Carmen," Mary Ellen requested. "We heard it was a bit strained."

Conrad nodded, "It was all due to her alcohol and drug use. Most disturbing and disheartening to me—to us both, actually—to see Carmen throwing her life away. Her addictions were ruining everything, and she couldn't see it. I'm afraid I said too much at the time, and she pushed me out of her life." Conrad stated sadly and his wife placed a comforting hand on top of his.

"But now," Cynthia tried to lighten her husband's mood, "she's clean, she has a new husband, and custody of the children."

"We had hoped things would go better for her, but now, the children are—" Conrad broke off, unable to finish.

"What can you tell us about Antonio Ibarra?" John asked.

"You've arrested him for the kidnapping," Conrad nodded. "We saw that on the telly."

"We always liked Antonio," Cynthia supplied, "but from the beginning it seemed to us that they were not suited to each other."

"No," Conrad agreed, "it was not a good match."

"Even so," Cynthia flashed them a look from under thick black lashes, "we're having a hard time believing he could have harmed the children." Her honey-colored eyes filled and her voice thickened, "We both adore our little nieces and we can't imagine what Carmen is going through."

"She called earlier about the ransom. We should never have waited to make amends for the past until something so awful—" Again, Conrad had to break off.

"Of course, we offered to help in any way we could," Cynthia said.

"Yes," Conrad stated. "I've already been in touch with my accountant and he's looking into how much the bank will give us using the dealership as collateral."

The FBI agents left soon after that. John was still angry and Mary Ellen felt the meeting had been a waste of time. Support was already checking into the Garcías' backgrounds and making certain of their alibi for Monday and Tuesday. Most likely, nothing would come of it; Mary Ellen believed the Garcías when they said they were at the dealership both those days.

In all likelihood, the Garcías were just as they seemed; a young married couple, still childless by choice, doing their best to make a living. They had worked hard for everything they had, beginning with their fortuitous opportunity to buy the failing dealership from Cynthia's father at his retirement five years ago, their undaunted determination to turn it around and make it grow, and scrimping every nickel to afford the house of their dreams. This house on Forget-Me-Not Lane had been that dream since they'd married in June of 1999. They finally moved in this Thanksgiving, and now hoped that they might soon start a family.

No way were the Garcías involved in their nieces' disappearance.

The finger of guilt still pointed at Antonio Ibarra.

Mary Ellen started up the Impala and drove away.

Friday, December 30

5:21 A.M.

Cripes, I hate kids! It's so good to get outta there.
If it weren't for the money, I'd a got rid of 'em before now.
How could I ever a thought stealin' 'em was a good thing? Is it
my imagination, or are they getting' fussier, crankier, noisier?

Ever since that dog showed up, Marisa had been going on
about Donna.

Cripes, how could it be Donna? Donna's back home with
Papi, where she belongs.

But no amount of telling could convince the kid it wasn't
her dog. It belonged to the boy who led it away, after all. And
even though they both agreed they never saw *him* before, she
just wouldn't quit, insisted it was Donna and wouldn't shut up
about it.

Until I gave her that backhand that sent her flyin'. She shut
up then, didn't she?

And Liana, with her constant nosebleeds.

Cripes, even with the damned humidifier goin' twenty-four-
seven! What more does she need?

But it was that damned dog that set them off. Now they were homesick and crying and yammering and he couldn't stand it any more.

Damn it, I hate kids!

He made great time on his trip back to Troy City and this morning after he stretched himself out on the couch in his own living room, he had to know what was going on. Back at the cabin with the kids hanging around all the time, he couldn't just put on the news. The children weren't stupid; they'd know something was off if they saw themselves on TV.

Then it woulda hit the fan!

Now, he turned on the television.

Yep! There it was; the Amber Alert for Marisa and Liana. *Now passin' as Mario and Leon.* He laughed out loud.

What came up next made him sit up straight. It was video tape of Antonio Ibarra being led away in handcuffs.

They arrested Antonio!

"Ibarra was arraigned yesterday on the charge of kidnapping and denied bail." The newscaster's disinterested voice said, "The children have still not been found. What we are about to show you now is a video tape of the mother's plea which was recorded earlier this week."

She wore a black leather coat with a long purple scarf wrapped around her neck. Her copper-colored hair spread out over her shoulders. Her large eyes were red and swollen. "Please, whoever you are," she was saying tearfully in her hoity-toity British accent, "I beg you. Please return my babies safely."

Such a sniveler! Sorry, Carmen. The girls are mine, now.

5:27 A.M.

Donna whined and scratched at the door. What the heck was she doing awake so early? Jet's eyes opened in the dimness of the cabin.

Geesh! Sun's not even up yet.

"Not now, Donna. It's too early. Go back to sleep." He turned over in the bottom bunk, pulled his thick covers up over his ear, and shut his eyes tightly. As he drifted away, something shook the world and he grabbed the edge of the bed to keep from falling off. His covers were roughly tugged from his body and the morning chill attacked him. He sat up and grabbed the blankets. Hank grumbled in his sleep from the bunk above.

"Go lie down, you bad dog!" Jet ordered, trying in vain to cover himself.

But the dog would not permit it. She leapt up on top of him now, and licked his face. He pushed her away, but it only made things worse. This was a game now. She lay on top of him, grabbed the covers and dragged them off with her as she jumped to the floor. Then she ran to the door whining, only to turn around and jump back on the bed. She wanted out. There was nothing to do but get dressed and take her.

Jet pulled on his ski suit over his pajamas and stuck his bare feet into his snow boots. With envy, he noted Hank still in dreamland and wondered if he'd be able to get more sleep when he came back with the stupid dog. He grudgingly grabbed her leash, and without thinking, opened the cabin door. The dog immediately bounded out and took off running.

"Donna!" Jet called after her, then immediately realized this early in the morning, people would still be in bed. "Come back here!" He modified his tone to a loud whisper.

She ignored him. He ran after her as he jammed his knit cap over his ears, wondering why he'd ever thought it would be fun having a dog to take care of. She already was well ahead of him and he did his best to catch up. In a moment, he was happy to see that he seemed to be gaining on her. In fact, she had stopped running. With dismay, he saw that she was back at the cabin with the unfinished snowman, sniffing around and making little crying sounds deep in her throat.

When he was close enough, he grabbed her and clipped the leash to her collar. With great difficulty, he managed to get her back to his own cabin.

Hank was still sleeping, Jet noted. Lucky! He stripped off his ski suit and got back into bed; but sleep eluded him. He lay in his bunk, eyes wide open, wondering what to make of Donna's strange behavior.

5:28 A.M.

In the darkness before dawn, before the five-thirty alarm had the chance to do its job, Mary Ellen was jolted out of a deep sleep when a huge Bengal tiger pounced onto her chest and started licking her chin.

"Me-ow!" said the tiger.

"Go away, Tillie," Mary Ellen muttered. She turned over to her side and drew the blankets up over her ear.

Although she'd been home by ten-thirty, Mary Ellen had stayed up until after midnight working online, and using the phone book to look up industrial cleaning companies in the Greater Troy City area. It was impossible to narrow down the search; she had no way of knowing if she was looking for a company that serviced professional buildings only, or if they worked in private homes as well. Consequently, she ended up with a long list of telephone numbers to call in the morning. Hopefully they'd know the kidnapper's identity before long.

"Me-ow-ow!" Tillie insisted, pawing the edge of the covers. At the same moment, the alarm started shrieking its annoying summons.

Mary Ellen groaned and sat up, "Okay, okay! You win! I'm up." She reached over to silence the ornery alarm, then flopped back down on the pillow and pulled the sheet over her head. "Two more minutes," she mumbled. But Aunt Tillie would have none of it. The cat found her way under the covers and started licking her human's ear and purring loudly.

It was no use. Mary Ellen dragged herself out of bed and went through her morning ritual completely by instinct and without conscious thought. By the time John honked and she took one last look at herself in the mirror, she was surprised to see how well she'd done. Her make-up had been neatly applied, and she had miraculously managed to put on matching earrings. For lack of a blow-dryer, she'd been forced to wear her hair in a ponytail; it was nicely tied with a scarf that matched her pink turtleneck sweater. The latter was neatly tucked into the waist of her black jeans. She even had on matching black boots. Apparently, judging from the dishes in the sink, she'd had breakfast; and from Aunt Tillie's satisfied expression, she had fed the cat as well.

The FBI agents arrived at the Ridgeport Police Station just before seven, but instead of going to their cubicles, they stopped by Support to see Frank Snell; the same Frank Snell who had been so abrupt with her on the phone yesterday.

Psychologically prepared to dislike him, Mary Ellen was not impressed by his physical appearance. She was reminded of a Weeble; an egg-shaped figure she'd played with as a child. The slogan sang in her head: "Weebles wobble but they don't fall down." Of course the Weebles of her childhood were not the same as those of today. She had the sneaking suspicion that some kid had choked on one of the smooth egg people and that the toys had been redesigned with arms that stuck out from their sides, or with protruding ears and hats that made them impossible to put into one's mouth.

Frank Snell resembled one of those egg-like Weebles of old; he was bigger at the bottom than he was at the top. He was a short middle-aged man with a round face, sagging jowls, and no neck. He wore an old-fashioned brown bowtie with yellow polka-dots under his double-chin. His thick hairy arms stuck out of the short sleeves of his tan and brown striped sports shirt that stretched over his bulging belly, testing the buttons that held it closed. The shirt was tucked into brown slacks with a very shiny seat and knees. His "egg-ness" was further emphasized by his smooth and shiny bald head. Now, Frank put on a pair of black horn-rimmed glasses with Coke-bottle lenses and waddled to the counter where he had placed identical tweed and leather suitcases.

The large bags were soft-sided with semi-stiff, reinforced

bottoms and brass studs for feet at the four corners. Two wide brown leather bands encompassed each bag from the bottom and continued to form double rope-like hand grips at the top. The bags were closed by means of heavy two-way zippers; the tabs could be joined in the middle and locked.

"These are the bags we'll be using to transport the ransom money," he explained in his smooth, sexy voice. The voice and body were so incongruous that Mary Ellen found that she couldn't look at him when he spoke. Instead, she focused on the object of his lesson. He unzipped one of the bags and opened it for the FBI agents to see inside. "We've installed tracking devices in these bags, completely undetectable by anyone but me and my staff. I defy you to find where we put them."

Even with this foreknowledge, neither FBI agent could discern where they might have concealed the transmitters. There was no sign that the Dacron lining had been opened and repaired. Nothing foreign, no irregularities, no wires could be felt through the fabric. All pockets were empty. After about five minutes of thorough prodding and examining, neither she nor John had found the hidden equipment.

"Show me." John gave up.

Frank gave him a cunning brown-eyed look out the side of his thick glasses. "I'm not telling you," he said. "If I gave away my secrets, they wouldn't work anymore, would they? You don't need to know where they are. If you can't find them, they've passed the test. That's good enough for me." He zipped the bags closed and picked them up by the leather rope handles, "Here you go!"

8:57 A.M.

Back at their cubicles, the FBI agents divided Mary Ellen's list of professional cleaning companies in half and started making phone calls. By nine, they still hadn't narrowed the list. All of the companies they'd reached used cleaners containing sodium hypochlorite or alkyl dimethyl benzyl ammonium chloride, and most used both. There had to be some way of using the kidnapper's work to trace him back to the crime; but that answer eluded them for the time being.

"How about some coffee?" John asked from his desk.

"Sounds good to me," Mary Ellen yawned and stretched.

She wondered how Carmen was doing getting the ransom together. In case she and Paul were being watched, and to protect them while they carried the large amount of cash, the police had provided the couple with undercover surveillance. Five of the plainclothes police—three men and two women—were to stay close by the couple without seeming to pay attention to them. They were to act casual, like people waiting for the bus or customers of the bank. Two more police officers were to observe the bank from an unmarked vehicle and follow the Thibaults wherever they went.

Mary Ellen was in the middle of dialing Carmen's cell phone number when she was interrupted by Glenda Baldwin who appeared in the doorway of her cubicle. She quickly hung up the phone.

"Sorry I'm late with this. I expected to be done by the time you got in this morning." Dr. Baldwin apologized.

"Any luck?"

"Yeah," the scientist nodded, "A few things, really. Although when I look at them, I wonder what you're going to make of them. Some of this stuff just brings up more questions to my mind." Glenda Baldwin opened the manila folder she carried in her hand. "Let me start with the easy one first. We identified the saints on the medals. One is St. Christopher, and the other is St. Luis Bertrán." She looked up at Mary Ellen, "I'm not Catholic, but I've heard of St. Christopher."

"Yes," Mary Ellen said, "He's the patron saint of travelers."

"I don't have any idea who this Luis Bertrán is."

"Neither do I," admitted Mary Ellen, "but I can find out easily enough. Anything else?"

"We found a hair with the root under the flap of the envelope that went to Antonio Ibarra. We were able to determine a number of things from that hair. First, we know it's a Caucasian *male* who has been working with harsh industrial-strength cleaners. No matter if you wear gloves, if you breathe in that stuff, it starts to show in your fingernails and your hair follicles," she explained. "The guy who sent the ransom notes has inhaled fumes consistent with the traces of the chemicals we found in the glue used to stick the letters to the paper."

"So we're looking for a white male. Anything else on that?"

"Yeah. He's a natural blond."

"Okay," Mary Ellen nodded enthusiastically. That certainly left Antonio Ibarra out of it.

"But don't get too excited," Dr. Baldwin cautioned. "This is where things get weird."

"How do you mean?" Mary Ellen asked the smile vanishing from her face.

"Remember, I told you last night that the hair we found on the gold chain had no root and that we could only eliminate people, rather than actually pointing a finger at the perp?"

"Yes, I get it," Mary Ellen said.

"Well, it doesn't match the hair from the ransom note at all. But we did find other strands as possible matches to the hair in question. A few of those hairs were among those found in the Ibarra girls' bedroom; those that didn't belong to either Antonio or to the girls. The weird thing is, the *best* match came from a doily on the bureau in one of the bedrooms at Ibarra's house. That hair had a root. It belonged to a dark-haired female."

9:29 A.M.

By the time John returned with their coffee, Dr. Baldwin had left and Mary Ellen was speaking with Father Francisco Gomez, the pastor of Our Lady of Guadalupe Church. She motioned to John to put the cup on her desk, waved her thanks, and gave the priest her full attention. Father Gomez was fairly knowledgeable of the saint.

"Luis Bertrán?" the priest said, "Yes, of course I'm well-acquainted with that saint, due primarily to my work with Hispanic immigrants. Here in the U.S., we anglicize his name and call him St. Louis Bertrand. Luis Bertrán came to South America in the mid-1500s when the Spanish were colonizing that continent. He was responsible for the conversion of many of the Indians of Cartagena. He traveled around the Caribbean with the Christian message, and he's pretty popular among the people of Caribbean countries and Latinos, especially Colombians. He's the principal patron of their homeland, after all."

Something about the information seemed to sizzle in Mary Ellen's brain, causing the hairs on the back of her neck to rise and a thought took shape in her mind; something she should have thought of earlier. As soon as she hung up with the priest, Mary Ellen commanded her computer to connect online. Although she knew it wouldn't take but a moment, she dug into her personal notes from the interviews she and John had had on Tuesday and Wednesday while she waited.

"John!" She called over to where he was busy on the phone. "You've got to drop what you're doing. Have Support finish making the calls. I think I'm onto something important and I need your help."

From his cubicle across the way, John gave a startled look to her frantic demand. He put down the phone. "What's up?"

"Are you online?" she asked.

"I can be in a second," he tapped on his keyboard.

"We've been wasting our time. How could we have neglected to check this out earlier?" Mary Ellen berated herself as her fingers flew across the keyboard. "We made the mistake of assuming the information we got was factual and *current*. We should have checked this out earlier when we spoke with Cabot, Carvalho, and LaRue. There are just too many connections for this to be a mere coincidence. I just hope to Heaven our delays haven't cost Marisa and Liana Ibarra their lives."

"Slow down and tell me what you're talking about," John

demanded.

While the search engine worked, she turned her chair to face her partner. "John, think about it. The intruder has a key and is familiar enough to the family that neither the children nor Donna find her being there strange."

"Her?" John questioned.

Mary Ellen didn't answer him but continued enumerating the facts as she knew them. "She knows Liana needs the humidifier and takes it. She even takes the time to pack the children's clothes; both indications that she loves the children and wishes to take care of them. The last time anyone saw her, she had a Plymouth Sundance; and Jet says the car that drove off in the middle of the night was either a Plymouth or a Dodge. To top it all off, the gold chain not only holds the medal of the patron saint of her homeland, but also a hair is found that matches one collected from a doily on the bureau in her old bedroom at Ibarra's. The chain is found half buried beside the road in front of the vacant lot placing her at the scene. John, I can't believe we didn't put it together sooner." Mary Ellen sighed deeply, "The kidnapper has to be Adelina Aguilar."

He seemed to be trying to place the name.

"John, it's the former nanny."

9:58 A.M.

Jet and Hank left the Lodge after devouring a large country breakfast of fresh-squeezed orange juice, flapjacks drowned in pure maple syrup, scrambled eggs, crisp bacon strips, sausage links, toasts with lots of jelly, and tall glasses of chocolate milk.

"I'm set until lunch," Hank pronounced as they crunched over the crystallized snow on their way to their cabin.

"I don't know how I'm gonna be able to ski on such a full stomach," Jet commented.

"Well," Hank sighed, "Pat and Becky have chores today, to prepare for tomorrow's New Year's Eve party. They won't be coming, so the pace doesn't have to be as grueling as yesterday's."

Jet made no answer. He was watching the man and the two little boys trudging down the driveway that led out to Route 302: The snowman builders. The same ones Donna had frightened yesterday. Luckily, Donna was safely locked inside the cabin. Otherwise, he imagined she'd be making a fool of herself, chasing the little boys, harassing these people.

He thought about the boy he'd seen in the window, peeking between the chintz curtains. Those large, dark brown eyes, looking at the dog with such emotion. Such—

What emotion was that? Not fear, but something else. Excitement. No, more than excitement.

It was joy! The child was *happy* to see the dog, not afraid of it.

The child had cried out when he'd seen the dog charging through the snow at them, but Jet had been too far away to make out what he'd said. Yet, even as they scrambled for the safety of their cabin—or rather, as the man jostled them into the cabin— Jet had not discerned any fear or panic in the kid's tone. Now that he understood the emotion he'd seen in the boy's eyes, Jet realized that the child's tone had been joyful as well.

Excitedly, happily, joyfully surprised.

Of course, the smaller boy had started crying and the man quickly grabbed him and tucked him under his arm as he ran toward the cabin. When he caught the other one by the hand, the kid fell to the ground, and the man bodily dragged him along in the snow. But now that he thought about it, Jet wasn't certain if the children were being rescued, or if the man simply did not want them to have any contact with the dog.

Why not?

Even as he tried to think of possible answers to the question, his mind kept returning to the look in the child's eyes. Haunting and beautiful eyes. Large dark pearls fringed with long black lashes. Grams would say such pretty eyes were wasted on a boy. A girl should have such eyes…

Jet had no time to ponder the thought for as Hank unlocked the cabin door, Donna took the opportunity to slip past them.

"Hey!" Hank called out to the dog. "Get back here!"

Jet took his time going inside the cabin to get the dog's leash, and Hank looked at him incredulously. "Come on, Jet. Hurry up."

"Why hurry?" Jet asked. "We already know she's going to Cabin 3, the snowman cabin."

Sure enough. Moments later when they arrived at the cabin, the boys found Donna exactly as Jet had said; sniffing around the snowman.

"What's she doing?" Hank demanded about the dog's odd behavior.

Jet shook his head and allowed Donna to do as she pleased.

"We should get her out of here," Hank urged.

"It's okay, Hank. They went out. I saw them leave just a few minutes ago," Jet said. "This gives us a perfect opportunity to find out why she keeps coming over here." Jet left Hank standing there and went around to the other side of the cabin to make sure the dark colored car he'd glimpsed parked there was gone. When he returned, he surreptitiously approached the door and tried the knob.

"What're you doing!" exclaimed Hank in shock. But of course the door was locked.

Meanwhile, Donna busied herself digging in the snow at the base of the snowman. Jet went over just as she uncovered something.

At first, he thought it was a piece of red and white cloth. He reached around the dog's large black body to rescue the cloth from Donna's heavy claws. It was rather damp from being under the snow, and when he tugged on it, the fabric started to shred. Jet handled it as carefully as possible to keep the thing intact.

As he spread it out in his gloved hand, he realized that it wasn't cloth at all, but a soggy piece of facial tissue. The cold and snow had kept the bright red spots from darkening and browning as they would once they dried. He knew that the large, irregular, lop-sided stains were blood.

Blood. Could this be why the child was crying yesterday? Did his crying and the hurried departure into the cabin, have *nothing* to do with the dog, and *everything* to do with the blood on this tissue?

Jet had grown up with the proper procedure one followed for handling blood at school. He knew the janitor always wore latex gloves to wipe up the spill and the spot was scrubbed with bleach. With this in mind, he retrieved from his pocket the sandwich bag from yesterday's cookies, and slipped the blood-ied tissue inside being careful not to destroy the delicate paper. Then he gently placed the closed bag back into his pocket.

This discovery did nothing to alleviate the disquieting thoughts that consumed him. Jet quickly covered up the hole that Donna had dug while Hank stood over him asking bewildered questions. Exasperated, Jet got up and turned his back on his cousin as he headed back to their own cabin. He bit back a harsh response to Hank's incessant talking.

Shut up, Hank. He wanted to say. *I really don't know what to make of all this, so just get off my back, okay? I can't think with you constantly asking stupid questions!*

Instead, Jet said, "I'm sorry, Hank. I know you're confused by this crazy stuff going on. I don't know what to think about it myself."

"Maybe it would help to make one of your lists?" Hank suggested.

"Great idea!"

Back in their cabin, Jet took out his laptop and the boys worked together.

```
Question #1: What's up with Donna?
Possible Answer #1: She's nuts.
Possible Answer #2: She's confused. She
misses Marisa and Liana and has transferred
her "affections" to these little boys.
Possible Answer #3: She misses the girls
and simply wants to play with anyone will-
ing.
Possible Answer #4: She's mixed up and
actually thinks these kids are her girls.
```

"Geesh!" Jet said.

"Yeah." Hank agreed, "Possible Answer #4 is crazy think-ing, isn't it? She couldn't get *that* confused, not when she gets close enough to smell them! Could she?"

Jet typed in another question for which Hank helped him arrive at a number of possible answers.

```
Question #2: Why did the man act so
weird?
    Possible Answer #1: Is afraid of dogs.
    Possible Answer #2: Has allergies to
animal hair.
    Possible Answer #3: Felt threatened by
Donna. A threat to the children? A personal
threat?
    Possible Answer #4: Wasn't afraid of
Donna. He was reacting to the blood.
```

That spawned yet another question.

```
Question #3: Who was bleeding?
    Possible Answer #1: The man. He took the
kids inside because he didn't want to leave
them with a possibly vicious dog?
    Possible Answer #2: The little boy. Cut
himself on?
    Nothing there except snow. How else can
a little kid bleed besides getting cut? A
scrape? A loose tooth?
```

"A bloody nose?" Hank offered.

The cabin door flew open and Christine and the twins spilled into the little house uninvited. "You guys ready to hit the ski trail?"

Reluctantly, Jet saved his work and put away the laptop. But thoughts of the beautiful girlish eyes filled with joy, Donna's excited reaction to the children, and the blood-stained tissue kept Jet's mind working, preventing him from enjoying the outing.

11:09 A.M.

Mary Ellen was having trouble finding the whereabouts of Adelina Aguilar.

Although the Registry of Motor Vehicles website provided her with a good picture of the woman for the evidence board, the information on her was sketchy. Aguilar's Plymouth Sundance had been registered in Massachusetts until the end of August, when Antonio Ibarra terminated her services as nanny for his children. After that, the Registry's trail went cold. There was nothing regarding the VIN of that car anywhere in the United States.

Mary Ellen's call to the Colombian embassy had come up empty. According to them, Adelina Aguilar left the country in August and had not returned. It looked like Aguilar went home to Barranquilla, Colombia, as Mary Carvalho had said. A little more digging backed that up; telephone and electric service had been established in Barranquilla on August 16th under the name of Adelina Aguilar.

So that's that, she thought.

But Mary Ellen had to make sure. She dialed Adelina Aguilar's phone number in Colombia.

"*Adelina Aguilar, por favor,*" Mary Ellen stretched her very limited Spanish regretting she had not had the time to find someone who could have made the call for her.

The only word she grasped from the woman's rapid Spanish response was "No."

Weakly, Mary Ellen asked, "*¿Tu hablas ingles?*"

"*Si.* Yes. *¡Lo siento!* I speak a little bit of the English—but not too good," the woman said apologetically.

"Oh, but you do much better with English than I do with Spanish, I'm afraid," Mary Ellen spoke slowly and clearly. She willed the woman to understand her and struggled to refrain from talking loudly as one often did when trying to express oneself to someone unfamiliar with one's tongue. "I'd like to speak with Adelina Aguilar."

"*¡Lo siento!*" the woman said. "I am Adelina's *hermana,*"

ah, sister, Carmella. I am sorry, but Adelina is not here."

"I see," Mary Ellen said, "Would you have her call me when she returns?"

"No, I am sorry. You do not understand," Carmella Aguilar said slowly, "Adelina is not here in Barranquilla."

"Not in Barranquilla? Where is she, then?"

"She is in Canada."

Carmella was happy to volunteer information without any prodding. She explained in hesitant, heavily accented English, "Adelina be here only three weeks. Together, we rent apartment. But she have more money than me, so we put apartment, everything, in her name. I get good job now and can pay rent, so Adelina leave Barranquilla. She be nanny, now."

"Do you have the name of the family she's working for?" Mary Ellen hoped.

Carmella provided the address and telephone number of Adelina's employer in Coaticook, Quebec.

Mary Ellen's next call was to the François Lemieux residence. She faired better with Madame Lemieux; Mary Ellen's French was much better than her Spanish. All the same, the woman honored her by giving English her best shot.

"*Pardon, mademoiselle*," Jeanine Lemieux said in her soft, feminine voice, "But Adelina works for us no longer. She— how you say?—quit. *Les enfants*, the children, after all, are older than she liked. Adelina likes the babies, the little ones, you know? Céleste, she is fourteen and Louis, he is twelve. They insisted they did not need a *bonne d'enfants*, a nanny, *et je regrette*, they treated her with lack of respect. I do not blame her for wanting to leave. You are fortunate to reach us, though *Mademoiselle* Kelly; we move to *Paris* tomorrow. Adelina was welcome to come with us, but she did not want."

"How long ago did she leave you?" Mary Ellen asked.

"*La veille de Noël*—how you say?—the Eve of Christmas was her last day."

Mary Ellen's mind raced as she asked her final question, "What kind of car does Adelina drive?"

"*C'est une Plymouth*," she pronounced it 'plea-moot'.

Mary Ellen's last call was to Carl in Support. She knew John relied on him to get information such as what she needed now.

"What can I do ya for?" Carl answered lightheartedly.

"How difficult is it to get information on cars registered in a foreign country—say, Canada?"

"Gee, I thought you were going to ask me something hard," she could hear the laughter in his voice. "Russia, Cuba, China, now those places take a little work. But Canada's a cinch."

11:15 A.M.

Why the heck did Jet even come with us? Hank wondered.

His cousin seemed so distracted it didn't look like he was enjoying himself. More than once Hank had roughly jostled Jet to force him out of his deep thoughts. For a few moments, Jet would seem to be with them, yet he barely commented on what the others were pointing out to him; like the deer drinking at the lake, or the lacey ice crystals hanging from the slender birches. Hank knew what was on his cousin's mind; the stupid Ibarra case.

Jet should leave solving the case to the FBI. Uncle Jules wouldn't be happy if he knew. Then, *Jet should have stayed behind with Donna.*

The group was following the snowmobile trail through the woods and had come to a large clearing. The tracks crossed the entire length of the field, then turned and came back forming a giant U. The hard-packed snow made going easy on cross country skis, and the cousins followed the snowmobile tracks until they came to the bottom of the U.

There in front of a metal rail fence they saw a large white sign with bold red letters: Danger! Approach at own risk. Beside it was an engraved plaque mounted on a pole.

"For Cornelius Patrick Tate and Walter Edmund Tate, November 28, 1936." Denise read the inscription.

"What's that all about?" Danielle asked.

"Wow," Christine said in wonder as she placed a gloved hand on the plaque. "It's for Cornelius Tate and his son, Walter. Don't you remember Daddy's story, Jet?" she asked excitedly, "How they both died on the same day in a hunting accident?"

Jet shrugged, "Yeah. Dad's always telling stories."

Christine pressed her lips together in derision then told the story as best she could. "Walter Tate was our great grandfather, making Cornelius our great-great grand. Cornelius is the one who built the chalet for his bride." She glanced toward Jet, and he merely nodded, leaving her to tell it. She continued, "Anyway, Cornelius and Walter went out hunting and somehow, Cornelius lost his footing at the edge of this cliff, his gun went off, and he accidentally shot Walter dead on the spot. Then the recoil of the gun sent *him* over the edge and he fell to his death, too."

"Ouch!" Hank exclaimed.

"How awful!" Denise and Danielle remarked together.

"Dad tells it better," Jet put in. "You guys should ask him about it."

Christine shot Jet an angry look but Hank didn't hear if she made a retort. Hank was distracted by his sisters who had approached the metal rail fence and were looking over the edge.

"This is scary," commented Danielle.

Hank went over to have a look, too. The snow was piled high along the fence rail, not only from numerous snowfalls, but from the snow thrown over by snowmobiles as they made the sharp turn. Now, instead of a waist-high railing, the top of the fence came only to Hank's knees. He peeked over, careful not to come too close to the edge.

A lumpy but untouched blanket of white lay over everything, softening the appearance of the jagged rocks it covered. A flat ledge jutted out of the rock wall about twenty feet down forming a table about ten feet wide; after that, Hank estimated it was about seventy or eighty feet to the bottom.

"A nasty drop," Denise observed.

"You guys shouldn't get so close," Hank warned.

Denise made a face at her younger brother and defiantly took another step. Suddenly her arms were flailing as she lost her footing. Hank grabbed the sleeve of her jacket. His quick action was all she needed to regain her balance.

Denise regarded him wide-eyed and frightened by the close call. "Thanks," she said.

Hank gulped only now realizing that if she'd gone over the edge, she might have dragged him over with her. "It's alright," he said in a husky voice, "but I think we should go back; I don't feel so good."

12:27 P.M.

They opted to use the white Impala because it looked less official, less police-like, than the Crown Vic. Parked at the west end of South Park under some pine trees at the picnic area, Mary Ellen had a perfect vantage point. She raised her binoculars and trained them on the area around the Dumpster beside the ball field.

The earlier promise of sunshine had been rescinded, replaced instead with a steel gray sky and a brisk icy wind. The thermometer had not risen above freezing, yet despite the cold, others had come to the park today. Mary Ellen scanned them each briefly.

A woman pushed a baby carriage on the paved walk along Park Street, just north of the ball field. She took a seat at the bus stop beside a man in a Bruins jacket who was deeply engrossed in the *Troy City Herald.* In the playground east of the snow-covered ball field, a couple of guys took turns dribbling a basketball across the unevenly cleaned-off court and shooting through the basketless hoop. Close by, a young man pushed his girlfriend on a swing. In the snowy area south of the ball field, a young woman threw a Frisbee for her German shepherd; the animal romped happily after it and eagerly jumped high to catch the toy and retrieve it to his mistress. To anyone who saw them, they were ordinary citizens enjoying the park on this cold winter day. But in reality they were undercover cops ready to move at the first sign that the suspect was taking the bait.

Carmen and Paul had gotten to the Ridgeport Police station around a quarter to eleven. With the help of the Garcías, Paul's business, and Antonio acting through his advocate Charles Cabot, they had managed to gather the entire amount demanded in the ransom note. The couple dumped the contents of two suitcases onto John Turner's desk and the four of them started stacking the straps of twenties and fifties into the tweed and leather bags provided by Frank Snell.

This was always a touchy area as far as the FBI agents were concerned. On the one hand, one hated meeting the demands of the kidnapper. It set a precedent for future extortionists and terrorists. It became an easy way to dupe desperate people out of large amounts of cash, and even with the best-laid plans, the kidnapper could get away. Even with these bugged cases, the perp could slip though their fingers. There was always the chance that he might instruct the Thibaults to transfer the money from the rigged bags to others at the drop-site. And what guarantee was there that the children would be returned safe and unharmed?

Yet on the other hand, if one tried to plant bogus money or stuff the bags with paper instead of cash, there was the real chance that the children would be killed when the perp discovered the double-cross; that's if they weren't already dead. And that scenario was completely unacceptable to everyone concerned. Hopefully, the transmitters in the bags would work and even should they lose track of the subject, the FBI and the police would be led to the right place.

A few minutes before noon, with the undercover police already in place, Mary Ellen and John watched Carmen and Paul drop the two tweed and leather bags into the Dumpster beside the ball field as the ransom note had instructed. Once their task was complete, the couple drove away in Paul's red Mustang. Twin green blips on the monitor secured to the dashboard assured the FBI agents that the tracking devices were functioning. The unnamed subject should make his move within the next ten minutes.

The minutes ticked by.

Mary Ellen's cell phone chimed.

"It's me, Carmen," said the woman. "We just got home. Has he picked up the money yet? We haven't heard anything at this end. No instructions regarding the return of the children."

Mary Ellen could tell she was trying to be calm, trying to hold it together. This had to be maddening for the poor woman. Mary Ellen tried to sound optimistic, "It's too early; we have to give him time. He hasn't picked up the bags yet, and I wouldn't expect him to make contact until he had the money in his hands, and has verified that it's all there."

Nearly a half-hour later, still nothing had happened and the FBI continued their surveillance. Mary Ellen couldn't help feeling there was something amiss. If he didn't come for the money, there would be no contact. Without further contact, there was no way to get the children, or to know if they were even still alive.

"I don't know, John." Mary Ellen commented at last, "I'm getting the awful feeling that our man isn't going to show up."

"Give him time," John said, repeating to her almost the same words she had used with Carmen, "He's probably noticed all these people who have suddenly decided today's a good day to come to the park, and he's being careful, waiting for some of them to leave." On that note, he spoke into a walky-talky, "Dave, why don't you and Kathy take a little walk? Don't go too far; just give this guy some breathing room." Almost immediately, the young couple at the swings left that area, hands joined. The pair walked slowly in the direction opposite the ball field, seemingly with eyes only for each other. "Bud and Rick, you guys can take a little break. Why don't you get a drink at the water fountain?" One of the basketball players grabbed the ball and tucked it under his arm. The two of them jogged off.

Mary Ellen continued to watch the park from their hiding place under the trees, hoping she'd spot some sign that the kidnapper was coming for the money, and her mind worked on the puzzle. Forensics had evidence suggesting that the kidnapper and the person demanding ransom were two different people. The question was: How were they connected?

Just then, a Troy City Department of Public Works truck drove up in front of the Dumpster, and both FBI agents lifted their binoculars. John spoke to his team on his walky-talky.

"Heads up, people. It's show time."

Twin rods protruding from the front of the truck entered the slots under the Dumpster and began to lift the trash bin over the top of the truck. The team of dumfounded undercover police watched the entire contents of the trash receptacle empty into the garbage truck.

"Something's wrong," John said to Mary Ellen. "Move! Move! Move!" he commanded into the walky-talky.

The white Impala came out of hiding, slid and bounced over mounds of snow, and blocked the truck's forward movement. At the same time, a Troy City police car closed in from behind. The German shepherd and his handler were suddenly on duty; the dog, now leashed, was ready, waiting for the order to attack, and his handler had her gun trained on the driver of the truck. The Frisbee, the baby carriage, the newspaper, the basketball, the swings; all were abandoned as the team quickly advanced and surrounded the truck with weapons drawn.

"Freeze!" John shouted with authority, "FBI!"

12:44 P.M.

"What's your name?" John demanded in the Interrogation Room at the Troy City Police Station.

"Leroy Jackson," the subject, a young African-American stated, his frightened eyes watching John's every move. He wore an official-looking one-piece brown jumpsuit with the appropriate insignia emblazoned across the back: The city seal surrounded by the words Troy City Department of Public Works.

Mary Ellen sat quietly to the side, observing, hoping John would hold it together this time. She had a gut feeling that this poor man was actually who he said he was; Leroy Jackson, a city employee, collecting the trash from the various bins in the park. A background check was being made, and someone from the DPW was coming to the station to give a positive ID of the man and vouch for him. She was certain he'd be cleared, that they were again wasting precious time. Besides, Glenda Baldwin had been sure the man they were looking for was a blond Caucasian male. Clearly, Leroy Jackson, a black man, was not their suspect. Yet despite this knowledge, John insisted on questioning him, believing that the perp had paid him to retrieve the ransom money.

For the umpteenth time, Mary Ellen Kelly wished she had a clone. *To be anywhere else in the world would be better than here.*

Mary Ellen got her wish.

There was a tentative knock on the Interrogation Room door. John Turner gave her an irritated look that meant he resented the interruption and that she should handle whatever it was that was so important.

A young Troy City rookie looked at her nervously; as though afraid of disturbing the FBI agents in their questioning of a suspect. "Sorry to interrupt you, Special Agent Kelly. Captain Rosa would like to see you upstairs. Right away."

"Special Agent Turner is not finished—"

"It's okay. Cappy only wants you."

Although the door was closed, the blinds on the office door were open, giving her an inkling of what the Troy City Police captain wanted. The burly Portuguese, noted for his mild, easygoing manner, was standing in front of his desk engaged in a heated argument with a tall, dark-haired woman wearing a skirted black suit and low heeled shoes. Since the woman's back was to her, Mary Ellen could not see her face; however her stance—feet braced and slightly apart with arms akimbo—indicated that she was extremely unhappy with Rosa.

Rosa, however, was facing Mary Ellen and she got a good look at *his* face. His olive complexion was bright red and the color seemed to spread from the roots of his thick black hair down to where his tanned football player neck disappeared inside his uniform shirt. His angular jaw clenched with constrained ire and his hands were shoved deeply into his uniform pockets. *Probably to keep from striking the woman,* Mary Ellen thought.

The raised voices of both parties could be heard half-way across the squad room, but the closed door muffled their words so that Mary Ellen could not discern what they were saying. She loathed disturbing them, and she suddenly understood how the young rookie had felt when he'd gotten her from the Interrogation Room. Bracing herself, she knocked assertively. The voices ceased immediately.

The woman quietly stepped aside to allow the police captain to open the door. Captain Rosa gave Mary Ellen a relieved but stern look and made the introductions.

"This is Margaret Sunderland, advocate for the Civil Liberties Union. Ms. Sunderland, FBI Special Agent Mary Ellen Kelly."

Margaret Sunderland had piercing dark brown eyes under severely sculpted eyebrows, a straight, narrow nose, and thin red lips. She looked to be in her mid- to late- thirties. Her handshake was firm, almost painful. It was only after they'd shaken hands that Mary Ellen realized that Captain Rosa had left his office and closed the door behind him.

The meeting with Margaret Sunderland took less than ten minutes.

Sunderland was unhappy with everything the Troy City Police and the FBI had done that day. "You've entrapped an innocent man, falsely arrested him, and now you are detaining him, questioning him without benefit of counsel," Sunderland finished haughtily.

Mary Ellen Kelly countered, "I can assure you, Ms. Sunderland, that the Bureau, the TCPD, the RPD, and the State Police are interested only in finding two kidnapped children. I'm sure you've seen the Amber Alert on TV, or heard the report on the radio."

"Yes, I heard about that," Sunderland allowed.

"We are only questioning Mr. Jackson with regard to that case. We do not believe he is a suspect in the kidnapping; only that he may have been in contact with the kidnapper. Mr. Jackson's civil rights are not being abused; I can promise you that. But, as an added precaution, we need to verify his credentials. He will be released as soon as someone from the DPW arrives to vouch that his ID badge is authentic and he is really in the employ of the city."

Both women remained cool throughout the exchange and by the time they each finished their piece, the short, balding Dan Waterman, boss at the Troy City Department of Public Works, had arrived waving a stubby cigar. His brown jumpsuit visibly strained over his round belly. His sparse black hair was slicked back over his skull and his dark eyes regarded everyone contemptuously. Once he'd grudgingly complied with the "No Smoking" rule and put out the smelly stogie, the women followed him and his police escort to the viewing room. He took very little time to look at the black DPW worker seated on the opposite side of the one-way glass.

"Yeah, that's him," the portly Waterman asserted. "Geez-Louise, you guys really know how to screw up a good day," he complained. "Jackson's a good man, and now you got him all off schedule. He has a route, ya know. Because of you, he's gonna be working until after dark and now I gotta keep the dump open until he gets in."

"Aw, that's too bad," muttered the cop who had escorted him.

Margaret Sunderland glared and Mary Ellen gave the mouthy cop a warning look as she hastily interjected, "You may take him back to his truck at South Park as soon as we cut him loose, Mr. Waterman."

True to her word, moments later, the visibly shaken DPW worker was allowed to leave.

"Don't go too far, Jackson," warned John Turner as the man was released into the custody of his boss, "in case we need to ask you a few more questions."

The entire morning had been a complete waste of time.

John and Mary Ellen had to face facts. Apparently, the team of cops had been made in the park and their as yet unidentified subject had thought better of picking up his money. He'd chickened out. Mary Ellen wondered what that meant for the children.

There were a number of questions niggling at the back of her mind: Why had the perp chosen to send a letter rather than make a phone call? Did he think the letter would never be traced back to him? Did he think it was a safer way? And then to chicken out; what was he thinking? Would he try again?

A very dismaying thought came to mind: It could all have been a hoax. The demand might not have been made by the kidnapper or a partner in crime, but by some stupid jerk trying to use the kidnapping as a way of extorting money from desperate parents. This was just as hateful a crime as the kidnapping!

Well, you creep. Rest assured, whatever it is you're up to, we'll figure out who you are, and when we do, you'll be sorry. Very sorry.

1:23 P.M.

Carmen had just put away the vacuum cleaner when the front doorbell rang.

"Coming," she called as she hurried to the front of the house. She was quite surprised to find Mary Ellen Kelly and John Turner standing on her doorstep holding the two garbage-smelling satchels of ransom money.

"We brought your money back," John Turner said.

She opened the door wider to allow them to enter and looked at the two FBI agents, not bothering to hide her dismay, "I don't understand. Why didn't he pick up the money? What does this mean for Marisa and Liana? Do you think he'll try again?" A lump rose to her throat and hot tears pricked her eyes. "Or did we miss our chance?"

"There's really no way to know," Agent Kelly seemed sympathetic, "If he really wants his money, he won't hurt them." She paused and Carmen wondered what the agent was not telling her. Then, "It's possible he'll try again. We just have to sit tight and wait."

"Where's Paul?" Agent Turner asked.

Carmen gave him a wry smile, "I sent him to work." She shook her head, "I don't need him to help me feel miserable. He just knocks about here and gets under foot."

"You should have somebody with you—" Agent Kelly began.

Carmen waved her off. "I'll be fine."

"We could send a couple of operatives—"

"No," Carmen said firmly. "Besides, I have an appointment with Dr. Solomon at two. My regular weekly therapy session; he checks up to make sure I'm still going to A.A. meetings. I was going to cancel it, but he wouldn't hear of it. He said that now more than ever, I need to see him." *Most likely we'll be talking about the kidnapping and how that's impacting...* She shook her head and told the agents, "By the time I get back, Paul will be coming home from the shop." She shook her head again, "No, I really don't need a babysitter, thank you."

After the FBI agents left, Carmen looked at the satchels of money, wrinkling her nose in disgust, "I can't keep these smelly things in the house." *At least, not in the house proper.*

She lugged the heavy bags one at a time to the closet in the entry and set them on the floor beside the vacuum cleaner, then locked the closet for safe keeping.

She glanced up at the kitchen clock: 1:33.

Perfect. She had just enough time to freshen up her make-up.

1:51 P.M.

Hank turned on the TV set and was about to flip channels when Jet grabbed the remote from his hand and motioned for him to be quiet.

They were interrupting regular programming to make an emergency announcement. The anchors for the local TV station were a young black man and an older white woman, both wearing grim expressions.

"We are interrupting our normally scheduled program to report breaking news concerning the area-wide Amber Alert, now in its fourth day," the lady anchor said, her brown eyes seeming to penetrate the viewer. "Although authorities have not yet located the missing children, police have just issued a new bulletin. Andrew?" She looked over at her co-anchor who took over the story.

"That's right, Diane. For everyone involved, it's been a frustrating case. However, just now, the FBI named a 'person of interest' in the disappearance of Marisa and Liana Ibarra of Ridgeport, Massachusetts," Andrew stated. "Police and FBI are looking for this woman, Adelina Aguilar."

"The nanny?" Hank blurted. Then: "Yipes! That's a bad picture."

The close-up of the face was grainy and blurred; apparently blown-up from a snapshot. She looked to be about forty years old, tall with a large built, wearing unbecoming green sweats. Jet had the fleeting thought of the mythical Amazon warrior women they'd spoken of in Mr. Crocker's Greek mythology class. The enlargement was replaced by the actual snapshot of the woman standing beside a dark blue car as the screen divided in half and her vital statistics were posted beside it.

The voice of the anchor read the facts aloud, "Adelina Aguilar is forty-five years old, six-feet-two and weighs approximately one hundred and ninety pounds. She has dark brown eyes, dark brown hair that could be streaked with gray; the hair could by now have been dyed a different color. Ms. Aguilar's most distinguishing feature is a dark dime-sized mole on her left jaw. Born in Colombia, her native language is Spanish and her English is heavily accented. She was last seen in Quebec, Canada where she worked as a nanny until Christmas Eve. Anyone who knows her whereabouts should contact the FBI hotline. That number appears at the bottom of your screen. If Ms. Aguilar sees this broadcast, she is urged to report to the local police. Ms. Aguilar is wanted for questioning at this time and is, I repeat, considered only a 'person of interest' in the disappearance of Marisa and Liana Ibarra."

The FBI hotline number remained on the screen as the picture changed to show the photographs of Marisa and Liana Ibarra that Jet had by now memorized; Little Liana with her brown ringlets, tawny brown eyes and deeply dimpled round cheeks; and Marisa's round, long-lashed black eyes, dark brown curls, and her coy, impish grin with the missing front teeth.

The female anchor was talking now, "The FBI has also revealed one more concern, this one regarding the health of one of the girls. Liana, the younger of the sisters, is prone to spontaneous nosebleeds. Normally, this would not be a serious problem; however, if proper care is not given, it can quickly become a health-issue, probably even life-threatening." The pictures of the girls vanished to be replaced by the anchor. "We have Dr. Stephen Nesbit with us to explain. Dr. Nesbit is an expert in pediatric hematology."

"Yes, thank you, Diane," the camera switched to a sophisticated-looking, middle-aged, balding man wearing an expensive charcoal pin-striped suit, white shirt and navy blue tie. He was clean-shaven and wore wire-rimmed glasses over his deep blue eyes. He looked straight into the camera, giving the viewer the impression that he was speaking directly to them. "Lots of kids get nosebleeds," he began, "and for the most part, it's not a serious problem—"

But Jet was no longer listening.

The broadcast had reminded him of things he'd pushed to the back of his mind; things that now crashed to the fore, demanding immediate interpretation.

First, the blood-stained tissue Donna had found at the base of the snowman. The spots of blood were large, as though the flow of blood had been heavy and sudden. Could those be, as Hank had innocently suggested, from a child's nosebleed?

Second, the large brown eyes of the boy he'd glimpsed briefly yesterday in the cabin window bore a close resemblance to Marisa's. Spooky.

They had to be merely coincidences. That Liana had heavy

nosebleeds, and someone playing in the snow had been bleeding badly. And that the boy at the window had eyes similar to Marisa's. Happenstance, right?

And now there was the dark blue car in the photo he'd just seen on TV. It was either a Dodge Shadow or a Plymouth Sundance. The picture had been poor, but he was certain it was a Chrysler product. A 1993 or four; maybe a '95. Could it be the car he'd heard starting up as he'd fallen off to sleep? What about the car he'd glimpsed parked behind the cabin? He hadn't paid attention, really, and now he mentally kicked himself for that. All he knew was that it was dark in color. He'd thought it was black; but could it have been dark blue? If only he'd looked more closely. Then again, at the time, he'd had no reason to. Earlier, it was gone. Maybe it was back now. He'd have to go look.

Finally, there was Donna's strange behavior to consider. A normally obedient and quiet dog suddenly is compelled—no, *obsessed*—with "visiting" the very cabin where those little boys were living. Suppose Donna *wasn't* crazy? Suppose those boys were really Marisa and Liana?

Should he call the cops?

Suppose he did and it turned out that he'd falsely accused some poor, innocent man and that all the similarities *were* coincidences? If he made a mistake, if the man was everything he seemed to be, a man on vacation with his family, it could be traumatic for the kids to witness and an awful experience for the man himself. Suppose he sent the cops off on a wild goose chase? How could he ever be trusted in the future? He'd be the boy who cried wolf; how could he ever call for help again? No. He couldn't just go off half-cocked and have an innocent man arrested for kidnapping two little girls and passing them off as boys.

He needed to be sure.

He needed proof.

2:38 P.M.

No doubt about it, I have to start eating better.
This steady diet of fast food had to be unhealthy. Mary Ellen crumpled the wrappings from her McDonald's takeout and tossed it into the trashcan as the phone on her desk started ringing.

It was Carl from Support, "Hey! I found your car. A blue 1994 Plymouth Sundance is registered to Adelina Aguilar of Coaticook, Quebec."

Mary Ellen quickly jotted the characters as he read them off, thanked him and as soon as they disconnected, she put out an APB for the blue Plymouth with the Quebec registration. It would be attached to the report given the media regarding Adelina Aguilar.

Mary Ellen rolled her desk chair over to the evidence board and took down the white sheet of paper with the question mark. On it she printed in bold strokes: Blond, Caucasian male—ransom notes. All she needed now was a name. She tacked it back up to the wall beside a photo of Adelina Aguilar.

Mary Ellen felt confident that soon they'd be closing in on Aguilar and her friend.

2:47 P.M.

John hung up his phone and called over to Mary Ellen in her cubicle, "Hey, I think I got a hit from one of the professional cleaners, possibly the author of the ransom letters."

"Great!" Mary Ellen waited for him to continue.

"On a hunch, while I had those cleaning companies on the phone, I started asking for a list of people who didn't come in to work on Tuesday. Support's been doing background checks on these people. Because of the Holidays, a lot of them are on vacation. A few of them are actually sick; out with the flu. But after a bunch of misses, we hit pay dirt." He paused, making sure he had her attention, "One guy who works for Rosebud

Cleaners didn't show up for work for his Tuesday night shift, and hasn't been in all week; no explanation, and the office can't seem to reach him." John's voice rose with excitement, "Get this. He's on the night crew that cleans the public restrooms in the Troy City Medical Center complex in the industrial park. We got a warrant and a black and white is going over to his address as we speak."

"So," Mary Ellen grabbed her coat from its hook, "what are we waiting for?"

3:01 P.M.

Located at Troy City's South End, 95 Malcolm Street was a tenement house, dating back to the early 1900s during Troy City's heyday as a leading textile producer, when mill owners built row upon row of cheap but sound housing for their employees. Each identical replica was situated side by side like Monopoly houses, leaving little space in between for yards, barely enough room for sidewalks.

Unfortunately, this one looked its age. The brown paint had lost its luster while the peeling white trim had turned a dingy gray. A couple of broken basement windows had been closed up with plywood; but at least the windows of the upper levels were intact. Banisters and railings seemed sturdy enough, though on the grimy side. On the whole, the property looked old but good enough on the outside. A little maintenance on those basement windows and a new coat of paint would be an instant face lift for the place.

The Crown Victoria pulled up to the curb and two uniforms stepped out of a Troy City police cruiser. As they climbed the squeaky steps to the front door, a thin woman with stringy gray hair tied back in a meager ponytail met them in the doorway, effectively blocking their entry. She wore an oversized red sweatshirt over skin-tight black stretch pants, making her legs look like matchsticks. A cigarette hung from her red lips.

John Turner and Mary Ellen Kelly produced ID badges,

"FBI, ma'am. We're looking for Richard Humphries." He held up a photo of the man.

The woman's brown eyes flitted briefly over the IDs and the photograph, then squinted, peering at them through the strands of her bangs as she blew out a long stream of bluish smoke. "What's he done?" she asked taking another drag.

This was none of her business. John was about to tell her so and push his way through, but Mary Ellen responded, cutting him off, "We only want to speak to him, Mrs. Ah—"

"Name's Cora Carpenter," she said, yanking the cigarette out of her mouth with the left hand, and holding out the right to shake theirs each in turn.

"Are you the proprietor?"

"Yeah," she shrugged, "for what it's worth." She blew out more smoke.

"Is he in?"

"Not now," Mrs. Carpenter shook her head, sucking on the cigarette again, "though he was in earlier."

"When do you expect him back?"

"Dunno," she blew out smoke again, "Ain't none of my business."

"We'd like to see his apartment, please," Mary Ellen pulled out the warrant.

Cora Carpenter unfolded the sheet of paper and barely looked at it. She handed it back to Mary Ellen, took one final drag on her cigarette, tossed it neatly into the street, and led them up the bare and gritty steps to the third floor as she blew out the last of the smoke. She dug a ring of keys out of her pocket and fingered through the collection until she reached the one she needed. "I don't know anything about the man except that he's quiet and pays the rent on time. Besides that, it don't matter to me what he does up here, so long as I don't get no complaints," she unlocked the door, but before she could push it open, one of the police officers pulled her out of the way.

John Turner kicked the unlatched door inward and stepped away from the opening. When no shots fired back at them, the FBI agents entered the studio apartment with weapons raised and ready, covering each other's backs. It was a quick matter to ascertain that the two rooms and bath were indeed empty. The weapons returned to their holsters and Mary Ellen went back to ask Mrs. Carpenter another question.

"You said he was here earlier," Mary Ellen reminded her. "Does that mean he came in this morning? Has he been away?"

The woman blinked behind her long stringy bangs, "Yeah, well he works nights, but I know he hasn't been around for a couple of days anyway. Until today, his mailbox was over-flowin' and I usually hear him when he leaves for work at night, and when he comes home in the mornin'," she stated. "I heard him come in this mornin'; must've been some time around five."

"Okay. Thank you very much, Mrs. Carpenter. We'll let you know if we need anything else from you," Mary Ellen dismissed the woman.

"Just lock up when you're done," Mrs. Carpenter reluctantly left them to their investigation.

The FBI agents slipped on latex gloves, not touching anything yet, but taking in everything of the tiny space that did double duty as Richard Humphries' living room and kitchen. Heavy, latex-backed draperies were closed over the front window, casting a gloom over the place; but it was easy to see that the studio was appointed with the castoffs and mismatched articles typical of furnished apartments: A tattered sofa, a patched recliner, a worn, threadbare area rug. Articles of clothing, magazines and newspapers lay discarded about the room. A dish containing the remnants of a meal sat on one end of an abused coffee table. Unwashed dishes were piled high in the porcelain sink. A greasy pot and large spoon sat on a cold burner on the gas stove.

But these things did not concern them. Rather, the FBI agents were interested in what lay on the Formica and stainless kitchen table: Copies of the *Troy City Herald* and the *Riverton Journal* with big holes cut out of them, a jar of rubber cement, a ream of white copy paper, scissors, and a pair of rubber gloves.

John pulled his cell phone out of his pocket and called Ruth Wilson, "I need you to send a team…"

As he spoke to the CSI detective, Mary Ellen checked the bedroom. It was in no better condition than the living room/kitchen had been. The blankets were twisted, the sheets rumpled on the unmade bed, with pillows flattened and lying askew against the headboard. Through the open closet door, Mary Ellen could see that it was all but empty; a few metal hangers on the rod and a pair of beat up Reeboks on the floor. The shoes might be of interest to the CSI people.

Next, noting that the top of a chest of drawers had been cleaned off, except for a gritty, dusty doily and an overflowing ashtray, she checked the contents of the bureau: empty. Apparently, Mr. Humphries had abandoned his apartment without giving notice to his landlady.

As she was about to leave the room, Mary Ellen noticed a framed picture on the nightstand beside the bed. She went over to examine it.

It was a blown up snapshot of two people; a man and a woman, apparently a couple in love. They looked to be in their late thirties or early forties. The tall man, a ruggedly handsome blond with well-developed biceps accentuated by his snug-fitting T-shirt, had his arms protectively wrapped around a dark-haired woman only a couple of inches shorter than he. The woman, though one might not call her a beauty, had an attractive smile and a flirtatious look in her dark brown eyes. Although the large mole that darkened the edge of her left jaw was a distraction, it did not detract from her appearance. On the contrary, it seemed to give her an exotic quality. With a lurch, Mary Ellen realized she was looking at a picture of Richard Humphries and his girlfriend, Adelina Aguilar. A much more flattering picture than those she and John had on file.

"Mary Ellen!" John called from the living room, "Come here. I want you to see this."

Knowing that the forensic people would want to examine this as well, she replaced the picture on the nightstand and joined John in the other room. He had raised the shade at the large front window, and was holding aside one of the draperies. From the window, Mary Ellen could see the South End Post Office, just down the block; Humphries could have easily mailed the ransom notes before he had even taken the children from their beds. But more interesting than that was the fact that from this window one had a perfect view of the ball field and the Dumpster in South Park.

"I'm beginning to understand what happened," Mary Ellen began. But she was interrupted by her cell phone. She grabbed the device from her purse.

It was Paul Thibault.

4:02 P.M.

They found him sitting in a chair in St. Luke's emergency room waiting area with his head in his hands. Mary Ellen sat down on his left while John took the seat to his right. Even then, he did not look up.

"Paul?" She placed a gentle hand on his arm.

"Why?" He raised his head and asked no one in particular, his eyes haunted and bewildered.

"Tell us what happened. Can you do that?" Mary Ellen asked as John took his tape recorder from his coat pocket.

Paul Thibault sighed heavily and seemed uncertain where to begin. He shook his head and started to cry.

Mary Ellen cleared her throat and tried again, "We went by your place earlier and Carmen said you were gone to work."

He nodded. "I couldn't get anything done," he said miserably, "I called Carmen and she told me you'd been by, that I had just missed you. After that, I kept thinking about Marisa and Liana, and the botched ransom thing." He groaned, "So I locked up and came home."

"And what time was that?"

"Three, three-fifteen. I'm not sure," he shook his head again. "Something wasn't right. I could feel it when I came up the back porch. The kitchen door was ajar. I know I locked it before I left. I had this awful feeling that something was wrong." He sobbed again into his hands, but forced himself to continue, "I pushed the door open, and that's when I saw her, lying on the floor. I don't know how long she'd been lying there like that. I could see she'd been hit with something hard across the face; nobody could hurt her like that with their bare hand."

Mary Ellen recognized his searching eyes as a need for understanding. When she nodded, Paul swallowed, and continued.

"There was blood from a large gash on her cheek. Her eye was swollen, too. It looked like she had an egg under her eyelid. And her face was so white, so frighteningly white," He whispered, "I thought she was dead at first. But when I took her in my arms, I could feel she was warm and I could see her pulse beating in her throat." He was in control of himself now, and the story came easily from his lips as he relived the experience, "I called 9-1-1, then I called you, Agent Kelly, because I found your number in the speed dial. Right after I hung up with you, a couple of agents were at the door. They'd heard the call on the wire tap. They waited with me until the ambulance came to take her away," he swallowed again as more tears threatened. "She regained consciousness a little while ago, but she seemed disoriented. They've taken her down to X-ray her head. They told me she has a concussion; now they're trying to determine how badly she's hurt." Again, he searched their eyes for answers, "What am I going to do?"

"Did you notice anything out of sorts in the house, Mr. Thibault?" John asked.

Paul met his brown eyes, "Yeah. Somebody broke into the closet in the entryway. I don't know what they could have been looking for. It's where we keep the vacuum cleaner and cleaning supplies."

"Mr. Thibault," John said carefully, "when we went by earlier, it was to bring back the bags of ransom money—"

"I didn't see—" Paul seemed to be thinking, and suddenly, he appeared to come to some realization. "Could it have been the kidnapper coming back for the ransom?"

"Most likely. A team has been sent to your house to look for evidence. I told them to look for the money."

"Oh, God," Paul moaned as he bowed his head in his hands again.

"If that's what's happened, Mr. Thibault, then our kidnapper has taken the bait." John said confidently. "We left the money in the bags with the tracking devices in them. Anywhere he goes, we'll be able to follow."

"I don't care about the money. That's not what's important to me," Paul said miserably.

"We know," Mary Ellen said, "but he could unknowingly lead us to the girls.

4:24 P.M.

By the time they left St. Luke's Hospital, the sun was already lowering into the western sky so that the hospital cast a long shadow over the parking lot. Back in the Crown Victoria, John filled Mary Ellen in on what he had learned from the detective who had been sent to the scene.

"Unfortunately, the surveillance camera didn't 'see' who actually invaded the Thibault house," John said. "Footprints in the snow in the backyard indicate that the perpetrator gained access to the property by sneaking in from Greenwood Drive. Then he left the same way."

"Did anyone on Greenwood notice anything suspicious?" Mary Ellen asked.

"Some of Troy City's finest are canvassing the neighborhood to find that out. It'll be good to have witnesses for the prosecution when the time arrives, but we don't need them to chase down the suspect. Frank Snell's tracking devices are working," John pointed to the green blips moving slowly across the dashboard-mounted computer screen. "King and Dunne are with us on it at the moment. They actually have a head start. They started tracking the subject while we were still talking to Paul Thibault."

King and Dunne, a team John always secretly thought sounded like a sixties folk group, were Special Agents Leonard King and Carolyn Dunne. King was a seasoned twelve-year veteran who had joined the Bureau as a field agent after serving five years on the Boston police force. Dunne had only about three years with the Bureau. But she was intelligent and dedicated; a true asset to the Bureau. Both agents had outstanding records. Turner and Kelly were fortunate to have their help chasing down the suspect.

At the moment, it looked like the perpetrator was heading north on the Interstate. John turned the Crown Vic around, left the parking lot by the Main Street exit, and headed north to Highland Avenue, then east. He knew there was an entrance to the highway just up the road. Not too much farther now and they'd be on the Interstate in pursuit of the little green flashing lights on the computer screen.

With one hand on the wheel, he reached out and he stuck the magnetic bubble light on the roof of the car, then turned on his flashing headlights and the siren. He stepped harder on the gas pedal and the Crown Victoria responded eagerly, grimly reminding him of another time when he'd done the same thing with dire consequences. He noticed Mary Ellen check that her seatbelt was firmly clipped as he veered around slow-moving vehicles while others in his path prudently got out of his way. John pushed that other incident out of his mind and focused on the encouraging prospect of nabbing the ransom thief and Carmen Thibault's assailant; Antonio Ibarra's accomplice.

Soon. Very soon.

4:43 P.M.

Although Patrick knew he was mincemeat if either of his parents caught him peeking in the guest files for personal information, the boy was completely lured by the cloak-and-dagger aspect of Jet's request. The opportunity finally presented itself late in the afternoon: His mother was occupied with the cook, his father had gone out to get last minute supplies for tomorrow night's New Year's Eve party, and Becky was upstairs with the girls; one always had to be wary of a sister who tended to snoop and tattletale on her younger brother. That's when Patrick finally got his chance to slip behind the reservation desk and get the information Jet had asked for.

Now, Patrick sat on Jet's bunk to give him his report.

Patrick remembered them; he'd been on the desk Tuesday night. The man's name was Richard Humphries. He and his wife, Lena, were traveling with their sons. They had come in after dark while supper was still being served. Initially, they'd rented Cabin 3 for only two nights, "But I noticed that they've extended their stay until tomorrow," Patrick said.

"Can you describe them?" Jet demanded.

"Mr. Humphries is a big guy, muscles, well over six feet, maybe six-five or -six. He has blond hair, but I can't remember the color of his eyes. Mrs. Humphries is a big woman. Not fat; just big. She's tall, but not as tall as her husband. She has dark hair. The boys are young, maybe four and six years old; dark hair, dark eyes. I guess they take for their mother."

"Anything else you can remember? Did they speak with any kind of accent? Was there anything strange or odd about them?"

"Humphries did all the talking, and he spoke English. He sounded normal to me; I couldn't hear any foreign accent." Patrick rolled his blue eyes, "And as far as finding anything strange about them, well, gee-whiz, Jet. We get all kinds in here! I mean, there's odd, and then there's Odd with a capital O." When he caught Jet's impatient look, he shrugged and continued, "Look. The man came in totally beat; he'd been through a lot. They'd been caught up in the blizzard, for Pete's sake! He was tired and upset. The wife and kids were quiet; I didn't pay much attention to them. I showed them to the cabin, made sure they had clean towels, turned up the heat and lit the water heater for them. Then I left. A little while later, they came back to the dining room to have some supper, but to tell you the truth, we haven't seen much of them since then. That's what efficiency cabins are all about; people doing their own thing without too much interference from the inn. Sometimes they take boxed meals from the kitchen and eat them in the cabin. Nothing strange in that; people do it all the time."

"What about distinguishing characteristics, like a mustache, whiskers, tattoo? Any blemish or mole?"

"Gee-whiz, man. You sound like a cop." Patrick complained raking his fingers through his black hair. He rubbed his forehead and closed his eyes, then shook his head, "Sorry, man. Can't remember."

Jet sighed in disappointment and tried to think of what should be his next step, but Patrick's voice broke his concentration.

"On the way to the cabin, one of the boys got a wicked nosebleed."

"Which one?"

"The smaller one." At that moment, Jet heard Uncle Greg's Jeep crunch over the ice and salt in the driveway, "Sorry, Jet. I gotta go help Dad unload the car."

"Hey!" Jet stopped Patrick suddenly thinking of one last question, "What about the car? Don't you take the make and registration of the car when people register?"

"Oh, yeah." Patrick frowned and dug a slip of paper from his jeans pocket, "I forgot." He threw the paper at his cousin. Jet tried to catch it but it landed on the floor. "I gotta go!" He ran out of the cabin, calling, "I'm coming, Dad!"

*****

Jet picked up the crumpled paper and flattened it out. It had been torn from a notepad that bore the Tate Lodge letterhead and logo. Patrick had scribbled the information on the paper. Richard Humphries' car was listed as a Plymouth Sundance with Quebec plates.

Jet's heart quickened and Hank jumped at his cousin's audible gasp, "Whaaa?"

"It's got to be the same car!"

"What car?"

"Adelina Aguilar's." Jet turned intent blue eyes on his cousin, "Hank, you know her car, don't you?"

"Yeah. It was a small navy blue Plymouth."

"A Sundance."

"Yeah."

"And in the newscast we saw before, they showed her in a snapshot, leaning against a dark blue car. They also said Adelina Aguilar was last seen in Quebec." Jet waved the slip of paper in Hank's face, "Well, the Plymouth Sundance Humphries was driving has a Quebec registration."

This could be the proof he needed. There were too many coincidences to be mere happenstance; the Plymouth with the Quebec plates, the girlish brown eyes in the window, the kid with the nosebleed, the dark-haired Amazon-type woman he'd mistaken for a man, Donna's excitement at finding the children. He had to be right. He dug his new cell phone out of his pocket, a Christmas present from his parents, given him with the understanding it was to be used for emergencies only. It was only the second time he was using it.

And this *was* an emergency.

4:47 P.M.

They were speeding up the Interstate, concentrating on the flashing green lights on the monitor. Neither of them spoke so that when the melodic chimes of John's cell phone sounded, it was like being doused with cold water.

John answered, using his hands-free hook up. It was Leonard King.

"You're not going to believe this," came the FBI agent's baritone voice. From his tone, John knew it wasn't good news. He knew of King's reputation as a serious and dedicated agent. If something had gone wrong, it wasn't due to any fault of his, or of his partner's, Carolyn Dunne.

"What happened?" John demanded with a deep breath.

"He gave us the slip."

John glanced at the computer screen. The little green blips flashed regularly, but now remained in the same spot. Apparently, the perp had stopped moving. "I can see the blips—"

"Oh, yeah. Snell's tracking devices worked like a charm. We followed those little green lights all over the place, until we finally caught up with them."

"I'm getting close myself. I'm taking the next exit," John said. King gave a low mirthless chuckle that made John doubt for the first time. "Where are you?" John asked slowly.

"At the city dump."

"What?" Still following the flashing lights, John turned onto a narrow, paved, but rutty road.

"The subject is smart," King was saying. "He must've figured the bags were wired. We got here just in time to watch a Troy City trash truck dump them out."

As John brought the Crown Victoria over a rise, he could see King's dark form standing beside his car. A DPW trash truck was just pulling away from a pile of refuse. John uttered a rare expletive. "Cordon off the area," he told King, "We'll have to get a team out here to find those bags. Maybe we can at least get prints to tie the suspect to the crime."

John swerved his car across the front of the trash truck, forcing it to stop. The dust was still rising in the air as he left the car running and got out. John approached the bewildered driver and his astonished partner with his picture ID held up in front of him. He knew he didn't have to look back to assure himself that Mary Ellen had him covered.

"Hold on a minute, sir! FBI!" When the driver rolled down his window, John continued, "Please step out of the truck."

The driver gave him a surly look and shrugged.

"Just do as I say," he ordered. When the man and his partner stood before him beside the garbage truck, John explained, "I'd like you to make me a list of all of the stops you've made since one o'clock this afternoon."

4:49 P.M.

John was still busy talking with the DPW driver and his partner when Mary Ellen's own cell phone rang. Observing that he was in no danger from either of the cooperative men, she allowed herself to relax a bit and answered the phone with her weapon still in her right hand.

Caller ID informed her it was Jet. She'd saved his number from his earlier call, intending on thanking him for his lead. *He must be checking to see if I got his voice mail.*

"Hi, Jet." At the mention of the boy's name, she saw John dart impatient eyes her way. Keeping the subjects within sight, she turned slightly to avert herself from John's condescending antics and expressions. "I was meaning to call you—" The boy was breathless and talking so fast she could make out little of what he said.

"Whoa, slow down."

4:50 P.M.

The two DPW workers were cooperative and helpful. The heavier, swarthy driver stood beside the truck as the younger, taller black one busily copied a list of all their stops that afternoon. John felt they posed no threat; he had already holstered his pistol, knowing that Mary Ellen had his back.

Or did she?

He dared an occasional glance toward Mary Ellen on the phone. It was the Tate kid again. What was eating him now? Why didn't she just let his call go to voicemail? This was important; she needed her attention focused on what they were doing now, not chatting with a teenager who saw himself as the next Dick Tracy. John couldn't imagine that anything the kid had to say was of any significance. It peeved him beyond words.

She'd turned so that he couldn't see her face, but her body language spoke volumes. She was listening attentively, her back stiff and straight. Suddenly, to his shock, she put her gun down on the hood of the Crown Vic. She had completely let her guard down. How'd she know this wasn't going to suddenly turn ugly? She was leaving his ass out in the wind! John could see her writing on a piece of paper, using the hood of the car as a table. Then she was thanking Jet profusely, and ending with a warning.

"All right, Jet," John heard her tell him slowly and deliberately, "I want you to listen to me carefully. You are *not*, under any circumstance, to approach this man. Let the law enforcement people do their jobs. *Do not* get in the way. Do you understand?"

John smirked. Fat chance *he'd* stay out of trouble, whatever it was. If they gave a prize for getting into the thick of things, that kid would get Highest Honors for Nose.

Mary Ellen glanced his way as she hurriedly punched another number on her cell phone. He wanted to ask her what was going on, but the man was handing him back the sheet of paper. He'd have to deal with her later.

John looked at the long list. It seemed to be made up of businesses and streets in the East End. The fifth name from the top of the sheet, glared like a red beacon: Greenwood Drive.

"Are these stops listed in chronological order?" John asked the men.

The driver regarded him blankly, and his partner translated for him in Portuguese. Then to John, the black man explained in English, accepting the role of spokesperson. "He's new from the Azores and doesn't speak a lot of English. His name is Francisco, but we call him Frank."

"Yeah," Frank looked quizzically from his partner to John.

"So when did you pick up Greenwood Drive? What's your name?"

"Russ," answered Frank's partner immediately. "We did that area after lunch." He shrugged. "Judging by the time we got in, we were on schedule; it had to be around 1:30. No later than 1:45."

Damn! John thought. The perp must've observed everything that had transpired from his window overlooking South Park. He'd realized all the extra people out there had to be cops. Maybe was tipped off by Ibarra himself! He'd waited while the DPW truck picked up the contents of the Dumpster. He'd mailed the ransom notes, so he knew where the Thibaults lived. All he had to do was wait to see if the money was returned to their house.

He'd waited. Patiently waited.

He probably saw Paul leave, observed him and Mary Ellen return the bags, knew that Carmen was alone, then, either by luck or again with certain foreknowledge, knew better than to come by the front where the surveillance cameras would spot him, and snuck in the back way to attack Carmen and steal the money.

Damn! He'd known the bags were rigged, or maybe, he hadn't wanted to take that chance. Either way, he'd known enough to take the money and get rid of the bags, and he'd ditched them in one of the trashcans that lined the street waiting for pick-up. And then King and Dunne, and he and Mary Ellen, had followed a decoy, thinking they were closing in on their man. They'd been duped, and John suddenly felt stupid. He wished he'd gone back to question Ibarra again. This time without Mary Ellen.

"Can we go home now?" Russ asked.

The man's words burned through John's thoughts, rudely bringing him back to the present. John regarded him and nodded brusquely, "Yes," then stopped them before they got back into the truck. "Wait. Did you see anything out of the ordinary on Greenwood Drive? Maybe someone running? Someone adding something to a trashcan just before you picked it up?"

Russ and Frank exchanged looks, then Russ answered, "Well, I almost got run over by a dark blue car. The truck was in the middle of the road, and I was getting the next can, you know? All of a sudden, like out of nowhere comes this blue car, tires squealing. Missed me by this much," he held his thumb and index finger apart to indicate inches. He shrugged, "Does that help?"

"Yes, it does, Russ. Thank you both for your cooperation."

John returned to the Crown Vic and shot Mary Ellen a disparaging look as she got into the car with him. He pulled forward to let the DPW truck pass, then threw the lever into Park and opened his mouth to sternly address his partner; but she cut him off.

"Jet has a lead for us."

John gave her an incredulous grimace. "Oh, really—?" he began.

"He's found Adelina Aguilar's dark blue Plymouth Sundance—"

"He what?"

"—And the cabin Richard Humphries rented on Tuesday night."

She was interrupted again as Leonard King stuck his large black face in John's window. John slid the glass down so that he could hear what the man had to say.

"We're through cordoning off the area where the truck just unloaded. The teams are here setting up lights so they can sift through the garbage. So if we're done here, we'd like to head back."

"Fine, Len. We were just leaving ourselves," John waved at Carolyn Dunne who stood beside their car. The pretty brunette smiled and waved back. "Thanks."

"You owe me a new pair of shoes, man," Agent King shot back dryly as he returned to his car.

John turned his attention back on Mary Ellen as he started the Crown Vic, "Continue."

Mary Ellen repeated everything Jet had told her: About how a woman fitting Adelina Aguilar's description and Humphries showed up at the Lodge Tuesday night with two little boys; that one little boy had girlish eyes and resembled Marisa, while the smaller one had nosebleeds; about Donna's obsession with seeking out those children. She ended with the fact that the navy blue Plymouth with the Quebec registration was gone this morning, although the wife and the boys remained at the cabin. And that the car had not as yet returned.

In spite of himself, John had to beat down his anger and acknowledge that it did indeed sound like important, pertinent information.

"Is that it?"

"No."

In the glow of the dashboard lights, John saw Mary Ellen's eyes flash with excitement. *She's enjoying this,* he thought; but he said nothing because she was explaining.

"Carl from Support gave me Adelina's tag numbers. John, the numbers Jet gave me match. It's Adelina's car."

While on the one hand he was glad they were finally making progress on the case, he couldn't help but feel resentment that again it was Jet Tate who had given them one of their best leads. He couldn't understand how it was that the kid seemed always to be at the right place—or the wrong one, depending on one's point of view—at the right time.

Sheer luck. Or fate.

"I've alerted the Manchester Office, but they don't have anybody in the area and those they have in the city right now are busy. It seems there was an attempted bank robbery with hostages and most of their people are on the scene. When I explained what was going down, they were sympathetic and promised to take a couple of operatives off the hostage thing and send them as soon as they could. The only thing is, they don't have any available choppers either." She was saying, "It's about a hundred miles from Manchester to Littleton; it's going to take them a good two hours to drive up there, even with sirens blaring. It's five o'clock; rush hour traffic could pose a problem."

"So what do you suggest we do?" he asked. The Crown Victoria bounced behind King's car as they followed the access road out of the dump.

"I made a couple of calls while you were busy with the DPW workers. The first one was to the State Police. They've been put on statewide alert for the dark blue Plymouth. While I was at it, I alerted the state police of all of Massachusetts' border states so our guy is pretty well bottled in. My last call was to Sheriff Matson. He's agreed to lend us of one of Troy County's helicopters. He'll pilot us himself. I would imagine he's already waiting for us at the Ridgeport Police Station."

John got back on the highway, heading south.

5:04 P.M.

Marisa sighed heavily. She had been sulking since yesterday. Since the slap.

This game isn't fun anymore, she thought.

In fact, it had stopped being amusing two days ago.

At first, it had been an adventure. It had been fun to spread out a blanket on the floor and make believe they were having a picnic, or that they were camping in the woods filled with scary creatures. The little cabin had been something like the playhouse back home; well, at *Papi's* house. Only without the dolls.

It had even been exciting pretending to be boys, and she and Liana had let *Tía* cut their hair. But now that Marisa realized she was stuck with the short curls, it made her sad. She had liked wearing pretty bows in her beautiful long tresses. She didn't think there was any way to tie bows into hair *this* short. At the time, it had sounded like a good idea, a great disguise. But now she was unhappy and she didn't want to be a boy any more either.

I want to go home.

But she wouldn't say so out loud. She didn't want another slap across the face like the one she'd received yesterday. It had stung and taken her by complete surprise, cutting off her breath and making her cry bitter, angry tears into her pillow. She couldn't recall ever having been struck before. The slap itself had not been all that painful, even if it had sent her against the wall. She'd been able to see the red mark on her face for the rest of the day yesterday, but today, there was no sign of it that she could see in the bathroom mirror. Yet she knew she'd remember that slap forever. She would not give anyone cause to hit her again. Not ever!

Nor would she complain for anyone to hear her.

But that didn't stop her from grumbling in her heart and shooting daggers with her eyes at *Tía's* back. She knew the way she felt now was disrespectful; but she also knew that no one could hear what went on in her head; except, of course, as Sister Dorothy said, God. But that was okay, because Marisa knew He'd keep her secret. She, herself, would never share this one, not even with *Tía*. And that made her sad because once she had loved her; but not any more. Not if she was going to let her nasty man friend, Rick (She refused to call him *Tío*), slap her that way.

This morning when they woke up mean old Rick was gone. And although that was a relief to Marisa, *Tía* was not happy about it; Marisa could tell. It had put *Tía* in a bad mood that had gotten worse as the day wore on and Rick did not return. So when she had asked *Tía* if she could go out, the answer had been no.

Marisa had been told they couldn't go out because Liana kept getting nosebleeds. Earlier, the three of them had gone out to the little store on the big road to get a few groceries, and on the way back, Liana got another nosebleed; so she supposed it was true. *Tía* had given her all the groceries to carry so that *Tía* could pick up Liana. Even though it upset her to have to carry all the clumsy items, and the jug of milk hurt her hand, she knew Liana couldn't walk all the way back with a bleeding nose. She had done her best without complaining.

If truth be known, she was worried about her little sister. Liana seemed to be getting more tired more often. Marisa had never seen her looking so pale and drawn. She looked skinnier than usual and her cheeks seemed to sink in. Something about her eyes wasn't right; they were shiny and sick-looking with dark circles underneath them. Also, Liana didn't want to eat, she took a lot of naps and didn't find anything funny. When had Liana ever not wanted to play? She said she was too sleepy. Something was really wrong with her. If the reason she couldn't go outside was because Liana was sick, then Marisa could accept that. After Liana had her nap, though, maybe she would feel better. Marisa truly hoped so.

If they were home, *Mami*—no, Mummy. Since August, she was supposed to call her Mummy. If they were home, Mummy would call Dr. Winter, and she would take care of Liana and make her better. That was one more reason Marisa wanted to leave this place and go home! She had *lots* of reasons for wanting to go home, the least of which being that she missed playing with her dolls. But more than that, she missed *Papi*, and Mummy, and Paul-Daddy. Even Donna. No matter that *Tía* and her bad man friend, Rick, forbade her and Liana from talking about them; she could still *think* about them. She could remember them and the last time she was with them.

Like yesterday, when she saw Donna.

Yes, she knew it was Donna; there was no way anybody could tell her it wasn't. She knew her dog, after all! Ever since Donna tried to play with her and Liana, they hadn't been allowed to go outside to play. They weren't even allowed to stand near the window any more! That wasn't fair. The snow was so pretty.

Okay, so Liana was sick, but there was nothing wrong with *Marisa*; so why did *she* have to stay inside on this cold but beautiful sunny day? Why couldn't *she* go out and play? She could amuse herself in the snow. She'd done it before. Maybe she could finish the snowman and when Liana woke up, it would make her smile to see him all done.

Maybe *Tía* felt it would be unfair to let Marisa out if Liana couldn't go with her. The problem was *Tía* had said no and Marisa wouldn't dare ask again; she knew better than that. That meant she was stuck in the cabin. Forever.

She couldn't understand why she couldn't look out the window, though. That had not been explained to her satisfaction. From the top bunk bed, through the space between the curtains, she gazed longingly at the pine trees, so beautiful with their branches bowing low with the weight of the snow. Pretty icicles hung from the edge of the roof where they had frozen after the sun went to bed last night. Today the sun had warmed them up, and drops of water dripped from their pointy tips. Now as the sun was going to bed again, the drops were starting to freeze once more, making the icicles longer.

So pretty.

But Marisa also knew it meant it would be too cold to go out now; with dismay she realized she had missed another day of playing in the snow. And although from where she sat she could not see him, the snowman they had started yesterday was still there, not finished. He must be so sad.

Suddenly, something moved among the lower, snow-encrusted branches of one of the big trees outside. Marisa quietly repositioned herself on the bunk so that she could have a better look.

5:12 P.M.

Adelina gently touched the sleeping child's forehead; it was hot, feverish. She had no idea how high the fever was or how serious it could be. But she did what she could; she freshened the cool damp cloth on Liana's forehead, and gave her a children's medicine that promised to reduce fevers. The child swallowed the medicine in her sleep, but otherwise did not stir.

It had been a mistake to take her out earlier; but they had needed groceries. And Rick had taken the car, so they had been forced to walk the half mile to and from the convenience store. The exertion had precipitated another nosebleed, this one the worst so far. And then Liana had slept almost the entire day.

Adelina also felt bad for Marisa. The poor little thing really wanted to go out and play and it had been such a beautiful day. It was a sin to keep a child in who wanted to go out so much. Marisa had been inside too much and she was unhappy. Adelina knew Marisa blamed her for everything; the haircut, the boredom, the injustice of the restrictions Rick had imposed on all of them. Maybe the child was right.

Had Adelina realized it would be like this, she never would have agreed to Rick's plan. But it had seemed like a good idea at the time. It was the only way she could be with the girls, like before, he'd said.

But it wasn't like before. Before, the children had been happy to be with her. They had baked cookies together, and had played and had run free like children should. They had been full of giggles and sweet smiles and loving kisses and hugs. Now Liana was too sick to do anything, Marisa was sullen and unhappy, and she, herself, was worried and frightened.

Now, they had to hide; it was never like *that* before.

She dared a peek out the window. The sun was fading from the sky and dusk was quickly settling in. Soon she'd have to turn on a light, but for now, she preferred to remain in the darkness.

She looked at the wall clock as she came away from the window. She could just make it out in the gathering gloom: Going on a quarter after five. She'd have to be starting supper soon. But when should she begin cooking? She had no idea. Rick would probably be hungry when he got back from whatever he'd been doing all day. If supper wasn't ready when he set foot in the door, she imagined he'd be angry.

But that's what happens when you don't give your partner any idea of when to expect you home. If I start supper too early, then it overcooks and dries out while I try to keep it warm; but if I start too late, then it's not ready on time.

Well, she'd wait until he called her cell phone, since she had no idea how or where to reach *him*.

She added more water to the humidifier and made sure the mist was directed toward the child, but not wetting her. Then she stretched out on the bed beside Liana. The girl's small body took up very little space on the bottom bunk. It felt hot where their bodies touched. Poor, sweet, little thing.

What on earth is he doing that could take all day?

5:26 P.M.

Agent Kelly had warned Jet to stay away from the people in Cabin 3 but he felt he had to spy on the place until the authorities arrived. At least that way if the occupants left in the meantime, he'd be able to give a report on when, how, and hopefully where they went. Toward that end, beneath a large spruce tree Jet and Hank had found a suitable hiding place with the perfect vantage point. From where he sat alone cross-legged on a thick, cushy bed of soft, dry needles, completely hidden from view by the tree's low-hanging boughs, he could easily see any activity that might transpire around Cabin 3. An added advantage afforded by the spruce tree was that its drooping boughs also sheltered him from the wind.

Yet, in spite of his comfortable hiding place, Jet was agitated. He'd called Agent Kelly over a half-hour ago, and although he knew he had to give them time to get here, he was worried that something might go wrong.

Just then, he heard the crunch of feet on the frozen snow. He dared to peek out between the boughs of the tree. At the same moment, Hank pushed into the hiding place in a shower of snow roughly loosened from the heavy limb.

"Geesh!" Jet brushed away the snow from his clothes. "You're like a mule in a china shop! Could you make any more noise?"

Hank stopped in mid-stride, dumfounded, "Hey, man. I figured you wanted your supper while it was still hot."

"Did you have any trouble getting it?"

"Na-aah," Hank shook his head, "Like Patrick said, they're used to people eating in their cabins. Nobody asked any questions, and I didn't offer any information. I did see Christine, though, and I told her we were eating together. I won't tell you the name she called me, and if your parents want to know why we don't show up at supper, I'm sure she'll volunteer her own version of what I said."

"Hmm. It should at least buy us some time before they come looking for us."

Hank took a flashlight out of his pocket, flicked it on, and stood it on end to give them light to eat supper by. "You think anybody will see the light?"

"We won't have it on very long. Let me have one of those." Jet pulled off his gloves and took one of the boxes from Hank's extended hand as the boy clumsily joined him on his comfortable cushion of spruce needles. The box was delightfully warm, and Jet inhaled the delectable aroma of chicken. "Mm-m-m!" Jet couldn't help exclaiming even before he opened the box.

Inside were half a succulent roasted chicken, mashed potatoes and gravy, fresh broccoli and baby carrots in garlic butter, a homemade buttered biscuit, and a small container of cranberry sauce. Hank dug a set of plastic utensils from the pocket of his jacket and the two boys attacked their supper with the fervor of starving men.

Suddenly, a sound just outside their hideout caused Jet to nearly upset his box of food. "Who's there?" he demanded. Pulling the bough aside, he grabbed their visitor's wrist and dragged the newcomer under the tree a bit more roughly than he'd intended.

Then he knew without a doubt that he was staring into the frightened face of Marisa Ibarra.

5:45 P.M.

Despite Agent Kelly's warning against making contact with the kidnapper and Hank's own objections to being left behind in the hideout, Jet accompanied Marisa back to Cabin 3. No amount of arguing could persuade him to reconsider.

Hank had told him that the former nanny was a devout Catholic. Then Marisa had said *Tía* Adelina was very worried about Liana. Based on both of these facts, Jet believed he could convince the woman to get medical attention for Liana and surrender herself to the authorities.

Hank watched in trepidation as Jet and Marisa left the safety of the hideout and trudged over to Cabin 3 in the snow. The door swung wide as they approached, and even from where he remained out of sight, Hank heard the woman's thunderstruck exclamation.

"Maris—Mario! What are you doing?"

Although his cousin spoke in a normal tone of voice, Hank

could hear Jet perfectly. "It's okay, Ms. Aguilar," Jet assured her, "Marisa and I have been talking. She wants to go home to her mother and father."

"It is no concern to you," the woman sternly replied in her heavily accented English as she reached to grasp Marisa's arm.

The child flinched and ducked behind Jet. Hank instantly recognized his cousin's predicament. How could Jet protect the child if this woman decided to fight for her? Certainly, she outweighed him by thirty pounds and outreached him by at least six inches. He was clearly at a disadvantage. Hank knew he'd been right; Jet should have left Marisa safely with him in the hideout.

Jet seemed aware of the danger himself, and Hank saw him draw himself up, as though to show the woman she did not intimidate him. But although his stance was assertive and unyielding, he continued to speak to her slowly in a subdued, non-threatening tone.

"Well, now, Ms. Aguilar, I think we both know that the children are not yours. You and your friend have stolen the girls from their father's house, and you know that is a sin."

The nanny gasped, evidently taken aback how much Jet knew. She blinked at him, "Who are you?"

"My name is Jet. I'm Marisa's friend," he said simply, "and Liana's. I've come to help them. I've come to help you do the right thing."

I'd better go help him, Hank thought.

But then, to Hank's horror, Jet and Marisa entered the cabin and the door closed firmly behind them.

6:00 P.M.

Everything the boy said made sense to her.

Adelina knew it was wrong to take the children away from their parents. She had known better all along; but she had allowed Rick to persuade her that she was entitled to some kind of rights because she had raised the girls from infancy.

Rick pointed out that she had spent more time with them than either of their parents had. And didn't the children deserve better than a drug-addicted alcoholic for a mother? Wasn't that why Antonio hired her in the first place? He had thrown Carmen out of the house because she was nothing more than a despicable reprobate, a lewd, lascivious, immoral woman; definitely not the kind of person to raise two beautiful angels such as Marisa and Liana. And Adelina had done such a remarkable job of instilling basic moral principles in the girls. They were good and obedient, respectful children. Rick had repeatedly praised her on her fine skills in child rearing, ruing the fact that, this late in life, Adelina would probably never have children of her own. Such a shame since she would have made such a wonderful, affectionate mother.

Rick also pointed out that although Antonio was a good man and a loving father, he just did not have time for them. It was a plain and simple fact that when one had to work five days a week and then come home and take care of a house and property, one had to be exhausted, and definitely not in the mood to play with two enthusiastic and rambunctious children. He must be feeling relieved now that he didn't have to dedicate all of his time caring for kids in addition to everything else he had to do. Rick imagined Antonio was just as happy to be rid of them; glad that Carmen had won custody. He certainly had not fought very hard to keep them if the judge saw fit to give them back to Carmen, given her past record.

It was truly a shame that the children she had raised from babies should be allowed to forget the excellent training Adelina had given them; for no doubt, they would stop saying their prayers, would forget their good manners, would become brats in no time, now that Carmen was in charge. They'd probably even forget their Spanish.

Rick had convinced her that she was doing the right thing for the girls. And she had listened with increasing interest as Rick explained how they could get the children, take them away, and the four of them could go back to Canada, then escape to Colombia where they would live together as a family.

The children would be hers.

Hers forever.

Adelina knew now that she had been a fool. She had allowed herself to be manipulated and had succumbed to temptation. By habit, her hand went up to her throat, searching for the crucifix and the medals she always wore; but they were gone. She'd lost them; or maybe her Savior and her saints had abandoned her because of the awful thing she'd done.

But maybe not. Maybe God had sent her this boy, Jet. *What a strange name!* Could this Jet be God's messenger, sent to remind her of things she knew deep down in her heart? Things she should have thought about before and resisted Rick's tempting plan? How could God ever forgive her for what she had done? How could Antonio? And Carmen?

There was something else Jet had said that made a lot of sense.

Liana needed medical attention. Adelina knew that, too. Had she still been their nanny, she would have taken the child to her pediatrician, or maybe even to the emergency room by now. So what was she waiting for? This nosebleed problem was definitely more severe than she'd ever seen it. Why hadn't she done something about it?

The answer was simple: Adelina was afraid. She knew that once she brought Liana to the hospital, it would be all over. She would never be able to pass her off as a boy; not for very long, at least. She would have to give the child's real name, and that would sound the alarm, and then—

"Ms. Aguilar!"

She started out of her ruminations. In the yellow glow of the tiny lamp on the table, the boy regarded her with imploring blue eyes.

"What are you going to do about this?" he demanded.

What, indeed? Fear and doubt overtook her like a giant wave and she shook her head as the words came out in Spanish, "What am I going to do?"

"Ms. Aguilar, you've got to turn yourself in," Jet was saying.

But Marisa's scream claimed their full attention, "Liana's bleeding again!"

6:14 P.M.

As the Troy County Sheriff's helicopter flew at top speed toward the Tate Lodge, Mary Ellen Kelly and John Turner kept in constant communication with Ground Support.

The state police on all of Massachusetts' borders were on watch for Adelina Aguilar's dark blue Plymouth but as yet the car had not been seen. Any number of reasons could account for this: The suspect might have ditched the car and was now driving a different vehicle; or perhaps he had slipped over the state line before all units had been alerted and positioned; or else the man realized he was being chased and had gone to ground. Whatever the case, the fact that he had not been picked up made the FBI agents uncomfortable. In all scenarios, if the subject suspected that he had been identified, he would now be in a heightened emotional state, desperate, and feeling trapped. The authorities had to presume he was armed and dangerous at this point, and that meant that any unsuspecting citizen who might innocently confront him would be in grave peril.

"How much longer, Sheriff?" Mary Ellen yelled over the chopper's engine.

"We're makin' good time," Sheriff Craig Matson replied. Serving his fourth term as sheriff of Troy County, Craig Matson was a fixture in county politics. His charismatic charm, handsome smile, and easy-going nature coupled with his no-nonsense, tough-on-crime attitude impressed men and women alike. He seemed unbeatable in every election. He also knew when to let the FBI take over. Clearly, this was their show now.

"We're over halfway there. I figure we should get there in about half an hour." Then he added grimly, "But this is the easy part." He squarely met her questioning gaze, "When we get there, we're gonna hafta find this place in the dark."

6:30 P.M.

Dr. Thomas Poole flashed a light into Carmen's eyes and regarded her with consternation. Despite his recommendations, Carmen insisted on going home.

"If there is nothing more that you can do for me other than 'observe me,' I can't see the point in spending the night in the hospital," she said. The truth of the matter was that since her bout in rehab, the thought of spending more time than absolutely necessary in a hospital environment was more than enough, thank you very much. "Paul will keep vigil over me, Dr. Poole," Carmen assured the ER doctor.

Paul squeezed her hand and nodded.

"Well, Mrs. Thibault," Dr. Poole slung his stethoscope around his neck, and replaced his penlight into the breast pocket of his white lab coat, "I certainly cannot keep you if you don't want to stay." He gave her a parting look as he left the examination room, "The police want to take your statement now."

As though they had been waiting at the door, the two Troy City officers entered the small room before the door closed behind the doctor. The woman, a small blond with hazel eyes, did the talking for both of them.

"I'm Sandra Lynch, and this is my partner, Larry Walsh," said the officer. Then glancing up at Paul, she added, "Perhaps you'd like to speak with us privately?"

Paul made to leave, but Carmen held onto his hand, "No, that's quite all right. My husband can stay; I have nothing to say to you that I need to keep from him."

Carmen gave the cops a full description of the man who had come to the kitchen door only moments after the FBI agents had left. He had flashed some kind of badge saying he had come to read the water meter. He was taller than Paul; she figured maybe six-five, six-six, blond hair around the edges of a navy blue knitted cap, and dark brown eyes. He wore a black waist-length jacket, zipped to the neck, with the name Mike stitched on the left breast.

"It seemed on the up-and-up to me," Carmen explained, "so

I opened the door to let him go down to the basement. That's when he pushed me up against the wall, pinning me there with his arm across my throat, cutting off my wind." Paul gasped and Carmen patted his hand until he relaxed. She continued, "He was strong and there was little I could do to defend myself, although I fought like the dickens. I suppose his jacket protected his arms from scratching and biting, because I couldn't seem to hurt him. I feared I'd pass out for lack of air if I didn't do something. So I tried stomping on his foot, but he only pressed harder against my neck and cracked my head against the wall. When my ears started to buzz, in a final act of desperation, I managed to knee him in the groin. He let me go then and I tried to get away, but I guess I was rather clumsy from having had my breath cut off for so long; I stumbled. I suppose I didn't hit my mark, either, for he recovered quickly and was back at me sooner than I had expected. This time, he struck me hard with his revolver. And then, I don't remember anything until I regained consciousness in the hospital."

When the police were finished with their questions, she was allowed to leave, but not before the ER doctor spoke to her one more time.

"Mrs. Thibault, you were very lucky. Had your assailant struck you with the same force on the temple, the story might have had a more unfortunate outcome. As it is," the doctor continued over her and Paul's shocked gasps, "you will probably be sore for a few days, but you should be none the worse for the ordeal."

When they got into the car, Paul suggested, "How about we go out to dinner?"

"Good Lord!" Carmen protested, "I'll certainly frighten away all the clientele. They'll think Scar Face has joined them for dinner!"

"Okay, then," he said. "How about some Chinese take-out?"

They said very little on the ride home. Carmen knew that Paul was worried about her, so she didn't mention the aching that seemed to involve her entire head. She was surprised when instead of driving up the driveway, Paul stopped the Mustang in front of the house and came around to open her door for her.

"Really, Paul. I'm not an invalid—" she started to object.

But he cut her off, "I think it's better if you come in through the front door. The kitchen is a bit of a mess, and I want to clean it up first," he explained as he helped her into the house. But instead of guiding her into the living room, he carried her upstairs to their bedroom.

The Chinese was good, what little Carmen ate of it. She found she had no appetite. Paul took the dishes away, and although he said nothing about the food she left on her plate, she knew he was upset.

Now, she was alone in the bedroom. The headache thrummed mercilessly in her head, the wound on her cheek stung, her eyes were heavy, and, early as it was, she wanted bed; not that her brain would allow her to sleep. Not so long ago, she would not have been able to get through something like this without a bottle of Scotch or a ball of crack. Thank God, there was nothing like that in the house to tempt her; the spirit was willing, but the flesh was always weak, after all.

In the bathroom, she found a bottle of ibuprofen in the medicine chest. She popped a couple of pills into her mouth and swallowed them down with a glass of water from the tap. They would have to do.

She stared at the stranger in the mirror over the sink with unseeing eyes. Her thoughts, of course, were full of Marisa and Liana, and she felt the weight of their disappearance on her heart. For the millionth time, the same questions flooded her mind:

Who has them? Where could they be? Are they all right? Are they cold, hungry? Alive?

And, as though she didn't have enough on her plate, since his arrest, she couldn't seem to get Antonio out of her thoughts either. How could the authorities believe he was culpable? How could they arrest him on such shabby evidence? Did that outburst against him on the first day contribute to their indictment of him? His indignant outcry in court when custody had been awarded to her made him seem like a ranting brute. Yet she knew he was, as her mum would say, all mouth and trousers. Antonio was a rule-follower. He never would have done anything to the girls. If he were indeed inclined to violence and murder, surely he would have killed her the day her found her high on crack and Scotch. She knew he wasn't guilty of kidnapping Marisa and Liana. But what would happen to him if…?

She deliberately pushed the unfinished thought out of her head and turned her attention to the poor face staring back at her in the mirror.

Thankfully, cold compresses had brought down the swelling in her left eye so that she could now open it if only a slit. Already, it was starting to color up; a lovely shade of deep violet-pink. It would be a veritable shiner by morning, probably dark purple with undertones of black. *How lovely. A suitable match for my dark mood.* An ophthalmologist's exam revealed no injury to the eye itself. *Thank God.*

The plastic surgeon on call had stitched up the gash on her left cheek and in his professional opinion felt reasonably confident there would be minimal scarring. A rather unattractive bandage covered his handiwork at the moment; she'd take a better look at it tomorrow. At the moment, it was pretty tender.

Luckily, the X-rays and CAT-scan revealed no damage other than a mild concussion, a bruised cheek bone, and a couple of small cracks along the lower edge of the ocular bone; she knew that only time would heal those injuries. She seemed to have escaped severe harm; she would suffer no lasting ill-effects.

Except right now, along with that bummer of a headache, she had a bad case of the weepies. She couldn't seem to stop crying. Her injuries only brought to mind again how vulnerable and defenseless were Liana and Marisa against any kind of brutality the kidnapper might choose to inflict upon them. The control she had used to face the public over the last few days had not just slipped; it had completely crashed and burned. Her heart felt like a giant crater had been gouged into it. So when the tears came, there was no holding back and deep sobs racked her entire body.

6:32 P.M.

As the car crunched over the ice and sand on the paved road that led to Cabin 3, the headlights momentarily swung in Hank's direction. Completely by reflex, he ducked quickly back into the hideout. Using the spruce bough as cover, Hank observed the dark-colored vehicle roll to a stop beside the cabin.

The guy was back!

As panic rose, it was all that Hank could do to remain hidden beneath the spruce tree. He pulled his cell phone out of his pocket and quick dialed Jet, but the call would not go through. *No service!* Hank could do nothing more than watch as the dark shape of the driver emerged from the vehicle and walked to the cabin. With his heart in his mouth, he saw the man fling open the door. Light poured out onto the snow.

The man yelled something like "What the hell—?" and the rest was cut off as the door banged shut.

The sound of the slamming door had the effect of a starting pistol on Hank. He scrambled out of his hiding place kicking up spruce needles and snow, and shot off down the road not knowing exactly where he was going or what he was going to do. The only thing he knew for sure was that Jet needed help.

Moments later, he ran to the Lodge where he found Patrick on duty at the desk.

"What's the matter with you?" Pat said as he took in Hank's frantic expression.

"Listen, you gotta call 9-1-1." Hank panted out the story as Patrick picked up the phone and dialed.

6:39 P.M.

Humphries was irritated that all he could find in the place was half a can of charcoal lighter fluid, but it would have to do. He squirted the accelerant onto the curtains and into the wastepaper basket, then he threw the empty can into the corner. With the flick of a neatly tossed match into the trashcan, flames blossomed like an angry orange flower. It wouldn't be long before fire spread throughout the cabin. By that time, he'd be long gone.

"Rick!" He heard Adelina plead as he closed the door, "You can't do this! I thought you loved me."

Love? Yeah, maybe he *had* loved her. Why else would he take the chance and come back for her? If he hadn't cared, it would have been a simple thing to just head southwest and get to Mexico where he could have lived like a king on the ransom money. Instead, he'd come back for her only to find out she'd betrayed him. She'd told that kid, whoever he was, all about the kidnapping. If she told this kid, how many others had she blabbed to? It made him furious just to think of it.

He would have shot them all if he could have been certain that no one would have heard and called the cops. But he'd kept his head. It was better this way. No one would get out alive. There would be no witnesses. Everyone was tied up good and tight; everyone except for Liana who couldn't seem to raise her head from the pillow. He hadn't bothered with her. That was a good thing; it had saved him some time.

Now, he had to concentrate on putting distance between him and the cabin. He could still hear Adelina yelling as he crossed the short expanse of snow to the car.

Better not to listen, not to think about it. Better to get away and not look back.

Heeding his own counsel, he ignored Adelina's cries and got into the car. *His* car, now. He backed the Plymouth out onto the road.

6:41 P.M.

The place was quickly filling with smoke and Jet could see flames climbing up the curtains. Soon the entire cabin would be engulfed. Jet knew this was no time to lose his cool.

Already his eyes burned and watered, so he shut them.

There was nothing to see anyway. He let his senses of hearing and touch take over. Over the crackle of the blaze, he could hear Marisa crying from where she was tied to the table leg, and Liana coughing weakly from her bed. Bound to the chair across the table from him, Ms. Aguilar was talking out loud in rapid Spanish, interrupted only by shallow coughs. *Saying her prayers?*

He tried to call out to her, but managed instead to inhale a mouthful of acrid smoke. *God, Ms. Aguilar! We've got to get out of here!* His brain screamed the words he could not say. Determined to free them all he tried to reach the knots; maybe he could work them loose with his fingers. But they were just out of reach of his fingertips. That wouldn't work. He needed help. Maybe if he could get around to Ms. Aguilar's back, he could undo *her* knots, then she could untie him.

Another problem was that Humphries had tied Jet's legs to the chair, limiting his ability to move. Maybe if he leaned forward a little, then pushed back. Not too much, though; it wouldn't do if he toppled the chair. He found that he could slide the chair maybe an inch at a time. The cabin was extremely hot, and he knew the flames were closing in on them. He wouldn't have time to get all the way around the table to her back at this rate. If only he could convey his thoughts to Ms. Aguilar. Her inch plus his inch. They could cut the process in half the time.

Overheated containers were popping now and he briefly wondered if any of them were explosive. He decided not to think about that and concentrated on the task at hand.

He tucked his nose into the collar of his jacket and found some breathable air. He sucked in a lungful then yelled at the woman across from him. "Ms. Aguilar!" No response. He sucked in more air and tried again, "Adelina!"

"I am here," she coughed.

"See if we can get back to back," Jet managed between coughs, "Maybe we can get each other free."

"*Si,*" she replied coughing. She gave a mighty push in her chair and sent herself back away from the table. For a moment, it sounded to Jet like she was going to fall over, but at the last minute, the chair righted itself. Jet heard the feet hit hard on the floor.

Jet got another breath of air from inside his coat and spoke again. "Easy does it, Ms. Aguilar," he warned, "If you head to your right, and I go to my left, we can meet each other halfway."

This time, the woman didn't answer, but Jet could hear her chair scraping on the floor. They made their way around the table, and before they bumped into each other, Jet tried squinting through his eyelashes to determine how to negotiate the last bit of their maneuver. He found himself looking at the back of her chair. All he needed to do was turn himself around, and they'd be able to get at each other's knots.

As he put himself to this task, he realized that Marisa's crying had subsided to a soft whimper. More troubling than that, he could no longer hear Liana coughing. Had she stopped breathing?

He frantically tried to hurry at turning himself around and again almost tipped himself over. As the chair miraculously righted itself, he wondered.

Where is Hank?

6:42 P.M.

The Troy County helicopter had arrived in Grafton County, New Hampshire, in good time, but Sheriff Matson's prophecy had proven true: In the darkness they had not been able to find Tate Lodge. Maintaining an altitude of one thousand feet over Route 302, they traced that road southward from Interstate 93. From there, the traffic below looked like some child's line of Matchbox cars. Special Agents Turner and Kelly used night-vision binoculars to peer over the tops of trees for any sign of the Lodge or a driveway that would indicate access to such a place; but their view was obscured by a thick canopy of evergreen branches.

Now, as the FBI agents continued to scan the ground, Sheriff Matson asked his Grafton County counterpart for directions.

"Hey, Special Agents!" He roared over the helicopter's engine, "Sheriff Gagne says they just responded to a 9-1-1 at the Lodge. Crew's on the way as we speak. Can you see any sign of them?"

The words were hardly out of his mouth when the flashing red and blue beacons of a number of emergency vehicles appeared over the horizon, approaching them from the south. The helicopter hovered as its occupants watched where the lead vehicle would go. They did not have long to wait, for at that moment, a car with a blue beacon took a sharp right, closely followed by the boxy shape of an ambulance. The parade continued with another large vehicle and more police cars taking up the rear.

The helicopter followed from up above. They had their escort.

6:43 P.M.

As Richard Humphries negotiated the wide curve down the serpentine driveway that led to Route 302, a splash of oncoming headlights against the trees that lined the road warned him of an approaching car. Instinctively, he hugged the right side and slowed down. At the same time, a flash of blue and red illuminated those trees and he knew this wasn't just another car; this was a cop car en route to some kind of emergency.

Could the fire have already been noticed and the alarm sounded? He doubted very much that that was the case; he'd just left the cabin. It would take a while for the call to be made and for the units to be dispatched.

It couldn't be, he consoled himself. *It's way too soon.*

But he took no time to stay there and deliberate. He quickly veered off into a space between a pair of tall pine trees and rolled a short way into the woods before the emergency vehicle came into view. He doused his lights and darkness enveloped him.

He figured he'd wait there unseen until all the rescue units had passed, then he'd slip back out behind them and make good his escape down the driveway. However, for whatever reason, it seemed that a sheriff's deputy had decided that the space behind him was a good place to park his own vehicle, effectively blocking his access to the driveway. As the vehicle's headlights washed his way, he ducked down in the front seat. The lights died and he heard rather than saw the cruiser's door open and close. He eased himself upright, and in his rearview mirror, he could only make out the dark form of the deputy walking his way.

Not waiting to see what he wanted, Humphries turned on his headlights and stepped on the gas, figuring he'd lose the cop in no time. The trail before him was covered in snow, packed down to a hard surface from countless snowmobiles. He found that the car could pass smoothly on this packed snow, even if it was a bit slippery. If he kept the speed down, he'd be okay. He followed the trail around an easy right curve.

His initial glance in the rearview mirror seemed to indicate that he was not being followed; however, just as he allowed himself to relax, the harsh glare of headlights and the intermittent flash of red and blue disabused him of that notion. The pursuing police car seemed to be gaining on him, and he dared to step harder on the gas, only to have his wheels spin uselessly on the icy surface. Panic shot up from his gut to his brain as he spun the steering wheel and regained control. He glanced again in the mirror in time to see the lights behind him dance crazily for a moment then shoot out sideways.

At first he didn't know what had happened, but as the gap between him and his pursuer widened, he realized the cop had spun out and was stuck in a drift.

"Right on!" Humphries chuckled malevolently. He continued deeper into the woods. It wouldn't be hard to lose these pigs and he'd be free and clear. Eventually, this trail would lead out to a *real* road and he could be on his way.

The dark trail zigged and zagged, presumably to give the

snowmobiler a more exciting ride. But for Humphries, with only his headlights to guide him, it was a true test of his driving skill. Suddenly he found himself veering off toward the edge and quickly turned the wheel. The car slid and he thought he'd land in the soft snow, but at the last moment, the tires caught and he remained on the trail. He realized he was driving too fast and forced himself to move more slowly. Knowing that he wasn't being chased made that easier to do. He let up on the gas and allowed himself to relax again.

That proved to be a mistake, for suddenly the trail climbed upward and curved at the same time. The tires lost traction and skidded on the icy surface. As the car slid sideways back down the slope, there was nothing he could do but helplessly go for the ride. The Plymouth slid for another ten feet or so, tires spinning uselessly in the opposite direction, then finally the entire right side sank down into the soft snow along the edge of the trail.

This couldn't be happening! He tried to move forward, but the car only sank deeper into the snow. Undaunted, he tried rocking the car back and forth, but now he found himself bogged down to the fender. There was no way around it. He had to admit he was stuck.

Uttering a string of expletives, Humphries clambered out of the car and pulled his two suitcases of money out of the back seat. He started on the uphill trail on foot but soon found it impossible to advance on the slippery slope. He stepped on an icy patch, lost his footing, and found himself on his behind at the bottom of the hill beside the disabled car. Clearly, the trail was too icy and dangerous for him to use.

He got up, brushed himself off, picked up the suitcases, and ventured into the deep soft powder along the trail. It would be difficult walking in this stuff, but even if the going was slow, at least he was going. Now, if only he could *see*.

At first, he stumbled about blindly using the edge of the trail as a guide in the darkness; but soon he realized that although this was the first night of the new moon, the whiteness of the snow provided enough contrast against the darker shadows of the trees for him to avoid bumping into them. As his eyes became accustomed to the total lack of light, he realized he could make out where he was going.

But the snow was deep and for each step, he had to lift his foot high over the top, as though performing some exaggerated march. Snow insinuated itself up inside the legs of his jeans and into his shoes, and he slipped and tripped often. The exertion made him breathe hard and sweat trickled down the inside of his clothes. To make matters worse, the bags seemed heavier than he remembered and were clumsy to carry. He hoped he wouldn't have to do this for too long.

Yet he wasn't about to leave the suitcases behind. They were his ticket to a new life; one without Adelina and the Ibarra children, now.

Well, good riddance to them anyway. The money will go farther without them.

He trudged along energized by the knowledge that his height was to his advantage. Even weighed down by the heavy bags, his stride was longer than that of his pursuers. He had already left them far behind.

6:44 P.M.

Jet had no idea how long he'd been working at the knots that bound Adelina Aguilar's hands behind her back. It was hot beyond belief and oily sweat poured down his face and stung his eyes already irritated by the thick smoke. He continued to try to get air from inside his jacket, but now even that seemed to have been polluted by the acrid smoke. He choked, expelling whatever air he had left in his lungs with no more clean air to replace it. If he didn't get loose soon, they'd all die here.

His fingers slipped inefficiently over the greasy knots, and he gagged and choked again, wondering momentarily where he'd gotten the air to do so. He felt dizzy and squeezed his eyes shut and played with the knots and then suddenly he felt something loosen. He couldn't believe it. The rope fell away from

Ms. Aguilar's hands and then the woman was undoing his bonds. He inhaled a breath from inside his jacket, but coughed it out almost immediately. He took another breath; this one he was able to hold. He leaned over and untied his own legs from the chair, then got down on the floor on his hands and knees. Was it his imagination, or did it seem easier to breathe down here?

He felt about him on the floor, but found only the bare legs of the chair beside him. No sign of Ms. Aguilar. He had no idea where she had gone off to. He continued feeling around him until he found Marisa's small form still tied to the table leg. He undid the ropes that forced her to remain upright and dragged the child's limp form with him as he fumbled to his left.

Dear God, help me!

If he remembered correctly, the door was that way. He inched his way across the floor, still towing Marisa behind him, but it seemed this place was even hotter and the smoke thicker. He couldn't breathe. He couldn't see. He felt dizzy for lack of air. Marisa had to be protected. He pulled her close to him and enveloped her inside his jacket with her face against his chest. He hoped this would shield her from the thick, acrid smoke. He moved again along the floor, maneuvering their bodies together as one.

He was so tired; too tired to cough. No air to breathe. So hot. He gagged and choked and his head hit the floor. Blackness enveloped him.

6:45 P.M.

Once the 9-1-1 call had been placed, Hank knew he had no choice but to inform his aunt and uncle of what he knew about the kidnapping and what Jet was up to with Ms. Aguilar in Cabin 3.

"What were you boys thinking of?" Jules Tate demanded loudly.

Sobered by what was transpiring, Christine and the twins

wisely said nothing and watched wide-eyed, waiting for what would happen next.

"I'm sorry, Uncle Jules," Hank apologetically regarded his aunt and uncle in turn as everyone shrugged into their coats. In the distance, he could hear approaching sirens. "I tried to stop him—"

Aunt Susan sighed heavily and put a hand on the boy's shoulder, "I know, Hank. Don't make excuses for Jet."

"What's important now is to get that little girl to the hospital as soon as possible," Uncle Jules said.

From the top of the stairs, Hank could see that many of the guests had heard the sirens and had already assembled to see what was going on. Some stood on tiptoes and peered out the front windows, while others gathered outdoors. The sirens were closer now and Hank barreled down the stairs. He wormed his way through the throng and ran to the cabin he shared with Jet, intent on getting Donna before the sirens drove her crazy.

He unlocked the door and ignored the dog's frantic and happy greeting, attaching the leash to her collar. Together they ran back out to rejoin the others just as an ambulance rambled up the driveway and into the large parking lot. A moment later, an old water tanker drew up alongside of it, immediately followed by a police car.

"Volunteers and trainees," Mr. Barlow explained, as he ambled out to meet them, "They go out for practice whenever there's a call. When it's the ambulance, they practice their EMT skills; when it's a fire, they do firefighting."

Mr. Barlow took the lead as he hurried to the ambulance. The driver rolled down the window and Mr. Barlow went up to him to give him directions to the cabin.

But that's not what Hank was concentrating on. There was something in the air. "Do you smell—?"

"Smoke!" Christine said at the same time. "Someone has set the woods on fire."

"That's not the woods," Mr. Barlow corrected her as the ambulance set off on its mission, "That's a house burning! One of the cabins is on fire!"

In the dark, it was hard to pinpoint the place where the smoke was coming from, but as they made their way down the plowed path the smell grew harsher, stronger. With increasing dread, Hank realized the smoke had to be coming from Cabin 3. By the time they reached it, wisps of black smoke were seeping out of the spaces around the windows and the door. Here and there, orange flames flickered around the edges of the windows. To all who watched, it was hard to imagine that anyone trapped inside that burning cabin could still be alive.

"NO! JET!" As Aunt Susan ran forward, a deputy's arm caught her firmly across the chest, preventing her from advancing any farther.

"Stay back, ma'am," he ordered with authority.

"Our son is in there!" Aunt Susan cried struggling to break free from the deputy's grasp, her blue eyes wide and frantic. He held her tightly and when she realized he wasn't going to let go, she pleaded with him tearfully. "Please! Please! Get him out!"

"Just stay back, ma'am," the deputy said in a gentler tone. Uncle Jules slipped a restraining but comforting arm around Aunt Susan's shoulders, and the lawman loosened his grip on her. Uncle Jules gave the policeman a meaningful look as he tried to reassure his wife, "Let the firefighters do their jobs. They're gonna do their best to get 'im out."

"If only I hadn't left to call for help… Or if I'd gone into the cabin with him…" Hank began.

But Uncle Jules cut him off, "No, Hank. You did the right thing. You might've become one more person to rescue."

Uncle Jules's words did little to comfort him. Everywhere Hank looked he saw panic and horror written on everyone's faces. Aunt Susan was tense, and her eyes were wild with fear. But she seemed to realize she had to stay where she was; huge, helpless tears rolled down her cheeks. She sobbed into Uncle Jules' chest. Christine and the twins, all too stunned to speak, held onto each other as tears rolled down their faces. Hank swallowed a horrible lump in his throat.

At that point, Donna jumped up on the deputy. He gently

but firmly pushed her back down, "Control your dog, there, son; or get 'im outta here."

"Yes, sir," Hank said horrified, "Down, Donna." To the deputy he said, "I'm so sorry, deputy. She's usually better behaved than this."

"Sometimes the smell of smoke can set off even the best behaved pets," the deputy acknowledged, "Just do the best you can, or as I said before, take 'er away."

Donna strained on her leash and started barking loudly at the deputy, until he gave Hank another stern look. "Quiet, girl," Hank admonished, "You're gonna get us in trouble."

Although the dog resumed her place beside him, she continued to tug on Hank's arm. Half to reassure the dog, and half to help soothe his own mounting fears, Hank stooped down to ruffle the dog's neck. She licked his face more exuberantly than the boy expected, pushing him off balance. He fell backward on his rump and the dog frantically hopped around until she got herself tangled in her leash so badly that Hank had to unclip it from her collar to unwind it from her legs. Donna used this opportunity to escape his grasp.

"Hey!" Hank yelled after her, "Come back here!"

Hank watched helplessly as the dog disregarded his order and ran toward the woods and disappeared among the trees. He had no choice but to follow her.

6:46 P.M.

Jet came back as the smoke momentarily cleared. It seemed to him he could feel a draft of cold air. At the same time, a new sound came to his ears; the hissing of something wet striking something hot, like a hot pot going into dishwater. He groped ahead with one arm and realized the floor was wet. *Water?* Encouraged, he squirmed along with one arm, the other holding Marisa close to his chest. As he dragged himself and the unconscious child toward was seemed like fresh air he gagged and choked uncontrollably. *I'm going to suffocate,* he thought dimly.

At that point his arm gave out and he fell flat on the floor again. Then he was floating away. One moment he was hot, the next he was cold. *Where is Marisa?* Suddenly, sweet air rushed into his body. He sputtered and choked and gagged until he had no more strength. He inhaled again and coughed some more.

Then there was a voice filled with concern yet insistent and demanding, "Jet!" Hands pawed at him, touched his face, squeezed his hands.

"Mom?" His throat was raw and it burned as the soundless word came from his lips. His eyes wouldn't open; they seemed to be glued shut. He was so tired. Another fit of coughing overtook him, and then he went away again.

6:49 P.M.

Richard Humphries emerged from the woods and into a clearing.

Cripes, this is tiring.

He put down his bags and sat down on one of them to rest for a minute. He had no idea how long he'd been trudging through the deep snow, but he felt confident that he had lost the cops.

In the distance, to his right, he could hear radio voices barking commands from the emergency vehicles at the Lodge. *Good.* Apparently they were too busy to be bothered chasing him down.

He wondered how far he was from Route 302. It couldn't be much farther. He stood up and listened for the rumble of traffic. It seemed like highway sounds were a ways ahead yet; that rosy glow in the distance could only be the lights of town. He comforted himself in knowing he was going in the right direction.

Good. A little farther and I'll be home free.

He picked up the two suitcases of money and continued toward the sound of traffic. He was in the middle of the clearing, and somehow, he was back on some kind of trail. Despite the darkness, he needed to hurry. Here he was vulnerable; even without a moon, anyone might see his dark shape contrasted against the whiteness of the snow. He tried to walk faster now that he was out of the deep snow and no longer slipping in icy patches.

Suddenly an odd sound caused him to stop and listen.

It sounded like the chuffing breath of something. Something large. A large animal. Coming from behind. Cautiously, he turned to look.

A first, he could make out nothing in the dark shadowy outline of the trees. But then he saw it; a large black thing emerging from the woods. With long, purposeful bounds, it leapt over the snow and was gaining on him quickly.

He shoved the suitcase in his right hand under his left arm and dug into his jacket pocket for the revolver he had used earlier to pistol-whip Carmen Thibault. He fired two quick shots at the animal as he ran toward Route 302. But the shots went wide and missed. The predator continued to close the gap between them.

Humphries realized he couldn't run and shoot, and still hang on to the two suitcases. So he dropped them both. With as much concentration as he could muster, he turned, and this time, with both hands on the gun, he took deliberate and calculated aim.

He fired. One single shot.

With a loud yelp, the animal crumpled and fell heavily to the ground.

A relieved chuckle rose in his throat.

He sighed deeply and was about to slip the gun back into his pocket when another sound—*whop-whop-whop*—caught his attention. It seemed to be coming from above and he instinctively looked up. Now, it was louder, and accompanied by the drone of a motor. *Whop-whop-whop!*

Just coming up over the dark line of trees was the black silhouette of a helicopter. A powerful search light turned in his direction and glared into his eyes. He shielded them with one arm as the helicopter closed in and bore down on him.

"Freeze!" a bullhorn-enhanced voice called from the helicopter, "FBI!"

Humphries aimed his revolver at the copter and shot repeatedly until the gun was empty. The helicopter continued to descend toward him. Frantic to escape, he threw the useless weapon into the snow, grabbed his two suitcases, and ran headlong, blindly toward the highway. He dared to look back once to see where the helicopter was and saw with dismay that it was close to the ground. Soon it would land, and the FBI would be chasing him on foot.

Blinded by the search light, he ran away from them as fast as he could over the icy trail, not really knowing where he was going. He simply knew he was headed toward the highway and possible freedom.

His eyes finally adjusted once more to the dark just at his right shin connected with the edge of something metal. It seemed to be some kind of a low fence, less than two feet high. No problem to clamber over it without even putting down the bags of money.

His feet set down on the other side of the fence just as he sensed the helicopter had landed behind him and he took one last look before continuing on his way. The chopper's spotlight would help him some, give him some light. He turned his attention once more to where he was going, but to his shocked disbelief, he could now see that the world ended directly in front of him. He was headed for a drop, but his foot was already in mid-step.

There was no way to stop. Momentum carried him over the edge.

6:51 P.M.

It seemed to take forever for Craig Matson to set the skids down on the ground. The heavy machine settled deeply into the soft snow, and the helicopter blades churned up huge clouds of the white stuff, sending it crazily into the air like some ill-directed blizzard.

The three in the helicopter had narrowly escaped injury as bullets zinged past the blades of the helicopter and pinged off the bullet-proof glass. All the while the helicopter had descended closer and closer to their suspect until finally, when it seemed as though they would apprehend him, they were forced to watch in horror as the man disappeared over the edge of the cliff. One second he was there, the next, he had vanished, suitcases held out from his sides like two great outriggers.

When it was safe to do so, Sheriff Matson and Special Agents Turner and Kelly clambered out of the helicopter and followed the subject's tracks to the fence at the edge of the cliff. Aided by flashlights, they carefully peered over the side, their weapons at the ready.

Their suspect lay facedown, spread-eagled in the snow on a narrow ledge. The suitcases lay only inches away from his inert body. One of them had opened in the fall, and the wind was flicking bills from their bands. Some had already come loose and were blowing off the ledge and into the canyon.

"You think he's dead?" Matson asked.

"The only way we'll know for sure is to get a team down there," Agent Kelly said. But at that moment, the sheriff's question was answered when the man stirred.

"We don't have time for a team," Agent Turner said. "Sheriff, do you have anything in your chopper that I could use to rappel down the side of the cliff?"

"I've got a length of nylon rope we used to rescue a kid who broke through the ice on Narrow Pond," Matson answered as he ran back toward the chopper. "If you can't rappel down, we can at least lower you."

"Are you crazy?" Agent Kelly demanded of John.

"We've got no choice, Mary Ellen. When he wakes up, he's going to try to run."

"But he's got no place to go."

"Exactly. He may be too dazed to realize that if he tries to run he'll fall to his death."

"Isn't there some other way?" she persisted.

"Look. I'm not going to do anything stupid," Turner explained, "We'll fasten one end to the helicopter, then I'll use the other end to go down to the ledge. Once I'm down there, I can keep him in place until a rescue team comes along. I'll hold him at gunpoint if I have to."

John Turner's mind was made up; there was no way she was going to change it.

While the two men worked together on their plan, Agent Kelly ran back to the helicopter where she radioed in the request for a rescue team with a stretcher to reclaim their injured suspect. As she was ending her call, a heart-stopping scream caused all of them to turn around.

6:53 P.M.

Hank had done his best to keep up with Donna, but the dog was just too fast for him. Instead, he had had to follow her footprints in the snow with the flashlight he had used earlier to light his and Jet's hideout. The dog's tracks had been easy enough to see in the soft, pristine snow. And if he listened intently, he thought he could hear something large snapping through dry branches and twigs up ahead. At least, he hoped it was Donna making all that racket.

It felt like he had hiked at least a mile when suddenly, he heard two loud cracks; the unmistakable report of gunfire. With an adrenaline rush of energy he propelled himself forward in a desperate run as yet another shot was fired, this time, accompanied by a yelp. His blood froze. Had somebody shot Donna?

"Donna!" he yelled.

Then he heard the sound of a helicopter hovering close by. More shots followed in rapid succession, then only the sound of the helicopter, evidently attempting to land. Hank couldn't imagine what that meant. He only knew that Donna had been hurt. He would never forgive himself if something bad had happened to her.

What will I say to Mr. Ibarra?

Janet Y. Martel

The thought was still running through his brain as he suddenly burst out of the woods and found himself in a large clearing where a helicopter idled, its blades moving slowly around in the wind. But his frantic mind did not take in what that might mean. Instead, his eyes landed on a dark shape a few feet away; a shape that resembled a castoff fur coat.

"Donna," he whispered as he ran to the dark inert form that lay in a crumpled heap. "Oh, God. Please don't let her be dead," he prayed.

As he knelt beside the dog, he was relieved to see that she was alive, panting quickly with short shallow breaths; a sure sign that all was not well. He yanked off his gloves and gingerly touched the matted patch of fur that glistened darkly in helicopter's spotlight. His fingers came away with a black sticky wetness. He shone the flashlight beam on his fingers. Blood. At his touch, the dog whimpered and tried to raise her head. Hank spoke to her in a soft reassuring voice, hoping he was telling the truth.

"It's okay, Donna. You're going to be okay," Hank put down the flashlight and using both hands, carefully examined the rest of the animal starting from her large head, working all the way down to her tail. Donna seemed to have only the single wound, but how bad it was, Hank could not tell. He only knew that the stain of blood on the snow was large and growing.

Suddenly, Hank realized there was someone standing beside the helicopter. He waved the flashlight. "Help!" he screamed with a choking sob, "Help me! Please!" Until that moment, he had not realized he was crying.

The next thing he knew, the FBI lady Jet knew was at his side. In the beam of the flashlight, he watched her apply pressure to the wound to staunch the bleeding, but it was obvious that the dog needed a bandage. She was telling him something, but his brain seemed to be far away. She pushed him roughly, shocking him back to reality.

"Here! Hold this right here. Press and don't let go," she ordered.

Hank again put down the light and dumbly let her place his

hands where she wanted them. He had seen that the FBI agent had made a compress out of his gloves folded in half. She was pressing his hands on those gloves over the wound on the dog's shoulder. Then Agent Kelly—*Yeah, that's her name*—was wrapping her own scarf around the dog's body to hold the gloves in place.

"Well, this is all I can do for now," she said wiping her bloodied hands off in the snow, "Hopefully this makeshift bandage will keep your dog from bleeding to death before we can get it to a vet."

"Thank you, Agent Kelly." She seemed surprised that he had called her by name, so Hank explained, "I'm Jet Tate's cousin, Hank Robert. This is Mr. Ibarra's dog, Donna. She took off running, and I went after her." Hank sobbed, "I thought she was chasing a rabbit or something."

"Apparently, she was after the kidnapper," Agent Kelly stood up and looked down at Hank as he cradled the dog's head on his lap.

Hank was incredulous, "You mean Richard Humphries did this to her?"

She nodded, then she sniffed the air. "Do you smell smoke?"

"Yeah," Hank replied, "it's the cabin. It's on fire."

"Which cabin? *Your* cabin?"

"No. Cabin 3. Where Ms. Aguilar and Humphries have been keeping the Ibarra kids. Jet's in there with them."

6:55 P.M.

Authorities ascertained from the innkeepers that the cabin had been rented out to a man with his wife and two children. The frantic parents of the teenage boy insisted their son was inside the burning building as well.

The volunteer firefighters quickly retrieved the first two victims, the boy and a young child, mere inches from the door, and a cheer immediately rose from the crowd before their condition was made known. As the two were brought safely away from the burning building, a large cloud of smoke followed them out the open door. Then, to everyone's surprise, another person staggered out close on their heels, carrying something wrapped in a blanket. The person collapsed as a firefighter took the bundle from the hero's arms.

The firefighters quickly identified the hero as a woman, presumably the man's wife. She had been carrying the second child. That meant the only person still missing was the man, and everyone seemed positive he had left the premises in his car. Since the vehicle was nowhere around, it made sense to believe that was so. However, once the woman had been revived, a deputy and a fireman questioned her to make sure.

"Is there anyone else in there?" they demanded of her, "Besides you, we have a teenage boy and two young children."

The woman managed to shake her head and form a soundless no before she lost consciousness. At that moment, something inside the cabin exploded sending a flurry of fiery sparks into the air. The firefighters resumed pouring water on the inferno, hoping to contain it before it caught in the woods.

In the meantime, one EMT kept busy monitoring three of the victims. She administered oxygen, checked vitals, treated burns, and made assessments about her patients. Clearly, all of the victims had inhaled a lot of smoke and would need additional medical attention for that, as well as the more serious burns of the adult female. The young male and one child seemed to be doing better, and would probably be held for observation overnight and released from the hospital in the morning.

Two other paramedics, however, were still working on the last victim, a little girl. By the time the woman had stumbled out of the cabin with her, the child was not breathing. Moments ago, the little girl's heart had stopped too, and the team was now performing CPR. While one paramedic pumped on her tiny chest, another squeezed a bag to push air into her lungs. Someone else charged the portable defibrillator. When it was ready, the paramedics cleared the way for the paddles which were applied to her bare chest. The shock made the child arch her back and lift from the stretcher. As soon as the charge had been given, one EMT felt for a carotid pulse.

Most of the tension left his face, and he allowed himself a tentative smile. The little girl had a pulse and she was breathing on her own. He gently fitted the mask of a non-rebreather over her face as one of the other paramedics hooked her up to an IV. Although she was breathing, she was not out of the woods yet. She was weak and her prognosis was questionable. The paramedic monitored her signs and when the child and the woman, the two most critical victims, had been loaded onto the ambulance, he stayed with them to make sure they had every chance of survival. The ambulance left for County Hospital as soon as the doors were secured.

Shortly, a second ambulance arrived to take the other two victims. By then, the boy was sitting up, but the little girl was lying back with her eyes closed, greedily sucking in oxygen.

As the second ambulance left, a crew of regular firefighters arrived with a newer and larger water tanker. Although by then the excitement was just about over, much of the crowd remained to watch the firemen working on the burning cabin. The newly-arrived support joined their comrades and continued to pour water on the smoldering cabin which was now nothing more than a charred black skeleton and a brick chimney.

6:58 P.M.

In addition to the nylon rope, Sheriff Matson also found a six-foot length of chain. By the time Special Agent Kelly returned, the men had fashioned this into a kind of sling and had tied one end of the rope through two of its links. Special Agent Turner stepped into this loop of chain as Sheriff Matson wrapped the other end of the rope around one of the uprights on the helicopter's right strut. This would give him enough friction to be able to lower the FBI agent down the sheer edge of the drop. The smooth round metal bar of the fence would prevent the rocky edge of the cliff from cutting into the rope.

There was no time to test their contraption, as the suspect, though still dazed, had regained consciousness. There was a good chance that once he had his bearings, he would make the mistake of trying to make a run for it and fall to his death. Turner was not about to let that happen. He looked at the sling critically. In principle, it should work, provided the knots were good and the rope sound.

Special Agent Kelly watched in silent dread as her partner pulled the chain up to his buttocks and tested his weight against the tether. The rope tightened as Sheriff Matson fed just enough to allow Turner to ease himself over the ice-encrusted edge. John Turner braced his feet against the lip of the cliff expecting to maintain the semblance of a sitting position as he descended the precipice. He bounced experimentally, but suddenly, his foot slipped on the ice.

"John!" Agent Kelly screamed as Agent Turner spun off the edge.

The sudden jolt threw Sheriff Matson off balance and the lawman lost his grip on the rope. Despite the wraps around the strut, the rope slipped out faster than planned.

John Turner helplessly swung outward and dropped.

6:59 P.M.

"You're gonna be okay, Donna," Hank whispered to the dog as he gently stroked her, "Everything's gonna be all right—"

A scuffle up near the helicopter distracted him. Something was going on over there. Somebody on the edge of the cliff. Did they need help? Torn between comforting Donna and going to lend a hand, Hank hesitated; but only for a moment. Special Agent Kelly's scream made him jump and he sprang into action.

He half-ran half-crawled the short distance to help the policeman near the helicopter. Immediately perceiving the nature of the problem, Hank threw himself on the rope as it sped away. Somehow, he managed to get a grip. It slipped through his gloveless hands, burning into his flesh. Ignoring the pain, he held on tightly as he was helplessly dragged along the slippery ground. His weight seemed to have slowed it down somewhat and he managed to get his feet out in front of him. He dug in his heels, plowing the snow to get some traction. But Special Agent Turner on the other end of the rope outweighed him so that gravity plus momentum pulled him irrevocably along the icy surface. For one panicked moment, it seemed to Hank that he would be carried over the side.

7:00 P.M.

The rope suddenly lurched to a stop. Turned sideways, Special Agent Tuner was unable to keep himself from slamming into the rock wall. The concussion knocked the wind out of him and he saw stars. His entire left side screamed with pain; his hip, his shoulder, his head. A wave of nausea overtook him. He breathed deeply to calm his stomach and ease his racing heart.

As his head started to clear, he became aware of shouts from up above; Mary Ellen asking if he was all right, shining a light in his direction. He managed to collect himself enough to reassure her, although his voice was not as steady or as loud as he would have liked it to be.

"I'm okay. Let me down some more," he croaked.

He descended, gratefully more slowly, for the remaining ten or so feet to the ground and was relieved beyond words when he felt his feet planted on firm terrain. "Okay. I'm down," he called up sounding more like himself.

He allowed the sling to slip to the ground as he pulled his service pistol out of its holster; but even that movement of his right arm caused the left one to scream in pain.

Could it be broken? he wondered.

The hand hanging uselessly at the end of his injured arm throbbed and tingled. Gingerly, he used his right hand to put his left hand into his coat pocket. That small amount of support seemed to help somewhat.

Turner could not linger over the pain or feel sorry for himself. He had a job to do. In the glow from Mary Ellen's flashlight, John Turner approached Richard Humphries, Antonio Ibarra's accomplice, who was writhing in the snow and moaning. Turner knew that with his useless left arm, there was no way to search the man for any weapon, even if Mary Ellen covered him from up above. Turner limped cautiously toward his prisoner, the pistol trained on him, ready for any sudden moves. This could all be an act.

"You can sit up, Humphries, but don't try anything cute, or I'll save the taxpayers a lot of money."

Humphries groaned and winced as he carefully sat up, obviously in at least as much pain as John Turner was himself. Blood dripped down the man's face from a deep gash on the right side of his head, and a large raw bruise swelled from his cheekbone, distorting his features. He gently cradled his right arm in his lap.

"Don't worry, man. I ain't goin' nowhere," he said through thick lips, "and I got no gun. I threw it away; no more ammo."

"You mind if I ask you some questions?"

A grimace that was supposed to be a smile stretched Humphries' face. "Nah. Ask away."

Turner wondered how much the man would actually tell him; nonetheless, the numb fingers of his bad hand could feel his little tape recorder in the bottom of his pocket. He bit his lip as he painfully moved his fingers and made them push what he hoped was the record button. Then he sat on a nearby boulder and reminded Humphries of his rights.

"What d'ya wanna know?" Humphries asked.

"I want to know what Antonio Ibarra's plan was." John said.

Humphries laughed, winced, "Ow!" Then sobered, "You're kiddin', right?" Turner said nothing and Humphries remarked, "You know, I saw that on TV; that you guys arrested Ibarra for kidnapping his daughters. That's too funny!" His laugh ended in a groan and he winced again.

"I see nothing funny in that," commented Turner.

Humphries sighed deeply, "No, I guess you wouldn't. What? When you become a cop they take out your sense of humor?"

Turner glared at him and Humphries continued, "Cripes. I never meant the kids no harm. It was just a child stealin'. I convinced Adelina that they were better off with us, and we were gonna raise 'em as our own. Ya see, Adelina was so sad after she lost her job as their nanny, I had to do somethin'. It was easy enough to convince her we should take the girls; Carmen bein' such a loser of a mother, and Antonio not fightin' harder for 'em than he did. We were gonna go to Mexico or some other Latin country and pretend they were ours. It woulda been easy enough; the kids speak Spanish like natives. I figured the ransom money would buy the girls some passports and fake birth certificates, and the rest would set us up for a new life. Give us a new start, and we'd live good. But first, we were gonna get 'em out of the country, go to Canada and lay low for a while.

"And we woulda made it too, if it hadn't a been for the blizzard! Cripes! The first day, we never got past Manchester; we had to hole up in a motel. That's when we cut the kids' hair to make 'em look like boys. I had bought some baseball caps and boy's jackets at a Goodwill store. The kids thought it was great; like Halloween.

"Anyways, by the time we got back on the road again, I figured there was an Amber Alert out for them, and I didn't know if anyone had seen the car. We shoulda got outta there clean, but Donna— Cripes! The damn dog was supposed to be asleep; I gave her a sleeping pill in a hot dog. She practically swallowed the thing whole. I thought I shut her up inside the house, but she got out somehow, and howled after we put the kids in the car and I started 'er up. I just beat it outta there as fast as I could.

"Anyway, like I said, I didn't know if anyone'd seen the car. Couldn't take that chance, so I figured it'd be safer if I kept off the Interstate. Those old routes are okay, but they're not kept up as good as the major roads. Make a long story short, I kinda got lost. Liana got another bleeding nose and we had to stop. This is where we ended up.

"By then, too much time had passed; getting' to Canada seemed stupid just for me to turn right around and head back to Troy City to pick up the ransom. So I didn't say nothin'; I just left Adelina here with the kids, got my money, and came back just in time to hear her tellin' that boy all about our plans."

John Turner cut in when Humphries paused to catch his breath, "So when the dust settled, Antonio was going to go to whatever Latin country you chose and meet you there."

Humphries gave Turner a puzzled look. "I never had plans to get back to Ibarra. I had the money and the kids, and we were keepin' 'em. They were gonna be ours. Didn't I make that clear?" He shook his head, his voice incredulous, "Were you thinkin' I was in this with him?" Humphries laughed despite the pain. Then he sobered and shook his head, "No. Mr. Special FBI Agent, you owe Antonio Ibarra an apology. The money and the kids were for me and Adelina." Humphries eyes widened, "That's until I heard what she said to that kid. She was gonna turn us in! I couldn't believe it! After all I done for her, she was gonna give it all up." He shook his head, "I just snapped. All of a sudden, I couldn't think of nothin' else but cuttin' my losses and runnin'."

8:43 P.M.

It seemed like forever to coordinate everything so that Donna could be taken out of the woods and transported to a vet.

First, while the rescue team hoisted Special Agent Turner and Richard Humphries up the sheer cliff, Special Agent Kelly radioed for assistance for the dog. Apparently, Mr. Barlow, even while one of his cabins was burning to the ground, overheard her call on the police radio and suggested they bring the animal to Doc Hubert, the vet who cared for the Tate Lodge horses.

The rescue team used special stretchers on runners to haul their patients over the snow, and one was used to move Donna out to the road as well. As the EMTs loaded the two injured men onto their ambulance, Donna was carefully placed on the back seat of a Grafton County Sheriff's car. Agent Kelly got into the ambulance with Agent Turner and their prisoner while Hank got into the back seat of the police cruiser and gently held Donna's head on his lap.

"Here, kid. Use this to keep her warm." The young black deputy had identified himself as Tim Coleman. He was shorter than Hank with closely-cropped black hair. Deputy Coleman handed him a wool blanket he got from the trunk and helped Hank tuck the edges around the dog. Then he got behind the wheel.

As the ambulance headed north en route to the county hospital, the deputy's car turned south, its own siren howling and emergency lights flashing.

Doc Hubert met them as the police cruiser pulled into the empty parking lot of the veterinary clinic. The veterinarian was a short, rotund man with round bald head and bulldog-like jowls. He waddled quickly out of his clinic with surprising agility and the police car's back door was open even before the siren had completely silenced. Experienced hands carefully picked up the injured dog, blanket and all, and Hank followed Doc Hubert into the animal hospital, answering the vet's rapid-fire questions as completely as possible.

Then, to Hank's shocked dismay, the vet carried Donna into a room and kicked the door shut behind him, effectively shutting him out. That was over an hour ago, and since then, Hank fidgeted nervously, trying to make himself believe everything would be okay.

Deputy Coleman stayed with him in the clinic's waiting room, trying to be supportive. Earlier, he'd shaken Hank's hand and mumbled something about him being a hero, but Hank couldn't see how that figured. It was all his fault that the dog had gotten loose and had run after that Humphries freak.

The way Hank saw it, it was Donna who was the hero. Hank saw himself as a loser, a failure, an irresponsible person who had allowed a beautiful animal to get hurt.

For the millionth time, Hank asked himself, *What am I going to say to Mr. Ibarra?*

Hank got up and paced a while, sat down, then got up and paced some more.

Suddenly, the door opened and Doc Hubert emerged still wearing his bloodstained surgical clothes. He was drying his newly washed hands on a towel. Hank froze in mid-stride and regarded the vet intently.

"Well, we got the bullet out," he wiped his round face with the same towel. "We took some X-rays, and she was lucky. The bullet grazed the shoulder bone and lodged in her chest against a rib, but missed the vital organs. She's lost a lot of blood and we're giving her a transfusion and an IV. I can't tell if this will affect how she walks; she may favor that leg from now on. She's young, though; that's what she's got going for her. She needs rest, and we'll know better tomorrow."

"Can I see her?" Hank asked.

"She's sleeping off the anesthesia now—" began Doc Hubert. Believing he was going to refuse him, Hank opened his mouth to plead, but the vet raised a beefy hand and continued, "—but I guess under the circumstances, you can go in and have a peek. She might hear you if you talk to her softly, let her know you care. But don't try to rouse her."

Hank stood beside the large black dog still lying on her side on the gurney. Since Doc Hubert had told him about the IV and the blood transfusion, the boy was ready for the tubes that carried fluids to the dog's inert body. He was relieved to see that her breathing was calm and steady, now; not the frantic panting she'd been doing in the clearing. Her tongue lolled out of the side of her mouth and Hank could see her eyes moving behind her closed lids. Part of a white bandage peeked out between strips of red tape that started at the shoulder, went over her back and around her chest, and wound all the way down her front leg; all that tape to insure that she wouldn't pull it off before it was time.

Hank extended a hand and gingerly touched her furry neck, "It's gonna be okay, Donna. You're gonna be just fine." Donna whimpered in her sleep and her tail twitched, giving Hank the feeling she was responding to him. He felt it was a good sign.

It seemed to him that he had only just arrived when his visit was cut short.

"And now for you, young man," said Doc Hubert. "Let's see what we can do about those hands of yours."

9:05 P.M.

John Turner sat on the edge of a gurney in Treatment Room A as Dr. Iwata flashed a penlight in his eyes.

"How's the shoulder?" asked the thirty-something Japanese ER doctor, "Very painful?"

Turner cast a disgusted eye toward his left arm cradled in a sling. The slam against the rock wall had dislocated his shoulder and earlier, Dr. Iwata had popped it back into its socket; an excruciating experience. Although X-rays had detected no breaks or fissures in the arm, his elbow was badly bruised and swollen, causing numbness and tingling in his fingers. He forgot and shook his head only to have a nauseating arrow of pain shoot through it. He winced, "Not as bad as my head."

Dr. Iwata smiled crookedly, "You're lucky to have such a hard head, Special Agent Turner. Most men would have suffered a fractured skull. All you got was a slight concussion and a couple of stitches."

"Without anesthesia," Turner pointed out.

Iwata shrugged and patted the FBI agent's good arm, "I'm sure you'll live."

"When can I interrogate Adelina Aguilar, Doctor?" Turner asked as he gingerly stepped down from the gurney favoring his bruised hip and being careful not to jar his head.

Dr. Iwata frowned. Although a full head shorter than Turner, the physician spoke firmly and with authority, "Ms.

Aguilar is not well enough to have you tiring her with your questions. She has been through a very exhausting ordeal; her lungs are still trying to rid themselves of smoke, and her throat is painful and raw. She can't speak above a whisper and the effort knocks her out. I will not allow you to interrogate her tonight. Or any of the other fire victims. Come back tomorrow."

Turner was eager to get corroboration of Humphries' story, but knew better than to press the doctor further. For the time being, he would have to accept what Humphries had said as the truth. It didn't make sense that Humphries should take all the blame. Misery loves company, after all. Yet, he had vouched that the kidnapping had been entirely his idea and Adelina knew nothing of the ransom. And Ibarra was definitely not in it. John shrugged, then winced against the pain. He had to admit it; it didn't make sense that one of Ibarra's partners would try to incinerate the kids.

Then he asked, "How's Richard Humphries?"

Dr. Iwata inclined his head slightly, "Mr. Humphries has a broken arm, a fractured cheekbone, and a concussion, but he's is going to be alright. Although I'm sure the fall was not enjoyable, he's lucky it happened in wintertime and there was a good cushion of snow to soften the impact. I'm afraid had it occurred at any other time of the year we'd have him on a cold slab in the morgue. He is getting his arm set at the moment; but as soon as Dr. Pearson is done with that, he will be released into your custody." The doctor turned to leave, then gave Turner a candid parting look, "You need rest yourself, Agent Turner. I suspect the arm will bother your sleep tonight."

Mary Ellen Kelly was sitting outside the treatment room when John came out. Immediately, his partner was up out of her chair and beside him. Her concern was touching. "How are you, John?"

"I'm fine, Mary Ellen," he said.

"While you were busy, I called off the Amber Alert and let Carmen and Paul know that the children had been found." She smiled, "I imagine they're on their way here as we speak."

"You were right."

"Huh?"

"About Ibarra being innocent," John explained as they walked out to the hospital lobby, "I said you were right. According to Humphries, Antonio Ibarra was not involved in the kidnapping. At first I didn't want to believe him; but what does the man have to gain by lying for him? Humphries is going up for two counts of kidnapping, transporting minors across state lines, child endangerment, extortion, arson, not to mention four counts of attempted murder." John shook his head and winced at the pain in his head, "He's going away for a long time. Why protect Ibarra if he was involved?" He was so tired. All he wanted was sleep. He rubbed his forehead with his good hand. But he couldn't rest yet; there was something else he had to do.

He pulled out his cell phone and searched for a number in memory.

"Who are you calling?" Mary Ellen wanted to know.

"First, Charles Cabot. Then Anita Pimental," John answered as he pressed the send button. "So go ahead. Say it."

"Say what?"

"That you told me so. I moved too fast on the arrest." He shut his eyes as the phone started ringing at the other end. "Poor man. I feel awful about what I put him through."

"You were doing your job, John. You did what you thought was right."

Then John heard Charles Cabot on the phone. "Sorry for calling so late, Mr. Cabot. This is Special Agent Turner. I have some good news."

Saturday, December 31

Special Agent Turner, sprawled in the recliner in the hospital room, opened his eyes and groaned. He ran his hand over the rough stubble of black beard. His teeth were fuzzy, his mouth dry and as foul-tasting as the bottom of a septic tank. He reached over for the cup of water with his good arm. The movement caused a knife of pain to slash through his bad elbow. Dr. Jiro Iwata had been right; his arm had kept him awake despite the pain pills.

Last night, Turner had been disappointed that Adelina Aguilar's interrogation would have to wait until this morning. He hated to leave her questioning to Lester and Bonelli of the Manchester office, who'd finally appeared on the scene after the excitement was over with some lame excuse about traffic; but he had no choice if he was to catch his ride back to Troy County. He'd get his shot at the woman when she was transported back to Massachusetts.

But Mary Ellen had a different idea; one that allowed him to stay in New Hampshire.

"The helicopter can carry only so much weight," his partner explained.

So when Humphries was finally released into their custody, Sheriff Matson and Mary Ellen took the prisoner back to Troy County via helicopter, leaving John behind. Mary Ellen would come back for him in the morning.

Turner jumped at the chance and had spent the night, with Dr. Iwata's reluctant permission, beside Adelina Aguilar's bedside.

Adelina had had a restless night herself, and he supposed his lack of sleep was due in part to her frequent coughing. At times she choked so badly he thought she'd never be able to inhale. But finally, she'd cough up black phlegm and flop back down on her pillow, completely spent. Moments later, she'd be breathing deeply, asleep again.

Turner's eyes closed as he started to drift off, but suddenly they flew open again at a new sound in the room. A voice coming from the bed. Turner struggled out of the recliner working against his protesting hip and hurting his arm again. He stood beside her bed and hoped he didn't look too scary to the bewildered woman.

"Ms. Aguilar," he said softly, "you're in the hospital." She regarded him with large black eyes. "Do you remember the fire?"

"*Si*," she nodded.

"Do you remember carrying out Liana Ibarra?"

Her eyes widened. "Liana," she whispered. She started off in rapid Spanish, but Turner held up a hand. She understood immediately and repeated in English, "How is she? Is she all right?"

"She's alive, but she is very sick," Turner took the liberty of opening the blinds at the window. Soft morning sunlight streamed into the room. He limped back to the bedside, clicked on his little tape recorder, and looked at the woman intently. "I'm Special Agent John Turner of the Federal Bureau of Investigation. The FBI, ma'am. I'd like to ask you a few questions. You have the right to remain silent…"

8:17 A.M.

Something in the room changed waking Carmen who'd been sleeping in the chair with her head on Liana's bed. She raised her head and peered blearily at the form that blocked the light from the window. A pretty, young nurse with short curly black hair held one of Liana's tiny wrists and timed her pulse. She gently put down the child's hand and checked the flow of the IV.

"How is she…" Carmen asked reading this new nurse's ID badge, "Ms. Fiore?"

Nurse Fiore nodded, "Please. It's Jane."

"Jane," Carmen reached across Liana and shook the nurse's hand, "I'm Carmen."

"Much better," Jane Fiore smiled showing pretty white teeth. Crystalline blue eyes crinkled. She was soft-spoken and her manner sweet. "Her vitals are good, she hasn't had a nose-bleed since the one in the emergency room, she's pinking up. The doctor will be in later, but I think we'll be moving her out of ICU today. We need this place for really sick kids."

The last was meant to cheer her up, and Carmen appreciated the nurse's attempt. "Thanks. You people are angels."

"You're welcome." The smile again. "You should get something to eat. We can't have moms passing out from hunger. It gives the hospital a bad reputation."

Carmen shook her head, "I can't right now. I'm waiting for her to wake up."

Jane Fiore's eyebrows rose slightly, "How about if I have a tray sent in for you?"

"That would be wonderful. Thank you."

The nurse left on silent shoes and Carmen looked down at her sleeping child. Liana did look better than she had last night. When she and Paul had finally arrived around midnight, Carmen had been shocked by her frail and deathly appearance. The child had been so weak, so pale; gray, really. Too weak even to cough up the smoke that had infiltrated her lungs. They had done everything they could to help her purge herself of the smoke, then they had put her in the Pediatric ICU. The rest would be up to Liana.

It had been so frightening to see her lying so still in her bed. Just a tiny bump under the white blanket. A small, drawn face with oxygen prongs in her nose, tubes in her arms, one for blood, the other an IV for fluids and an antibiotic. Sensors stuck to her thin chest under the flimsy johnny, a clamp on one of her fingers, hooked up to monitors and electronic gadgets for God knew what. And she didn't move. Except when the coughing wracked her little body unmercifully.

Carmen left Liana's bedside to use the bathroom. Under the harsh glare of the light over the mirror, she examined her reflection as she washed her hands.

Her mum would say she looked like she'd been dragged through a hedge backwards. She wondered what the sweet and polite Miss Jane Fiore had thought of her partially-closed black eye; not purple as she had predicted, but truly black. And the grotesque bandage on her cheek. She looked like somebody's punching bag, and figured with a shrug that that's actually what she *had* been.

She was glad they'd caught the ruddy bastard. Glad also that with her assailant's capture, Antonio had been cleared of all charges. Poor Antonio. What she had put him through, keeping the girls away from him, taunting him, punishing him that way.

Well, that won't happen again. Next Christmas will be different, she vowed. *He would have liked to take them to Puerto Rico for* la Noche Buena. *We'll see what we can do about that. Maybe not every year, but every other, perhaps.*

Feeling somewhat better, she sighed and redirected her attention to her reflection in the mirror. She lifted the corner of the tape that held the bandage in place and gently pulled it off. It smarted only a wee bit. She was pleasantly surprised by what she saw. The mark was raw and red on a sizeable purple bruise that swelled on her cheek; but she looked no worse than she'd expected. The plastic surgeon had done a superb job; his stitching hardly showed. It would all go away in time. She threw the bandage into the bio-hazard bin and came out of the bathroom.

Her eyes immediately went to Liana's bed, and grew wide in astonishment. The child was actually sitting up and moving; she was trying to pull the tubes out of her arms and making fretful, wordless little sounds. Carmen rushed the few steps over to her side.

"Liana," she spoke softly, not wanting to startle her, "Liana, my sweet, sweet girl."

At the sound of her mother's voice, the child stopped and looked up. In a matter of moments, the expression in her brown eyes changed from consternation, to disbelief, to relief, to joy. Then came the tears. Delicious, sweet tears of happiness. Carmen gently but firmly embraced her little girl, and Liana's arms threaded themselves around her mother's neck, tubes and all.

How long they held each other, Carmen didn't know, nor did she care. It was a wonderful and glorious reunion that neither mother nor child wanted to end.

Until a sound interrupted them.

Carmen reluctantly broke away, but still held Liana's thin shoulders. She turned toward the sound she'd heard. There, in the doorway, stood Paul, a mischievous, boyish grin on his adorable face, with Marisa sitting in the compulsory wheelchair, eyes glowing with emotion just barely restrained.

"Marisa," Carmen whispered.

The word had hardly left her lips and the child sprang from the wheelchair and into her mother's waiting arms. Then Paul was there, too, making it a four-way hug.

11:33 A.M.

As planned, Mary Ellen Kelly picked up John Turner in front of the Grafton County Medical Center. He looked like he'd had a tough night.

The white bandage wound around his head and the arm in the sling made him look gaunt and vulnerable. He was disheveled and in need of a shave. His clothes were rumpled and the knee of his pants had a hole, probably from his rock climbing experience. Mary Ellen had never seen her partner in such a state. But he looked a lot better than he had last time she saw him.

His eyes were serious and unsmiling as he painfully got into her white Impala. Mary Ellen helped him clip his seatbelt. Aunt Tillie meowed loudly from her carrying case in the back of the car.

"Hello to you, too, cat," he said as Mary Ellen pulled away from the curb.

"I got you some shaving gear and toiletries from the drug store—"

He interrupted her, "My Spanish isn't too good, but Adelina corroborated everything Humphries said. She was shocked when she learned about the ransom, and cried when she found out that Antonio had been arrested for the kidnapping. She kept asking for forgiveness."

"So what's going to happen to her now?"

"She'll no doubt be State's witness against Humphries, maybe work out a deal." John sighed. "Maybe she'll serve time or be deported. I don't know which; but she'll never get another job as a nanny, at least not in the States. Anita Pimental will make sure of that." He sighed again, "I like it when all the loose ends have been tied up in a nice little bundle." He looked at her squarely, "So what's the plan?"

Mary Ellen smiled, "We need to go to the mall and get you some clothes for the weekend. You can use the public restroom to clean up and change. Then we can be on our way."

"On our way where?"

"To my parents' New Year's Eve dinner," she gave him an impish grin.

"I feel like Sidney Poitier in *Guess Who's Coming to Dinner.*"

12:18 P.M.

The Roberts were unloading their luggage from Uncle Phil's Explorer when Dad drove Mom's Voyager into the parking lot of Tate Lodge. It looked like everyone had come out to greet them with hugs and kisses: Christine, Danielle, Denise, the Barlow cousins, and Hank wearing preposterous red mittens. Even a wobbly Donna all bandaged in red tape was out, tongue waving from her grinning muzzle, tail wagging gently.

When the Voyager came to a stop, they all rushed over. The door was flung open and Jet noticed as he poked his head out of the car, that the air still carried the faint smell of smoke. He ventured out, his legs still feeling a little shaky. Then he was being hugged and kissed and squeezed and overwhelmed by everyone's concern for him.

"Oh my God, Jet!" Christine kissed his cheek and squeezed him tightly.

"I'm fine. Really," he shrugged away from his sister's exuberant and unexpected display.

Hank made to shake Jet's hand and extended one of his crazy mittens. He ended up by hugging him instead. That's when Jet realized they weren't mittens at all, but bandages that covered his cousin's hands, leaving only the ends of his fingers sticking out.

"Rope burns," Hank explained, "Doc Hubert bandaged 'em up with vet wrap, just like Donna. They make everything a challenge; eating, dressing—"

Further explanation was interrupted when Uncle Phil shook Jet's hand, "A hero." He said, "Danielle and Denise called us last night to let us know about the Ibarra kids and your part in their rescue."

"I didn't do much," Jet frowned as he bent to pat the dog who'd been licking his fingers, "I almost got us all killed. If I hadn't been there, maybe Humphries wouldn't have started the fire. Maybe the FBI would've gotten there and surprised them all having supper. Maybe—"

"He had a gun," Hank cut in. "Maybe he was planning to

do away with them all anyway. You don't know."

"All I know is every time Jet gets involved with these FBI agents, he ends up in the hospital," Dad said. "It's a good thing the Union has a good health plan."

"Sorry, Dad," Jet said sheepishly, "I'll try not to let that happen again."

"What's important is that everything came out all right," Mom said. "The kidnappers were caught and will face trial. The children are safe and with their parents. Mr. Ibarra has been cleared of all charges and should already have been released from jail. Donna is going to be okay."

"And Hank and Jet are both heroes," Uncle Phil said.

"I think it's a great way to start the New Year," Aunt Claire put in. "All of us together and certainly blessed."